Norman Mailer

BARBARY SHORE

Norman Mailer was born in 1923 in Long Branch, New Jersey, and grew up in Brooklyn, New York. In 1955, he was one of the co-founders of *The Village Voice*. He is the author of more than thirty books, including *The Naked and the Dead*; *The Armies of the Night*, for which he won a National Book Award and the Pulitzer Prize; *The Executioner's Song*, for which he won his second Pulitzer Prize; *Harlot's Ghost*; *Oswald's Tale*; *The Gospel According to the Son*; and *The Castle in the Forest*. He died in 2007.

Books by Norman Mailer

The Naked and the Dead
Barbary Shore
The Deer Park
Advertisements for Myself
Deaths for the Ladies (and Other Disasters)
The Presidential Papers
An American Dream
Cannibals and Christians
Why Are We in Vietnam?
The Deer Park—A Play
The Armies of the Night
Miami and the Siege of Chicago
Of a Fire on the Moon
The Prisoner of Sex
Maidstone
Existential Errands
St. George and the Godfather
Marilyn
The Faith of Graffiti
The Fight
Genius and Lust
The Executioner's Song
Of Women and Their Elegance
Pieces and Pontifications
Ancient Evenings
Tough Guys Don't Dance
Harlot's Ghost
Oswald's Tale: An American Mystery
Portrait of Picasso as a Young Man
The Gospel According to the Son
The Time of Our Time
Why Are We at War?
The Spooky Art
Modest Gifts
The Castle in the Forest
On God

BARBARY SHORE

BARBARY SHORE

Norman Mailer

VINTAGE INTERNATIONAL

VINTAGE BOOKS

A DIVISION OF RANDOM HOUSE, INC.

NEW YORK

FIRST VINTAGE INTERNATIONAL EDITION, OCTOBER 1997

Copyright © 1951, 1979 by Norman Mailer

All rights reserved under International and Pan-American
Copyright Conventions. Published in the United States by
Vintage Books, a division of Random House, Inc., New York, and
simultaneously in Canada by Random House of Canada Limited,
Toronto. Originally published in hardcover in the United States
by Rinehart & Company, Inc., New York, in 1951.

Library of Congress Cataloging-in-Publication Data
Mailer, Norman.
Barbary shore / by Norman Mailer.
ISBN 0-375-70039-0
I. Title
PS3525.A4152B37   1997
813'.54—dc21   97-6683
CIP

Random House Web address: http://www.randomhouse.com/

Printed in the United States of America
10 9 8 7 6

To Jean Malaquais

BARBARY SHORE

Pㅅᴏʙᴀʙʟʏ I was in the war. There is the mark of a wound behind my ear, an oblong of unfertile flesh where no hair grows. It is covered over now, and may be disguised by even the clumsiest barber, but no barber can hide the scar on my back. For that a tailor is more in order.

When I stare into the mirror I am returned a face doubtless more handsome than the original, but the straight nose, the modelled chin, and the smooth cheeks are only evidence of a stranger's art. It does not matter how often I decide the brown hair and the gray eyes must have always been my own; there is nothing I can recognize, not even my age. I am certain I cannot be less than twenty-five and it is possible I am older, but thanks to whoever tended me, a young man without a wrinkle in his skin stands for a portrait in the mirror.

There was a time when I would try rather frantically to recall what kind of accident it had been and where it had occurred. I could almost picture the crash of an airplane and the flames entering my cockpit. No sooner had I succeeded, however, than the airplane became a tank and I was trapped within, only to create another environment; the house was burning and a timber pinned my back. Such violence ends

3

with the banality of beads; grenades, shell, bombardment—I can elaborate a hundred such, and none seem correct.

Here and there, memories return. Only it is difficult to trust them. I am positive my parents are dead, that I grew up in an institution for children, and was always poor. Still, there are times when I think I remember my mother, and I have the idea I received an education. The deaf are supposed to hear a myriad of noises, and silence is filled with the most annoying rattle and tinkle and bell; the darkness of the blind is marred by erratic light; thus memory for me was never a wall but more a roulette of the most extraordinary events and the most insignificant, all laced into the same vessel until I could not discern the most casual fact from the most patent fancy, nor the past from the future; and the details of my own history were lost in the other, common to us all. I could never judge whether something had happened to me or I imagined it so. It made little difference whether I had met a man or he existed only in a book; there was never a way to determine if I knew a country or merely remembered another's description. The legends from a decade of newsprint were as intimate and distant as the places in which I must have lived. No history belonged to me and so all history was mine. Yet in what a state. Each time my mind furnished a memory long suppressed it was only another piece, and there were so few pieces and so much puzzle.

During one period I made prodigious efforts to recover the past. I conducted a massive correspondence with the secretaries of appropriate officials; I followed people upon the street because they had looked at me with curiosity; I searched lists of names, studied photographs, and lay on my bed bludgeoning my mind to confess a single material detail. Prodigious efforts, but I recovered nothing except to learn that I had no past and was therefore without a future. The blind grow ears, the deaf learn how to see, and I acquired both in compensation; it was natural, even obligatory, that the present should possess the stage.

And as time possessed the present I began to retain what had happened to me in the previous week, the previous month, and that became my experience, became all my experience. If it were circumscribed it was nonetheless a world, and a year from the time I first found myself with no name in my pocket, I could masquerade like anyone else. I lived like the hermit in the desert who sweats his penance and waits for a sign. There was none and probably there will be none—I doubt if I shall find my childhood and my youth—but I have come to understand the skeleton perhaps of that larger history, and not everything is without its purpose. I have even achieved a balance, if that is what it may be called.

Now, in the time I write, when other men besides myself must contrive a name, a story, and the papers they carry, I wonder if I do not possess an advantage. For I have been doing it longer, and am tantalized less by the memory of better years. They must suffer, those others like myself. I wonder what fantasies bother them?

There is one I have regularly. It seems as if only enough time need elapse for me to forget before it appears again:

I see a traveller. He is most certainly not myself. A plump middle-aged man, and I have the idea he has just finished a long trip. He has landed at an airfield or his train has pulled into a depot. It hardly matters which.

He is in a hurry to return home. With impatience he suffers the necessary delays in collecting his baggage, and when the task is finally done, he hails a taxi, installs his luggage, bawls out his instructions, and settles back comfortably in the rear seat. Everything is so peaceful. Indolently he turns his head to watch children playing a game upon the street.

He is weary, he discovers, and his breath comes heavily. Unfolding his newspaper he attempts to study it, but the print

5

blurs and he lays the sheet down. Suddenly and unaccountably he is quite depressed. It has been a long trip he reassures himself. He looks out the window.

The cab is taking the wrong route!

What shall he do? It seems so simple to raise his hand and tap upon the glass, but he feels he dare not disturb the driver. Instead, he looks through the window once more.

The man lives in this city, but he has never seen these streets. The architecture is strange, and the people are dressed in unfamiliar clothing. He looks at a sign, but it is printed in an alphabet he cannot read.

His hand folds upon his heart to still its beating. It is a dream, he thinks, hugging his body in the rear of the cab. He is dreaming and the city is imaginary and the cab is imaginary. And on he goes.

I shout at him. You are wrong, I cry, although he does not hear me; this city is the real city, the material city, and your vehicle is history. Those are the words I use, and then the image shatters.

Night comes and I am alone with a candle. What has been fanciful is now concrete. Although the room in which I write has an electric circuit, it functions no longer. Time passes and I wait by the door, listening to the footsteps of roomers as they go out to work for the night. In fourteen hours they will be back.

So the blind lead the blind and the deaf shout warnings to one another until their voices are lost.

TWO

I SUPPOSE even a magic box must have its handle. Yet once the box is opened, I wonder if it is too unreasonable that the handle is then ignored. I am more concerned with the contents. If I begin with Willie Dinsmore, it is because he served as a handle; and I, who was to serve for so long as the sorcerer's apprentice, forgot him quickly.

Let me describe how I was living at the time. I had a bed in one of those young men's dormitories which seem always to be constructed about a gymnasium and a cafeteria. Since such organizations are inevitably founded on the principle that people should be forced to enjoy each other's presence, I suffered through a succession of bunkmates, and found once again the unique loneliness which comes from living without privacy. I would hardly have chosen to stay there, but I had little choice. Through all that year, in which I received no mail and moved beyond a nodding acquaintance with very few people, I worked at a succession of unskilled jobs and with a discipline I would hardly have expected in myself put away regularly at the end of the week a sum of ten dollars. I was driven with the ambition that I should be a writer, and I was grubbing quite appropriately for a grubstake. My project was to save five hundred dollars and then find an inexpensive room: calculated virtually to the penny, I found that if the rent were less than five dollars a week, I would have enough money to live for six months and I could write my novel or at least begin it.

The cash finally accumulated, I searched for a cheap place of my own, but the place was never cheap enough. I flushed corners for thirty dollars a month, for forty dollars, and more, but they would have exhausted my savings too rapidly. I was growing somewhat desperate until Willie Dinsmore, after weeks of jockeying me on a puppeteer's string, gave me his room.

Dinsmore was a playwright. Being also a husband and a father, he found difficulty in working at home and therefore kept a small furnished cubicle in a brownstone house in Brooklyn Heights. Once, in passing, he told me he would let the room go when he went away for the summer, and I had coaxed a promise that I would get the vacancy. Since we knew each other only casually, I made a point afterward never to lose contact with him for very long. Dinsmore's niche cost only four dollars a week, and there was not another so inexpensive to be discovered.

I would pay him a visit from time to time and note with all the pleasure of an eager customer each small advantage the house had to offer. Certainly I was easy to please. Although I would be situated on the top floor beneath a flat roof and have for ventilation but a single window, opening upon laundry lines and back yards to the fire escape of an apartment house upon the next street, it never occured to me how oppressive and sultry a hole this might become.

A small room, not more than eight feet wide, one had to edge sideways between the desk and the bed to reach the window. The paint was years old and had soiled to the ubiquitous yellow-brown of cheap lodgings. Its surface blistered and buckled, large swatches of plaster had fallen, and in a corner the ceiling was exposed to the lath. Cinders drifted up from the dock area below the bluffs to cover the woodwork. The sash cord was broken, and the window rested in all its weight upon two empty beer cans which served as support. Even at four dollars a week the bargain was not conspicuous, but I was enamored of it.

I would sit on the bed and watch Dinsmore sort his papers, scatter dust from the desk to the floor, and mop his face. He was a short stocky man whose favorite position was astraddle a chair, chin resting on the back, and his body bent forward. He looked like a football lineman in this posture, and his head, which resembled a boxer dog, could hardly contradict the impression. Having told him nothing about myself, and indeed I was hardly in the habit, he made the assumption that I was a war veteran, and I never bothered to explain there might be some doubt. Dinsmore was happier this way in any case. Like so many writers he had very little interest in people, and if they could serve his didactic demands, a pigeonhole was all he required. I had been installed immediately in the one he undoubtedly labelled Postwar Problems.

"I'll tell you, kid," he would say, "it's a shame the way people got to live doubled up in rooms, and lots of you GI's" —his voice was pitched deferentially when he spoke about veterans—"the ones who're married and living with their in-laws and their marriages are going to pot all cause they can't get a lousy apartment. It's the fault of the real estate interests, and it's a crime that we fight an anti-fascist war and don't clean out the fascists in our own house, but I'll tell you, Mikey, they're making a mistake, they're cutting their own throat, cause the veterans aren't going to stand for it."

I never knew whether he believed this, or if it came from the desire to vindicate his plays. The poorest strain in his writing had been the kind of superficial optimism prevalent during the war, which still lasted posthumously among the many playwrights and novelists whose lack of political sophistication was satisfied by dividing all phenomena into Dinsmore's categories. At bottom it was only a temporary mode of that great crutch to the simple-minded:—the right guy and the wrong-o—and already to the confusion and the eventual danger of men like Willie the names had changed.

Willie kept his head down, however, and his eye to the measure. His hero was still the young anti-fascist who had come back from the war and gave the speech about the world he fought to make. The speech was not new, but an old speech never hurt a playwright, and Dinsmore doubled his success in a thematic sequel whose young veteran told the audience what kind of world he wanted for his infant.

It will be apparent by now, I fear, that I was not precisely infatuated with Willie. He had a home, he had a family, he had a reputation, and any one of the three was more than I could expect. But Willie found other homes as well. He had the kind of mind which could not bear any question taking longer than ten seconds to answer. "There are the haves and the have-nots," Willie would declare; "there are the progressive countries and the reactionary countries. In half the globe the people own the means of production, and in the other half the fascists have control."

I would offer a mild objection. "It's just as easy to say that in every country the majority have very little. Such a division is probably the basis of society."

Willie reacted with a hurt smile and a compassionate look in his face. Whenever I contradicted him, he would change the subject. "You take the theatre. It's sick, Mikey, you know why? All commercialized. What we need is a people's theatre again, you know where you pay a quarter, tie-ups with unions, school kids, where you can show the facts of life. A worker's theatre."

"Precisely."

"The problem is to give it back to the people. The classical theatre was always progressive. Art is a people's fight."

To elaborate at such length upon Willie is not completely necessary, but I wanted to give a small portrait of him because he was the first person to mention Beverly Guinevere to me, and his description had its effect long after I knew it was untrue, and colored many nuances. If I had had any judgment, I would have known that Willie was innocent and his perceptions about people had no more chance of being accurate than a man who hurls a stone at a target he cannot see. But to possess judgment was another matter. My face allowed people to think that I was only twenty, and in a reciprocal of that relation I often felt like an adolescent first entering the adult world where everyone is strange and individual. I was always too ready to mistake opinion for fact.

The first time I heard Guinevere's name Willie was in the process of using it as a springboard for one of his lectures. "Someday," Willie threatened, "I'll sic the landlady on you." He paused, rocking the chair on its legs. "She's a character, wait'll you meet her. I'll tell you, Mikey, when you find out the score you'll stay away from her."

"Why?"

"If she gets alone in the same room with you, you won't be safe." He paused again. "Guinevere's a nymphomaniac."

I remember that I grinned. "What happened to you, Willie?"

"Nothing. She's not my type. You know she's kind of old, and she's fat." He pursed his lips judiciously. "And then I'll tell you, Mikey, extramarital relations are different when you're married, I mean there's the psychological angle to consider. And when you got kids there's always the danger of disease, of going blind, having a leg fall off. I may not have been a GI, but I saw that venereal movie, too." And intrigued, he shook his head. "You remember the guy who couldn't talk, who just whistled? Holy Cow, I tell you we need Health Clinics all over the country, especially in the South. I made a tour

11

through there last year to gather some material, and *Jesus*, the ignorance."

He massaged his chin, fully embarked upon a lecture. "Conditions are brutal in this country—slums, juvenile delinquency. I mean when you add it up there's an indictment, and that's just counting the physical part of it. You take Guinevere, someone like that, it's a psychological problem, a psychological casualty I think of it. I mean I can see her side of it, Mikey. She's lonesome, that's all. You know she made sort of an advance, and I repulsed her with a few well-chosen words, just a couple of gags, but I guess it hurt her feelings. People always want you to think well of them, so she started to tell me her side of it, and she hasn't got any intellectual resources, and there's a lot of housework cleaning up this barn. You know the typical American housewife with the success story in reverse. I'll bet she reads *True Confessions*."

"You don't make her sound very attractive."

"Oh, she's got sex appeal of a sort, but she's a crazy dame. I might have entertained ideas, but there's her husband involved, and although I never met the guy I think it's kind of sneaky seeing a dame when her husband sleeps in the same building."

This is the woman Dinsmore advertised as having the power to give his cubbyhole away. Witness my surprise—for I had become convinced that he would finally end by awarding his room to some other acquaintance—when Willie came to the dormitory one morning, and told me he was leaving for the country. I dressed quickly and ate breakfast in the cafeteria while Willie sat across from me, scattering his cigarette ash in my saucer. "Look," he said, "Guinevere could have already promised the first vacancy. We'll have to figure out a plan."

"I hope it works," I told him.

We walked over to the rooming house. For a June morning the sidewalks were still cool, and the brownstone houses

were not without dignity. The spring air contained a suggestion of wood and meadow, and it was possible to imagine the
gardens and the trellised arbors as they must have existed fifty
years ago. We were on a street which led toward the bluffs,
the docks beyond, and the bay. Across the harbor through a
morning haze the skyline reared itself in the distance, while
down the river an ocean liner was approaching its dock.

Mrs. Guinevere, I discovered, had the basement apartment with its customary entrance tucked beneath the slope of
the front stairway, its private gate and miniature plot whose
stony soil was without even a weed. As Dinsmore pressed the
bell, I could hear it ringing inside.

From the apartment there was the sound of footsteps approaching, then a suspicious pause. A voice shrieked, "Who is
it?"

Willie shouted his name and I could hear the bolt slide
slowly open. "Come on, come on," he said raucously, "what
do you think, we got all day?"

"Oh, it's you," a woman screeched back. "Well, what
the hell do you want?" The door opened a crack, a set of plump
little fingers curled around it, and a pair of eyes and the tip of
a nose appeared in the slit. "You always have to pick a time
when I'm busy." Slowly, provocatively, the face protruded a
little further and two curls of extraordinarily red hair peeped
around the door.

"Come on out. I want you to meet a writer friend, Mikey
Lovett." Dinsmore made the introductions to the doorpost. I said
hello somewhat foolishly, and her eyes stared back at me. "I'm
pleased to meet you, Mr. Lovett," she said in the unexpected and
dulcet cadence of a telephone operator. "I hope you'll excuse the
way I'm dressed." With that, she swung the door open as though
to unveil a statue. I was startled. Dinsmore had poorly prepared
me. She was quite pretty, at least to my taste, pretty in a flam-
boyant cootchy way, so that my first impression was of no more

13

than a fabulous crop of red hair and a woman beneath, waggling her hips. Undeniably short and stout, her limbs were nevertheless delicate, her face was not heavy, and her waist, respectably narrow, tapered inward from her broad shoulders in an exaggeration which was piquing.

"It takes me forever to get dressed," she grumbled. "Boy, you men are lucky not having to fool around with a house." Her voice began the first sentence as a telephone operator and finished the second as a fishwife; once again she was shouting. Yet in the silence which followed this, she closed her large blue eyes for several seconds and then opened them again with counterfeit simplicity. Obviously she considered this to be of considerable effect, but since her eyes protruded a trifle, the benefit was somewhat doubtful.

The silence served as a floor upon which she and Dinsmore could exchange a minuet of looks and glances and innuendo, while a smile flickered between them. Standing to one side, I had the opportunity to look at her closely. It was impossible to determine her age, but I was certain she was less than forty.

"Yeah, it's tough," Dinsmore grinned at last. His voice rasped more when he spoke to her. "Still, you look good... good."

"Aw, you." After the introduction she had paid me no attention, but now, hand on hip, she wheeled in my direction. "If I was to listen to this guy's line," she said, "he'd be up my skirts in two minutes."

"You hope," Dinsmore said.

She laughed loudly with boisterous good humor, and I had the impression she might have nudged him in the ribs if I were not there. Her thin lips pursed, but this was beneath the other mouth of lipstick which was wide and curved in the sexual stereotype of a model on a magazine cover, and seemed to work in active opposition to the small mobile lips beneath. "Boy, you writers," she snorted, "you think you own the world."

Dinsmore threw up his hands in a pantomime of being rebuffed, and then, the manner satisfied and the preamble concluded, his tone changed. "Listen, Guinevere, you're a pretty good scout, how about doing us a favor?"

"What?" It was apparent the word "favor" had few pleasant connotations to her.

"I'm giving up my room for a couple of months. How about letting Mikey have it?"

She frowned. "Listen, I can get five dollars extra if I put up a sign and rent it out."

"Why should the landlord be the profiteer?" He waved his finger at her. "Suppose I kept paying for the room, and Mikey stayed in it. That'd be okay."

She shrugged. "I can't stop you."

"Well, why make me go to the trouble? Why don't you just let the kid take it." He whacked her playfully on the hip. "Come on, be a good sport."

"Aw, you writers, you're all nuts," she jeered. "No sooner get rid of one of you, then I get another."

"I really could use the room," I said. I smiled tentatively. Perhaps she was examining me. After a moment or two she nodded her head angrily, and said, "All right. You can have it. But the rent's got to be paid every Thursday, four dollars paid in advance of the week to come, and no hot air about it." In the correct style of a landlady her voice had been flat and authoritative, although immediately afterward as though to salvage someone's good opinion, she whined defensively, "I can't be bothered chasing around after you guys, I've got a lot of work to do here, and Lord knows I get paid little enough for it, and you got to co-operate."

"I'll pay the money on time," I said.

"Well, let's hope so." She had yielded grudgingly, but now that business was terminated, she smiled. "I'll see you around, Mr. Lovett. Linen day is also on Thursday. You get one new sheet a week, and you can help me if you strip the bed before I get up there." This, however, was said with heavy allure.

We exchanged a few more words and left for Dinsmore's house. He clapped me on the back. "She likes you, kid."

"How do you know?"

"She just likes you. I can tell. Good-looking kid like you. You'll be having your hands full with her."

Unwillingly, in the customary reaction to just this situation, my hand strayed up to the scar tissue behind my ear, and I was taken again with a desire to study that face Dinsmore had called good-looking. "No," I answered him, "I won't be having my hands full with her. I've got to work."

"Stick to your story, Lovett."

We walked slowly, the day already warm. "She's absolutely weird," Dinsmore said. "A complex character." He sighed, pushed the hair off his forehead. "Basically she was good stuff," he lectured, "but you get human beings caught in a profit nexus, and it turns them inside out. The structure of society is rotten today."

"Yes, it is."

When we reached his house, he paused, shook my hand, and smiled. "It's been great knowing you, kid, and I'm glad I did you a favor." Before I could reply, he went on. "There's something I'd like to say, because right now like everybody else you're at the crossroads, and the thing you want to ask yourself, Lovett, is which way are you going to go? Will you be against the people or will you be for them?"

"I'm afraid I haven't thought that way in a long time."

"You'll have to. Wall Street will leave you no choice." He smiled wisely, and something hard and smug came into his face. "There's just one thing you got to remember, Mikey. It's the basic issue, it's the basic trouble with this country. Do you know what it is?"

I confessed I was not completely certain.

He prodded his thumb against my stomach and in a sepulchral voice he stated, "Empty bellies. . .empty bellies. That's the issue, kid."

Thus, unlike most partings, ours was on a basic issue. I turned once to wave at him from down the street before he went inside his house, and then I continued back to the dormitory and gathered my belongings. It was time for me to move.

My few possessions transported and unpacked, I lay on my new bed and mused about the novel I was going to write. Through this long summer I could turn back upon myself and discover. . .but I had seen so much of the world and, seeing, had so disconnected it, that I had everything to discover.

I daydreamed only a little while about my novel. Instead I was thinking of Guinevere. She was a nymphomaniac, he had said. Such a curious word. I had never applied it to anyone. It was difficult to forget her breasts which had thrust upward from their binding in copious splendor, so palpable that they obtained the intensification of art and became more real than themselves.

A jewel. But set in brass. This morning she had sported a house dress and covered it with a bathrobe. Her red hair, with which undoubtedly she was always experimenting, had been merely blowzy and flew out in all directions from her head. Yet there had been opera pumps on her feet, her nails had been painted, her lipstick was fresh. She was a house whose lawn was landscaped and whose kitchen was on fire. I would not have been startled if she had turned around and like the half-dressed queen in the girlie show: surprise! her buttocks are exposed.

The nymphomaniac. As I was about to fall asleep for the first time in my new room, I realized that I wanted to take Guinevere to bed.

THREE

THE attic, as I have indicated, was up three gloomy flights of stairs. Once, many years ago, the house had been a modest mansion, but now it was partitioned into cubicles. On the top story, a masterpiece of design, no window gave upon the landing, and at the head of the stairs, burning into perpetuity, one weak light bulb cast its sallow illumination upon my door, upon the doors of the two neighbors I had not met, and upon the oilcloth of the bathroom we shared.

It was a big house and gave the impression of being an empty house. Downstairs there were ten names arranged in ten brackets next to as many bells which did not ring, but a week could go by and I would pass no one upon the stairs. I hardly cared. In the last months I had come to know fewer and fewer people, and by the time I quit the dormitory, for better or for worse I was very much alone. At first this did not matter. I began my novel, and for a few days, completely isolated, I made progress. Since I could assume that a sizable portion of my life had been spent in one barracks or another, a room for myself was more than a luxury. Temporarily I felt free and rather happy. As though to exploit all the advantages of my new situation, I ate meals around the clock and slept as my whim directed.

Such a period could not last for long. A day passed and another, while pages of new manuscript collected on the desk. And about me, with patient regular industry, dust accumulated everywhere. Whatever plans I might have entertained for Guinevere were not to come passively to fruition. I never saw her. Conventional landlady, she never bothered to clean, and the dust in my room increased from minute to minute in competition with the hall outside. The entire house was filthy.

Except for the bathroom. This bore the evidence of regular attention, and even presented a certain immaculacy at times, a mystery to me until I met McLeod.

One morning I found a man at work washing the bathroom floor. He looked up and nodded, his cold clear eyes staring at me from behind his spectacles. "You're the one who took over Dinsmore's room?" he asked finally.

I answered his question, and he rose from his knees, introduced himself and made a short speech in a dry ironic voice. "I'll tell you," he said, pinching his thin lips primly, "this place is always a mess. Guinevere don't get off her bottom long enough to wash a handkerchief, so I've taken over cleaning the bathroom twice a week, and far as I see there's small profit in it." He scratched his chin sourly. "I've asked Hollingsworth, the gentleman who resides in the other room up here, to pitch in once in a while, but he's always got a hangover, or else he's sprained his wrist, or there's a mole on his belly." He shrugged. "If you want to, Lovett, you can help me keep this clean, but I can tell you from the outset that if you don't want to co-operate, I'll still be doing it because unfortunately I've got a mania about neatness."

My introduction to McLeod. On completing the discourse, he folded his long slender hands over the top of a broom handle, and pursed his mouth. At the moment he bore an astonishing resemblance to a witch, his gaunt face nodding in communion with himself, his long thin body stooped in thought. When I did not reply immediately, he filled the gap by running a comb through his straight black hair, the action emphasizing the sweep of his sharp narrow nose.

"You're a writer, Dinsmore told me."

"More or less."

"I see." He gave the impression of listening carefully to what I said, evaluating my words, and then discarding them. "I've got a proposition," McLeod said to me, "which you can take or leave. You clean up the bathroom on Wednesdays, and I'll keep doing it on Saturday." With little effort he gave the impression of saturating each word with a considerable weight of satire. I sensed that he was laughing at me.

Annoyed, I yawned. "What do you say we draw up a contract?"

His mouth, severe in repose, became mocking as he smiled. He looked at me shrewdly. "I'm getting you down a bit, eh?" Laughter altered his face so that for an instant he could appear young and merry. He drawled out his next offering with a self-satisfied air as though he were sucking a candy-drop. "Well, now, that's a thought, Lovett. It's a thought." And still chuckling, he examined the bathroom floor, found it to his satisfaction, and stowed the broom in a corner. "I'm across the hall. Drop by when you're dressed," he offered.

I did, and we talked for an hour. I had thought he might be taciturn about himself, but he belied this impression by talking freely, or more exactly by conveying a series of specific details much as he might have furnished a dossier. He was forty-four, he told me, and he worked in a department store as a window dresser. He had grown up in Brooklyn, he had always been a solitary man. He had a father who lived in an Old Folks' Home. Rarely saw him. Possesed a high-school education. Obtained in Brooklyn. "I've lived here always," he said with his mocking smile. "I've never been out of New York with the exception of one small trip to New Jersey. That's m'life." And he burst into laughter.

"Just that?" I asked.

"I see you don't believe me. People rarely do. It's because I give the impression of having some culture. I've studied, you see, by myself. I'm not a joiner, and I don't put my education to work, but I am a great reader, it must be said."

And with that, subtly yet unmistakably, he directed me to the door and shook hands, his eyes studying me in amusement.

I dropped into his room again the next evening and the next. I think I talked with McLeod five or six times that first week. However, I would not say we became friends quickly. He had a brutal honesty which made it difficult to speak casually with him. He would leap upon some passing statement I might make, and figuratively twirl my words about his finger as if to examine them from every aspect. I found myself continually on the defensive, and though with a left-handed fascination I was always providing matter for his mill, nonetheless I resented him for it.

What glee the process gave him. Once I mentioned a girl with whom I had recently had an affair, and I shrugged and said, "But it didn't mean much. We got a little bored with each other, and drifted out of it."

McLeod gave his sly grin, the side of his mouth sucking on the imaginary candy-drop. "You drifted out of it, eh?"

Irritably, I snapped, "Yes, I drifted out of it. Didn't you ever hear of anything like that?"

"Yes, I've heard of it. I hear it all the time. People are always drifting in and out of things." He leaned back on the bed, and pressed his finger tips together. "I'll tell you the truth, Lovett, I don't know what those words mean. 'Drifted in and out, drifted in and out,'" he repeated as though the phrase were delicious. "When you have to, it's pretty convenient to think of yourself as driftwood."

"I can explain it to you."

"Oh," he said, grinning, "I know you can explain it to me. I just want to try to figure out m'self what it signifies drifting out of an affair. Because in the old days when I used to cut a figure with the women I had my share of it, and it seems to me now that when I broke up with a woman it was often somewhat nasty."

"With a sadist like you," I said in an attempt at humor. My answers were invariably dull, my temper ragged. He had a facility for wearing one down, and it was not surprising that when I swung I was wild.

McLeod nodded. "Oh, yes. When I'd examine my motives, I'd find elements which were ugly enough. I've been a bad piece of work in my time." He said this with great severity.

Almost immediately, however, he would be prodding again. "Now, I don't know about you, Lovett, but when I'd drift out of an affair I'd find if I started to think about it that the reasons were somewhat interesting. There were women I quit because I made love to them ineptly, unpleasant as that may be to admit. And then, taking the converse of the proposition, there was a woman or two in love with me and wanting to get married." He began to laugh, quietly and ferociously. "'What? Get married?' I would say to them. 'Who, me? Why I thought it was understood from the beginning that this was on a give and take basis.'" His mouth curled, his voice whined in a grotesque of outraged innocence. "Girlie, you got the wrong number. I thought it was understood we were modern individuals with a modern viewpoint." He roared with laughter now. "Oh, my mother." And then, his mouth mocking me, McLeod said, "That's another one belongs with the driftwood."

"Now, look," I'd object, "does a man have to get married every time he starts a relation with a woman?"

"No." He lit a cigarette, amused with me. "You see, Lovett, there's a difference between you and me. You're *honest*. I never was. I'd start off with the lady, and we'd have a nice conversation at the beginning about how neither of us could afford to get tied up, all understood, all good clean healthy fun." His voice was steeped in ridicule. "Fine. Only you see, Lovett, I could never let it go at that. The old dependable mechanisms would start working in me. I'd begin operating. You know what I mean? I'd do everything in my power to make the girl love me —when you think of the genius I've squandered in bed. And sure enough there'd be the times when I'd talk her into being in love, when I'd worry her to death until there was never a man in the world who made love like me." He coughed. "But once she admitted that. . . . finito! I was getting bored. I thought it was time we drifted apart." He laughed again, at himself and at me. "Why, when the little lady would suggest marriage you should have seen me go into my act. 'You're welshing on the bargain,' I would tell her, 'I'm disappointed in you. How could you have betrayed me so?' " Once more he roared with laughter. "Oh, there was a devilish mechanism in it. You see, she betrayed me, you get it, she betrayed *me*, and it was time for us to drift apart."

"I'm to take it that the shoe fits?"

McLeod looked out his window at the apartment house beyond. He seemed to be listening intently to the clanging of the steam donkey on the docks below the bluff, working overtime into the night. "I can't say, Lovett. It's always a good idea to know oneself."

"I think I do."

His face was still impassive, his thin mouth straight. "I suspect in your case there are special conditions." Casually, he flicked the next sentence at me. "Mind telling a man how you got that patch on your skull?"

I was caught without guard. "It's not your business," I managed to stammer, and I could feel myself blushing with anger.

He nodded without surprise, and continued in the same casual tone. He could have been a scientist examining a specimen. "My guess is that there're other tattoos on your skin."

"Guess away."

"You need maintain no front with me," McLeod said quietly. "It's friendly curiosity."

"Anything you want to know," I murmured.

He did not answer directly. "The analysis I gave of your motives and mine in drifting out of an affair is very curious."

"Why?"

"Because it's not the least bit true for either of us. I presented it merely as a construction. I, for example, have never been tormented by excessive sexual vanity."

"Then what were you getting at?"

McLeod shrugged. "I was interested in the way you spoke so casually. It would not be surprising if the affair with the little lady you mentioned were more painful than that to you."

He was not far wrong. Casual it had been for her, and painful for me. "Possibly," I admitted with some discomfort.

"You see, Lovett, the thing I noticed from the beginning is a certain passion to pass yourself off like anyone else. Perhaps someday you'll tell me why you choose to stay in this rooming house, a lonely proposition I should think."

"I want to be by myself, that's all," I said.

McLeod went on as if I had not spoken. "A young man might do that who was seriously alone, and had lost most of the normal forms of contact. Or"—and he puffed at his cigarette—"it's possible that somebody like you stays here and talks to me because it's your job and you're paid to do that." With a startling intentness his eyes looked into mine, waiting for some informative flicker perhaps.

"I don't know what you're talking about," I said.

"No . . . Well, maybe you don't, m'bucko. Maybe you

don't. You're not the type, I expect," McLeod said cryptically. "More like you to drift," and he was silent for a long time afterward.

Such conversations were hardly soothing. I would leave him to spend troubled hours by myself while the questions he had asked so easily went wandering for an answer. There were times when I shunned his company.

And days after I moved in, I found myself still thinking of Guinevere. She would be so fine for me. Her hips waggled in invitation; she was obtainable. In retrospect I understood that I had gone to visit McLeod the first time with some idea of learning about her casually. Guinevere's name, through lack of opportunity, had not been mentioned, and now it was impossible. No matter how flatly I might inquire about her, McLeod would be certain to appreciate the reason for my curiosity.

By shifts I did my work, went for long walks through the hot streets of Brooklyn, and apportioned the sixteen dollars a week I allowed myself for meals in a lunchroom, a few drinks, and a movie. It was quiet, it was lonesome, and the last evenings of spring I tasted vicariously, watching the young lovers parade the streets of the vast suburban mangle which extends beyond the border of Brooklyn Heights to the dirt, the popcorn underfoot, and the quick sordid gaiety of Coney Island, sweet and transient, soon to be swept away in the terrible and superheated nights of midsummer.

FOUR

AFTER a week Mrs. Guinevere came to the room with a change of linen. Once again she was dressed uniquely. Although it was nine o'clock in the evening, she wore a nightgown over some underclothing whose complex network of straps could be seen upon her shoulders. This ensemble of slips, girdles, gowns and bands was covered by a short flowered bathrobe open at the throat to exhibit her impressive breast.

"Oh . . . hello," I said, and found it difficult to add anything. I was too absorbed in what I had been writing to make the transition smoothly. "I guess I owe you four dollars," I managed to say.

"Yeah." Guinevere seemed uninterested in the money.

I rummaged through my bureau drawer, came up with my wallet, and paid her. In the meantime she had stripped my bed and tossed a fresh sheet and towel upon it. When she finished, she sighed loudly and purposefully.

"How're things going?" I asked.

"So-so."

This would hardly do. "You look tired," I said intimately. "Sit down."

Guinevere glanced at the pile of folded sheets upon her arm and shrugged. "All right, maybe I will," she said, "seeing as

27

the door's open." The sentence was invested with a wealth of vulgar gentility.

Perched beside me on the bed, she sighed again. I lit a cigarette and discovered that my hands were not at all steady. I was very aware of her.

"How about letting me have one?" she asked.

Inwardly, I was shaking. I did something she must have found surprising. I picked up the pack and the matches, and placed them in her lap although we were sitting not a foot apart. She opened her large blue eyes then, glanced at me, and waved the match to the tobacco. I had no idea what we would talk about.

Guinevere solved that for me. "What a terrible day I've had," she sighed.

"The linens?"

"No." She shook her head dramatically and stared at me. "No, I've been having trouble with my nerves." Her lipstick, an experimental bluish pink, had been applied this once to conform to the real shape of her lips, and it made her look less attractive. "What's the matter with your nerves?" I asked.

She fingered a curl in her red hair. "I'm just too high-strung, that's all." Her eyes came to rest on my typewriter, and I have the idea that for the first time since she entered the room, she knew where she had seen me before. "You're a writer, aren't you?"

I nodded, and she said what I expected her to say. "You know, I could be a writer. I tell you when I think of all the real-life human dramas I've lived among"—her voice took on the shadings of a radio announcer—"and the experience I've had, for I've lived a full life although you wouldn't know it to look at me, why I tell you I could make a fortune just putting it all down on paper."

The lack of contact between us was considerable. Her voice

sad and reflective, she recited to an unknown audience. I coughed. "You ought to sit down and write."

"No, I couldn't. I can't concentrate." Her hand played over the pile of sheets. "Today is linen day, and do you know I haven't been able to do a thing. I just sat and looked at those linens until my husband came home, and he had to cook supper for me—oh, I had a horrible experience last night."

"What?"

"It gives me the creeps to talk about it."

"Well, what was it?"

She fingered her bosom, adjusting the brassiere to conceal a quarter inch more of the gorge between her breasts. "Well, you know I got the downstairs apartment, and we keep the windows open in this weather, and guess what happened? A cat got in and crawled over the bed around four A.M., and I woke up and saw it looking me in the eye." She sighed dolefully again. "It's a wonder I didn't wake the whole house with my screaming. My husband had to calm me for an hour. And this morning I opened the cupboard, and that same cat, a big black thing, jumped out at me, and scratched my face. Look!" She showed me a faint red line on her cheek.

"It happened, and now it's done," I said.

She blinked her eyes against the unshielded glare of the light, a single bulb which hung from a cord above the desk. "No, it isn't." Dramatically she whispered, "Do you know what that cat was? It was the Devil."

I didn't know whether to laugh or not, and so I grinned doubtfully.

"Yessir," she went on, "you may not know it, but that's one of the manifestations of the Devil's spirit. A black cat. It's in the Good Book that the Devil, the Lord's disinherited brother, is a manifestation as a cat, a black cat. That's why black cats are unlucky."

I wondered if this were a joke. Her words had tumbled out in a pious breathless voice which had little relation to the first picture I kept of her, hand on hip, jeering at Dinsmore, "All you writers are nuts."

"Well, how are you sure of this?" I asked.

"Oh, it's in my religion. I'm a Witness, you see. My husband and myself, we're Witnesses. And the reason the Devil came is because he's making a last attempt to catch me. You see I've got a lot more knowledge now, and the more you got the less chance *he* has to catch you. So he's putting Temptation in my way."

I could not help it. This time I smiled.

"Oh, you don't believe me, but if I were to tell you the kind of Temptation I've had this last week." Here she gave a practical example. "Honestly, every time I've turned around, there's been another man propositioning me."

Her plump hand darted into the space between her breasts and gave the brassiere a hefty tug. It began immediately to slide down, and I found it difficult not to stare.

"If they propositioned you, they must have had some reason," I suggested slyly.

"What?" she cried raucously. "You don't mean to tell me you characters need any help. You run after us like a bunch of hound dogs."

Sensing that the continuation was not meet to what she had been saying, her voice became sad again. "I don't know," she said, "the world is so full of sin. Nobody loves his neighbor any more. On Judgment Day, the Witnesses teach that Christ is coming back, and we'll all have to stand up and be counted."

"Not many of us will pass."

"Exactly. That was what I was telling my husband. You know, you're not a dumb fellow. I could tell from the first moment that you had brains." As she blew out the smoke, she pursed her mouth, and I had the passing idea she expected a kiss.

She continued, however, to talk. "Now, I don't know anything about politics, but it seems to me that everything's going wrong today. Everybody's turning his back on the Lord. We're going to Gethsemane, that's the truth. We're going to be destroyed."

I listened to an automobile roar through the street below. Its muffler was broken, and the blast of the exhaust quivered through the warm evening and stirred the air in my room. I could see the royal blue of the summer sky as it deepened into night. I sat there trying to remember the biblical meaning of Gethsemane. "Yes," she continued sadly, "you're all goners because you've deserted the true way. I tell you there's going to be a world catastrophe." In the same tone, without transition, she asked, "What religion are you?"

"I don't have any," I told her.

"Then you're damned."

"I'm afraid so."

She shook her head. "Listen, I used to be like you, but I found out there's going to be wars and plagues and famines, and the Witnesses'll be the only ones saved because they bear true witness to the ways of the Lord, and they don't have false idols. You know I won't salute the flag, and nobody can make me cause it's in my religion."

"The Witnesses are the only ones to be saved?"

A fair question. She seemed perplexed. "To tell you the truth, I'm not sure." She could have been a clubwoman discussing the best method of running a benefit. "Probably it's just going to be our organization, but there might be a couple of other organizations, and maybe, this could be, a combination of our organization and a partial membership of one or two other organizations."

Guinevere lit another of my cigarettes. "It's funny you being here," she said casually; "I mean just taking this room."

"Have to live somewhere," I murmured.

"Yeah." She considered this. "You writers are weird guys.

Never know what to make of you." Her speech completed, she dumped the sheets on her arm, and stood up. "I got to go," she told me. "Pleasant talking to you."

I tried to detain her. "How would you like to clean up the room for me?" I offered.

"Clean the room?" she asked flatly.

"I know you're not obliged to do it, but I was wondering—is it worth a buck to you?" Immediately, I was horrified. The dollar would come out of my meals.

"It isn't the money. You know I'm very busy," she said. "This place may not look like much, but it's a man-sized job."

"You can find time." Now that she was reluctant I had lost my regrets over the dollar.

"I don't know. I'm going to have to think about it, Lovett."

Merely by using my name, she created another mood between us. Suggestions of her rough intimacy with Dinsmore were bandied. "I don't know, you crazy guys, didn't you ever hear of cleaning your own room and saving a buck?"

"We'll talk about it," I said smoothly. "I'll see you in a day or so about this, I suppose . . ."

She nodded with disinterest. "I'm not hard to find. I never go any place." Kicking the open door with her foot, she mumbled something about, "Work, work, every goddamn day."

On the stairs she called back a last time.

"You better clean the room yourself." I could hear Guinevere clumping down in her bedroom slippers.

FIVE

MY friendship with McLeod progressed in no familiar way. I grew to like him, but I learned no more than he had told me the first time. I knew where he worked, I thought I knew where he had been born, and with dexterity he managed to offer nothing else. It seemed as if we always ended by talking about me; to my surprise I discovered myself telling him one day about the peculiar infirmity I was at such pains to conceal from everyone else. He heard me through, nodding his head, tapping his foot, and when I was finished he murmured, "I suspected as much, I have to admit."

His next remark astonished me. Sniffing the air as though it were a sample to be tested, he added in a soft voice, "Of course you're presented with a unique advantage."

"What?"

"You need furnish no biography for yourself. And if you think that's not a benefit for certain occupations . . ." He let the comment die in a silence he created, and asked no questions.

Yet there were incidents, trivial enough, upon which he placed curious emphasis. At night he was often out of his room, and apparently concerned that I should not be curious about his absence, he would go out of his way to present the reason. "There was a particular party I had to see last night," he might say. "Feminine." The corner of his mouth curling with mockery,

33

he would go into his solitary laughter while I waited with an uncomfortable smile, not knowing at what it was directed.

He interested me a great deal. I was certain he was relatively uneducated, yet his intelligence was acute, and from passing references, it was apparent he had read and absorbed a surprising number of books. I had a theory McLeod had begun his serious studies—it was difficult to think of him reading for pleasure—comparatively late, and had spent his time with major works. The collection in his bookcase indicated little personal taste. I said something about this once and he answered glumly, "Taste, m'boy, is a luxury. I don't have enough money to dance around with this and that. Nor the time either." It was obvious, I deduced, that he must set aside perhaps a dollar a week, gleaned from petty sacrifices, and when he had saved enough he would buy the particular book he wanted at the moment. Such denial would cost him something, but he gave little evidence how it might pinch, cocking his sneer at the world and seeming oblivious of any other existence beyond the stale cabbage smell of our dark and dusty rooming house.

In everything he did there were elements of such order, demanding, monastic. He was unyielding and sometimes forbidding. Dressed in the anonymous clothing of a man who buys his garments as cheaply as possible, there were nonetheless two creases always to be found in a vertical parallel upon his buttocks. The straight black hair was always combed, he never needed a shave. And his room, clean as any cell could have been in our aged mansion, described an unending campaign against the ceiling which sweated water and the floor which collected dust.

I made a number of assumptions about McLeod. At the department store his salary was small, and I wondered why he should have been content with so little when he was intelligent and probably efficient. I ended with an hypothesis developed from what I knew of his room, his clothing, and the way he

34

bought his books. Everything about him, I decided, was timid. His horizon bounded no doubt by the image of a house in some monotonous suburb, he would sell the birthright he had never enjoyed for regular work and security. "Bury the rest," I could hear him say, "I'm only a poor noodle in search of a sinecure."

It is true that in many of our conversations he worried ceaselessly at a political bone, but I showed little interest. He spoke in a parody of Dinsmore's words, saying almost the same things but with an odd emphasis that made it difficult to know if he were serious or not. Once I told him, "You sound like a hack," and McLeod reacted with a rueful frown. "An exceptional expression for you to employ, Lovett," he told me softly. "I take it you mean by 'hack' a representative of the people's state across the sea, but I'm wondering where you picked up the word, for it indicates a reasonable amount of political experience on your part."

I laughed and said somewhat heavily, "Out of all the futilities with which man attempts to express himself, I find politics among the most pathetic."

"Pathetic, is it?" he had said, and directed at me a searching stare. "Well, maybe it is. And in answer to your question, I'm hardly a hack. I've told you already, m'boy, I'm not a joiner." He grinned sourly. "One might call me a Marxist-at-liberty."

This, too, has been an excessive preamble. But as Dinsmore was to muddle my impression of Guinevere, so McLeod was to mislead me about Hollingsworth, our neighbor on the top floor. The morning McLeod and I met in the bathroom he had said in passing that Hollingsworth was lazy, and I was to learn that the word meant nothing at all. Afterward, McLeod was more specific.

One day he introduced the subject. "You met our little buddy, Hollingsworth, yet?"

When I shook my head, McLeod said typically, pinching his words, "I'll be interested in your reactions when you do."

35

"Why?"

But he would not tell me so easily. "You're a student of human nature."

I sighed and sat back in my chair.

"He's a fascinating case," McLeod continued. "Hollingsworth. A pretty sick individual."

"I'm bored with sick people."

McLeod's internal laughter twisted his mouth. I waited for his humor to pass. He removed his severe silver-rimmed glasses and cleaned them leisurely with his handkerchief. "You know, Lovett, you can't talk without nonsense. I don't suppose you've said ten words to me you've ever meant."

"I have nothing to say."

"Neither has Hollingsworth." He whinnied again, his tongue probing with relish a tooth in his upper jaw. "He's got a mind like a garbage pail. My private opinion of him can be summed up in one word. He's a madman."

There he let it lapse and we talked of other things, but as I left that evening McLeod was to repeat, "Just let me know what you think of him."

The meeting, when it came, was accidental. I crossed the hall next evening to knock upon McLeod's door, and to my chagrin he was not there. I stood in the hall for a moment, disappointed because I did not want to work that night, and now there was no other prospect. For luck, I knocked once more.

Instead, a young man who I guessed was Hollingsworth peered out of the adjoining room. I nodded to him. "I'm sorry," I said, "I guess I tapped too loudly on McLeod's porthole."

"Oh, that's all right." He peered at me in the dim light of the hallway. "Are you the fellow who moved in just recently?"

I affirmed this, and he smiled politely. There was a pause. He broke it by saying without embarrassment and in great seriousness, "The weather's been mighty hot, hasn't it?"

"It has, I guess."

"I do believe it's going to let up though," he said in a soft mild voice. "I think it's fixing to rain, and that should clear a lot of the humidity out of the air."

I grunted something in return.

Hollingsworth seemed to feel that the necessary liaison had been established, and we were no longer strangers. He said, "I'm having a drink now, and I wonder if you'd like to have one with me?"

When I accepted, he invited me in and opened a can of beer. His room was somewhat larger than McLeod's or mine, but there was little more space, for the bed was big and an immense bureau covered a sizable area of the floor. I pushed aside some dirty shirts to sit down, and as if their touch remained against my finger tips, I was aware for seconds afterward of something odd, or out of place.

His room was unbelievably messed. There were several piles of soiled laundry, and two drawers in the bureau stuck open with linen hanging over the edge. His closet door was set at an angle, and I could see a suit tumbled upon the floor. Empty beer cans were strewn everywhere; the wastepaper basket had overflowed. He had a desk littered with pencil shavings, inkstains, cigarette butts, and a broken box of letter paper.

Yet the floor had no dust, the woodwork was wiped, and the windows had been washed within the last few days. Hollingsworth took care of himself as well. His cloth summer pants were clean, his open shirt was fresh, his hair was combed, he was shaved. Later I noticed that his nails were proper. He seemed to have no relation to the room.

"It's nice to have a sociable beer once in a while," he said. "My folks always taught me not to go in for heavy drinking, but this can't hurt a fellow, now can it?"

He was obviously from a small town: the talk about the weather, the accent, the politeness were unmistakable signs. The simple small-town boy come to the big city. His body expressed it: less than medium size with a trim build, he suggested the kind of grace which vaults a fence in an easy motion.

The features were in character. He had straight corn-colored hair with a part to the side, and a cowlick over one temple. His eyes were small and intensely blue and were remarked immediately, for his nose and mouth were without distinction. He was still freckled, which made me wonder at his age. I was to learn later that like myself he was at least in his middle twenties, but there must have been many people who thought him eighteen.

Standing in the center of the floor, the light reflected from his blond hair, he was in considerable contrast to his room. It seemed wrong for him. I had a picture of the places in which he had slept through his boyhood: a bed, a Bible, and in the corner a baseball bat perhaps. As though in confirmation, the only decoration upon his wall was a phosphorescent cross printed on cardboard. It would glow in the darkness when the lights were out.

I had the fantasy that each morning he cleaned this room, dusted the woodwork and beat the rug. Then after he was gone, a stranger would enter and make a furious search for something Hollingsworth could not possibly possess. Or else . . . There was the picture of Hollingsworth making the search himself, ripping open the drawers, hurling clothing to the floor. This was fanciful, and yet the room seemed to be visited more by violence than by sloth.

After a few minutes I asked him where he worked, and he told me he was a clerk in one of the large brokerage houses in Wall Street.

"Do you like it?"

He made a characteristic speech. "Oh, yes, I can't complain," he said in his soft voice. "They're all very nice over there, and they lead one to believe—although of course they may have their reasons for it—that there's a lot of room for advancement. But I like a job like that anyway. It's clean work, and I always prefer clean work, don't you?"

"I haven't thought about it much."

"No? Well, I can see that not everybody thinks about it the way I do." His politeness was irritating. He added, "I suppose there's a lot to be said for an outdoor occupation, and the healthful qualities involved."

"I'd hate the idea of being cooped up in an office."

"Mr. Wilson—he's the man over me—says there are all kinds of inside jobs, and if you can work with people instead of paper, it's very different. He's going to prepare me to be a customer's man, and that I would like more."

"Do you think you'd be good at that?"

He considered my question seriously. "Yes, I do. I'm very good at selling. My folks have a store in Meridabet—that's my home town—and I've always been able to sell people the things they wanted, and then sometimes the things they didn't want." He gave an uncertain smile which voided his last sentence of any humor, and said, "I don't suppose that's a very nice way to do business?"

"It's a rough life as the man said."

He guffawed loudly with a hir-hir-hir that lasted for many seconds. But his laughter lapsed so abruptly that I realized there was no real merriment. He was making just another gesture. "That *is* a clever way of putting it," he told me. In one of his excursions he had picked up a pipe and a tin of tobacco, and he played a match carefully over the bowl. I could see by the way he held it in his mouth that he found little enjoyment.

"You smoked that long?" I asked.

"No, I'm learning. I've noticed that Mr. Wilson and some of the men over him like Mr. Court tend to smoke a pipe a great deal. College men mainly smoke pipes, don't they?"

"Probably a case can be made."

"I don't like the pipe much, but if it's necessary, I suppose

I'll have to learn." He tapped the stem in resignation against his teeth. "Do you mind if I ask you a personal question?"

"No."

"You're a college man, aren't you?"

Indeed, why not? So I nodded, and he smiled with pleasure. "Yes, I thought so," he went on. "I've trained myself to observe people. Which college is it?"

I named at random a famous university.

He bobbed his head in admiration as if I had built the place. "Sometime I'd like to have a few talks with you about college. I've been wondering . . . Do you make many contacts there?"

I resisted the impulse to be flip, and said noncommittally, "I think it depends on whether you want to."

"That could be a big help for a career I would say. Most of the big men in the place I work at are college men. I'm intelligent, everybody tells me that," he added in his colorless voice, "and maybe I should have gone, but I hated to think of all the years I'd waste there. Wouldn't you?"

I merely said, "It *is* four years."

"That's what I say." He produced an image. "If you all start a race together, and there're too many men, you can get licked even if you're good." He regarded me seriously, and I discovered again how unusual were his eyes. The pupils were almost submerged in the iris, and reflected very little light. Two circles of blue, identical daubs of pigment, stared back at me, opaque and lifeless.

The sockets were set close together, folded into the flanks of his thin nose. Front-face, he looked like a bird, for his small nose was delicately beaked and his white teeth were slightly bucked. There was a black line between his gums and the center incisors in his upper jaw, and it gave the impression of something artificial to his mouth.

"Do you mind if I inquire what you do?" he said to me.

"I'm a writer, although don't ask me what I've published."

Again he produced his excessive laughter, going hir-hir-hir for some time and then ceasing abruptly. I had a passing image of the mechanical laughter in a canned radio program, the fans whirring, the gears revolving, the klaxons producing their artificial mirth and halting on signal. "Oh, that's good," he said. "I think that's very humorous." He tilted the beer to his mouth, and gurgled at the can. "You know a lot about books then."

"Yes. About some."

His next question was more tentative. "Do you know any good books I could read?"

"What kind do you mean?"

"Oh, you know."

I noticed a few magazines and a book on his desk. Because I was curious I said, "If you could let me see what you're reading now, I'd have a better idea of what you want."

"I guess you would." As though exposing his chest to the stethoscope, he gathered up the publications on his desk, and deposited them beside me. "You can see there's quite a bit of reading matter."

"Yes." He had a pocket book with the cellophane carefully peeled from the jacket. It was an anthology of the letters of famous people. Underneath, I found a pile of pulp magazines, a radio amateur's handbook, several Westerns, and a series of mimeographed papers which contained lessons on ballroom dancing.

"I don't suppose I ought to be reading things like that," Hollingsworth said.

"Why not?"

But he only tittered. I leafed through the pile and put them aside. "What kind of books do you want?" I asked again.

"Well . . ." He seemed hesitant. "In the Army there was an awful lot of literature that I liked. You know things with the facts of life in them."

I gave the name of an historical romance which had been a best seller.

"N-n-no. I don't remember the titles, but there were you know things about American fellows and girls. The real stuff though. You know the way we feel."

I mentioned several of the major novels which had been written by Americans between the two wars. This seemed to satisfy Hollingsworth. He made a list very carefully, writing each title into a little notebook he carried in his hip pocket. When he was finished, he asked, "Do you know where I could get them?"

"I can loan you one or two," I offered.

"Oh, I'd appreciate that. It's awfully neighborly." He had sat down in the chair by his desk, and was fingering the crease in his pants. "And there's lots of real things in them, isn't there? I mean, you know, . . . *foolish* girls, and boys who are willing to . . . to take a chance." He grinned.

"You'll probably find some."

"I'm really surprised they print things like that. I wonder if they should allow it. Atheistic things, and the Bolshevists, I understand, write for them a lot."

"For what?"

"Oh, for them, you know." He picked up another can of beer and offered it to me.

I had decided he annoyed me. "No, I think I'd better get back to my room and work."

"Do you make things there?"

"No. I . . . ?" I realized that he had forgotten. "No, I write."

"Oh, well that's a clever occupation." He followed me toward the door, and stood talking to me in the hall.

"I've been in New York for two months," he said suddenly, "and do you know I haven't found any of the evil quarters. I understand that Harlem is quite something, although they say that the tourists have ruined it, isn't that true?"

"I don't know."

"It takes all kinds to make a world, I suppose."

"Yes."

He leered at me suddenly. "I've had some interesting experiences with the lady downstairs. Mrs. Guinevere. She's a fine lady." The leer was shocking.

"I've heard a lot about her," I said.

"Oh, yes. She's an experience. Something to put into one's memoirs as they say."

"Mmm." I shuffled a step or two away. "Well, back to work for me."

"Oh, yes, I understand," he said in his soft voice. "One has to work, doesn't one?" He sipped his beer reflectively. "Sometime I'd like to talk over my experiences with you, would you mind?"

"No."

"It's been very enjoyable having this little discussion." He retreated almost completely into his room. As I left, he said one last thing. "You know that Mrs. Guinevere?"

"Yes."

"An extremely colorful person. Typical of New York, so I've heard."

I had no idea at all what to think of Hollingsworth.

SIX

IF I was a very lonely young man in New York that summer, it could be only my fault. Outside the rooming house I had not many acquaintances, but still there were people I could have visited. Yet as time went by, a week and then another, the tenuous circle of my acquaintances withered and fell apart. Entering Dinsmore's room with the intention to see no one until I had completed some work, I did not realize that actually I was feeding a wish, and in effect making it more difficult to break the bonds I fashioned myself.

This may sound extreme, and in fact it was. I did not have to disappear so completely, nor was I obliged to feel an insuperable weight at the prospect of seeing some indifferent friend for a few hours. A man in such a pass is hardly interesting, and there is no need to recount the hours I spent imagining a series of rebuffs and insults. In my mind I would telephone to somebody and he would invite me to his house, but from the moment I entered I would know it had been a mistake. Conversation would languish, I would stammer, I would be in an agony to depart. And so, in thinking of those people I knew in the city, I would discard them one by one, convinced as I considered each person that he was without interest, or without friendship.

44

Across the blur of the past, I have a memory which returns over and over again, and I am almost certain it happened. Perhaps it was during a furlough from the Army, although that is not important. I knew a girl then who was in love with me and I very much in love with her. We spent a week in a tourist home at some seashore resort, and that week provided more happiness and more pain than I could have thought possible. For the girl love had always been difficult and clothed in a hundred restrictions of false delicacy. She had been ashamed of her body and almost indifferent to men. What combination of circumstance and myself could bring it about I no longer know, but I adored her, so completely, so confidently, that my admiration seemed to accomplish everything. The room we shared burgeoned for her. She came to love her flesh, and from there it was but a step to loving mine. We lay beside each other for hours on end, brilliant with new knowledge. I had discovered magic to her and reaped the benefit; I could shine in the reflection of her face. Never, as she would assure me, had a man been more ardent, more thoughtful, and more desirable. She blossomed in that week, and I was so proud of myself. We were very close. We fed upon one another, we talked, we made love, we ate sandwiches she brought to the room, and we stole out to the beach for long solitary walks. We lived under the shadow of the war and perhaps that furnished its spice.

While I was with her I was very happy, but the moment I had to talk to someone else, an agony of shyness beset me. To order a meal from a waitress became a minor ordeal, and I remember that I could not bear to talk to the woman who owned the tourist house. Once on a hot afternoon we had wanted some ice water, and I had pleaded with the girl to go for it herself because I sensed myself incapable of managing such a transaction.

"But, Mikey," the girl had said—if I had another name it is not recollected now—"Mikey, why don't *you* get it? You make so much of it."

And I had refused, actually sweating at the prospect. "No, I can't," I had said. "Please, you go get it. I just don't want to talk to her."

I had won and therefore lost, and the girl got the ice water. When we parted, and I believe I never saw her again, she whispered a phrase not devoid of literary ambition, "Mikey, you know the room is the trap of the heart," and the extravagance of the words was not completely without meaning.

This is one of the few memories I possess, and I offer it for what explanation it may provide. If I lived in a close relation with the few people I knew in the rooming house and became progressively less capable of doing without them, there is after all a precedent. I was a dog on a chain, and the radius circumscribed a world in which I was able to provide for many of my wants and most of my needs. I had begun again to think about my week with that girl, but the image of Guinevere, no matter how incongruous, often accompanied her, and I find it hardly surprising that a·few days after seeing Hollingsworth I felt compelled to make the trip downstairs and ring the bell of Guinevere's apartment.

It was after three o'clock and Guinevere was in the midst of lunch. I was greeted at the door with a surprising reception. "Oh, Mr. Lovett, you're just the man I want to see. Come in, won't you, please?" I shall not bother to describe her costume in detail; suffice it that she was clothed with enough variety to suggest everything from breakfast in bed to a formal evening. "I had an idea you might be coming down," she said, her voice lilting through high notes and modulated carefully through the lower tones. "I'm just finishing eating. Won't you have coffee with me?"

"Well, all right. I'd like to talk to you about a business matter." As the pretext for visiting, I intended to ask her again to clean my room.

We walked through the hallway of her apartment into the

46

kitchen whose sink and stove were covered with what seemed all the unwashed pots of all the meals of the last week. Upon the kitchen table was the litter of this repast: a half-eaten sandwich, a sliced tomato somewhat squashed upon the oilcloth, and meandering through it a pool of spilled coffee.

"A business matter?" she repeated belatedly, and it was obvious my words had a poor effect. Business was reality. "Oh, you got to excuse this place," she groaned. "I never can get in gear. Here, sit down, have some coffee." The open sleeve of her imitation Japanese kimono trailed through bread crumbs. She reached over to the sink, found a rag, and flopped it upon the table to wipe a clear space for me. "Monina," she bawled abruptly, "say hello to Mr. Lovett."

"Dello Ditter Luft," a voice piped at me. In an alcove between the refrigerator and the window, a child was sitting in a high chair, a child of exceptional beauty. The sunlight illumined her golden hair and steeped her face and arms in a light so intense her flesh appeared translucent. In one small hand she grasped a spoon and was in the process of transferring some oatmeal to her lips. The maneuver was difficult and swatches of cereal mottled her tiny mouth and pouting cheeks. I had for a moment the whimsy that she was an angel come to earth, but a sullen angel, perplexed by the mechanics of living.

"Why, she's lovely," I exclaimed.

"Oh, she's got the looks," Mrs. Guinevere told me. "And don't think she don't know it, that little bitch."

Monina giggled. A sly expression formed beneath the oatmeal. "Mommie said dirty durd."

Guinevere groaned again. "Oh, that kid, you can't put nothing over on her."

"How old is she?" I realized she was big to be in a high chair.

"Three and a half going on four." As if she guessed the reason behind my question, Mrs. Guinevere said with no attempt to conceal anything from the child, "I want to keep her a baby. I'll tell you, I've got it all figured out. In about another year or two, I'm going to have enough money put together to head for Hollywood, and Monina's a cinch. Only she's got to remain a kid. There's not so many roles for kids five years old as there is for infants, you know, one year old and up. So I want her to stay young." She raised her forearm and kissed the flesh above her wrist. "Oh, is it chafed. I got to get my watch fixed. Here, look at that." And Mrs. Guinevere gave me her arm to examine. "Just touch it there. Gee, it's sore."

I could see a faint red mark. I pressed it and trailed my fingers over her arm. "It's very smooth," I murmured.

"Yeah, I got good skin." Her eyes closed and she leaned back, a look of sentience upon her face.

Abruptly, she whipped her arm away. "Oh, hell, I forgot."

"What?"

"You ain't supposed to tell anybody."

"Tell what?"

"That Monina is three and a half. That's a secret. You promise you won't tell."

I shrugged. "Yes, I promise."

"Well, I guess you got something on me now." Her painted mouth in its broad sensual curves grinned at me provocatively. "You could hurt my chances if you wanted to."

"Monina don't want doatmeal," the child said.

"You shut up and eat it," Guinevere screeched. "I'll get the strap if you don't."

But Monina had made her bid for attention and was temporarily content. She sighed like an old woman and applied the back of the spoon to her cheek.

"You know I've missed opportunities with her. When I think of the money I could be making now." Guinevere shook her head, and sipped her coffee. "You just can't trust nobody. I've

48

had promises galore, and where did it get me?" She extended her hand. "Let's have a cigarette, Lovett."

We smoked in silence for a moment. "Why do you want her in Hollywood?" I asked.

Guinevere's bald blue eyes stared at me, and she said in a mysterious voice laden with self-love, "What do you know, Lovett, of what a woman goes through? Do you think it's fun taking care of a household with a no-good husband, and behind me I've had conquests after conquests, lovers and night clubs and gay exciting times. I could've been married to a Maharajah, do you know that? And what a lover he was. The whang he had on him." She paused as though talking to a foreigner, and said, "That's what I always call it, a whang."

But I was becoming accustomed to conversation with her, with leaping up stairways and tumbling down them. "Yes, I know."

"He begged me to marry him, and I turned him away, you know why? His skin was dark. I could have been a Maharajess, but he had odd ways about him, and so I missed the boat. I tell you if I met another nigger with as much money as him, I wouldn't make the same mistake. I'm a young woman, Lovett, and I'm wasting my life. Boy, there was a time when I could pick and choose among you characters."

"How can you go to Hollywood?" I persisted. "What about your husband?"

"I'll leave him. I only married the sucker out of pity." She stared about the kitchen, surveying the dirty dishes. "I've got too good a heart, that's my only trouble. If you saw me dressed up, you'd realize how easy it is for me to make a man. There isn't one of you I can't get if I want to lift a finger."

"Lift a finger for me," I essayed.

"Oh, you, what do you want with an old woman like me? I'm twenty-eight you know." She drew a design in the bread crumbs. "Boy, if I told you my husband's name, you'd fall out of the chair."

"Who is he?"

She smiled secretly. "Catch me telling you."

Through the open kitchen window a warm breeze drifted into the room, carrying with it the smell of leaves and tar from the streets beyond. A delicate anticipation stirred through my body. Somewhere people were making love, the heat moistening their fluid limbs, the balm of summer carrying them through this languorous hour. I almost stretched out my arm in a caress.

"Lovett, you want to do me a favor?"

"What?"

She placed a hand confidingly on mine. "Look, I got a taste for some root beer. Be a good guy, and go out to the store, and get me a bottle. And I can give you the empties to return at the same time."

"I don't see why I should." I was annoyed at the way she had shattered my mood.

"Aw, come on. Look, I'll tell you what. I'll give you a nickel if you do it." She said this with some reluctance.

I laughed. "How young do you think I am?"

She shook her head. She was quite serious. "Fair's fair. You go out in the sun, you're entitled to it."

"I don't want your nickel."

"Come on, do it anyway."

This was childish. "All right, all right." I picked up her quarter, and left with ill-humor. I was furious with myself for doing her errand. She was absurd, an overblown woman whose attractiveness was almost submerged by the rubble about her person. Yet I wanted her. We could be alone in my room under the baking heat of the roof, and all through this summer we could have a succession of trysts.

I bought two bottles of root beer and a candy bar, and

50

hurried back. "Here's your quarter," I told her. "It's a present."

"Aw, that's swell of you." She accepted the quarter greedily as an unexpected bounty. "See, I changed for you." She had, indeed. My heart leaped. She wore a tropical halter and short pants, and her flesh bulged wantonly.

"Dressed for me, huh?"

She guffawed. "I can't stand wearing clothes in this heat. If there's nobody around I'd like to be without a damn thing on." She thought about this. "You know those nudists got something."

Monina was out of the high chair, and walking about. Once or twice she examined me with the unabashed stare of a child. "Ditter Luft doodooking," she said to her mother.

"What's that?" I asked.

"She says you're good-looking." Guinevere laughed. "You know, you ain't bad, Lovett." Now, both the child and the mother were looking at me. I was hardly comfortable, and Monina, who had seemed somewhat retarded to me with her baby talk, had created a presence far larger than herself. "When does she take her nap?" I asked.

"Oh, that kid don't nap. You never saw anything like her. She keeps the same hours I do. I swear she don't go to bed half the time till midnight." Guinevere swigged the root beer, and handed it to Monina who parodied her mother, throwing back her tiny blonde head and tilting the bottle. She did not hold it against her mouth however, and a considerable quantity splashed upon her chin, dribbled down the undershirt, and trickled to the floor. "You slob," her mother shrieked.

Monina giggled. "Ditter Luft doodooking," she said again.

"Why don't we go into the other room?" I suggested. "And Monina can play in the bedroom. You want to play in the bedroom, don't you, Monina?"

"Nooo."

"She follows me everywhere," Guinevere said. "Monina

can't be without me." She yawned. "All right, come on, we'll all go in the living room." But "living room" was apparently more than just a word and her manner became haughty again. With a ridiculous gesture, Guinevere pointed to the ashtray, and said, "You can take that with you if you wish, Mr. Lovett," implying by the action a cornucopia of servants, brandy, and cigars.

Actually, to my surprise, her living room was not in execrable taste. The furniture was modest, but she had achieved some decent effects. A mattress and spring on legs was covered by a dark green spread and served as a couch. There were several old armchairs with new print materials, and a dull tan rug was set against tomato-colored drapes. There were more mirrors than she needed upon the wall, the lamps were shabby, and needless gewgaws were clustered upon every end table, but altogether one could notice a certain unity. Yet, like people who build a house when at heart they desire a monument, I had the impression that she was seldom here.

She paced about uneasily before settling in one of the chairs. "This is a nice room," I told her.

"Yeah, I like it; I worked hard on it," Guinevere said dispiritedly. "If I had more money I could do something with these things." Then she lapsed into silence, unaccountably depressed, her eyes staring at the carpet. "Boy, the work I put into this," she muttered. Her hand fretted into the money pocket of her shorts and turned it inside out. "But does he appreciate this? No." She leaned back, her breasts lolling heavily in the halter, her fingers pinching a rope of flesh about her waist.

She lay there dormant, but her restlessness was conveyed to the child who pranced about the room. I watched Monina. She halted before a mirror and preened her body, kissing her wrist with the absorbed self-admiration she had seen in her mother. "Dashtray," I heard her whisper. "Dake dashtray." Her little arms fluttered, her head nodded politely, and she extended an invitation in pantomime, glowing with satisfied laughter at the portrait of herself in the mirror. She pirouetted away to stand in contemplation before a set of china knickknacks upon a table. Selecting a tiny bowl of cheap porcelain, she stared at the decoration painted about the rim. "Mommie, Monina, Mommie, Monina," she said aloud. A smile set upon her face, she approached me, and repeated the same formula, holding the bowl before my eyes and pointing to the cupids painted upon it.

Guinevere stirred heavily in the armchair. "Put it down, Monina," she shouted at the child. But the command was too ambiguous. What was meaning and what was sound?

Monina smashed the bowl upon the floor.

"Oh, you little bitch," Guinevere shouted. "Go to the bedroom."

"No," Monina screamed.

"Stand in the corner."

"No!"

Guinevere stood up threateningly. "I'll get the strap," she shrieked. Monina pouted, her eyes glaring at her mother.

"All right," she conceded at last. She trailed reluctantly to the door, and then turned about and pronounced anathema. "Mommie-diggie, mommie-diggie."

"I'll get the strap!"

And Monina disappeared.

Guinevere groaned. "Oh, that kid'll drive me crazy." Eyes closed, she laughed, her belly shaking in jollity. "Oh, murder." After a moment she stirred herself and began to pick the pieces off the floor. She was less than a yard away from me, and knelt in such a position that it was impossible not to stare at her breasts. Chuckling, she seemed in excellent humor. "That kid," she murmured.

She looked up, and a broad coarse grin formed upon her mouth. "Well, Lovett, here we are alone," she jeered.

"Yes, I got what I wanted," I drawled.

53

"Oh, you." She dropped the pieces in the ashtray by my side, and went back to her chair. This time she sprawled with her legs akimbo, her hands kneading her breasts. "Mmmmm," she purred. Slowly she massaged her bare shoulders against the print of the seat cover in a slow luxurious motion from side to side. "You ever rub your back against velvet?" she asked.

"Don't think so." My voice was husky.

"Oh, I love it. Mmm," she purred again. "Boy, I wish this was velvet. This is just cotton, scratches a little." She yawned pleasurably. "You know I'll tell you something, I don't know why I'm telling you, I never told anyone else, but when I'm alone, I love to take off my clothes and lie in velvet."

Was this a secret vice, or something she had invented on the spur of the situation? "Interesting," I murmured. I was hardly concerned with what I said.

"Oh, the times I've had," she told me. "Brutal!"

I stood up and walked toward her. She tasted my kiss for a few seconds, and then pushed me back, and hummed a breathy, "Whew." She smiled. "That was nice."

I reached out for her, and she caught my arm. "Aw, now hold on."

But like the bull who has passed the pic, and felt the flank of the horse collapsed by his horn, I must gore and gore, reach out and pin to earth. My hands clutched various parts of her body. "Whew," she said again, and pushed me away competently, standing up from the chair in the same motion.

We stood face to face, my arms about her. "What the hell is it I got?" she demanded in pleasurable anger. "Boy, you guys can't leave me alone."

"No," I mumbled.

She sighed and walked away. "I tell you I've had all kinds of men, and there hasn't been one of them who didn't fall in love with me. Just must be something chemical I got." She turned around and examined me. "You know, Lovett, you're not

54

a bad-looking guy. I could go for you, but I'm not fooling around any more. I don't know why, it isn't my husband, but I play it close to the vest." Her voice exuded satisfaction. "Now you and me could get together, but what profit is there in it for me? You tell me."

"Oh, the hell with that." I reached forward and kissed her once again. She closed her eyes indolently and moved her mouth against mine as if she were eating candy.

"What Mommie done, what Mommie done." Monina stood in the doorway and pointed an accusing finger.

To my surprise Guinevere taunted the child. "What Mommie done," she mimicked. "I'll get the strap! Go to bed."

"Mommie bad, mommie-diggie." It was impossible to know what the child felt. She quivered, and hot furious tears stood in her eyes. Yet suddenly she coquetted at me. "Kiss Monina, too," she demanded.

Guinevere patted her bottom. "Go to bed, or I'll get the strap," she shrieked automatically. And once again, reluctantly, the child withdrew.

"See what you've done," Guinevere grumbled. "That kid'll have something on me now. Wait, she'll let me know about it."

"I'm sorry," I said.

"Lot of good that does," she whipped at me. "You guys give me a pain in the ass." She turned away to light a cigarette and laughed. "Here," she said unexpectedly, "here, you want to feel my breasts, here, feel them," and she took my hand and placed it. I kissed her again, and indolently she raised the arm which supported the cigarette and returned the embrace.

She was not without response. The kiss must have lasted for over a minute, and my hands moved in a crescendo about her. When we paused, her breath was coming quickly too.

"Hey," she said.

"Come on." Nothing was going to stop me now. "Come on."

"We can't."

"Right here."

She stiffened. "Look," she whispered, "the kid's around. Are you crazy?"

I would not be thwarted. "Upstairs in my room."

"I don't know."

"You've got to come upstairs."

She pinched me suddenly. "All right, I will."

"You promise?"

"I'll be up." She groaned. "Oh, my God, what you guys get me into."

"You promise?"

"Yes, I'll be up in ten minutes. Now, get out of here, and let me get Monina to bed."

Battered, drunk with lust, I stumbled to my room.

G UINEVERE did not follow.

I was furious. In the next miserable hour I lay on my cot under the baking heat of the roof and stared at the wall. The hot summer afternoon dragged by, carrying me with it in torpor. I tried to read, I thought of working, but neither was practicable. At last I took a walk.

I was gone for hours and ended at the docks where I sat on a deserted quay, flipping pebbles into the oily water which swirled about the piles. Twilight came, and across the harbor, skyscrapers reflected the sun. I ate my solitary meal in a lunchroom and returned to my desk in an attempt to write.

It was hardly productive. After several hours in which I was able to do very little, I went out again to pace through the dark streets. I was in the kind of mood where I made resolution after resolution. I was not doing enough work, I decided; then tomorrow I would begin a new schedule. I would get up early and work till evening, and I would do the same in the following days. I would leave Guinevere alone. Certainly I would not go to see her without some invitation.

Yet perversity is not without resource. I could detect in myself beneath twenty mattresses of frustration the small hard pea bean of relief that Guinevere had not kept her word. For an image came to me of the two of us in my room. The door is locked, and I lie with my head at her breast while summer air shimmers over us. We are happy, we are content, and we are safe. Suddenly there is a knock. We start up, look desperately at one another, search for an escape. There is none. The door is the only door to the room, and the window is a hundred feet above the ground. We make no sound and draw the bedclothes to our necks. The knocking ceases, and there is silence. Then a key is inserted in the lock, turns back and forth. We wait, petrified, and the door opens, and on the threshold stands a stranger. His arm lifts in a menacing gesture, and I close my eyes and turn my head to the pillow.

This was a conscious fantasy, but even so, walking the street on a June night, I shuddered and there was a sweat on my back. Several minutes passed before I felt calm enough to light a cigarette, and I dallied beneath a lamp-post.

When I came back to the room, I picked up my novel, and on an impulse reread everything I had written. I intended a large ambitious work about an immense institution never defined more exactly than that, and about the people who wandered through it. The book had a hero and a heroine, but they never met while they were in the institution. It was only when they escaped, each of them in separate ways and by separate methods, that they were capable of love and so could discover each other.

I had never stated it so baldly before, and as I put the novel down, the story seemed absurd and I was abysmally dejected. Some of the chapters I had read were good, but I knew that as a whole the concept was sentimental, and that I hardly knew where I was led. In the morning, after a miserable night, I deserted my first resolution and went for a long breakfast, read a paper slowly, and delayed coming back to work. I did a page or two, tore them up. New ideas were forming on the novel, confused and often destructive; there was nevertheless a ferment.

For several days I worked steadily, alternating between excitement and depression, burrowing at a mountain whose girth I could not conceive. I thought of Guinevere frequently, but my reluctance equalled my desire, and the stalemate aided my determination to keep working.

Finally, the white flag appeared. I came back to my room one morning and found a note from her. In a small careful hand she had written:

> Dear Friend,
>   Where you been? I got something important to tell you. Come see me. This is something we got to talk about. G.

The note decided my attitude. I changed my clothing, brushed my hair, and walked downstairs.

Guinevere opened the door with a tremulous smile. "*Hello*," she said. Her voice was soft and husky. She might have been a maiden greeting her first lover, eyes downcast, body articulated in yearning. I would not have been startled if she had said demurely, "How can I look you in the face again?" She maintained the pose for several seconds, but when I failed to respond, she shed it like an overcoat. "Where the hell you been?" she demanded.

"Upstairs. Waiting for you. Waiting for seventy-two hours." I had prepared this speech.

A gleam of satisfaction could have appeared in her face. Almost instantly, she began protesting. "Aw, listen, that was a mix-up the other day. Monina got sick right after you left. You know I had two doctors here, and it cost me twenty-five dollars. Honestly, what a day I had. First you getting me all *upset*"—she said this with great fondness, as if I were a bad boy whom she adored—"and then Monina. My husband had to give me a sedative that night."

"What was the matter with Monina?"

"Nerves." Guinevere sighed. "Come on, let's go in the kitchen. I'm having my coffee."

I shook my head. "Let's take it in the living room. I'll have one with you."

So we took coffee in the parlor. Really she was like a cat who stirred at every sound, darted here and there at a footstep, and never gave herself wholly to any direction. A round table was set between us, a cloth was put upon it, and a silver service. She poured with her little finger crooked, her face set in poised, determined gaiety. Yet again she wore a bathrobe, and a loose strap from one of her voluminous undergarments slithered over her breast.

We drank in silence for a time, and then she sat back and stared at me with her provocative grin. "You know...Michael, you shouldn't have done that the other afternoon. I could go for you."

"Look, you called me Michael. What's your first name?"

"Guinevere."

"Well, what's your last name?"

"Smith, Smith's my husband's name."

I was dubious, but I nodded. She leaned forward for an instant. "I'll tell you," she said, "I was born Beverly Guinevere, but when I was on the stage, I just used to call myself Guinevere, you know one name, like Margo or Zorina. And I like it, I keep it, you know it's not like other names."

"You were on the stage?"

She nodded profoundly.

"What plays?" I asked.

"Oh, I was in burlesque, I was a queen. Boy, they used to go for me." She glanced with distaste at her body. "I was a lot slimmer, not skinny, I never been skinny, I always been good to feel, but you know pleasingly plump. *Svelte.* They used to announce me, 'and now presenting the svelte siren of sensation—

Guinevere.'" She caressed her arm abstractly. "They'd all go for me. There was an old gink, sixty-two years old, and he offered me a thousand dollars to go to bed with him once."

Monina had appeared in the doorway, and Guinevere glanced at her. I looked about uneasily. The child was completely naked. "See Monina," the mother said, "you see the way she's built. That's the way I was, but since I been married I let my figure go." Emerging from the reverie, she shrieked suddenly, "Monina, put something on."

But Monina coquetted, her arms raised, the tiny hands at her neck. I found myself reluctant to look at the child, for her body was extraordinary. She was virtually a miniature of a girl of eighteen, the limbs round, slender curves flowing from shoulder to hip, her luminous blonde hair lovely against the pale flesh. "No," Monina pouted.

"I'll get the strap."

Monina sighed. She seemed bored with the strap, and although she retreated, I could swear she was listening from the hall.

Guinevere poured me another cup of coffee. "Someone was telling me you're an author, Lovett," she said.

"He was mistaken."

She passed this by. "You know I been thinking there's a way you and me could make a lot of money," she said. "I got a story that's worth a million bucks."

"Well, then why don't you write it?"

"I can't. I can't write. I haven't got the patience. But here's my idea. I'll tell you the story, you write it, and we'll split the money. I swear. When I think of the hundreds of thousands of dollars this book is worth, and it's all in my head."

She was not to be halted. "Listen, you really ought to listen to this. It's a natural. I read lots of novels, and I never seen anything to compare to this." Her voice became matter-of-fact again. "And you know it covers a span of years, it's a serious story." She closed her eyes and rested her forehead against her fist, face twisted into concentration. "I've been trying to make up my mind which stars ought to play it, but so far I'm not sure, although I suppose they decide it all in Hollywood anyway. Just to think about it gets me excited.

"Here," she offered. "It takes place in this city in New York State, and the main characters are a doctor, a real good-looking guy with a mustache, big you know, and his nurse, she looks like some of those blonde stars, and then he's got a girl-friend, a dark-haired girl, any feature player could do that part." Guinevere lit a cigarette. "Now, this guy, the doctor, he's a pretty good guy, good heart and so forth, and he's a wow with the women. He's got the biggest whang on him in the whole town, and maybe he don't know it. He's got dozens of girl friends, and there isn't one of them who won't surrender herself to him, you know. But he's got a favorite, the blonde star one, his nurse, and she's a good kid too, worked hard all her life, and she goes for him. You know she's really in love, but she don't show it, puts up a tough front." Guinevere sighed with content. "Now the other one is a society girl, hoity-toity, and she comes to see him about something or other, woman trouble maybe, and he seduces her in his medical chambers, and they really tie a can on. You know for weeks he just goes around with her, to night clubs and to the beach, the country club, and he can't get her out of his system, it's chemical. Only all the time, at the same time, he still keeps the nurse on the string, and they get together once in a while, and it's love with them, it's just passion with the other."

"That is," I interposed, "it's the blonde star one he's really in love with?"

"Yeah." Without missing a breath, she continued. "Well, all this time, there's been a hullaballoo with the brunette society one's parents, you know they don't like the doctor because he's also from lowly origin like the nurse. But there's nothing they can do, it's real flaming youth." She halted, and murmured in

62

aside, "Some of this I'm drawing from my own experiences." Guinevere tapped the ash from her cigarette. "Well, this goes on for a while and there's a climax. One night just for the hell of it he has one on the house with the society girl, and she gets pregnant. Only in the meantime before she finds out, he's decided that he's really more interested in the nurse, and they're thinking of getting married. When the society girl comes in, you know, knocked up, he talks to her for a while and convinces her he's not in love, and that she ought to have an operation. And so here's the first big scene. The doctor makes an operation on this dame he's had a hot affair with, and the nurse, the woman he's in love with, assists him right at it. I mean you can see how this would make a movie even though they'd have trouble with such a scene. I imagine they could work it out though. She could have a brain tumor, or something of that nature. It would be a good scene the operation, you know with him giving directions to the nurse, scalpel nurse, forceps nurse, sponge, acting cold because he's a good doctor, and he's got lots of responsibility." Guinevere stared at me blankly. "The operation turns out a failure. She isn't going to have the baby any more, but at the same time he does something, he makes a mistake, and the society girl can't make love any more. She looks perfectly okay, but she's crippled there, a beautiful girl and yet she can't do it any more. Well, when she finds out, she's mad, and she's going to expose him, but the nurse who's a wonderful character convinces him he ought to marry the society girl, and he does even though there can't be anything between them, and for a while they all keep living in the same town, and he keeps up his affair with the blonde nurse. They're still in love, and it's gotten very chemical like it used to be with the society girl, he goes down on her and everything, and she loves him. But the wife who's now turned out a bitch is going to expose him all over again, and so the nurse takes off and goes to New York, and the doctor gets richer and richer, fooling around with a lot of dames on the

63

side, but his heart is still with the blonde nurse. Only they don't see each other for years." She stopped. "Guess what the ending's going to be?"

I was not to hear it so quickly. Guinevere went on developing wondrous detail upon detail; my attention flagged, and I listened indifferently. For Monina stood in the hall entrance performing a dance. The child was still nude, but somewhere she had picked up a coaster for a highball glass, and now in a posture of unbelievable provocation, she held it like a fig leaf, writhing her limbs sinuously through a parody of amorous advance and retreat. She would approach a few steps, her blonde head cocked to one side in sensuous repose as if she were stirred by an exotic music, and then abruptly with a tiny pout upon her lips, she would draw back, an attitude of feigned horror in the pose of her limbs. As her mother spoke she danced silently, an interpreter. The story drew to a close, and with it the dance. Monina reclined against the doorway, her arm caressing her thigh. She never looked in my direction, yet everything was done for me. Her blonde eyelashes fluttered upon her cheek, her eyes opened to gaze boldly at the wall. And all the while, Guinevere, unheeding, continued to talk.

"They meet again in New York, just about a year ago, the nurse and the doctor, and the doctor's wife is dead, and whammo do they get together. I mean drinking and making love, nothing can stop them. And the nurse doesn't tell him about that baby she had from him after she left cause she knows he won't believe her; he'll think it belongs to some other guy. And the doctor wants to get married, and she holds him off cause she doesn't know what to do with the kid. And then what do you think, she can't tell him so she murders the kid, her own child, and she's caught, and the doctor too. I forgot to say he made out the death certificate cause she brought him in on it at the end, and then in prison, which'll be the last chapter, they're brought together for a final hour by the warden who's a pretty good guy, and there in the cell behind the bars they have a last one that really makes it worth while being killed."

And Monina, resolving the chord, ran toward me on tiptoe, nude nymph, halted within the reach of my arm, and in a child's counterfeit of a leer raised the fig leaf above her head, exposed and triumphant.

For the first time she stared at me as though I were real.

In the next instant a look of confusion mounted upon her face, deepened into terror. Abruptly, her mouth crumpled, her eyebrows knotted, and she began to wail in panic. Within a minute she was hysterical.

EIGHT

WE made hot milk for Monina, we put her to bed. Guinevere sat beside the child and stroked her hair, crooning fragments of love ballads in an absorption so great that I am certain she was unaware of me. And the language, conventional enough—"Oh, go to sleep, baby, cause Mommie loves you, go to sleep"—was startling from Guinevere. A tear which might have been genuine coursed down her cheek. "You're all I got," she murmured once, and that compassion which is just one degree from self-pity shone upon her face.

Monina quieted at last and fell asleep. Fingers held to our lips, we tiptoed from the room, closed the door, and went into the kitchen.

I was shaken. Like the spectator at an accident I wanted to talk, but Guinevere gave me small opportunity. "Whew," she said, "I never saw her that way before." She leaned an elbow on the table, and munched a crust of bread. And whatever she might have revealed with Monina was not to be revealed again. "Lordy, that was something. I don't understand the kid," she said in an offhand tone.

She had acted somewhat differently the moment Monina had begun to cry. Then she had started from the chair, picked the child up, and spanked her once with fury across the bottom.

"How long was she doing that?" Guinevere had shrieked at me. When I stammered that Monina had been in the room for several minutes, Guinevere scorched me with fury. "Why you lousy no-good son of a bitch," she screamed in her harsh voice, "why didn't you do something?" She had clapped her forehead. "Oh, my God, I'll go crazy."

It was not an appetizing scene. While Monina sobbed and wailed, her body trembling, Guinevere abused me for over a minute in a more formidable rage than I had believed she could muster. And conscious that I had allowed Monina to continue, I stomached her outburst, humiliated, yet too shamed to make any response.

Guinevere collected herself finally, and carried the child into the bedroom. Now, half an hour later, she revealed no dregs of her tantrum. "Honest, Lovett," she said, "it's hell bringing up a kid," speaking in a conventional voice which might have belonged to any housewife on the street. She seemed almost in a good humor.

"Here, I'll make some more coffee for us," she offered.

"I've had enough, thank you."

"Oh, I haven't. I could drink it all day long."

We chatted at random for several minutes, or more exactly Guinevere talked. I listened indifferently, my attention wandering. As I nodded my head, she told story after story about this man and that lover, about presents she had accepted and presents spurned, of drinking bouts and happy license, and then occasionally if she sensed my belief flagging or my detachment growing, she would parade a special attraction and describe with relish the baubles of a particular lover. "I been every kind of woman you'd want, Lovett. There isn't anything I haven't done. But times change. I can tell you it's a damn shame you didn't know me a couple of years ago. Why we'd a been together after two hours or two minutes, but now you know I'm different. There's the child to think about," she said smugly.

"And then," I suggested on an impulse, "you're religious now, too."

For an instant I could have sworn Guinevere looked at me in perplexity. She shrugged dubiously. "Oh, yeah, that. Yeah, I'm religious." For conversation like this, her footing was always stable. She might have stumbled, but without visible effort she drew to a gallop, and spoke once more of the Witnesses. "And you know, it was my husband who first converted me. He's a religious man, religious as they come." She bent forward and chuckled. "When I think about him in private, I call him the deacon. If you ever met him you'd be amazed I married a man like that, but then opposites attract, you know there's some truth in that."

"He's Monina's father, isn't he?"

She nodded carefully as though debating her next words. "Lovett, I'll tell you something. I don't know." She held up her hand. "Not that I was fooling around with anybody else at the time, but I could swear it wasn't him. She don't look like him, she looks exactly like me, and she ain't got any of his temperament." Her voice lowered; this, the deepest of secrets, to be revealed, she bent forward again, confiding. "Now, you know I ain't a Catholic, but there's times when I think they got something, like with Mary. I'm not saying Monina was born the same way they claim for Jesus, but you know it might have been a similar kind of thing, the doctors are always discovering new secrets, and who's to say?" Reflectively, sensuously, she caressed her arm, her large blue eyes staring at me in calculated innocence.

I offered my small fagot. "Lots of odd things happen."

"That's what I think. There's always something fishy going on. If I was to tell you some of the things that happened in this house. You know I just can't keep up with it all, and I'm supposed to keep a lookout."

"Well, what do you care?"

She snorted. "I got a pretty good setup here. We get our rent for nothing, and I don't want to lose it." Guinevere lit a cigarette with great deliberation. "Now, I don't know what's going on upstairs, but you're three single men up there, and who knows what kind of floosies you guys are bringing in."

"There's an orgy going on every night."

She shook her head. "Listen, you're all right, Lovett. It's not you I'm thinking about. I can see you're a man of honor, and anyway you go for me so you're accounted for. It's those other two jokers. McLeod's a queer fish, and Hollingsworth, although he seems okay, could have an ace or two up his sleeve. He's still waters." With her hand she molded a curl in her red hair. "Now, what I was thinking is maybe you'd care to keep an eye out on them, and let me know about it." She was casual, deliberately casual; she yawned as she finished.

I had the impression that this finally was the purpose, if there were a single purpose, behind her note. "In other words," I said, "you want me to spy on them."

She shrugged. "What's wrong with that? Everybody does it all the time anyway."

"Well, I don't care to assume the role."

Her manner altered. "I'm just asking you to let me know what's going on." Cunningly she added, "You mean you wouldn't do me a favor?"

"Not one like that."

Guinevere put her hand over mine and squeezed it. "I thought there wasn't anything you wouldn't do for me." She sighed. "Well, let's forget about it. I'll lose my job when the cops come in some night and find out what's going on, but that's none of your affair."

I grinned. "You can always go back on the stage."

"I'm too fat now."

"You're incredible," I said.

I have no idea what passed through her mind. Conflicting

expressions molded her mouth and eyes. "Aaah, you stink, Lovett," she said at last. "Why do you think I wrote you that note?"

"So I'd look after your boy-friend, Hollingsworth."

She started. "What do you mean by that? You know a lot of people talk about me, but that don't mean nothing." She crushed my empty cigarette pack and tossed it on the floor. "I'll tell you something, something a woman should never tell a man. I wrote that note cause I wanted to see you again, and this time I intended to surrender. I was going to break all my resolutions. I really had it for you, and I was going to slip."

"Sure."

"But, now, it's impossible. You hurt something in me. A woman's not a machine. Why I could no more look at you now than if you were a cripple." She spoke the word with venom.

From a depth in me, fatuous and self-pitying, I heard myself say, "I am a cripple." Anger followed. My voice quivered. "And you, why don't you stop playing Mata Hari? You're very bad at it."

I might have lashed her across the face. Her eyes contracted. "You can get out of here, Lovett. I didn't invite you down to insult me." Her voice became strident. "Get out, get out, you son of a bitch."

"Oh, I'm going. And you can come upstairs next time."

"Get out!" she screamed.

So, once again, completely bewildered, I climbed to my room and re-enacted our little drama to exhaustion. And if our fight had been serious—for I hardly understood it—then I was still without Guinevere for my bed, the two of us locked in hothouse warmth. When noontime came I would go down the street to the lunch wagon, eat, and return here. Outside, the heat of summer afternoon would bake the roof. Thus suspended, my mind dallying with the empty hour to follow, I sloughed through empty hours of the past.

70

I could almost remember another summer when I had lived in a hotel converted to a hospital. Had it been Paris? And was it the summer of victory? There, too, I would have lain on a cot through hot afternoons, staring at the ceiling, while about me in that, the summer of victory, soldiers ate at a groaning board of black-market treasure and women in profusion, and in the limitless appetite of those days everybody was making a deal or setting up a household, establishing contacts, seducing actresses, losing or winning a half-year's wages in the nightly poker games. For those few months heat rose from the silenced machines, and if like shavings, men were blown about, one could easily mistake it for a dance.

While it lasted, I was virtually inactive. I see myself in that period as moving about, even capable of leaving the hospital for a few hours, but I did nothing. I read only the newspapers, I ate the food which was served me, I never approached the black market. Once a month went by in which I did not stir from my cot.

Occasionally there were eruptions. I must have gone out with most of my face bandaged, and I think I was drunk in one of the bars of Pigalle. I spent fifty dollars that night, and there were soldiers yelling in my ear, and I can almost recall the words from the song of a chanteuse, can almost touch the drowsy whore who scratched herself before she began to dress. Or did I only languish in the summer heat of Paris, my mind inert, my body in torpor?

At times I am certain I used to lie on the bunk and stare at a photo of myself taken in England or was it in Africa? I would examine the face which the doctors assured me would be almost duplicated. Yet I must imagine this, for of all the hours I looked at the snapshot I cannot remember that face at all, and I do not know if I think of it now or whether, lying in that cot, I saw all the endless children who waited for our leavings on garbage lines, all the whores we abused, the peasants we cursed because they could not understand us and we were drunk. It almost comes back, the diarrhea, the trench foot, the boots we polished, the men who got killed. The machine stopped at last, but I stopped first, and lay on my cot that summer in a Paris which might be mythical, and counted the cracks in the wall. Empires had fallen, kingdoms been reshuffled, but that was over the horizon. I played a closet drama in which the machine would let me go. . .go where?

Here I lay upon another cot, drowsing through a hot forenoon, while outside upon the city streets men came and passed, errands were completed and work begun. I went down for lunch and came back to sit at my desk, driving myself dully through the hours which passed. I felt at a crisis in my work, impulses so contradictory, understanding so scattered, that an hour could go by and I would produce no more than a line or two and then discard it. By evening I felt the need to talk to McLeod.

CHARACTERISTICALLY, he sat upright on his hard chair, arms folded upon his chest, his knees crossed, his eyes boring into me from behind his silver-rimmed spectacles. Once or twice, in an unconscious gesture, his fingers would sharpen the crease of his trousers, and he would nod his head as if he had heard what I said many times.

I was talking about Guinevere, recounting in detail everything which passed between us. McLeod listened, a small smile upon his lips, chuckling from time to time in a manner I found disconcerting. Only once did he make a comment.

"What's this about Jehovah's Witnesses?" he asked.

I repeated some of the gospel she had preached, and McLeod shook his head. "She was making it up," he said.

"I don't know."

"She was." He fingered his lean jaw for an instant. "I've known her for some time, and I've never heard her speak about them. It's inconceivable. She probably read something in a magazine, and then fed it back to you."

"Well, what about her husband?" I protested. "She says he's religious."

McLeod chuckled again. "I don't believe I've met the gentleman," he said lazily.

I went on with my story, and under McLeod's scrutiny, so

dispassionate, so balanced, I found myself admitting details which normally I would have found distasteful. In his presence I could find enthusiasm for the balm of confession as if nothing I might relate would ever provoke a dishonest reaction. The story launched upon the ways, I searched out facets I had almost forgotten, recalled conversations with an accuracy which startled me.

McLeod listened, soberly and quietly, a tight smile pinching his thin lips. When I had finished, he removed his eyeglasses, wiped them carefully, took out a comb and smoothed his straight hair. "Well," he murmured. Abruptly, he began to shake with laughter. He controlled himself by an effort and murmured in a slow unsteady voice, "So you're finding it hard to work, eh?"

This tipped his mirth again. Jeering at me, he continued to laugh. "What a woman she is," he said at last, and then with a look at me, "What a duet." He replaced his eyeglasses, stared through them at me. "The fat ghost and the pale ghost," he stated. "Tell me, Lovett, do you think she'll bestow the ultimate pleasure upon you?"

"I don't know," I admitted. "And by now I don't think I care."

"Oh, you'll care again. She'll expire before she'll let you get indifferent. She needs a spy." With a transparent pleasure, he paused before he spoke again, his finger uplifted. "Tell me, Lovett, will you go and report our conversation to her? That'll round out the picture, you know."

"What are you talking about?"

He shrugged, his face impassive. "It's conceivable, it's conceivable."

I disregarded what he had said; other questions pressed upon me more. "Look, what do you make of her?" I asked.

"Lovett, I'll give you some of my wisdom," McLeod drawled. "You'll have to find out for yourself. Not everything can be learned by taking a pill."

"Well, thanks."

He grinned. "I'll give you a tip to further your scientific inquiries along. If you want to know about her, you've got to imagine what her husband is like."

"But neither of us has ever met him."

"Nevertheless," he said, "you have to fabricate a picture of him. When you do that, you'll be able to see her better."

I applied myself to the speculation. "He must be a retiring man, overshadowed by her." But this game was impossible. "He could be just as easily seven feet tall with a big red face, and whip her every night."

McLeod chuckled with glee. "You know, Lovett, you're not bad." He touched his finger tips together. "I've constructed a somewhat similar portrait, putting the two together. A man, therefore, who minds his own business, who's meek. You'd never notice him, but when he's alone with her, she's terrified of him."

"Why?"

"Ah!" He raised his arms and quivered them in a parody of a meek man in a fury. "Because he could murder her when they're alone." A moment later he was talking once more in his slow mocking voice. "Now, that was as far as I got for a while, but it don't satisfy me. Why did the gentleman marry her? Why?"

I shrugged. "He found Guinevere attractive."

"A profound observation," McLeod said with a grimace. "He was attracted to her. And you"—his words flicking me—"being also attracted to her find that completely comprehensible." A pedagogue reaching the climax, his hands went up in the air. "Why are people attracted to each other? Because they fulfill things reciprocally, be they nice things or sentiments which don't bear examination. Now, I don't have too much to do. I have my work, and when I get back I do a little reading, or I sit here and think. And one of the subjects which occupies me now and again is why a certain Mr. Guinevere, whose last name nobody has ever discovered, decided to marry her, and then set it up for the kind of relationship it is, one where he is never present, and she is practically a queen bee. What kind of individual do you think he is?"

"I have no idea."

"He's almost dead, that's what he is. Why does he marry her? Because she gives out an emanation, call it what you will, that makes him think he's close to something alive. He knows he's frozen, and he wants to be laid against a body that's nice and warm. He sees it as an experiment on himself. That's the kind of man he is, I'm convinced. Only what he doesn't know is that she's frozen too."

"Why did she marry *him*?" I asked.

"A good question." He held up his hands again. "Why? That's a chestnut, isn't it? Well, maybe she needed security. Economic matters have to be taken into account, foreign as they may be to your way of thinking." He removed his spectacles again and squinted judiciously. "But that doesn't account for it all. The mental goes along with the economic, and I keep returning to Mr. Guinevere. A moral man, I'm convinced. He wanted to punish himself, so he married her, and therefore she in turn, we might suppose, wanted to be in a position to punish somebody. And that's only half of it. I'll tell you," he said, virtually talking to himself, "I picture him further as a gentleman who can see through her. He sees through her, and yet he doesn't. I don't suppose you could understand how much that means to the lady in question. He keeps her in place, but she can still fool him from time to time."

"I should think she'd resent him for holding up the mirror."

"Oh, does she? I should say so. But that's it. Nothing is perfect. And if she's afraid of him, that's fine too. She's always wanting to be made a woman."

"Has she ever approached you?" I asked.

He clucked his tongue noncommittally, and grinned. "Now these hypotheses I leave to you, Lovett. You can do what you will with them."

McLeod started to yawn, but he did not finish.

For someone scratched upon the door.

It was one of the most curious sounds I had ever heard, light, rapid, and with a persistence that spoke of an animal's claw. McLeod revolved in his chair, his body stiffened, an attitude of intense concentration upon his features. What he expected I could not guess, but his reaction was extreme—all blood left his face. He sat transfixed for many seconds while the scratching repeated.

With what effort he replaced his eyeglasses, adjusted them upon his nose. "It is Hollingsworth then," he whispered incomprehensibly. And all his will and all his strength apparently necessary for the next action, he straightened himself in the chair, and froze his face into a surface of composure, his lips supporting a mild distaste. "Come on in," he called suddenly in an even voice.

Hollingsworth proffered his polite smile as a token of admission. He eddied toward us, dressed in his tidy fashion, a clean shirt, light summer pants, and for the jaunty note, a pair of black-and-white sport shoes. "I'm awfully sorry to disturb you," he said in his remote voice, "but I heard people talking, and I thought that I might share in whatever you're saying." To me, he nodded. "How do you do Mr. Lovett? It's nice to see you again."

"Take a chair," McLeod told him.

He sat down after hoisting his trousers carefully, and for over a minute we gazed judiciously at one another in unavoidable proximity. Except McLeod. He consumed Hollingsworth with his stare.

I wondered if Hollingsworth had left his place in the same clutter I had seen it last, the clothing upon the floor, the bureau drawers jammed and overflowing. I could see him giving a last survey, and then convinced everything was in order, turning the key, pausing to listen to us, and scratching for entrance.

He cleared his throat now, and leaned forward, his hands cupped over his knees, the palms arched to avoid deranging the crease of his pants. "If you fellows don't mind," he said without preamble, "I wonder if we could discuss politics."

McLeod grinned, but weakly. "Anything we can clear up for you in a couple of minutes?"

He considered this seriously. "It's hard to say. I've noticed that political discussions have a way of becoming very long and drawn out if you know what I mean." When we did not respond to this, he said, "It's mainly about the Bolshevists I'd like to talk. I heard Mr. Wilson and Mr. Court discussing them at the office the other day, and I realized I have a great deal to learn on the subject." With modesty, his opaque blue eyes upon us, he added, "I have to keep well informed on all subjects, and it makes a fellow hop sometimes."

"What makes you think I know anything about it?" McLeod asked. Color was returning to his face, but he was still pale.

In the ingenuous voice of a child, Hollingsworth said simply, "Well, you're a Bolshevist, aren't you, Mr. McLeod?"

"Do you mean a Communist?"

Hollingsworth looked perplexed. "They're the same thing, aren't they?"

McLeod yawned violently. "Call it the egg and the dinosaur," he said, closing his lips in a cryptic smile.

"That's an interesting way of putting it," Hollingsworth said. "And you'd say you're both?"

Once again McLeod could dissect him with his eyes. There was a pause, and behind the impassivity of their faces, I could sense the rapidity with which their minds were working. "Yes, both," McLeod said. "Yes, absolutely both. Absolutely."

His face was impassive, his body draped carelessly upon the chair, but like a safety valve shrilling its agitation, his foot—so disconnected from him—tapped ever more rapidly, ever more nervously upon the floor.

"Well, then you can answer some of my questions," Hollingsworth said pleasantly.

"Possibly I can," McLeod admitted. "Yet first let me ask one. What made you decide to do it this way?"

Hollingsworth looked puzzled. His eyes seemed to pinch the thin flanks of his nose as he pondered, and his answer was not exactly responsive. "Oh, I couldn't say. You talk sort of differently." He glanced about the room. "And the other time I was here when we talked about the bathroom—I'm awfully sorry we've never been able to work out a schedule for that—I noticed you had so many big books on the shelf." He had withdrawn a tiny pad of paper from his jacket, and this he balanced on his knee, his pencil playing over it in the motions of a man sketching idly. "Would you say then that you're an atheist?" he asked politely.

"Yes." The pencil flicked lightly upon the pad.

McLeod, a grin cemented to his jaw, murmured, "As a matter of fact, I'm more than that. I've been head of the church dynamiting section in my time. We've knocked over several in the past."

"And you're against free enterprise?"

"Completely." As if passing from acceptance of the game to active encouragement, McLeod delivered himself of a long exposition, his voice never altering from the acrid tone with which he began. "You might say that I am against free enterprise because it sucks the workers dry, turns man upon his brother, and maintains the inequities of a class society. This poison may only be met with poison, violence with violence. A campaign of vigorous terrorism must be undertaken to wrest the seats of power from the buh-geoisie. The president must be assassinated, and

79

congressmen imprisoned. The State Department and Wall Street must be liquidated, libraries must be burned, and the filthy polluted South must be destroyed nigh unto the last stone with the exception of the Negroes." McLeod halted, and lit a cigarette for himself. The first match went out, and he struck another one, brought it to the tip, his hands cupped in an excess of care. "Do you have any more questions?" he asked.

Hollingsworth scratched his head. "Well, you've given me a great deal to think about. This is all extremely interesting I should say." Carefully he brushed a cowlick from his forehead. "Oh, yes." He leaned forward, phrased the next question diffidently. "Would you feel that your first allegiance is not to the Stars and Stripes, but to a foreign power?"

McLeod betrayed no humor. "I would admit that is generally correct." He stared at his hands in a curious way, as if resigning himself to whatever he saw portrayed there. After a moment he looked up. "Does this conclude the political discussion?" he asked.

Hollingsworth nodded. "I must say you have it all at your finger tips."

"I've prepared it," McLeod said. "For years."

"I appreciate your co-operativeness."

McLeod leaned toward him. "Wall Street is interesting, isn't it?" he asked in an amiable tone.

"Oh, yes. Very much so. I really feel as if it's an education."

Subtly, perhaps unconsciously, McLeod was parodying him. "Yes, that could be said." With a sudden motion, he reached forward and flipped the pad from Hollingsworth's knee. "Don't mind if I look at this, do you?" he asked.

But Hollingsworth performed the ritual of a man who obviously did mind. He started in his chair, his arm extended in pursuit of the pad, his fingers closed and opened to articulate his frustration. Slowly his tongue licked over his lips. "Do you think a fellow ought to play that kind of trick on one?" he asked me quietly, his neutral voice washed faintly by righteousness. I was watching McLeod. He sat back in his chair and studied what Hollingsworth had written. From time to time he chuckled without amusement. Then he passed me the pad, and I read it with my heart beating stupidly. Hollingsworth had made the following list:

> Admits to being Bolshevist.
> Admits to being Communist.
> Admits to being atheist.
> Admits to blowing up churches.
> Admits to being against free enterprise.
> Admits to encouraging violence.
> Advocates murder of President and Congress.
> Advocates destruction of the South.
> Advocates use of poison.
> Advocates rise of the colored people.
> Admits allegiance to a foreign power.
> Is against Wall Street.

Silently, I handed the pad back to McLeod. In a flat voice, not without mockery, he said to Hollingsworth, "You made a mistake. I never advocate the use of poison."

Hollingsworth had recovered. Diffidently, but not without firmness, he shook his head. "I'm sorry, I don't like to disagree with a fellow, but you did say that. I heard you."

McLeod shrugged. "All right, leave it in." He took a long puff at his cigarette. "Tell me, old man," he drawled, "is there anything else I can do for you?"

"Why, yes." Hollingsworth adjusted the belt of his trousers. He leaned forward again, and his face which had been in shadow entered the cone of light cast by the bulb hanging from the ceiling. Upon his mouth he exhibited his apologetic smile.

But there was little of apology in his other movements. Firmly, he pointed to the pad. "I wonder if you would affix a signature to this," he said formally. "I would like to keep it as one of my souvenirs, and that would"—he searched for a word—"enhance the value thereon."

"Sign it?"

"Yes, if you don't mind."

McLeod smiled, tapped the pad upon his knee for a moment, and then to my astonishment, took a pen from the breast pocket of his shirt, scribbled a few words, and scratched his signature. He read aloud, "Transcript of remarks made by William McLeod—signed—William McLeod. Does that do?"

"Oh, that's fine," Hollingsworth said. "It's nice to meet people who are so co-operative." When neither of us replied, he looked at his watch with great seriousness. "My, I've stayed longer than I thought." He stood up, and took the notes which McLeod extended to him. "Well, I'd like to thank you fellows for being so nice about it all."

"Any time we can help you, any time," McLeod nodded.

Hollingsworth still remained at the door, fingering the pad. With a certain gentleness, he ripped off the top sheet on which they had written, and tore it in two. "You know," he said, "on second thought perhaps I really don't want this souvenir."

"It is valueless," McLeod drawled again.

"Yes, so it is." He dropped the pieces to the floor, and was gone.

When the door had closed, McLeod rested his head on his hands and laughed wearily. Upon his head beat the glare of the light bulb, seeming to burn through the frail thin hair at the peak of his scalp, and thrusting beyond him across the floor a distorted shadow of himself, elongated and bent, eloquent in its shadowed head and emaciated forearms. I became aware that the shades were down, and in this stifling room, nothing moved, nothing stirred, the books along the wall in silent witness beside myself. He raised his head and stared at the light as if he must excoriate himself like a fakir searing his vision into the sun.

With what seemed an intense effort, he tore his eyes from the light, and looked at his hands. "You ever wait for anybody?" he asked quietly.

I did not understand at first what he meant, but from some recess of my mind leaped again the image of the stranger, the door opening, the obscured face hovering above my bed. "I don't know," I said.

He stood up and leaned against the bookcase, the end of his cigarette still pinched against his fingers. When he looked at me there was small recognition in his eyes. "One thing I'd like to find out," he said. "Which team does he come from?"

"I don't follow you," I said.

Something flickered in his stare. Perhaps he was aware of me again. "That's right, you wouldn't know, would you, Lovett?" And then for an instant he grasped my wrist. "Of course it's one of the techniques to leave the innocent behind, and he's the one who carries away the valuable piece." But as I met his look, he relaxed his grip upon me. "No, you're not in it, I'm certain of that." He snickered. "I suppose I have to be."

I stammered out a question and McLeod made no response. Instead, he laughed again to himself. "I'll tell you, Lovett," he said, "I'm tired. Do you mind leaving here? I want to think for a while."

I went away with McLeod sitting in the chair in the middle of the room, the light bulb above his head, his eyes looking without expression at the peeling plaster upon his wall. I had the impression he would remain in this position for hours.

TEN

Tʜᴀᴛ evening I lay awake for a long time and watched the random play of city lights across my ceiling. And in such an abstract game with nocturnal sounds as my only diversion—a woman's heels clacking slowly upon the sidewalk, a window somewhere being opened and shut again—I found myself constructing an imaginary childhood.

Could it not be possible that I was born in an old house in the center of a Midwestern city, the house going quietly to seed, while the distinction of being one of the oldest families became less important to everyone but ourselves? This would be a city whose suburbs were constantly expanding and whose industry, nurtured by congenial tax rates and an amiable political machine, could grow and double within a decade. Institutions altered, and with them, men, and there would be a new country club and insurance brokers who peopled it. My parents would talk about such things with distaste for they lived in the memory of an earlier world, illumined in the transitory splendor of a calendar sunset, and they would assure me that forty years ago the city was lovely, adorned by small quiet streets and brownstone houses in the first rich maturation of their colors, small gardens between the buttressed stone stairways, and the inevitable corner grocery which lasted beyond its time like an old

84

relative on pension until it emitted at last only the rich odor of unground coffee out of a once-magical assortment of smells. Spring mornings the men would walk to work, and on Sundays the entire family was in black, the quiet afternoons in the back yard annotated only by church bells.

It is a sweet picture, but it is a false shore. The only brownstone houses I ever knew were in disrepair and skived by landlords. I was born into a world which would move forever faster, and if I had to create for myself a tropical isle, I could not render it perfect, for I would always find the darkening clouds of typhoon, and hear the surf lashing the shore. It was possible to engage in such a voyage, but only to return to the hard cot beneath the dirty window of my narrow room.

So I lay there that evening while McLeod across the hall must also have stared at the ceiling, and I dreamed that I was in another room in a vast dormitory for children, and while we slept a fire had begun in the cellar and was sweeping along the dry wood of the walls and through the deep vent of the staircase. Soon it would reach the great room in which we slept and sear a passage through the door, and we would awake to the sound of children's screams and hear our own voice.

Thus, restlessly, I slept.

In the morning Guinevere came to visit me, and as I might have expected she was not alone. Behind her, more vivid than a shadow, yet linked as inseparably, followed Monina. They came in together after a cursory knock, Guinevere's arms laden with a pile of sheets which she deposited quickly upon my bed. "How're you doing, Lovett?" she bawled.

I nodded a greeting. There was nothing to suggest that the last time we parted she had been screaming at me. Monina, no more abashed than Guinevere, ducked her head, babbled something, and then proceeded to examine the room. She did this with great care and some insolence as though she were unobserved, lifted a corner of the rug and looked under it, peered behind my armchair, and finally, paused at the desk and went through my papers, clucking to herself in some child's game of words.

While this went on, Guinevere prattled at me. She had also had a dream the night before, and she proceeded to tell it in detail. "And you know I thought I was a turtle, can you make that out, Lovett?"

"No."

"Boy, it was murder. I was a turtle, and there I was lying on my back, and I couldn't get up again. You got any idea how that makes you feel? This morning I had to go out to the drugstore, and get myself a bromo." She lit a cigarette and drew the smoke into her broad painted mouth.

"Well, it was just a dream." I was irritable this morning.

"Yeah, but you didn't have it. I can't get over that, being a turtle." Without altering her position, she shrieked suddenly, "Monina, you leave Mr. Lovett's stuff alone."

The child paid no attention, but I do not think Guinevere expected any response. She merely groaned and turned to me. "That kid's got hell in her blood. She takes after me. Honestly, Lovett, the things I've done."

I squinted at the sunlight lancing through the window, and made no answer. "You know when I was in Hollywood," she told me, "I ruined my career just cause I was so wild."

"When were you in Hollywood?"

"In the middle of my burlesque career. They gave me an option. You know about the time they were making stars out of burlesque queens. They took me on too, and if I'd had any sense, if I'd been smart about it, I'd be making five thousand dollars a week today." She sighed and exhaled some smoke. "But I threw it away by being wild. You know I put out for everybody, not cause I figured they could do anything for my career, but because I've always had a good heart, and you got to realize there were a lot of handsome stiffs out there. I used to be

86

crazy about making love in those days. And the fellows out there they really got whangs on them cause they use it so much."

She snuffed her cigarette, and turned to the child. "Monina, where's the radio?"

"Doutside."

"Well, go get it. What's the matter with you anyway? If you leave it out there, somebody's going to steal it."

Monina sighed impatiently, signifying she was weary of her mother, but she obeyed. Gone for a moment or two, she reappeared in the doorway staggering under the load of a portable radio which in proportion to her child's frame must have been as unwieldy as a suitcase. "That's a godsend," Guinevere said. "On linen day it keeps me from going nuts." She reached down and hefted it from the floor to the bed. As she played with the dials, she continued to talk.

"You can understand, Lovett, being as you go for me, that for a lot of them out there I had It. You wouldn't believe if I told you the names of some of the famous stars and producers who wanted to marry me, but I ruined my chances by being too nice to all of them. They knew about me, and even then a couple of them wanted marriage, but I loused up my career and that made it impossible."

"How?"

"Well, by playing around so much. The breath of scandal can't touch a luminary; if it does you're cooked. And I mean I can see their side of it. They would have invested millions of dollars in me, and they never could have known when some jealous star would have bought off the police and had me framed in a love nest. So they didn't renew my option." She smoothed the sheets with her hand, and stood up, and without transition, looking at me with her head to one side, she said, "How would you like to dance, Lovett?"

"I'm not very good."

"That's all right. I can show you." She had found some

music on the radio, and now she closed her eyes, hummed to herself, and approached, arms outstretched. We drifted about the room in a slow shuffle, her body draped upon me in what was virtually an embrace. Leisurely we swayed, back and forth, the fresh warm air of summer morning eddying through my open window. "You're not bad," she murmured.

Guinevere moved quite well, her body light, her rhythm sensitive. At heart, however, it was not a dance. She applied her body to me, coquetted, withdrew, her motions an invitation. But of course there was nowhere to go. While the music played, Monina withdrew into a corner, knees against her chest and arms about her knees, the tiny face stricken in loneliness. When the song ended, it was followed by another tune with a faster beat. Guinevere wriggled in my arms, oscillated her hips, and grinned wantonly at me. Only Monina did not stir; her nature minted into the same coin as her mother, she must exhibit characteristically the other face. Her head an inch from her knees, she stared at the floor and began to whimper.

"Scared," she cried, "I scared."

The music ended, and with it the program. A voice began to talk about a canned food. Guinevere withdrew her body slowly, stood a short distance from me, her eyes looking into mine. "Let's dance some more," she said softly. With a glance over the shoulder, she bellowed without irritation, "Keep quiet, Monina."

Monina responded by blubbering.

"Oh, that kid," Guinevere whispered. Her eyes were bright and provocative. I had the impression that if Monina were not there, the hide-and-seek which Guinevere must play with me would be finished. For this instant she seemed younger and more attainable, lavish in the promise her eyes conveyed. "If only the kid wasn't around," she said into my ear.

We were standing still. She turned away to find other music on the radio, and Monina grasping the pause to advantage ran toward me and threw her arms about my legs. I patted her head, felt her clutch me more firmly as Guinevere stood up and said, "Oh, this band is smooth."

"I don't want to dance," I told her.

Nevertheless she approached, her eyes fluttering to the music. "Aw, come on, Lovett."

Monina released me and pummeled her mother's thigh with her fists. "Mommie-diggie, mommie-diggie," she shrieked with rage.

"What the hell's got into her?" Guinevere demanded. She began to chuckle. "I bet she's jealous." With a deft swipe of her arm, she pinioned the child against her. "Now, take it easy, Monina," she cautioned. "Boy, I bet she's made me black and blue."

The radio, unadjusted, blared too loudly in the room. I turned if off, and listened to Guinevere saying, "You know you got no idea, Lovett, how I bruise. I tell you I got the whitest flesh, and you can't imagine how delicate it is. Every time a man puts his hands on me, it leaves marks." The child, pacified, was now hugging her mother. Guinevere winked at me. "I'll let you know something I never told anybody—when a man starts pawing me, I can tell there's going to be bruises, and I feel like a white sheet or a carpet or something, and a guy with muddy boots is just walking all over it. What do you think of that?"

I made no response. I sat down at the desk, and Guinevere, the child at her knee, ensconced herself in the armchair. "You haven't been thinking about . . . you know, what we were talking about yesterday?" she asked casually.

"What do you mean?"

Guinevere was insufferably cunning. "Well, you know, about just keeping an eye out, seeing what happens."

"I told you I don't spy."

"Who was talking about that?" She made a small attempt

at righteousness. "I wouldn't dream of asking you such a thing. I just thought maybe like everybody else you got curiosity about this person and that person." Monina had placed herself at her mother's feet and was trailing her hand idly over her legs.

"Go to Hollingsworth. He's got more aptitude for it than I."

"Now, why do you say that?" Suddenly her face exuded an air of manufactured mystery. "You know I'll tell you something funny. I've been wondering about Hollingsworth myself."

"You have?"

"He's a sneaky son of a bitch," Guinevere said, fingering her bosom. "There're things I could tell you about him."

I shrugged, having the idea that behind her elaborate digressions, something demanded voice. She was in a state where she sought information, but if balked would end by furnishing it. "I think he's masquerading," she suggested.

"I don't understand what you mean."

"Well, there's something about him." She had lit a cigarette, and was waving the extinguished match at me for emphasis. "Sometimes I think he's the son of a prince, now I don't mean that exactly, but you know, a magnate, or a . . . a potentate, and that he's living here in disguise."

I laughed. "What gave you that idea?"

She was quite serious. "I got my intuition about it. There's something fishy with that character."

"Something fishy?"

She was reluctant to expose her evidence, as if once removed from the fertility of her brain it must wither in my barren room. "Things," she said ominously.

I laughed again.

Annoyed, she finally admitted in a grudging voice, "There's a joker that's always going up to visit him. I don't like that a bit."

"What does he look like?"

"Oh, I can't tell. He wears a dark blue suit, and he's got a hat he pulls down over his forehead. My theory is that he's the guy who comes to pay off Hollingsworth."

"For *what?*"

"Well, I figure that's the way his father gives him his allowance, you know in the form of a stipend."

"Guinevere, I hope you realize how silly this is. Why can't the man be just anybody?"

She caressed her forearm, mouth puckered in suspicion, uncertain how well she could trust me. "You know I've seen a little bit of Hollingsworth," she confessed. Her expression was sullen. "I don't trust him," she repeated. With an abrupt gesture, Guinevere smoothed her dress upon her thigh, and stated dramatically, "I asked him about his buddy. Do you know what he said?"

"I don't."

"He said nobody ever comes to visit him." She was triumphant. "What do you think of that?"

"How do you know he visits Hollingsworth?" Yet I was uneasy. Somehow she had created a mood where anything was conceivable.

Without embarrassment, Guinevere mounted her proof. "I followed him up the first time. I like to know what's going on." Her mouth was cherubic in its pride.

"Did you and Hollingsworth ever become friends?" I asked suddenly.

She was very casual. "What's it to you?" she yawned.

"Not much."

Guinevere looked at me, her eyes wary, denying the sense of her words. "He's just like the rest of you," she said raucously in one of her sudden modulations. "He wasn't above trying to get up my skirts either."

I made no answer. I was ruffled she had lumped me in the same basket with Hollingsworth. A minute dragged by, and Guinevere to fill the pause went on at length with one of her inexhaustible stories about a lover and his whang, developing ever more lavish detail as if I were a kitten to be enticed by brightly colored ribbons. At her feet, Monina, bored amanuensis, sketched designs in the dust.

The child began to complain at last, and Guinevere stood up and hefted her pile of sheets once more. "Well, I got other things to do besides talking to you," she said. Still, at the door, she turned around coquettishly. "You'll keep an eye out, won't you?"

"No."

Visibly irritated, she departed, yanking Monina behind her.

ELEVEN

WHAT a long day was to follow.

After Guinevere left, I had my solitary meal at noon, and came back to write for several uninterrupted hours. When I finished, the afternoon was at its height, and in a lethargy of self-satisfaction I lay on my bed and watched the air flutter along the pitch of my ceiling. The door was open to the hall for any breeze which might wander through, and after a while I began to drowse.

A voice woke me, a soft husky voice whose overtones were sweet. "I'm awfully sorry. Would you get up?"

I roused myself to a sitting position. A girl was standing in the doorway, her slender body balanced awkwardly, much as though she would leap into flight if I stirred too quickly. "Come in," I offered.

"You looked so comfortable sleeping there," she said, "that I hated to wake you. I guess you have the secret of knowing how to sleep."

"I was just drowsing," I mumbled foolishly.

She took my desk chair, and sat down upon it. "No, you mustn't be ashamed. I thought you were beautiful."

I rubbed my head, dazed by awakening in the afternoon

heat. Apparently, she expected no answer. "Oh, it's wonderful," she went on. "You're awfully lucky."

"Why?"

"To have this room. I love it. If I could, I'd buy it from you."

I grimaced. "It's dirty enough and cheap enough."

"But that's what is good about it. It's *so* dirty," she said in her husky voice. "I hate clean rooms. I hate people who are always afraid of leaving a trail. That's why this place is wonderful. You live here and you leave your marks, and after you stay long enough it's going to be in the walls, and the air, and a part of you is never going to leave here."

On the strength of this speech, I examined the girl more closely. Her face, narrow and delicate, with a childish nose and mouth, a soft chin, and gentle brown eyes, made it difficult to determine her age. Like Hollingsworth, like myself, she might have been twenty; it was not unlikely that she was ten years older. My stare was returned candidly, a small smile rendering her lips tremulous, while she fished awkwardly in her purse for a cigarette, lit it, and passed it over as if we were old friends. I accepted the gift, but I was hardly prepared for such abrupt intimacy.

"Don't *you* want one?" I asked.

"Oh." She seemed startled. "Oh, yes." Once more she fumbled through her pocketbook, and struck a match with hands that shook perceptibly. I noticed her fingers then, long and slender, potentially beautiful, but the nails were bitten, the cuticle was ragged, and deep tobacco stains yellowed the skin. She smoked like a man, palm upward, the cigarette held in the crotch between her fingers, the smoke drifting through the interstices and curling about her wrist. With her delicate features she could have been attractive except that her complexion was dull and beneath her eyes discolored, and her brown hair, unadorned, dropped lankly to her shoulder. I had the impression she was not wholly aware of herself, and even the most elemental grooming would be performed spasmodically. Certainly her clothing would carry the stains of everything she touched.

In confirmation, some ash fell from the cigarette, and she rubbed it into her skirt. The suit she wore, a brilliant violet poorly chosen for her mouse-brown hair and sallow color, was frayed at the elbows, ravelled at the collar.

"You're a poet, aren't you?" she asked.

"No."

"Oh, but you are, I can tell." When she smiled, her childish mouth turned pensive and wise, conveying to me the uneasy suggestion that she knew more about me than I had discovered myself. "A poet with a typewriter," she mused, "oh, things are sad." The smoke curled upward over her hand into the air. "You should never use a typewriter," she said.

"I like to," I confessed gruffly.

"No, you don't understand," she informed me. The cigarette had burned to within a half-inch of her knuckle, but she seemed unaware of the heat.

"Hadn't you better put it out?" I asked.

She looked at the butt in some surprise. Probably she had forgotten how it came there. Yet, obediently, she opened her hand and let it fall, and if I had not ground it down, I believe she would have watched the ember char my floor.

Realizing at last that she must have had some reason for coming into the room I asked her purpose. She placed a hand over her pocketbook. "I noticed," she said slowly, "that there's a place to let in this building. I saw the sign outside."

"Oh, I didn't know that."

"Who could rent me the room? I came into the house, and I couldn't see where I could find the janitor, and I just walked and all the doors were closed."

I smiled to reassure her. "I'll take you down to the landlady."

"I've got to have it," she said, a pressing note in her voice. "You see I don't have any place to live."

I shook my head. "If it's one of the lower rooms it's probably expensive."

"But I'm just loaded with money," she said in a wan attempt at gaiety. "If I pay the money, she can't refuse me. That's a law, isn't it?"

I led her downstairs to Guinevere's apartment. Before I could knock on the door, the girl clutched my elbow. "I'm named Lannie," she said, "Lannie Madison. Will you tell her that we're friends, and that it would be wonderful if she would give me the room." After a pause, she smiled. "It's not really untrue. I liked you the moment I saw you."

I nodded. "All right." After I rapped, there was a long pause in which I could hear Guinevere approaching, her slippers flapping slovenly upon the floor. She opened the door a crack, and peered out with suspicion. "Oh, it's you," she said ungraciously.

I made the introductions, and Guinevere, clasping her bathrobe over her bosom, nodded indifferently. "What the hell do you want, Lovett? I'm busy with Monina."

Her rudeness angered me, but I said quietly, "Lannie's an old friend of mine, and she saw there's a room empty, and she'd like to rent it." As I finished, I felt I had made a mistake. Guinevere's face became guarded. "That would be a nice cosy setup for you, wouldn't it, Lovett? When the police come, you can tell them you two are playing house." And apparently determined to extract the last chiché from her role, she announced, "Listen, Lovett, and you . . . Miss Madison, I keep an orderly house here without shenanigans, and I don't intend to start any."

Lannie had turned pale. In a small voice, she murmured, "Why are you so cruel? You don't mean it. I can see that you're kind, and that you're ashamed of it."

"I'm ashamed of nothing." But Guinevere was staggered. I sensed that the cliché of the blusterer with the heart of gold was not entirely without attraction to her. "What do you want the room for?" she temporized.

"I don't have anywhere to live. I found a job today, and I have to have a bed."

"Why don't you go to a hotel?" she asked, examining Lannie in detail.

"I don't have enough money."

Guinevere folded her arms. "Well, then you don't have enough for this. It's fifty dollars a month, and the bath is in the hall."

"But I do. I can get enough money." As if she had just remembered—"I have enough now."

Guinevere shook her head. "There's nothing I can do for you. Room's rented."

The reaction surprised me. Lannie stood with her back straight, her head high. "Oh, you're a wicked, silly woman," she said with sudden passion. "You don't understand yourself. You don't understand the good there could be in you. Why do you lie, and why must you bully?"

Guinevere's face reddened. "Listen, Lovett, you don't need to bring your friends around to insult me. I've gotten enough lip in my life."

Lannie put her hand in mine. "Well, let's go." There was indifference in her voice. But at the door she paused and, with what I suspected was artistry, said, "You know you should give me that room. You're going to feel terrible later, because you suffer when you've been unkind."

"Wait a minute," Guinevere said. "You sure there's no monkey business, Lovett, between you and her?"

"No business at all," I drawled, and abruptly the strain in Lannie's eyes dissolved, and she began to peal with laughter. Guinevere, reluctantly, began to snigger. "You'll be the death of me, Mikey," she said, and for the first time since I had brought Lannie down, there was recognition in her bald blue eyes, and a hint that she might wink at me. "Oh, you give me a pain in the ass, all of you," she grumbled.

Yet nobody laughed genuinely. When we finished it was on a wary note. Guinevere sighed heavily. "You sure you got sixty dollars?" she asked Lannie.

"I thought it was fifty," I said.

Guinevere folded her arms. "It is fifty . . . after the first month. There's a joker wants to rent this place, and he offered me ten bucks. I'm not letting that go for anybody, no matter what my personal feelings may be."

"Oh, I'll give you the ten," Lannie said. "You deserve it, you should have it." She fumbled through her purse once more, and extracted a small sheaf of bills. "Let me pay you now."

"Don't you want to look at the room first?" Guinevere asked.

Lannie seemed surprised as though this had not occurred to her. "Oh. Oh, no. I know what it's going to be like, and I know I'll take it. I could tell it was a wonderful room from the sign outside."

"Take a look at it anyway," Guinevere said.

"No, no, I want to pay the rent now," Lannie said in a breathless voice. With her stained fingers, she counted off sixty dollars, the last ten in singles. I do not believe she had five dollars left. "Can I have the key?" she asked.

I intended to leave with Lannie, but Guinevere delayed me. "You don't mind, Miss Madison, if I keep your boy friend for a while?"

"Of course not." Lannie turned to me. "You'll visit me, won't you?"

"I'll drop by when I leave here. Probably I can help you."

When we were alone, Guinevere shook her head. "That girl friend of yours is an odd dame," she said.

"Mmm."

A nudge in my ribs. "I suppose it's all over between you and me now."

"There never was anything."

Guinevere smiled sadly. "There could have been. Fate kept us from getting together and throwing a little party, but I've thought about you, Lovett." She grinned. "I'll say one thing. You like them older than you. First me, and then Lannie, or should I say, first Lannie and then me?"

"You've got it all wrong," I said indifferently.

"I like that Miss Madison," Guinevere mused aloud. "There's something a little out of the ordinary about her." She allowed her voice to trail over the words. "You know I could tell you something."

"But you won't."

She deliberated. "Yes, I will. You know there was no vacancy sign up. What do you think of that?"

"Then how did Lannie know there was a room?" I asked automatically.

"Yeah, how did she?" Guinevere shrugged, and pointed a finger up the stairs. "Go ahead, go after your girl friend."

"Who offered you ten dollars?"

How coy Guinevere could become. "Oh, that don't matter. He won't get it now, anyway."

"Who?" I persisted.

She fingered a lock in her red hair. "It'll all come out in the wash. That's my philosophy. And you might just as well go ahead. I can see I'm passé as far as you're concerned."

TWELVE

I MOUNTED the stairs to Lannie's new room. She opened the door for me, her face shining, her greeting rippling forth so easily that the questions Guinevere had asked seemed not important.

"This is a wonderful place. Oh, you were marvelous. The way you talked to her."

"I don't see how."

She gave the sad smile which illumined her face. "I knew you would be modest," she said cryptically in a manner to indicate one had heard about me for years. "But it's wrong. When we have something, we should be proud of it." Lannie looked about the room, and sprawled in an armchair, her legs extended before her. "I can't tell you how happy I am."

Certainly, it took little to please her. The room was large and had a high ceiling, but that was the best to be said for it. The windows, which rose from the floor to the molding, opened upon the back court with its clotheslines and fire escape. Here, too, a scale of cinders had bedded the woodwork, and the gray light diffused between the buildings could hardly improve the dull nap of the aged sofa and armchairs. For decoration there was only a calendar left by the last occupant, its nude maiden curling at the edges. Across the room was a washstand, and above, a metal dish, a piece of soap moldering within, its underside turned to jelly.

Lannie sat contentedly, obviously ready to wait until I suggested what we should do. The ragged violet suit was tailored poorly to her bony frame, sagged to her knees, unpressed and wrinkled. Perhaps she had lost weight. The suit seemed to alienate her head from her long legs so that the young ravaged face with its dark eyes appeared to exist yards away from the brown scuffed moccasins where a large perforation in one sole exposed extravagantly the soiled flesh of her foot.

"What about your baggage?" I asked. "Won't you need help in moving it?"

She shook her head. "I couldn't dream of that. You've done enough for me already." Her long stained fingers curled around a cigarette. "I've got friends. They'll help me."

"I'd be glad to do it," I insisted.

"Oh, no."

"I would."

Lannie laughed at last, a husky contralto, and her brown eyes stared mischievously at me. "I don't have any baggage."

"None at all?"

"It's with my father." She laughed again. "With Father Pawnbroker."

"But what'll you wear?" I exclaimed.

"Oh, I saved something." She rummaged through her pocketbook, and pulled out a rumpled pajama top and bottom.

"You've got to have something else."

This only made her sullen. She laid her head against the top of the chair.

"What are you going to do?" I insisted.

Lannie was aloft in a private study. "I don't care," she said. "This morning I woke up, and I thought of all the dresses I had, and my typewriter, and all those little chains. I'm a cat. I don't want strings to my legs. I gave them away to Father

Pawnbroker." She smiled. "Like Vincent I cut off my ear and gave it to my beloved, and now I hear sounds I never knew before."

"That was the money you gave for the rent."

"I don't know, I suppose it was." I might have been the fat man and she the sprite, and as I blundered after her, the audience she had assembled for herself must have roared with approval.

"How will you eat?"

"Oh, Mikey, I don't care. Tomorrow I'll eat. I've got money, money." She dumped her purse upon the floor, and nudged the few singles with her foot.

"And after tomorrow?" The weeks had gone by, each to the eye-dropper of twenty dollars. At bottom, I was jealous.

"After tomorrow . . . people will feed me. People are good, that's what no one understands."

"Who will feed you?"

She laughed at me. "Mrs. Guinevere."

"She even begrudges me a cup of coffee."

"But that's because she doesn't love you, Mikey. She'll love me."

I was exasperated. "Do you want a loan of some money?"

"You see, Mikey," she pealed, "people always take care of me." Lannie shook her head. "No, I can't take your money; I'd never pay it back." But then mock-seriously, finger to her chin, she reconsidered. "No, I *would* pay it back, I'd work and slave to pay you back because you're so virtuous, and you'd make me ashamed. I hate bullies." She puffed at her cigarette, and watched the smoke trail to the tips of her broken nails. "I love the color nicotine gives to your hands," she said. "It makes them look like rich old wood." She sniffed. "My father's shirts always used to smell of tobacco. He was a wonderful man, a wonderful old drunk. He would have loved Mrs. Guinevere just as I do."

At the look of bewilderment on my face, she laughed. "Poor Mikey."

"I don't like being called Poor Mikey."

She shook her head. "And you shouldn't be. You're proud. I love proud people. You can see the pride in Mrs. Guinevere." Lannie's voice was eager. "She knows so well she's a woman she's so big and her coloring is so beautiful, and she *trumpets* it. 'I'm full of life, don't hold me in,' she cries, and all her life people held her in, and so she's unhappy. I love her. I want to talk to her."

Somehow she wove an obligation to accept her verdicts, to feel she had discovered truths one had never discerned before. For a few minutes I could accept all the qualities she had bestowed upon me. I could be handsome, and I could be proud, and I could be even a bully. And in parallel to me, Guinevere would become beautiful, her coloring vivid, the large body assuming its strong curves with confidence.

Under Lannie's influence what could avoid its transformation? She had stood up and was pacing about the room. At the mantel of the dummy fireplace she halted and drew an imaginary face in the air. "He's cute, isn't he?" she demanded, and then before I could answer, she had gone to the window and was playing with the fastener on the middle sash. "It's like a finger," she said. "Look!" and crooked her hand. "When they finished the house, there were no locks for the windows, and so the builder, a cruel capitalist who later built a house at Newport, cried at the top of his lungs, 'Cut off the fingers of the workmen, and nail them into place.' And this is a poor workingman's finger." She stroked it. "It's all that's left of him now, his finger and his thumb."

I could not respond. At another time, in another mood, I might have entered the game, but behind the gaiety, her mouth was strained, her eyes were vacant. Abstractedly she would finger the ends of her bedraggled hair.

"We ought to dust the place," I suggested.

Lannie surprised me by nodding her head. With an effort she roused herself. "You find something to clean with, and I'll open the windows," she told me. "We can move the furniture around. I love rearranging. That will make the room mine."

I went into the hallway and found a broom and a cloth that Guinevere had left in a corner. When I returned, the windows were indeed open, and Lannie stood on the broad low sill and stared into the courtyard below. I made no sound. There was such absorption in her study that I hesitated to interrupt it. Arms on the window frame, her body inclined outward, a bird prepared for flight. Slowly she leaned forward, leaned forward even more, until one brief unclenching of her hands, and she would have plummeted to the concrete below.

With a sudden gesture she pushed herself back into the room, and started when she saw me. "I like the view," Lannie said quietly, all animation gone. "I looked down, and I thought, 'It's the bottom of the ocean. It's deep, and you're all alone there.'"

I nodded casually, as though nothing untoward had passed, and went to the sink, filled a glass with water, sprinkled it on the floor. Industriously, I swept. Lannie tugged feebly at an armchair, and then with a sigh perched herself upon it.

"The furniture will be too heavy for you to move."

She moved her head in agreement. "Sit down with me, and let's talk."

"I'll continue sweeping. I can still talk, you know."

Her chin rested on her hand. "I wasn't lying about getting a job," she told me.

"I believed you."

"Well, you shouldn't have. I usually lie. But this time I did get a job. I walked in on Mr. Rammelsby and told him I was an expert advertising woman." She began to laugh. "I think Mr. Rammelsby's real name is Ter-Prossamenianvili, or something like that. Poor little Turk. He's so fat and he sweats so much, and he's going to lose his job for hiring me. If there had been anyone but him, some lean efficiency expert, I would never have been taken." She sighed.

"What will you do there?"

"Oh, I have to make slogans. You know they get hundreds of little men who work deep down in the earth trying to find new inventions, and then when one of them does, it's given to hundreds of people like me who try to find slogans. And then when we find one, a product is made and sold to millions of people, and finally it works for somebody and the product is a success." She smiled wearily. "I can do the job, but I hate it. I've had so many things like it, yes I have"—much as if I had contradicted her. "I was supposed to start this morning, but when I woke up I knew it was more important to find a room. Poor Mr. Rammelsby. He always puts his faith in the wrong people. But maybe they'll fire him this time, and he'll have to go back to Turkey, and he can sit on a hassock and have lots of wives with beautiful navels." She watched me ladle the dust into her wastebasket. "Let's arrange the furniture," she said.

To move the sofa and two armchairs took a disproportionate amount of effort. We had to discuss where to put each piece, and whenever we came to a decision, she would change her mind. We shifted the sofa several times—to the windows, against the fireplace, by a wall—but nothing pleased her. She agreed at last to place the armchairs with their backs to the window, and when we had accomplished this, she looked up and surveyed the room. "Why don't we leave it?" she asked. The sofa was temporarily facing a wall, its back to the center of the room. She tugged it away perhaps a yard so that someone sitting there could touch the baseboard with his feet.

"I think this is wonderful," she announced.

"Lannie, you can't leave the sofa that way."

"Why?"

"It's separated from the rest of the room."

She nodded dumbly at this, her face stricken for a passing moment. "Oh, of course, how stupid of me," she said airily, waving her hand in the air. "Come on, let's turn it around."

So we tugged and hauled again, reversed the sofa's position, and rested when we were done, perspiring from the summer heat. "It's another room now," she announced.

But of course this was not true. The big bare chamber was still dirty, still gloomy, and the dull faded furniture rested stolidly in its new positions, heavy and inert. We were silent for several minutes, and I looked up to see her mouth trembling. "What's the matter, Lannie?"

"I don't know." She smoked a cigarette restlessly, the ashes tumbling into the fold of her skirt, and not until the ember touched her fingers did she let it fall to the floor.

"I'm going to put some pictures into the room," she said, "and I'm going to make some drapes. And for that, they won't be able to stop me. And then"—her mouth curled, her small teeth were exposed for an instant—"I'm going to turn the sofa around, and leave it where it belongs, facing the wall." She coughed, and said in her husky voice, "I wish you'd go now, Mikey."

I was startled. "Go?"

"Yes, Mikey." She sat still, not looking at me.

"Well, maybe tonight or tomorrow we can…" I hardly knew how to finish.

"Yes, yes."

She did not turn around as I left the room.

THIRTEEN

I n the evening I stopped by Lannie's door, and no one answered. She would be sitting in an armchair, her legs tucked beneath her, chin upon her hand, the sound of my tapping penetrating so slowly through her reverie. Startled, she would come to let me in.

But nothing stirred. Probably she was not there. I went downstairs and into the street, paused for a moment beside the brownstone balustrade, looking at the lights in Guinevere's cellar apartment. Her husband must be home now, and between them was passing the daily exchange of their marriage, casual words I could not hear. On an impulse I thought of ringing her bell.

Instead I walked through Brooklyn Heights and came to rest at the end of a little street which abutted the bluffs. My arms resting on an iron railing, I stared out across the docks and across the harbor to the skyline of New York deepening into the final blue of night. Among the skyscrapers, windows here and there were lit, the charwomen had started their work, and throughout those pinnacles of stone the fires were banked, the offices bare.

The ferryboat to Staten Island had begun its trip. From where I stood the boat looked very small, its deck lights twinkling across the water to form the endless flickering legs of a centipede. An ocean freighter nosed across the harbor seeking anchorage, and in the distance bridges arched the river, supporting in a stream the weight of automobiles. Through the summer night, ships sounded their warnings, clear and unmuffled.

I looked at the water and my thoughts eddied aimlessly.

While I dreamed at the railing, an hour passed, night came. The outline of the ships which moved through the harbor could be discerned only by their lights.

"Well, hello, it's a fine evening, isn't it?" a voice murmured. I must have started. Hardly had I been waiting for Hollingsworth.

"I see you like to stand here, and think about things," he insinuated softly.

"Once in a while."

"I do myself." He took a cigarette from his pack and offered it to me in a motion so persuasive I could hardly refuse. Then a lighter sprang from his pocket, and he clicked forth the flame, patently waving it before me to solicit my admiration. The gadget was made of silver with a black shield upon which were engraved two letters. "When did you get that?" I asked.

"Oh, a day or two ago. You see the initials for my name. Leroy Hollingsworth. L. H. I think that's very clever of them, don't you?"

"Yes." With some regret I realized that he intended to keep me company. "Well, where did you buy it?" I asked.

"Oh, I don't know." He smiled apologetically. "You see, it was a gift. A lady presented it to me." He gazed complacently at the water, his blond hair and small curved nose illumined by the moonlight. "I don't know why," he said in a smug quiet voice, "the girls seem to like me a great deal." Filling his pipe bowl, he drew the lighter again, and sucked reflectively at the stem. "Yes," he said meaninglessly.

Perhaps as a result of what happened the night before, I had become agitated at the sight of him. How he could have sensed this, I do not know, but when he opened his mouth it was to say, "Last night was interesting, wasn't it?"

"Mmm."

"That McLeod's an odd fellow. I thought he had, if you'll permit me, a lot of crust." Hollingsworth paused delicately after this pale vulgarity. "But then, some of his ideas are interesting."

"What ideas?"

"Well, the blowing up of people and poisoning them. Sometimes I can understand how a fellow can get to feel that way. Don't you sometimes?"

I decided he was going to question me now. "Invariably."

But he merely laughed. "I'd like to make a study of the Bolshevists," he told me. "I think there's a lot to history. It broadens your outlook." He puffed at his pipe, released the smoke with a pouting motion of his lips as if he parted with something valuable. "What would you say to a libation?" he asked formally.

I could not think how to refuse him, and so we walked back the street, Hollingsworth chatting about his job, about opportunities for himself, about the weather. We picked a bar finally, and at his insistence, installed ourselves in a red-leather booth. I ordered a beer; Hollingsworth, to my astonishment, a double Scotch. When the waitress brought the drinks, he insisted on paying for them. Then he smiled at the girl.

Rather, he leered. The change smacked of alchemy. If he had comported himself with the politeness and formality of a divinity student who is without promise, that now vanished. As the waitress counted out the change, Hollingsworth cocked his head on his hand, cheek almost parallel to the table, and stared coolly at her, humming a phrase of music. "I've seen you somewhere," he said without preamble.

"No, I don't think so," she told him.

"You dance, don't you?" he asked. "Yes?" Hollingsworth smiled, crafty, almost jeering. "Sure, I saw you dancing somewhere," he announced, "you're a good dancer, you like to dance, don't you?"

The waitress was young with a coarse attractive mouth. "Yeah, I like to dance."

"I like to, too," Hollingsworth murmured. "I like to dance and dance." He hummed his song again. She had finished making change, and he passed a quarter to her for the tip. "There's more where that came from," he assured her. "You'll be here to serve the next round, won't you?" and when she nodded, he leered again, "Okay, there's something I want to talk to you about."

He was in a curious mood. When the waitress was gone, he looked across the table and winked. "I guess I'll be able to slip a little present to her, as they say." His opaque blue eyes stared blankly at me.

"You'll like that, won't you?" I asked.

"Well, it's the thing to do." He yawned, and made a point of looking at his wrist watch. "Once in a while I come into these places, and strike up an acquaintance with one of the girls." He gave his smug diffident smile. "They put out, too."

I sipped my beer judiciously. "What happens if they don't? I should think you couldn't make a connection every time."

He fingered his straight corn-colored hair. "Well, now, that all depends. If they've led me on, and given me reason to think there's something doing, then I just won't take no." He paused as though deliberating whether to illustrate this remark. "Now, there was a lady I met in one of these places, a real lady, well-dressed, but not above having her good time. We got to talking and she invited me to her apartment for a drink, and then in what might be called the crucial moment, she changed her mind." He gave a small reflective shrug, "So I just forced her to do it."

"Forced her?"

"Oh, yes, she knew she would have gotten hurt. Sometimes I can be very stubborn."

I hardly knew what to say. He had told me this with such finality. "But do you think that's worth anything? I imagine the next time you saw her things didn't go so well."

"I never saw her again. I don't care to see these women again. I mean, you know, I always think it's much duller the second time." He caressed his small curved nose. "How many girls have you done it with?" he asked baldly.

Before his curiosity, I found myself uneasily compliant. If it had been possible I might have made a count. "It hardly matters," I said.

"I bet I've had more," he told me.

The juke box, primed with a coin, had begun to blast our ears. "I'm sure I don't care," I said. "I've never gone in for matching chips."

He roared at my reply with his odd hir-hir-hir, and stopped abruptly. "You think that's bad manners to ask a question like that, don't you?"

"I really never have thought about it," I said frostily.

Hollingsworth smiled widely, revealing the black line at the root of his four front teeth. "I've noticed that the people with good educations act like this," he said. "I suppose I'm lacking in manners, and that's why you don't like me."

I could hardly have told him I did, and yet for the first time since I had known him my antipathy flagged. "I wouldn't say that," I muttered.

"Oh, yes." He nodded his head in confirmation. "I'm not a child, and I can see these things. With Mr. Wilson and Mr. Court I can sense a difference. They're made of a finer mold than me." He nodded his head wistfully. "You see I'm of humble birth."

His china-blue eyes held a hint of aggression. "I'll tell you something, Lovett," he said, "I'm really not concerned with whether you like me or not." He drew designs through the wet ring of his glass. "I've got other irons in the fire. Bigger irons than you."

"Probably, you have. I'm no one to emulate."

"In your heart you think you are. Don't deny it. You think I'm dirt."

As the waitress came by, he held up his glass. "Refills, okay, honey?" he asked, the leer once more upon his face. Again he insisted on paying the check, and passed the waitress another quarter. "You work long tonight?" he asked.

"Till one."

Hollingsworth seemed to be deliberating. "Well, now, if I came walking by at one o'clock, would you be outside waiting for me?"

She laughed doubtfully. "I might, I don't know, I might," she giggled.

"When's your night off?" he drawled.

"Oh, it's almost a week away," she told him.

He shook his head. "Well, I think I'll come walking by tonight, Gloria."

She giggled again, "Alice, you mean."

He snapped his fingers. "That's right, of course, Alice, I knew I'd met you somewhere; it all comes back to me now, Alice. Well, now, my name is Ed Leroy, and this is the beginning of a beautiful friendship," he said softly, the axis of his head parallel again to the table, his eyes boring up at her from an angle.

"Oh, you're a card," she tittered in some confusion.

"That's right, I'm a card, and I don't take any wooden nickels, and I don't give any. You know what I mean?" he asked cryptically.

"Oh, I know what you mean, but if I answered you, would you know what I meant?" she asked.

Communicating by questions so they talked for another minute. When she left, the date arranged, Hollingsworth swallowed a large draught of his Scotch. "I think that's always the best policy not to give your right name," he told me. "Complications can set in."

I did not answer him, and a silence grew between us. Taking out the cigarette lighter he began to play with it, his forefinger tracing over the embossed initials. Obviously, he was feeling cocky. "I wonder what you think of your friend McLeod now?"

"Can't say as I've thought about it."

Hollingsworth shook his head. "I have. I thought he showed the white feather."

This penetrated my reserve, and left me furious. "I thought he was making fun of you," I said.

Hollingsworth showed his teeth. "Well, now that's interesting you say that." He flicked the lighter viciously, and gulped the last of his drink. With the whiskey in him, his eyes assumed a trace of expression; the pupils seemed to narrow. "I suppose you guess you know a few things about the people in our house," he told me.

"A few things."

Hollingsworth snickered, and slid the lighter across the table to me. "What would you say if I told you that was given to me by your lady friend?"

I stared at him in bewilderment.

"Oh, yes," he continued. "It was. It was given to me by the lady downstairs, by Mrs. Guinevere." He laughed triumphantly. "Yes, she had the initials put on specially for me."

With what effort I managed to grin. "And did you get around to seeing her a second time?"

He lit his pipe again. "I think you're scouting for information," he reproved me, his voice quiet and stiff. However, he could not maintain the attitude. "I will say that I have had some very pleasurable experiences with the lady in question." And as he smiled, I sensed finally the extent of his hatred for me. It left me not wholly unfrightened. He was smoking his pipe so calmly, his elbows relaxed upon the table.

Slowly I was beginning to appreciate what he had told me about Guinevere. I was stunned. My vanity bled. I could imagine her discussing me with Hollingsworth.

As if to probe the wound, he added, "Yes, she told me many things." He yawned delicately, one of his fair hands at his thin mouth. "She's a very unhappy woman, and a great deal of it is her husband's fault. I have lots of sympathy for her."

I swirled the last inch of beer in my glass. "Oh, yes," he went on, "it's a very interesting marriage. I was surprised to find out who her husband was."

"Did she introduce you?" I asked flatly.

He deliberated as if deciding what story to tell. "No," he said, "I discovered it. I happened to look in the window one night, and then, well, I put one thing and another together."

"You mean you spied." I was acting like a cuckold, reshaping to my misery all that had passed between Guinevere and myself. She had wanted me to spy on Hollingsworth. "I guess that is the only way you could do it," I whipped at him.

"Do you want to go over there now?" He sneered, his mouth ugly.

"All right, let's go." We might have been two boys jostling one another in preparation for a fight.

"Come on," he answered.

And with exaggerated gravity we stood up, each in turn, and left the bar, walked up the street, our bodies a stiff yard apart. Neither of us said anything. We strode along at a rapid pace, breathing heavily, our mutual animus almost tangible. When we came to the house, we halted irresolutely. My heart thumped in stupid anxiety, and I knew I did not want to go in. Once again we repeated the formula.

"Well, come on."

"Come on."

Puppies snarling over a bone, we rang the bell together, our fingers colliding, stood waiting, panting.

I could hear it peal inside, boring through layer after layer of protection.

There were footsteps on the other side of the gate, and the light went on in the entrance-way under the stone stairs. Guinevere appeared. She opened the gate a crack and stared at us. "Well, I'm a son of a bitch," she shouted heavily. "What do you jokers want?"

But Hollingsworth pushed her aside, and started in. She flung herself on his back, pummelling him with her heavy fists, and shrieking, "Who invited you in? You got a nerve," her voice close to panic, her bathrobe trailing. It might have been a scene in a bawdyhouse, the madam roughing futilely the latest of her drunken clients. We landed all three in the living room, all of us puffing, all of us glaring at one another. "Well, I'm a son of a bitch, I'm a son of a bitch," she kept saying.

Hollingsworth held her by the arm. "All right, trot him out," he told her.

"Trot who out?"

"Get him out. Your husband. I want to show this character over here."

Hollingsworth was much more drunk than I had realized. His skin was pale, his blond hair sagged upon his forehead, and his eyes burned. "Come on, trot him out," he snarled.

"You can go shove it," she shrieked.

Hollingsworth lashed Guinevere across the face with enough force to send her staggering backward into a chair. Her robe flew open, exposing her body even as her mind must have been stripped, and frantically her arms swam out and pulled the wrapper about her again, her modesty desperate. This once accomplished, she put her hand to her cheek, sat swaying, her emotions visibly balanced on the point of the blow. She might have cursed, she might have wept, she might have thrown herself upon him, but instead she remained motionless, her face blank.

"Cut that out," I shouted furiously, belatedly. I think I was the one who might have wept.

Monina was tugging at my arm. Her eyes wide and delighted with the tumult, she pulled me from the room. "Come meet Daddie, come meet Daddie," she sang.

I had no idea where I was led. I left Guinevere and Hollingsworth staring at one another, locked in their positions, strange animals confronted suddenly. Pulled behind Monina, I could only follow her into the bedroom. She ran immediately to the man who stood in one corner, and shouted with glee. "Daddie—Ditter Luft, Daddie—Ditter Luft," drawing us together to shake hands.

The man was in shadow, but I knew him immediately. He came forward into the light, sweat upon his forehead, mouth warped into the silly grimace of a man caught hoisting his longjohns in the midst of a raid. Drily, he said, "Well, Lovett, the lassie's uncovered me."

FOURTEEN

THE grin compressed into the thin line of his mouth. He looked no longer foolish. In a dull voice he muttered, "Once you've found a father, you'd do better not to track him to a brothel."

After this, neither of us could say a word. "McLeod," I blurted at last, and whatever it was I thought to tell him—that I was sorry, that I wished it had not happened—choked into silence. I turned around, started toward the door, and retraced my steps through the hall. Behind me, I could picture Monina still clutching him about the knees.

In the living room I paused for an instant. Hollingsworth had left, and Guinevere was collapsed into an armchair, her slim arms and legs thrust out at odd angles from the bulk of her body. The ruddy face was white now and bore the red signature of Hollingsworth's hand. She looked bloated and defenseless. "Oh, why do they do this to me?" she groaned, the fleshy tip of her nose pointed into the air. All at once I could not bear to look at her, and hurried outside.

For the second time in the same night I came to the railing which overlooked the docks, and stood there, holding to the iron posts, gazing down on the harbor below, while through my body coursed the reaction to the drink I had swallowed, to the hours spent with Hollingsworth, and the minute in the apartment. Why relate how my limbs ached or my stomach raced or my head whirled—there is something comic in such a catalogue. Suffice it that I was wretched, and if I had found a balance of sorts, the balance was lost now.

Guinevere McLeod.

So I stood at my distance above the river, and watched a dirty moon yellow the water. Somewhere, today, I had read in the newspaper, a woman had killed her children, and a movie star had enplaned from the West to be wed in a tiny church upon some hill. A boy had been found starving on a roof, a loaded rifle in his hands. The trigger squeezed, the shot rang down the street, and I could have been holding the rifle. I could even hate the boy because he had missed.

The tread of my foot heavy on the heat-softened pavement, I walked back at last to the house. As I came up the street, McLeod was sitting on the steps, a cigarette in his hand, elbows resting on his neatly creased pants. I nodded at him, feeling a considerable desire to pass him by, climb the stairs, and fall into bed. With an upraised hand, he detained me.

"Sit down," he said. "Don't you want to talk for a while?" He exhaled smoke carefully.

I squatted beside him while he gazed soberly into the illumination of the street light across the gutter, his body seemingly at ease. One might have thought him weary from his day's work and content to rest in the cool wind which drifted across the harbor. We did not speak for several minutes.

"Brothels," McLeod said abruptly. "I find their existence a fascinating subject. Ever considered it, Lovett?"

"No."

"You might. I've seen your kind dead-drunk more than once on a whorehouse floor. There's a certain requirement only a brothel can satisfy. To fornicate without emotional involvement—for the man in the street that's wish fulfillment."

He laughed, his eyes set straight ahead, his mouth pinched

over the cigarette. Some sequence played itself out in his mind for first he sighed, and then as though to correct himself, grimaced. "Come on," he murmured softly, "let's take a walk."

I obeyed him, fell into stride with his long legs. We moved along at a rapid pace, unwinding a little of the constraint each of us felt. When we came to the foot of Brooklyn Bridge, he started across and I followed, our footsteps echoing over the planked boards. A heavy mist had come in from sea, and the lights from neon signs and the windows of office buildings flickered dully through the murk. Foghorns bayed, and the automobiles which passed on the ramp to either side were almost obscured.

"Considerable attraction Hollingsworth has for her," McLeod stated from the recess of his silence.

"You think so?"

"No doubt about it. I can understand the reasons."

I tried to detect some expression on his face, but it was too dark. "What are you going to do?" I asked.

"A stupid question, Lovett. Do you think I'm such a young chicken that m'sexual esteem has been cruelly scored? What's been going on for several years, man?" He scratched his chin. "You think there haven't been the months when I wished that she'd find her gentleman caller, and he'd take her away? No, friend, I was born with what you might call an analytical disposition, and the experiences of m'life have reinforced it. I'm a thinking man, and moreover I don't give a toot."

"Then why haven't you left her?"

"Ah." He held up his hand. "Perhaps I'm not sure. No, I'll sit around and watch. I'm curious toward the outcome."

"That isn't natural," I protested.

"Natural?" He mimicked. "Lovett, you've got no conscious past to hinder you, so need you carry all the impedimenta of a middle-class moron? Distinguish, man, between your own desires and the realm of political possibility."

"As you do," I jeered.

"Look," he told me, grasping my shoulder, "a question must have occurred to you last night: Why didn't I boot Hollingsworth out of my room? I'll tell you why. Somewhere a mistake's been made, and for some reason or other, certain parties must think I know or have certain things. I'll have no rest till it's worked out. To satisfy my impulse, which was to whop the bejesus out of Mr. H., would have been a very expensive gesture. I'd have been paid back and with a profit. Do you understand? I decide such minor issues on the lowest practical level."

"You didn't seem so indifferent last night."

"Certainly not. I was frightened, more frightened than you could know."

"What was it all about?" I asked directly.

He did not answer my question. "I consider possibilities, and I work within limits," McLeod stated dogmatically. "What I may want has nothing to do with it."

We were passing beneath the arch of a suspension pillar. At the edge of the boardwalk, which extended over the automobile ramp, I could discern a man peering through the mist at the city beyond. He was a bum wandered up from the Bowery to retch his whiskey into the water. As we approached, he uttered a liquid belly sound and sank to his knees, hands still clutching the iron paling. Then, slowly, ludicrously, he slid backward until his stomach touched the ground, and lay there, face propped upon his arms, staring at the city. The fog was lifting.

I bent over him, but he was sound asleep. A snore of contentment rumbled out of his throat.

"We ought to do something for him."

"Let him be," McLeod said. "He's happy." Taking up a position beside the drunk, he blinked at a red light on the dome of an office building. "I can remember I took a walk over this bridge twenty years ago, and there was a drunk in practically the same place." He ran his long forefinger back and forth over the narrow bridge of his nose, kneading the tip vigorously between thumb and forefinger as if he were milking it. "How old do you think I am?"

"You told me forty-four."

"I was lying. I'm fifty-near. I was twenty-one when I joined the movement."

"The Communist Party?"

He nodded. "And I was forty when I left. Nineteen years with the wrong woman."

"It took you long enough," I commented. "What position do you have now?"

McLeod looked at me carefully. "Oh, vaguely sympathetic to them, y'might say. I dropped out, that's all, became inactive. But vaguely. I wouldn't fight about it. I'm a retiring man." He chortled.

"Then why was Hollingsworth bothering you?"

"Who knows? Who knows?" We had come to a halt, and McLeod surveyed the girders of the bridge. "You see there was a time"—he was exceptionally casual—"when I was not without importance in the organization. So perhaps that's why they're interested in the mind and flesh of Bill McLeod."

"How important were you?"

I sensed that I had gone too far. McLeod's response was cool. "You know it's all down on paper in many a file. You just have to look it up."

"How could I?"

He started walking again. "Well, maybe you can't. There's no telling. It's just that it's difficult to trust . . . even myself, and that's the truth." McLeod began to whistle the snatch of a song.

I was furious, and from what experience I hardly knew, discovered myself arguing with him. "You were with them for over twenty years," I demanded rhetorically, sensing this as still another shock for what had been indeed a long evening, "over twenty years, and you're still sympathetic? What kind of man are you? What about the collectivization famine . . . the. . . the. . ." And I spluttered my indictment: the purges, the pacts, the exploitation of one class against another, the phrases coming from my mouth in a consecutive exposition. I might have been living for years in a house with one room locked, and when at last the door was opened, I found the furnishings complete. "Why," I cried at last, "they've turned socialism inside out, they've perverted. . ."

"Look, m'lad," he cut across me, "I've never creamed m'pants over the beauties of the land across the sea. I know what it is better than you, hard enough and ugly enough for ten million of your sort, but have you ever tried to jack a peasant from the mud in which he wallows?"

I was trembling. "Don't tell me how much blood is necessary to pour a ton of concrete. If you had any theoretical capacity. . ."

McLeod had stopped and was looking at me with a fixed smile. "You're the one who's had no experience with politics. It bores you, does it? I suppose you get this from a book."

"I don't know where I get it from," I said stiffly, the effort to remember drenching my back with perspiration.

"What a stinking two-penny left deviationist you are," McLeod said. "And you'll tell me about some friend of yours who was murdered by our men in Spain."

"Maybe there was, maybe there was," I muttered.

"Maybe a dozen. And do you ever stop to think that it's you and your ilk who have no theoretical capacity? What do you know of history in your soft, squeamish way? Have you any idea of how many revolutionaries have to be devoured to improve the lot of a common man one bloody inch." He blew cigarette smoke in my face. "Do you know what a dream that is, and what an agony?"

"Only you've lowered them."

"Temporarily. Temporarily. You can't see history. You

can't understand state ownership, and the absence of all contradictions."

We were almost screaming at one another. "State ownership indeed. State ownership for a bureaucratic class at the expense of the others. Who controls the means of production?"

"How you have the little formulas," he cried at me. "But to change mankind. How're you going to do that? It's the bureaucrat you despise who's got the job."

"It's all degenerated, it's been impossible for twenty years."

"Go on, go on," he sneered. "Tell me a tale of the Old Bolsheviks and how they were murdered, tell me about the forced labor."

I was almost carried away. For once I grasped him by the shoulder. "Look, that revolution was the greatest event in man's history, and if it had not been confined to the one country, if it had spread. . ."

"But it didn't."

"It didn't," I agreed, "and so it died, and ever since, the crisis of the world has deepened, until by now it's only your bureaucrat who can raise man as you put it, and it's a measure of the disaster that everywhere the bureaucrat has the magic power."

McLeod began to walk again. When he spoke, his tone was lowered, was almost amiable. "You have a little theoretical equipment," he said slowly in the tone of a headmaster, "but where does it lead you?"

"Nowhere."

He nodded, was about to say something and then paused. But as if our argument had unhinged his resolution to be silent, as if, indeed, he were incapable of holding the words to himself a moment longer, he blurted hoarsely, "It's out now. They know." Only by saying this could he feel the complete shock, for he gripped my arm suddenly with tense fingers. "You see, Lovett, for a long time they looked for a man who wasn't married. And then I got the idea they looked for a man who was married. Although actually it's unimportant, and how was I to know in any case? What counts is that it's out now, do you see? They know me, and I don't know them. Not yet." He might have repressed a spasm for the fingers on my arm dug in suddenly and were withdrawn.

"I'm beginning to ramble," McLeod said quickly. "Let's leave discussion to the side." He took a breath, and in what was almost a chatty voice, said, "Perhaps I'm not as sympathetic to the New Jerusalem as I've portrayed. I'd just rather not go into it, and prefer to ask a question instead. You're not politically active, are you?"

I shook my head. "It's hopeless."

"The period of revolutions is past, eh?" he asked. "To attempt to continue is merely catering to a myth?"

"I suppose so." The fog had thinned sufficiently for us to discern the darker bulk of skyscrapers against the night.

"And so you accept what you have here."

"I don't accept. I just recognize that we'll have no better. At least one's allowed a corner in which to write a book."

"For the moment."

"For the moment," I admitted.

"Of course the condition which allows you to write a book rests upon the continued exploitation of three quarters of the world, and the living standard of a worker here depends on the Chink and the black man missing a meal."

"It's no use," I said again.

He nodded. "Let's leave it this way. I was curious at the range of your political vocabulary, that's all. And I would caution you that your own problems are not the problems of the world, and one's state of mind may well determine one's political outlook. But we'll have discussions, you and me." He whistled the snatch of song again. "When I'm permitted leisure." And clapping me on the back, he said, "You see, laddie, we're

124

excrescences, and we're waiting for the stones to grind us between them. Let's not fight, you and I."

We had come to the trolley station at the foot of the bridge. Beneath a street lamp I could see his face more clearly, and he was haggard. There was moisture on his forehead, and his long black hair for once was unkempt. "Do you feel all right?" I asked.

"Passable." He gripped my hand and shook it formally. "I've enjoyed our little talk, but you must remember to have pity on the poor retired bureaucrat." He gave his short laugh. "If you don't mind, I'd like to walk by myself and think awhile."

"Take it easy," I muttered.

"I'm always careful." Tossing up his hand in a mock salute, he strode off into the darkness of the streets.

I returned alone across the bridge.

It was a long walk. I was exhausted from the argument we had had, so pointless, so stereotyped, and so demanding upon me. I had not talked like that for how many years? And with the labor of parturition, a heartland of whole experience was separating itself to float toward the sea.

I was an adolescent again, and it was before the war, and I belonged to a small organization dedicated to a worker's revolution, although that dedication already tempered by a series of reverses was about to spawn its opposite and create a functionary for each large segment of the masses we had failed to arouse. I was young then, and no dedication could match mine. The revolution was tomorrow, and the inevitable crises of capitalism ticked away in my mind with the certainty of a time bomb, and even then could never begin to match the ticking of my pulse. There was a great man who led us, and I read almost every word he had written, and listened with the passion of the novitiate to each message he sent from the magical center in Mexico. Of all the students in the study group, none could have been more ardent than I, and for a winter and a spring, I lived more intensely in the past than I could ever in the present, until the sight of a policeman on his mount became the Petrograd proletariat crawling to fame between the legs of a Cossack's horse, and a drunken soldier on a streetcar merged into the dream I was always providing of the same soldier on the breast of the revolution, shaking his fist in an officer's face as he cried, "Equality. I can't explain it to you, vile exploiter, but equality, that's what I want." There was never a revolution to equal it, and never a city more glorious than Petrograd, and for all that period of my life I lived another and braved the ice of winter and the summer flies in Vyborg while across my adopted country of the past, winds of the revolution blew their flame, and all of us suffered hunger while we drank at the wine of equality, and knew with what passion to be later buried that our revolution would beget the others, and in a year, in a week, we the ignorant giant would bestride the earth and refashion it until there was nourishment and love for every man our brother.

More than two decades later I could have the dream in all its purity, and if from the tenets of the organization which taught me, I could also learn how the great wave had crashed and the revolution been betrayed, our leader persecuted, those twenty years were thrown into a minute, and I from my own need and own hunger listened to the time bomb I had fashioned and was certain that tomorrow the people would crowd the streets, and from the barricades would come the victory that meant equality for the world.

So the memory came down to the sea, and across my back scar tissue burned ever new circuits with its old pain. Things had altered this night. With a pain throbbing in my head I continued slowly home.

FIFTEEN

AT the foot of the bridge I sat down to rest in a bare little park with concrete paths and a stunted tree. It was well after midnight, but a few automobiles still clattered over the broad cobblestone paving, and across the avenue a bum wavered out of an all-night bar, performed a slow blundering dance around an ash can and staggered down the street. An old man had gone to sleep on a bench near by.

In the distance, the sound carrying mournfully through the darkness, I could hear the El grinding over the rails as it approached a station, and for a moment I thought of the long ride out to the end of the line, and the Negro slums along the way where children sleeping on the fire-escape would turn in their slumber as the train passed, moaning a little in acceptance of its fury even as artillerymen will drowse beside their howitzer while a night mission is fired. And from the third-story windows, level with the track, the Negro women, arms upon the sill, would stare into the night, their liquid eyes passive, lidded with weariness.

I stared at the few people who rested in the park. There was a girl sprawled upon a bench not fifty yards away, and I passed her by, only to return with a start. It was Lannie, her face illumined in the cone of a street light. She lay stretched to full length, her body upon its side, cheek supported by her fist. I was certain she had not stirred for minutes.

I approached slowly, cautious not to invade her fancy too roughly. "Lannie," I said at last.

She looked up slowly, her legs drawn beneath her, her torso straining for an upright position. For the first instant Lannie's eyes contained no recognition. "Oh, . . . Mikey," she said and passed her hand before her forehead. "You know I didn't know you," she muttered; "sit down, I'm so glad to see you. I've been lonesome."

"I tried to see you again," I told her, "but you were out."

She nodded disinterestedly. "I took a walk. I guess I've been gone for a while." Her fingers patted my breast pocket. "Give me a cigarette." I placed it in her mouth, for her hands were trembling, and struck a match. She puffed deeply, and then exhaled without force so that the smoke eddied about her face seconds afterward. "What time is it?" she asked.

"It's almost one."

"That late?" She gave a helpless laugh. "What have I been doing all these hours? Oh, I'll never get up tomorrow."

"What about your job?"

"Who cares. I wouldn't like it anyway." She tossed her head. "If you must know, I lost it this morning."

"But I don't understand."

"They fired me." She shrugged. "Mr. Rammelsby called me in, and said somebody had been complaining about my work, and I told him that I would leave because I could not support whispers and discontent, and tonight I'm free. No one can force me to do anything tomorrow for it's mine."

"Why did you tell me you had a job?"

"Oh, because you're so solemn and serious, and you would have been disapproving." She yawned.

Abruptly I realized that she was dressed in the pajamas she had been carrying in her handbag. Of heavy cotton, they billowed about her slim body, at least a size too large, and wretchedly wrinkled. Her matted hair fell to her shoulders. In the litter of these externals, the delicate lines of her face were almost lost.

"Do you like my pajamas?" she asked.

"I was just looking."

"I feel wonderful in them. I feel so free. I was walking down the street a little while ago, and I knew that if I wanted to, I could let them fall, and I would be naked."

Various objections appeared. "You'll be arrested if a cop sees you," I said.

"But they can't. I'll say to a cop, 'Sir, these are beach pajamas, and I sport beneath them a fully equipped set of lingerie. If you do not believe me, you shall have to strip me, and are you, sir, prepared to bear the consequences?' and then his red face will swell, and I'll punch him in his ugly nose, and scream, 'Police.'"

"You're not wearing anything underneath?"

She shivered in answer. "Don't scold me, Mikey. I'm warm. I've had a wonderful evening." She picked up a bottle which had been placed beneath the bench, and jiggled the inch of liquid still remaining. "I went into a store, and I said in my worst voice, 'Give me a pint, kid, and make it the roughest, cheapest brand you got.' And I've carried it all night. I feel just like a bum. I would love to be drunk in a gutter, covered in my own spew, my head in filth, and then I would feel like Christ. What a happy man he was. All night I've been thinking about the crucifixion. You put your arms out and you're at rest, and if people spit at you then you can pity them." Arms folded, she hugged herself. "Oh, something has happened, something happened today, and then there'll be more tomorrow."

"What?"

Lannie shook her head. Instead of answering directly, she told me something else. "You know a couple of months ago no one would talk to me, and I didn't see anyone. Once in a while I'd hear somebody yelling, and I remember that I used to cry a lot. And then one day I was in a room all locked up by myself"—she went on, her voice devoid of color—"and in the corner there was a big fat woman with a hard face because all the girls were frightened of her, and this used to make her feel so terrible she would slap them. This time she was changing my linen, and her face wasn't cruel at all. It was a sad face." Lannie watched the smoke of the cigarette crawl along her fingers. "I went and looked at her, and she said, 'You know who I am now, don't you?' and then she put her arms around me, and she took me in her lap and ran hands through my hair, and she kissed me. I never loved anyone, Mikey, the way I loved her then. She was beautiful."

I twisted uncomfortably on my seat. "Why do you tell me this?"

"Because tomorrow and then after and then so long after I pull the cord and hang a man, and that's what they make me do." She trailed off listlessly, and I could barely comprehend her. A sodden breeze stirred through the park, and the newspapers which littered the concrete path yawed sluggishly before its passage. I could hear a drunk snoring on one of the benches, saw another right himself momentarily to shake his fist at a passing car.

"What time is it?" Lannie asked again.

I told her, and she nodded dumbly, her dark, stained fingers playing at her throat. "Oh, Mikey, I don't know," she said at last.

"What?"

She stared at me, and in her eyes apprehension stirred like the faun aware of distant hunters. "Will you take me home tonight?" she asked.

"Of course."

"I knew you would"—this impulsively—"I wonder if you

know, but of course you can't. You're the kindest man I've met in so long."

I was unprepared for this. "Kindest man?" I parroted.

"Oh, you are. You mustn't be ashamed of it. You know you're so fussy, and you're old-maidish, and you're proud, but underneath it there's such kindness in you." Trembling, she lit another cigarette. "I knew only one man who was kinder than you, and he was a middle-aged man, a teacher in a little school in a small town, and he had beautiful hands, and he used to love to touch little boys with them because the little boys were so beautiful, only he never did dare; he would keep his hands in his pockets. They used to nickname him Wing, and they treated him dreadfully."

"Why I read that," I blurted. "It's a story."

She looked at me like a child, a finger upon her lower lip. "It is, that's right." And she gave her husky laugh with its overtone of exhaustion. "I'm getting silly again." Her head was lowered. "Oh, let's go home."

We started out across the park, her palm dry and feverish against my hand. When we had gone a little way she halted, murmured, "I forgot something," and fled back to the bench. By the time I followed she had recovered the bottle and held it aloft with triumph. "It would have been a shame to leave it there. Let's find someone to give it to." She set off immediately, prancing from bench to bench to examine the sleepers, and stopped finally before an old man with a white stubble. He was snoring powerfully. "Listen to him." She mocked his sounds. "Here, old graybeard," she murmured, slipping the flask into his coat pocket, "with this for sustenance may your dreams be sweet." And she darted away with a delighted laugh.

I caught up with Lannie after running a few steps, and encircled her waist. Beneath the cotton of the pajamas, I felt her grow rigid. "Philanthropist," I murmured.

She smiled at me. Yet her body, independent of what she

might desire, would not bend, and along the length of my arm I felt its constraint. Soon I released her, and we strode along hand in hand toward the rooming house.

I can hardly account for the route I took. Call it curiosity. In any case I passed by the bar where Hollingsworth had made his date, and found him standing on the street with the waitress. His head lowered, he was plunged into a conversation directed at her throat.

"Well . . . *hello*," he broke off, as he saw us, his head going up, and his eyes flickering from the waitress to us and back again.

I introduced Lannie, and we stood around in a circle not saying anything at first. She and Hollingsworth examined each other closely, but with a surface indifference almost successful in its subtlety. The silence continued, uncomfortable only to myself and to the waitress, who was probably petulant at the interruption.

Then Hollingsworth began to perform. Cockily, he extracted his lighter for one of Lannie's cigarettes, and flourished it in my direction. "Well, I guess this has been a long night for certain people," he said at last.

Lannie puffed at the light he had furnished, her body inclined from the waist, her eyes staring at him. With her free hand she still held mine, the pressure intent.

"I'm the new roomer," Lannie said in a husky voice.

Hollingsworth put the lighter back in his pocket. He cleared his throat. "Well, I know I'll be pleased to have you for a neighbor, Miss Madison," he said. "I think you'll find our place a very interesting specimen of life in New York."

"That's what I've heard," Lannie said vaguely.

"Indeedy," said Hollingsworth. "And the roomers are generally a high class of people with some culture." He tapped the pipe against his teeth. "I've always been very concerned with culture."

132

The waitress, who was standing to one side, interrupted brusquely. "Hey," she said, poking him in the ribs, "I thought your name was Ed Leroy."

I had introduced him as Hollingsworth. He pivoted slowly, and said, "I told you, Alice. My name is Ed Leroy Hollingsworth. Perhaps you missed the last name."

"I don't like it," the waitress said. "Come on, let's get going. I'm tired." She stared with suspicion at Lannie's pajamas. "I want to get home."

"In a minute," Hollingsworth snapped at her. With a look at me, he bent toward Lannie and asked, "Miss Madison, what do you think of our friend, Mr. Lovett?" And in his manner he made the question part of a game which linked them together.

"Oh, I think he's been very kind to me," Lannie said, accepting his gambit.

Hollingsworth nodded. "He's one of the best. We're great friends. Lovett's more studious than I am, very bookish, but he's a capital fellow. And they're other capital fellows in the house too."

"What about you?" she asked.

"Oh, I'm wilder. I don't know why, but I'm very wild. Wine and women, you know, although nothing that's off-color." He spoke as if I were not there.

"I'm glad I moved in," Lannie said with a burst of feeling as strong as it was unaccountable. Hollingsworth nodded his head to this, but I had the idea he was hardly listening. "Yes," he went on, "I suppose I am the complex type. What do you think, Mr. Lovett?"

"I agree with Alice. I want to go home."

"Yeah," Alice chimed in.

Hollingsworth smiled. "I guess now is not the time to embark upon long conversations. But sometime I would like to talk to you, Miss Madison." He shook hands with both of us quite formally, and then stared again at Lannie. "You have an interesting dress," he said in his mildest voice. "I suppose that's the new advanced style."

Lannie looked up and nodded her head vigorously. "I knew you would like it, or at least I had hoped you would; there are so many fools and no one sees anything." We were all silent, and she was shivering.

After a moment we separated. Moving down the street, I heard Hollingsworth say to the waitress, "Well, come on, sister."

Lannie and I walked on for some distance without speaking. Her hand, still squeezing mine, gripped harder and harder, until with a sudden motion that might have signified a decision taken, she pulled it away. "He's very beautiful," she said without preamble.

"Oh, extremely," I said.

"No, you could never understand. He has no idea of himself, and that's what makes him so exciting. I love his pious little voice."

"I detest it."

Lannie stiffened. "Oh, you would. You don't understand anything." To my amazement, she was quite angry. "He's unique, and there are so few who are. And they're always being condemned."

After that we fell silent and walked back without another word. Her head was turned away from me, and I might have thought her in a study if the tension of her body whenever it grazed against mine were not so evident. We climbed the steps of the rooming house, mounted to her floor. At the door I paused, and to my surprise, she invited me in. She was shivering again.

"You must have a glass of water before you go to bed," she said in a poor attempt at whimsy.

I discovered that she had moved the couch to face the wall once more. It must have required some heavy labor, for the two of us had been able to shift it only with difficulty. Now she sprawled upon it, her heels jammed against the baseboard. I sat beside her uncomfortably, and the gray dirty wall, its plaster cracked, stared back at me.

"I love this," Lannie said, her voice going on and on as though to pause would mean collapse, "if I had a dime I'd go out and buy some popcorn and sit here eating it. And whenever I wanted I'd throw a piece upon the floor." Lazily, smoke drifted from her mouth. "The wall is so nice. I can make it anything I want. This afternoon when you left, I kept looking at it, and I decided it was Guernica, and I could hear the horses screaming." She sighed to herself.

With a stubbornness she seemed to evoke, I asked, "What are you going to do for a meal tomorrow?"

"I won't be bothered thinking about it now."

"Do you have any money left?"

"Millions." One foot was lifted into the air, and with a slow absorption she waggled her moccasin which was loose at the heel. After a moment she took it off, poked a finger through the gap in the sole, and twirled it about her hand.

"Let me lend you money," I persisted.

She flung the moccasin against the wall. "Do whatever you please."

I was busy with private calculations, wondering how much I could give her from my small cache. "Will you take twenty dollars?" I said at last.

"I'll take whatever you give me," she said passively. She yawned. "Oh, Mikey, you're such a guardian. You should be handling investment funds for silly widows." She cocked her arms behind her head. Abruptly, she giggled. "I ought to make love to you. I've always wanted to make love to a guardian and whip his behind with his watch fob. What could be more exciting?" She nudged the ash from her cigarette with a finger tip.

I said nothing. I carried the residue of this long day and

longer night. My limbs ached, my stomach was uneasy, my body was tense. As she talked my responses lost proportion. I would be indifferent to some of her most astounding declarations, and in turn would stifle the irritation she might summon by a passing word. I gazed at her wall, suffering its oppressive emptiness, discovering upon it none of the distractions she would claim.

When I looked at her again there were tears in her eyes. "What's the matter?"

"I don't know." She scoured her moist cheek with the back of her fist. "Oh. We always have to move, don't we? I know I'll have to leave this room, and Mikey I'd like to stay here and close the door and have my food slipped in through a trap. Tomorrow I'll have to go looking for a job."

"Lannie, where were you living last?"

She smiled ruefully. "I had an apartment." Somehow this was difficult to believe.

"How did you lose it?"

"I donated it to the enemy." Lannie gave a small laugh. "What a stupid girl I was." She looked at me, and then she drawled, "I got kicked out of my own bed this morning, and I was the one who invited him there. Never show kindness to a drunk."

"Why didn't you make him leave?"

She gave her smile of wisdom to indicate that I was innocent indeed. "Oh, I couldn't. That wasn't possible." Lannie tossed her head mockingly. "And anyway I don't remember, not exactly. I woke up, and then I don't know what happened except that I was on the subway, and I had been sleeping. He threw these pajamas at me as I was going out."

"But . . . ?"

"Oh, I took pity on him. He was just an old drunk, and they'd canned him from his job, and so I took him in. He'd worked in the same agency I was in once, and he had beautiful

136

black hair and fat red cheeks. And he just stayed, and I think he knew that I was getting bored with him, and he hated me because I was all he had. And today he just ordered me out. I'll never talk to him again."

"But why did you let him keep it?"

She shrugged. "Descend to cabbage and the pinching of a penny? How mean! Let him fight over some walls, let him come after me and take everything I have, one after another, and don't you understand in giving it away I win every time." She smiled with forced delight. "Besides I was bored with my apartment."

I laughed suddenly, explosively, as much from exasperation as from mirth. Lannie yawned. "You're much nicer when you smile," she said. She reached over and stroked my face. "You have a wonderful nose," she told me. "I love the way it's turned up and your septum is pink. I knew a girl once with a nose like that, and she was very cruel."

I yawned too, and stood up. "I'm going to bed," I announced.

"Oh, you can't leave me yet." She said this casually, but for an instant I had a glimpse into the hours she anticipated alone and the bare walls which weighed upon her.

"I've got to. I'm exhausted," I said.

Lannie led me to the door, and then halted before it, barring my exit. Her head was at the level of my chin, and I kissed her forehead almost automatically. With a quick motion she came into my arms, thrust her mouth upward, and kissed me. Her lips were feverish, and her slender body bore against mine, hugging me in a wiry embrace. Intoxicated with fatigue we clung to each other, swayed across the room to sprawl upon her bed.

Her body arched against mine, rigid to the touch, her mouth tight as though she must repel even as she would accept. I held her in my arms, gave her my body to which she could cling, and remotely without tenderness or desire or even incapacity I performed, riding through the darkness of my closed eyes while she sobbed beneath me in fathomless desperation.

If it were love, it was also fear, and we might have huddled behind a rock while the night wind devoured the plain.

"Save me," I heard her cry.

SIXTEEN

O NCE, McLeod had said to me, "You know, m'bucko" —his voice relishing the outrageous brogue he would affect whenever he said anything which he had considered for some time—"it's onanists the world is forever shaping, and if you have a taste for dialectics, it demands little more to see that it is only by onanism at last one can receive the world." He had vented the sound of his private mirth, and stared at me. "If this doesn't ring a bell for you now, it'll toll a mass someday, for ye're in the archetype."

I stayed with Lannie through the night, and it was almost dawn when I climbed the stairs to my room. Yet I did not fall asleep for over an hour, every nerve of my body protesting against the events of that long day which had just ended. I would dream, and then I would be awake again. And despite myself, deprived of the rest of afterlove, I exhumed the hours I had just spent, and twitched irritably in my bed.

I had not really wanted Lannie; I had driven myself, not once, but again and another. She had wept, she had . . . why recount the details? It was done, and I had my regrets. I would end it as soon as possible.

Unhappily, our decisions are more plastic than we would allow, and in the afternoon when I awoke, my night with Lannie lost what had been without attraction. If it had been with the image of other women I had scoured my loins for her, it was now with the thought of Lannie that I lay comfortably in my bed, and her face in recollection seemed beautiful. I could have the desire to hold her, to embrace her gently.

McLeod's words returned to me then, and more. Out of that long day and longer night, I could be troubled again by the talk we had had on the bridge and the memory which followed it. Where had I learned the words I said to him, and what remained of them now? I would force my mind to yield more, but nothing could be forced; from the effort I came up with no more than a question. What, I heard myself asking in the silence of the room, are the phenomena of the world today? And into that formal void my mind sent an answer, the tat to the tit; I could have been reciting from a catechism.

The history of the last twenty years may be divided into two decades: a decade of economic crisis, and a decade of war and the preparations for new war.

Hands at my forehead, I repeated this as though in rocking back and forth I might find momentum to carry me further, to provide, from that time when I had languished like a handmaiden before a revolution which did not come, one face, one friend, one name which might present itself and offer a thread for the maze. But nothing followed. Nothing but the single answer: a decade of economic crisis and a decade of war and the preparations for new war. My mind had its own pleasure and I could force nothing. After a while, I wearied, went down to eat a meal, strolled afterward through a short walk.

When I returned I stopped on an impulse at Guinevere's door and rang her bell, hearing it sound with such clarity that I could picture her apartment in all its confusion, the beds unmade, the bread crumbs upon the table, and somewhere on the floor a puddle of coffee. Would she be drowsing, or did she sit in the kitchen now, staring into space? I rang again and listened.

In one of the recesses I heard her footsteps, slow and listless, as she dragged toward the door. Then there was no sound at all, and I imagined her motionless in the hall, standing with her weight balanced, one foot to answer, and one to retreat. So I rang still again, and as if it were only a cumulative pressure which could summon her, the steps became heavier, and with a steady slovenly clumping of her slippers she approached the door, paused with her hand on the knob, and slowly opened it a crack.

We stared at each other. I was shocked. Face swollen, hair undone, her eyes stared emptily ahead as though I were not there. For two seconds, three, perhaps four, we stood looking at each other, a minim of recognition in her face, and then, her mouth pinched and small without make-up, she fluttered her lips in an attempt to speak, and instead, closed the door in my face.

I shrugged, and climbed the stairs to Lannie's apartment. But the encounter with Guinevere, delayed in its reaction, fell upon me as I knocked on Lannie's door. I was abruptly depressed. From inside her room, I could hear the sound of laughter, and though I continued to knock, I wanted to slip away.

The laughter ceased, and there was silence on the other side of the door. When she welcomed me, her eyes were without enthusiasm. She squeezed my hand, erected a smile, and that was all.

In the corner sat Hollingsworth. He had selected with his dependable instinct the only wooden chair in the room, and he sat upon it stiffly, his hands turned in upon his knees, his narrow backside biting no more than the last inch of seat, so that he might have been a cadet, his body frozen into an agony of immobility, his mind shrieking, "Brace! Brace before *they* make you brace."

The muscles at the side of his mouth tensed, his teeth were revealed in a greeting. "Well, this is a surprise and a pleasant interruption," he said.

Lannie dropped in a chair, her body twisted, her head lolling over the arm. Strewn about her upon the floor were a dozen cigarette butts. "Oh, Mikey, I've had so many visitors today," she said. "I woke up this morning, and there was a mouse upon the bed, and we talked for a while, and he told me many things, although I found him pompous and a bore at last. And although he would not admit it I knew that he was Christ, and I wept for him because instead of dying, he's come back, and now he's lived too long. I told him he should go back to his cross, and without a word, he put on his hat, jumped off the bed, and left through a hole in the wall." A wan smile passed her sallow mouth. "And then there was another visitor, come to bring a towel, and he was like the mouse too, only I hated him. He said his name was McLeod, and he was a friend of yours."

"McLeod?"

"Yes." Her yellow fingers fluttered a match at her unlit cigarette. "He sat, and he talk talk talked as if he thought that he could tell me something when I knew him immediately for what he was. And then he said as he was leaving that he was Guinevere's husband, and I should have said that I was sorry for her." Lannie's face, to my surprise, was venomous.

"He told you that?"

She inhaled nervously and expelled the smoke with uncharacteristic force. "She's so beautiful and alive, and he can say with that voice of his, in modesty no less, that he's no better than she, when all the time I was with him I wanted to scream."

Hollingsworth smiled. "And then it was yours truly who came to pay Miss Madison a visit."

"Yes." She beamed. "Oh, I don't know what I would have done without him. When *your* friend left, I walked around, and I knew that if I didn't have something to drink I'd be ill, for how long may a bee live without nectar?" Lannie hugged herself, her thin arms protruding like stalks from the soiled cotton cuffs of her pajamas. And her voice suddenly hoarse, she said, "Lovett, you said you'd loan me some money."

I handed her two ten-dollar bills.

"Mikey's my banker," she said to Hollingsworth with an ironic gesture.

The sum of many small frustrations exploded for me. "I'm not your banker, and if you think I don't need that money, you're mistaken."

She danced out of her chair and over to where I sat on the sofa and pinched my cheek once. "He is a banker," she said to Hollingsworth, "but he's a charming one, and though he suffers through investment, and the black hand of money grips his heart in the middle of the night, he cannot escape his desire to be charming, and so he must always raise bond issues for Bohemia and resent his fate." She whirled about with amusement. "Those are the worst bankers of all when they turn upon you."

I recognized without much elation that this performance was for Hollingsworth, and not a word of her speech, not a gesture in the dance of her limbs was uninspired; she might have been a geisha tracing the ritual of the tea ceremony. And Hollingsworth sat and watched her, his buttocks seemingly suspended a millimeter above his seat, a polite look upon his face, an expression of mild curiosity in his eyes as if he would be the hick who has paid money and now watches the carnival girls strip their costumes. This is the magical evil of the big city, but he is wary of being taken in: "I come to see pussy," he says to his neighbor, "and I ain't seen pussy yet." He will smash the carnival booths if he is cheated. Perhaps he has come to be cheated.

"I would say," I offered, "that Ed Leroy here knows more about banking than I do."

His eyes blinked at the interruption, and in a small severe voice, he said, "I don't like to contradict a fellow, but you know very well that my name is Hollingsworth, Leroy Hollings-worth." He took out the silver and black cigarette lighter, and clicked forth the flame. "Naturally, a fellow who employs his brain power will use another name from time to time, but that's only common sense." He turned to Lannie. "Somehow I find it less of a confinement, if you know of what I'm speaking about, when there's one name for such and such an occasion, and an-other for a situation that's not exactly the same." He smiled expansively. "I always feel as if I can take a deep breath upon such transfers, do you know?"

"Oh, of course I know," Lannie said breathlessly, "you're so wise"—an ecstatic look upon her face. She threw her head back carelessly. "That's so important and no one understands it, everybody runs and nobody breathes, and when I wake up in the morning I'm choking so." A nervous hand searching her pocketbook, she pulled forth a toothbrush, and held it up like a standard. "I never can get this in my mouth. I start to brush my teeth, and everything in me says no, no, spit it out."

With an abrupt spasm of her fingers she snapped it in half, throwing the handle to one corner of the room, and the bristles to the other. She yawned and murmured contentedly, "Tomor-row, I'm going out to look for a job."

I turned to Hollingsworth. "Why is it you're not working today?"

He seemed to raise his buttocks another millimeter into the air. "Oh, my vacation has started." For the first time since I had entered the room, he leaned backward, allowed his shoul-ders to touch the chair. "I suppose we'll all be seeing a great deal of each other now."

A small but apparent reaction was evident after this state-ment. His shoulders left the back of the chair, and he was sit-ting upright again, his eyes concentrating on something, some object, some motion in the wall behind me. I turned around and

144

saw the door handle move, first to the left and then to the right. This was done silently at first, but after several purposeless attempts, it was rattled violently, and then a second later, when this was without effect, a foot began to kick with steady application against the base of the door.

"Demme in, demme in," a voice demanded.

It was Monina. She entered the room with a smile of delight and pranced over to me. Then she curtsied and extended a finger in an aristocratic gesture. "Kiss the boo-boo," she told me, and I brushed my lips against her hand. Satisfied by this, she rose haughtily, moved toward Lannie, and unable to sustain herself as a queen a moment longer, climbed into her lap. "You kiss me," she commanded.

Lannie obeyed, and framed the child's face with her palms. "Oh, you're beautiful," she said to her.

In response Monina hugged her passionately.

Hollingsworth hawked his throat. "Hello, Monina," he said to announce himself.

The child twisted in Lannie's arms at the sound of his voice, and then buried her head. Unaccountably, she began to weep.

"Mommie frightened today."

"Why?" Lannie asked.

"Mommie's crying." To say this upset Monina even more, and panting and hiccuping she delivered herself of a long story which I could barely comprehend. She had picked up the rug, or so I translated it, and there were insects beneath. She had gathered a few in her fist and put them into a glass and poured some of Mommie's boiling coffee water upon them. Then she brought it to Mommie who was lying in bed and crying, and Mommie had thrown the glass to the floor, and screamed that she would get the strap. Monina began to bawl, and Guinevere clasped the child to her breast, and they wept together, and Mommie had cried, "I was afraid of him, but he was going to change our lives; oh, my baby, it would have been all different." In anguish, she had shrieked, "Oh, my lover's deserted me."

And Monina, her face wrinkled into a parody of Guinevere's misery, repeated in a high piping voice, "Oh, dover's durted me, my dover's durted me." Somehow, in saying the words she crossed the child's boundary from real sorrow to the imitation of it so that her delight in herself became greater than the woe she would project, and she luxuriated upon the phrase as if it were a jelly bean of incomparable flavor. When she finished she could contain herself no longer, and giggles, malicious and childwise, tinkled from her mouth. She gave herself to Lannie's arms, her small body shaken with mirth.

Hollingsworth had listened to this without expression, without movement save for his foot which slid back and forth upon the carpet. I heard the story through his ears, and it provided me a portrait of Guinevere, perhaps my own as much as his, face swollen with weeping, her features puffed from the hornet's nest of discovery which had beset her. Hollingsworth would watch her, eyes blinking to the metronome of his brain, his toe pawing her upon the carpet. She was the turtle tumbled onto her back, even as the dream had in advance prepared her. And slowly he wiggled his toe, debating perhaps, remotely tempted to flip the turtle upright again.

He looked at Monina who was sitting primly on Lannie's lap, the child at intermission who has forgotten already what is past, and cannot conceive what is to come. Slowly, she wriggled within Lannie's arms, and revolved her head to stare at Hollingsworth, her mouth sullen again.

"Monina," he said, "do you think that was a nice thing to give those bugs to your Mommie?" He smiled frostily.

Her reaction was unforeseen. I do not know if his reprimand excited her guilt, if indeed she contained any, or whether it was with a sure grasp that a rebuke from him, from *him*, was

146

too unjust to bear. In any case she was out of Lannie's arms and across the room more rapidly than I had believed she could fly. And like a missile whose fuse was her mouth, she buried her teeth into Hollingsworth's hand, emitting in advance one single shriek which graduated her at a bound from a child to an avenging banshee.

Hollingsworth was caught by surprise. Unguarded, a moan escaped from his mouth, his eyes opened in fright. What nightmares were resurrected? He sat helpless upon the chair, his head thrown back, his limbs rigid, a convict in the deathroom, his body violated in the spasms of the current.

"I'm innocent," he screamed.

And with the cry, Monina released him, ran weeping out the door and wailing down the stairs.

Doubled with pain, Hollingsworth grunted, his paw held out before him to reveal in bleeding outline the opposed small scimitars of Monina's teeth. He writhed back and forth upon the chair, and then tentatively his unmarked hand fumbled through his hair. There was no spot shaven, no electrode upon his skull. He groaned, and mother to himself, supported the bleeding hand with the other, kissed it gently, tenderly, through a welter of self-pity and adoration.

We sat transfixed. As his anguish receded, he sat back, arms dangling, his face pale, sweat upon his brow. "Ohhhhh," he shuddered. Then he drew upright in the chair, his mouth deadly. "When I see that kid again," he said, "I'll cut her fucking heart out."

Lannie stood and made a vague gesture toward him. "Does it hurt?" she asked inanely, her yellow fingers plucking at the corner of her mouth.

He extracted a handkerchief from his pocket. "I'm going to see a doctor," he said; "this can be a serious injury." His voice was recapturing the anonymity with which he cloaked himself. "I must apologize for swearing, being as there were ladies present." When Lannie made no response, her fingers only nipping her mouth more fiercely, he continued. "It was such a sudden shock, after all. These things have a way of taking a fellow by surprise." Deftly, he wrapped the handkerchief about his hand. "Some children are badly brought up, it's a question of manners I would say." He stood up, and in the way he grasped his chair for support, I knew that he was still shaken. "One can never tell. A child's bite can be poisonous, I've heard."

Lannie could restrain herself no longer. Arms at her side, she laughed helplessly, "Oh, what a fool . . I never dreamed," she gasped. "You're stupid."

Hollingsworth suffered through it, fumbling in his shirt pocket to find a cigarette, and managing at last to light it. "Some people have a very unusual sense of humor," he muttered.

Delighted, I joined her. We laughed at him without pause for almost a minute, while he remained motionless, his face losing at last even its caricature of outraged dignity, so that he seemed to wait, patient and resolved, until the insult had run its course.

"Are you done now?" he asked her coldly, and for its effect upon her he might have pressed a button. Her laughter stopped. She quivered through every inch of her body, and I realized suddenly how close she was to hysteria.

"Sorry," she whispered.

"I suppose I'll go now," he said. He started toward the door, and with his hand upon the knob, he sniffed at his bandage, and delivered himself of a speech.

"I have a great deal of interest in all my friends, and so after I left that girl Alice with whom I spent an interesting few hours, if you know what I mean, even though she was what I would call a coarse girl of low upbringing, the passion's creature sort of thing that one reads about in the newspapers . . ." The statement had become unwieldly, and he let it lapse to smile pleasantly at us, his youthful face without guile, his yellow hair blending pleasantly with his blue eyes. "In any case, upon my return, I happened to pass this room, and you know there were a few sounds of the sort a fellow can hear very often in New York around four in the morning if he keeps his ears open."

"Oh," Lannie said, "oh, you misunderstand; you do."

"Yes, I hope so," he said modestly, "but I think, Miss Madison, that between you and Mr. Lovett there's certain kinds of . . . intimate exchange."

"Now, do you want to get out of here?" I asked. A murderous discharge of feeling left my limbs powerless.

"Leave him alone!" Lannie cried out to me.

"Oh, I'm going," Hollingsworth said. He was alert, his weight balanced to parry attack.

"You're scum," I told him.

"No." An expression of wistfulness set his features in unaccustomed patterns. "No, I don't do this to be a mean fellow. I have to do it. You see that's the only way I'm safe." And with a curt nod, much as though he regretted what he had just said, he passed through the door.

Lannie, standing motionless, her arms rigid, her face white, sang after him, "I'm sorry, I'm sorry."

SEVENTEEN

No sooner had the door closed and the sound of his steps disappeared, than Lannie began in the same breath to laugh and to weep. "Terrible. It's terrible, terrible, terrible," she kept repeating in a monotonous voice.

What was terrible I could hardly have said. I followed her mechanically across the room, trying once to encircle her waist with my arm but she flung it off. And each time I attempted to soothe her, she appeared not to have heard me. "Oh, it's terrible," she kept saying.

"What, Lannie?"

"Ohh." She dropped into a chair, started to light a cigarette with her trembling hands, and when this proved impossible, threw it to the floor. I brought her a glass of water, and she gulped it with disproportionate effort as though her throat refused to swallow.

I allowed a few minutes to go by without saying anything, and slowly, measure by measure, she grew calm again. A tired smile widened her mouth. Limp and pale, she remained in her seat, her fingers still shaking. "We should never have treated him that way," she said at last.

"Why not?"

"Oh, Mikey, you could never understand him because he's

different, and do you know how rare that is?" She shook her head, watching with an abstract curiosity the quiver of her fingers. "You see he's consecrated, and we just wander, and every day is new to us and ends by being silly, but he has a purpose and so he's fortunate." This time she succeeded in applying a match to her cigarette. "He doesn't know what he possesses, and I could show it to him."

"Then why did you laugh?" I asked.

"Yes, why?" I thought she was going to answer me; perhaps she even searched a moment for the reply. "Oh, it's beyond you," she said finally.

Yet my question must have had its effect for Lannie became silent again. As the minutes passed without either of us furnishing a word, I sensed melancholy settling upon her. She smoked the cigarette dreamily, her head back, her eyes following the passage of the smoke toward the ceiling. Once or twice she sighed. "There's no rest," she muttered. And the smoke curled from her limp hand and clung to her sleeve before drifting upward.

"Why don't you tell me what it's all about?"

Lannie stood up and walked to the window. Her back to me, she stared through the dirty pane. "When night comes, I'll be able to see the courtyard better. There's a pool at the bottom, and I float in the middle with lily pads about my hair, and a bird calls for me. I can hear that clearly."

"What are you talking about?" I snapped.

"I don't know," she went on, "who comes before Mr. Ter-Prossamenianvili, and that isn't even his name. If I could find a record of myself I would tell you." She perched herself on the window sill, and held out her hand as if to capture the sunlight. "You see, Mikey, they were always putting me on a bed, and then there were hands and the shock. I know what they were doing because each time they gave me the shock it would leave a little less of my brain, and they wanted to render me stupid as others render fat. They hated me, and they made a record of everything they took from my brain, and there was the girl in the corner with the eyeglasses who kept writing everything on the pad, and now it's in some green filing cabinet. They hated me, and I loved them for their sins."

This outburst apparently finished, she remained leaning against the window. The afternoon sun had lowered, and the last rays of light shone from outside. The worn gray nap of the furniture was oppressive again, and the dust-laden air shimmered in the bare and empty spaces of her room. Against a wall the sofa still remained as she had left it, facing no one, its monumental back a reminder of how she must sit when she was alone. I could see her in another chair turned to hide in still another room, and she would be watching the glow of embers in a fireplace. The room would be dark and quiet, and as the coal turned to ash, a chill wind would blow about her. The fire would die, and she would sit there in the darkness, her hand extended toward the whitened embers. And behind the chair with the breath of malevolence, another presence would fill the room, and she could only wait, terror-struck.

Tears started in my eyes. I could have wept for her. "Lannie," I said.

The large brown eyes, liquid and unguarded, looked at me from across the room, and with a pity I offered to her in preference to myself, I heard my voice say, "Don't you understand? I think I love you."

I might have given a blow across the brow for she ducked her head and held her nose as if all the grief she were able to contain had lodged suddenly there. She was aware of me now, and for an instant there was a directness in her response which I had rarely seen. "Mikey, you're good," she said.

"No, look." I had crossed the room and was holding her by the waist. "Let me love you," I pleaded. "I want to, don't you understand?"

"Oh." Her mouth was tight. She stared fixedly past my shoulder.

"Don't hold yourself against me, Lannie."

She began to cry. I pulled her toward me, and she ceased to resist, and ended with her arms about my neck, the salt of her tears against my mouth. "I want to love you. . ." She was caught by a new paroxysm of grief. "But I can't. I can't love you." She tried to push me away. "I don't like you. And you don't need me."

"I do."

She shook her head, tears streaming over her narrow face. "I don't know, I don't know," she whispered.

I guided her to the bed and lay myself down beside her.

There is a wager always when we make love, and if I was without passion, I was not without feeling. In the certainty of my own affection I gambled that she would melt.

It was a brave essay I made, but in a lost cause, and I stalked the heels of others and was rutted in the scars they had left. I loved her with as much talent as I could muster, and with more warmth than I had summoned through long months, but she lay beneath me stiffly and suffered it with a smile, her face calm and patient, sweet suffering Jesus upon the cross.

Slowly my confidence faded, and I made love with a sense of dread which slowed my motions and stilled my heat, until at last, the clock run down, and a cold sweat upon my back, I withdrew and lay beside her shuddering.

She was brisk in her motions. She took the sheet and wiped my face, kissed me once remotely upon the nose. "All done now," she murmured, but whether it were a question or an expression of relief, I hardly knew. After a time I sat up in bed, and each of us in our fashion rearranged our clothing. Lannie stood up finally, lit a cigarette, and stretched her arms. "Well, you got what you came down for," she said with sudden savagery.

I was too bruised to answer, doubting any reply I could make.

She spread the counterpane and walked to the window, her body erect, her head held high. Disgust on her mouth, she said quietly, "I hate making love in the daytime, it's always so obscene, and I keep thinking I'm a little girl and I'm peeking through the keyhole to see fat papa on the john." Lannie was breathing quickly. "You have to peek at me, don't you? You have to find out what I'm like. There never is anyone who lets me alone. Once I fled with a book, and picked a little green hill that looked down on a little green valley, and all the village oafs came out and jeered at me because I was smarter than them, and how could they bear that?"

"I don't know whether you'll believe it or not, Lannie, but I wanted to make you happy."

She looked as though I were taunting her. "Then why do you bother me? Why did you come near me?"

"I don't understand you," I stammered.

"You know I'm not well. What were you trying to do?"

I might have been lashed across the face. I turned away from her and murmured, "Oh, you're wrong, you're wrong," but the words lacked assurance. "You can't be right," I protested. "I . . . I think I love you."

Her mouth curled again. "You can't love anybody, Mikey, for you're Narcissus, and the closer you come to the water the more you adore yourself until your nose touches, and then you're alone again."

I did not want to believe this. "It's true," I said, "but it's . . . it's not true. It's not all true." I caught her by the shoulder with enough force to have hurt her. "Don't you understand? I want to live." I caught myself on the point of weeping. "It's not all true," I heard myself repeating.

This made her furious. "You want to live?" she asked, flinging my arm away. "You can't, you don't know how to.

You can't." She intoned this with a rhythmic blow of her fist against my chest. "You came to me because I was easy, and you thought it would not cost you anything." Again her fist thumped me. "But we never buy anybody without paying the price." Her blows stopped, her body trembled.

"You're not telling the truth," I muttered furiously, taking her shoulders again. "You give me no credit," I said, "I try. And you don't try, Lannie. You don't try at all."

This crumpled her. She swayed lightly, and with a gesture of concealment turned her head away and began to sob. "Yes yes, yes yes yes," she said rapidly.

"Lannie," I said. I touched her with my finger tip. "Lannie."

She fumbled her way into my arms weeping piteously. I might have comforted a child. Her tears soaked into my shirt, close to my flesh, and I held her and rocked her slowly.

"I need you, Mikey," she cried, "I need somebody . . . I need protection."

We were not lovers, but father and child, and yet for me who had fathered nothing, this was man's estate. I held her, I comforted her, I smoothed her hair, and as she subsided, I felt rising within me that most savory of emotions, a certain small affection for myself.

If only it could have lasted.

But a vista opening to all that was impossible. She slipped out of my arms, and stood with her back to me, her shoulders drawing together in an attempt to achieve composure. "I told you it was no use," she said quietly.

I did not answer, and when she spoke again, she had succeeded in masking herself. No more would we talk directly to one another.

"Oh, so many things in the world," said Lannie, "and do we ever stop to count them, or would we be statisticians if we did? And are they the same once counted?" She darted toward the armchair where she had left her purse, and picked it up to examine the inside, holding a piece of paper aloft. "There's so little you know, and it would be so difficult to educate you. Last night, or was it the night before, or when was it? I sat down, and I felt some words, and I wrote them down."

Before my bewilderment, she laughed. "Here, here read this, you may as well. Even the dunce must not always sit in the corner."

She had written in a sprawling hand which followed no pattern. One line crossed another, and the letters would slope to the left or right as the whim seized her. I read it with great difficulty, and in the middle, when I realized who was the hero of her piece, I must have moved my body suddenly for I heard her laugh.

This is what was on the paper:

and once on a hot night with the cannon going rub dub a dub to the silver of the moon he had a filipino woman commit salacio upon him and afterward he drove her away with a whoop and a cry and no money for her battered mouth thinking of this the next day in the sun with his yellow hair reflecting the maize of the fields where he was born the sermon going on the chaplain smiling at him with a what a fine serious chap smile and he smiling back while the sunday hymn comes out of his mouth sweet jesus redeemer his yellow hair and blue eyes so devout the little smile upon his mouth as he mouths the hymn and hears the cannon of the night before going rub dub dub a dub in his young buck crotch and through the jesus redeemer he sees the woman at his feet and smells the caribao flop she has left behind her sensing the sun in his hair again smiling at the chaplain for he contains the night before and the present moment and it renders him exquisite so that he sings the love words of crabbed spinsters lover jesus lord redeemer while to himself he says and he is wholly in

love with his image as he cracks her black head with his
knuckle you do that you do that now

When I had finished, I read it through again, and handed
it back to her without a word.

"He told me this, he was very proud of it," Lannie said.
"And I was proud of him as well, for he is so slim and his
muscles are so hard."

"I see," I mumbled.

"No, you don't." She fingered a cigarette. "You can't
understand the peace of being with a man who looks at you
as if you do not exist, so that slowly you're beaten beneath him
and everything whirls and you're not there at all, and love has
finally come the only way I want ever to see it when it is smoke
and I am in the opium den and thugs beset me, but I do not
care for I feel nothing any more."

"When did it happen?" I asked with a dry throat.

"I don't know. I don't add time, I don't feel bondage."

"Was it here?"

"Oh, was it? Who knows? For this house is like the last
one I was in, and he has been with me . . . oh, maybe it is
two days, and maybe it is all of this summer. And he tells me
what to do and then I do it, and so everything is very simple
now."

"And you like this?" I said very slowly.

"There is a man of extreme turpitude," she said with great
detachment, "and we are here to punish him for his sins. I
opened the door, and now I must close it, and he will pay."
Passion came into her voice for an instant. "And you will try
to interfere for you know nothing, and you will not succeed for
we are righteous people." With that she closed her eyes as
though to banish me, and I could think of nothing to answer.
All that had been gained was lost again.

EIGHTEEN

DURING the war, if I am to assume that I was in it, there must have been a period when I was part of a squad, for I recall a series of marches with intermittent combat, and at the end of a month we had crossed a border and were in the enemy's country. That night the squad was assigned a guard post in the loft of a barn which overlooked a field of grain. We set our machine gun to command the field and a row of trees at the end of it, and each of us sprawled out in the hay to sleep until it was our turn to watch.

We slept, however, very little. The farmer's daughter, appropriately enough, came to see us with a pail of hot water, and our washing completed, stayed to collect the chocolate bars and loose cigarettes we could turn from our pockets. So that night the farmer's daughter kept company with seven travelling salesmen, and at dawn with the literal cock of the crow she slipped back to her house, and we took up our march again.

I had been with her somewhere in the middle of the night, and although it was too dark to see her face, she must have been a beefy girl for her limbs were heavy. I had lain upon her to the accompaniment of snores and giggles, even as there had been snores and giggles for the men before me, and would be for the men after. There was moonlight on the field, and I made love from the hip and looked across the meadow with open eyes, for I was also on guard. I never saw the girl. Above my head in magnification of myself the barrel of the machine gun pointed toward the trees, and once, hearing a noise, my fingers stole up to the trigger handle, and I was surprised to find it cold.

My ration consumed, I went back to the hay and stretched out in a nervous half-sleep which consisted of love with artillery shells and sex of polished steel. By the next afternoon we were ten miles away, and the following night we had no such luck, for the company assembled and we dug holes at the outskirts of a small city preparatory to the attack. There are times when I have the idea I was wounded in the action which followed.

Probably I dreamed of other things the night of the salesmen's convention. I may have thought of the girl at the seashore resort, perhaps I even carried a letter from her in my pocket. I know that after leaving Lannie, I brooded about that girl I would never see again, and as Lannie had recalled the farm girl to me so she could recall the other. I had been so happy, I told myself now. She had fallen in love with her body, and I had been the cause. The room came back in all its warmth. A lamp was on and our bodies were golden, we smelled of each other in a bouquet of glowing flesh. Soon we would embrace, loving the taste of our mouths, and we would exist only in what we could hold within our arms.

Where was that girl and what did she look like? I wanted her so badly I was almost ill. Frustration put me on the rack, and with the frustration came something worse. For I would never meet that girl, and if I did I would not remember her and she would not recognize me. And if all these impossibilities one by one were to be solved and the wheel presented a double miracle for the same chip, then undoubtedly the girl and I, having changed, would be magical no more to each other. So that was done and that was dead. There would be no solutions from the past nor duplicates found in the present, and I could have cried out in resentment against the implacability of this logic. To be presented my present regimen without a single luxury? I resisted myself and knew in all hopelessness that whatever I was to find could not come from the past.

Therefore I stayed up late, determined to work. After hours of intermittent effort during which I would finish a few lines and punctuate them by lying on the bed or walking the floor, I succeeded at last in completing a page. The next followed less slowly, and from early in the morning until dawn I wrote with more facility than I could usually find.

When the sun was up I went for breakfast, came back to my room and slept till evening. I scribbled again through the following night, and in the morning feeling comparatively fresh, decided I would not go to bed until dark. During all this time I hardly thought of the people in the rooming house, and scarcely cared how long I did without their company. Everything which had been at cross-purpose seemed to resolve itself in my work, and for those two days I was not unhappy. I had another meal before the city awoke and strolled over the bridge in the cool of an early summer day, content with myself and my labor. I thought of going to the beach, or visiting somebody.

Yet neither appealed to me, and on the walk home as a hint of depression to follow, I entered upon a long calculation as to how much money I had still in the bank, and how great an inroad had been made already into both time and cash. As I trudged through the old gully of standard worry and preoccupation, I knew by the time I reached the house that I had been deceiving myself, that my indifference had evaporated, and what I wanted at heart was to see Lannie and McLeod again. Delayed in its appearance and multiplied in its power, came a reminder of Lannie as I had left her in the chaos of her room, and an image of McLeod as he had strolled off into the darkness beyond the bridge. So I returned, lay down on my bed, and as time passed, my fancy had free run until I began to imagine the most exceptional events, and even the silence of my cubicle became oppressive.

As though to mock me, my mind pushed forward a familiar question. What were the phenomena of the world today? If I knew little else, I knew the answer—war, and the preparations for new war—but out of an irritability which could not find its itch, I was hardly satisfied. There would be millions asking and millions answering the same question, and that side lay idiocy. "Do we want to suffer a hungry belly?" they would be asking, "Do we want to be blown to bits?" and put the reply in the negative with a passion to deceive the question. For wanting the opposite they would swindle themselves, assume that by the sole force of their desire, they could shape the result.

That side lay idiocy, that side lay the hair which became the snake and the cow-flop which cured the heart. That side lay all the answers which men could read daily and dutifully repeat: It is the fault of our leaders or their leaders, ours who are stupid or theirs who are evil; it is due to the unfathomable ways of the Almighty; it is because we are selfish; it is because we are generous; it is because we live with machines, it is because we have not enough machines; it is because we have lost the way, it is because the others have not found it; it is. . .it is without an answer. Only patriotism is left and anger to burnish it. The enemy is at fault, the enemy is the destroyer of peace.

One enters the argument of The Only Recourse. The thing to do is to be more selfish, or less selfish; to have more liberty, or less liberty. We need a big army, and lower taxes; diplomats must meet, we must break diplomatic contact; it is our duty, it is our danger; our ideas are superior, we need ideas . . . so we will swallow simples for nostrum.

I think of a soldier who is not inordinately fond of killing, who hates his officers, and is weary to death of the particular war in which he finds himself. Nevertheless, he kills as opportunity demands, he obeys his officers, and he does not desert. His ideas move in one direction, and the sad feet which belong to society move in the other. Thus the actions of people and not their sentiments make history. There was a sentence for it, a sentence I had pondered through what experience I could remember and through much that was lost, and as it came to mind it left its trail of books I had once studied. "Men enter into social and economic relations independent of their wills," and did it not mean more than all the drums of the medicine men?

I had come this far, remembered this much, and felt again a faint glow of the ardor with which I had waited for the inevitable contradictions to burn the fuse. The proletariat which crawled to glory beneath the belly of a Cossack's horse, the summer flies of Vyborg, I could see it all again, and know with the despair which follows fervor that nothing had changed, and social relations, economic relations, were still independent of man's will.

Except for myself. I lived, and was it I alone, in relation to nothing? The world would revolve, and I who might exercise a will for so long as money lasted, exercised nothing and dreamed away hours upon my bed. Now, the silence about me could become doubly oppressive. I started up and crossed the hall to McLeod's door, knocked upon it as if I could summon him to be present. There was no answer, and when I knocked again, the door gave before my fist, swung slowly open.

My eyes were drawn immediately to the table which had been placed in the center of the room and was bracketed by two wooden chairs which stared blankly at one another across its empty surface. Adjacent to one of the chairs was set a floor lamp so arranged that it would shine into the eyes of whoever sat on the other side of the table. Everything else had been pushed to the side.

Then I realized McLeod had vacated the room. The cot was stripped of linen, the bookcase was empty, and his few spare possessions were gone. He had washed the floor before his departure. I stood in the doorway, my heart beating. I assumed instinctively that he had fled or harm had come to him, and it was several moments later before I realized the probable answer. He must have moved downstairs to rejoin his wife, and now they would suffer the proximity they had always avoided.

I closed the door and descended to the street. The iron gate to Guinevere's apartment was locked as always, and I rang her bell, and waited for the sound of her steps. On this occasion there was nothing faltering about them. She approached the door, opened it, and smiled broadly at the sight of my face. "Jesus, I haven't seen you in a dog's age," she bawled. "Come on in. I'm going nuts. Have I got a problem!" As I followed her through the foyer, I could catch the odor of heavy perfume and the hem of her purple velvet wrapper swished luxuriously along the floor.

She led me into the living room, and flopped into an armchair. "Oh, Lordie, I'll never get in gear."

"What's the matter?"

"Look." With a gesture of mock distaste she extended her arm about the room. Its customary order had vanished. At least twenty boxes and packages of varying size and shape were strewn about the floor. Opened, their contents disgorged, and in quick appraisal I counted two negligees, one black and one pink, a pair of fancy gloves, a spring coat, two lamp shades juxtaposed so violently in style that a hotel lobby could not have contained them both, a pair of shoes, a ten-pound tin of ham, a corset with lace for the hips, a sweater, a silver-plated cork opener, a brooch, an Hawaiian scarf, an oil painting of Spring in the Mountains, and a pastel-bound folio of three slim volumes whose titles I could not read but whose reputation I am certain was mildly pornographic. There were other items so confused with their wrappings that I was unable to classify them, but the ensemble of opened boxes and closed boxes, of white tissue and paper packing, of ribbons and odors grew so overwhelming that I might have thought myself submerged in a dressing room of chorus girls whose naked limbs and mascaraed navels, breasts and black net, peeked out at me through a chiaroscuro of yellow lights and cigarette smoke and costumes hung from the wall.

"Guinevere," I managed at last to say, "what are you going to do with all this?"

"I don't know," she groaned. "Boy, what I got myself into." And with that, as though to weigh the enormity of her disaster, she plunged her hands into a carton at her feet, and brought forth a length of cheap print material which she unrolled with a grimace between us. "And that, too? What did I get that for? Look at it, it's so cheesy. The damn salesgirl. I knew she was trying to put something over on me."

"How're you going to pay for all these things?"

Her blue eyes regarded me in innocence. "Oh, I'm not going to buy them all. I'm going to return them, and just keep a couple of things." She leaned forward in her chair. "But what things should I keep? That's what I can't decide."

I began to laugh. "Guinevere, if you knew you were going to return nearly all of this, why did you buy it?"

She looked at me as if my question were utterly without logic. "What has that got to do with it? Lovett, you're not a woman, so you couldn't understand."

"Well, while you were buying. . .your collection, did you think you were going to keep everything?"

She deliberated over this, reluctantly I would say. Probably she had never considered the question before. "I don't know, Lovett. I suppose so. I mean, you know, I thought how nice this would look and that would look." Her mouth tightened irritably. "You're no help at all. What a mess!" And she kicked over a box with her foot, stirred irascibly in the chair. Her coloring was so vivid at the moment, her energy so compelling, that I must have stared at her with evident amazement.

"What's the matter?" she asked. "What are you looking at me for?"

"I was just thinking of the change there's been since last I saw you."

"Oh, that." She yawned in a pretense of indifference. "Listen, that was a crisis. There's a saying of some sort which covers it. But I'm all over it now. I know where I stand." She said this smugly, and yet her restlessness was so pressing that it overflowed in another instant. "I don't know what I'm going to do with all this stuff when the next batch arrives."

"The next batch? How many days have you been doing this?"

"Just a couple." She lit a cigarette and burned her fingers with the match. "Oh, damn." In a rage to punish the pain, she flipped the match into an ashtray with enough force to bounce it out again, and squashed the cigarette after it. "There'll come a day when I'll keep this stuff," she muttered, and in the rapid shifting of her body from side to side in the chair, she knocked over a sewing basket on an end table. Spools and thread scattered into the debris of the room, but Guinevere paid no heed. With an uncomfortable grunt, she reached forward and picked up a small paper bag from the carpet. "This is one thing I'm not giving back," she told me archly.

"What is it?"

"Oh, I'm not showing it to you."

"Very well then, don't."

"I oughtn't to." With a begrudging air, she emptied the bag into her lap. I saw a khaki-colored object made of cloth.

"What is it, a brassiere?" I asked.

"It's a money belt."

"You expect to be handling large sums soon?"

Her mouth pursed. She exuded an aura of grave import. "I'm prepared, that's all."

"You're always prepared," I taunted her.

"Yeah, well you got your opinion of me, and I got mine of you," she answered in a surly voice. "You ain't so hot, Lovett." And then, the idea first occurring to her, she asked. "What brings you down here anyway?"

"I'm looking for your husband. I see he's moved."

"Oh, him. What about him?"

"I was wondering where he is."

"He's around." Even this she made mysterious.

"Then he's not working today."

"No." Guinevere looked at me. "He's quit his job."

"Why did he do that?"

"Search me. I'm no mind reader." Her features became twisted with exasperation. "Listen, the time I have been having with that guy. He's driving me nuts. He's become a bleeding heart. You ought to hear him talk. Do you know what he keeps telling me?"

"What?"

"That there's no time left. How do you like that? You'd think he was inviting me to his funeral."

"I should imagine you'd be concerned."

"Mikey," she said sadly, "there was a time when I was concerned. I've been impressed by him just as you are now. I thought he was a gentleman. You know, he's got brains." She snorted. "Try eating them sometime." She massaged a ripple of flesh beneath the velvet wrapper. "You know what he did—he stole my youth away, that's all; and now I got to look out for Number One. I'm tired of sacrificing myself."

"What are you protesting about?" I asked her.

She shifted heavily in the chair like a businessman about to embark on a new tack. "Lovett, there's something going on. I can't enumerate the details for you, so you got to take it on trust. But honest to God it's Monina I'm thinking of. She's got a future in Hollywood, a big future, and I got to provide for it.

And I know you like the kid, and you like me, so maybe you could help us."

I blew cigarette smoke in her direction. "I hardly know how."

"Well, you're his friend. You could advise him."

"What do you want me to tell him?"

Again she deliberated, mounting her profile for my delectation, and then furnishing a veiled glance of her eyes. "Mikey, am I still under your skin?"

"I would hardly know where to locate you."

But apparently this sufficed. Indeed, she must have been looking for any pretext to include me, as if, undoubtedly instructed that this was to be a guarded secret, some special dispensation ought to be found for so quickly relating it. "Now, Mikey, you don't know this, but he's got something he won't give up."

"What is it?"

She held up a hand. "Even if I knew I couldn't tell you. And I don't. Honest. I lived with the fellow for all these years, and I never knew. But he's got something all right, and it doesn't do him a bit of good, and if he'd only give it to the interested party whom it would really help, everything would come out fine, and we'd all be sitting pretty. It's as easy as that. Wouldn't you say he's unreasonable?"

"Don't you ever feel any loyalty to him at all?"

She did not answer my question directly. "Mikey, I can see that it's not fair to ask this of you. After all, I don't want you to be torn between us. You've had it bad enough probably." She massaged her hand slowly, ritually, as though to exorcise a wrinkle she had found there. "So let's put it this way. I don't ask you to do a thing. The interested party has his own methods, and there'll probably be something going on between them, discussions and who knows what. The important thing is that when he sees the sense of giving it up, that you—well, you know, that you don't keep me in the dark about it. I'm sort of curious, you see." And she crooked her hand in the air, holding an imaginary teacup with which she experimented, the little finger curled at an angle.

"I'm afraid I won't be of any aid to you."

"Well, I'm not asking you to commit yourself," she said quickly. "Just leave it an open issue. How's that?" When I did not reply, she folded her hand into her lap again. In the silence which followed, exasperation generated from exasperation until she burst out, "You're nothing but a sadist, Lovett."

I laughed at her.

"Oh, it's easy for you," she said bitterly. "What do you know of the worries I got? Everything's going wrong. Even Monina's turned against me. I've slaved my life away for her, and now you ought to see the way she runs after him. He never paid any attention to her since she was born, but that don't bother Monina. You'd think it was a love affair." She pulled at a curl on her head and readjusted it with a hairpin. "Right now she's with him."

"Where are they?"

Guinevere was sullen. "They went out for a walk, and they're probably back in his room."

"I thought he moved down here."

"He did. But his business appointments he keeps separate."

"Business appointments?" Ideally, a parrot would be her best companion.

"Well, not exactly. But whatever it is, he and the other party got some things to talk over."

"They're going to do it right now?" I felt so great a desire to be present that she must have discerned it without difficulty.

"In a couple of minutes, I suppose. Maybe ten, maybe twenty." She could afford to be casual. "What's the matter? You want to be there?" she asked.

"I don't know."

Guinevere smirked at this obvious lie. "Well, I don't see what's stopping you."

"Probably they would prefer no company."

She shrugged. "You can't tell. You're sort of different. There's no predicting what they'd say."

"Why won't you be there?"

Her mouth became pinched. "They both told me they didn't want me. So that's that." Almost instantly she concealed this resentment, but by an effort intense enough to suggest the frustration she felt. "Oh, brotherrrrr, it's a big world," she declared suddenly.

I stood up. "I'm going to try to be there."

She laughed. "Mikey. . ."

"Yes?"

"Be a good guy, and remember that I'm the one who told you all about it. You know, I do something for you, and you do something for me. . ." Her voice trailed off. "Just remember what I said anyway."

NINETEEN

Even as I came to the head of the stairs, I could hear squeals coming from McLeod's room. I opened his door and looked within, but for many seconds neither he nor Monina was aware of me. The child twisted in the air, giggling in rare delight, her thighs flailing, fists pummeling his bony arms which threw her up and caught her, threw her up within a handspan of the ceiling and caught her not six inches from the floor. They were both laughing, and when he set her astride his shoulders, she grasped his straight black hair, and jogged up and down. "Horsie, horsie, play horsie," she cried. He made a pretense of galloping, clumping his heels against the floor, and she was almost helpless with glee.

Then McLeod saw me, and his gaiety ceased. He removed the child from her perch, set her on the floor, and greeted me coolly. "Where have you been?" he asked.

"I just saw your wife."

"Mmm." He inclined his head. And did she tell you I've become a new man?"

"In a sense."

Monina was tugging at his pants, and he tousled her hair almost unconsciously. "Yes, I've been attempting to force a revolution into my life, and that's a touchy business at best." I have the idea he must have been a little drunk. There was liquor on his breath, and his speech had become slurred just perceptibly. Monina hopped restlessly from one foot to the other. She gave a sigh of boredom and began to poke at the mattress with her finger. "Bah, bah, blah, blah," she burbled.

"What's the matter, Monina?" he asked.

Her head was turned down. She would not look at him.

"I lived in this room for two years," McLeod said to me. "It's a long time."

"It's a very long time when a child is growing up. There's the trespass if one is looking for punishment. Do you know there'd often be a month go by, and I wouldn't see her more than once or twice. We're strangers to each other now." He caught Monina by the arms. "Do you love your daddie?" he asked.

She twisted uncomfortably and like a wild bird struggled to be free. "No." Once loose from him, however, she giggled.

"If her tongue were developed, she could well add that she loves no one and trusts no one for that is her birthmark. Yes, she's my daughter right enough," he said blackly. With scorn upon his mouth he reached forward and tapped me with one finger on the knee. "You see me as the sentimental parent, but there were other times. D'ye have any conception of the desperate anger which can come upon a man when he sits in his living room with a legally engraved spouse, the act of marriage having divorced them from all passion and all friendship so that they live in guilt and hate and very occasionally in love. And there before them on the floor is the sweet product of their distaste, an infant mewling with snot on her lip and turd in her seat. So a man like m'self sits there, and reflects that very few of the good years are left to him, and he's bound not only to the woman but to the child until it chokes him so much he could crush the infant's skull with his fist." The finger jabbed my knee again. "You draw back from that, do you? A horror. Yet I sat there, and

171

with impeccable reason I would not care to refute even today, came to the conclusion that to murder one's own child is the least reprehensible form of murder. For do in a stranger, and you know nothing of what lives you snarl and what grief you bestrew. But take the axe to your own brat, and the emotional price is yours alone. Murder is nothing and consequence is all." He took a breath. "I'd give an arm to have the child love me," he said abruptly, "and that's a barometer to my weakness which increases with the years."

"She may yet," I suggested.

He nodded. Perhaps he grappled a beast who threw him first to one side and then another, for he reversed everything he had said. "There's hope in the situation, Mikey. It's just that I've been starved too long, and I'm suspicious of food." Into his impassive eyes a glint of feeling wavered. "She . . . that is my wife . . . I would say that all capacity for feeling is not dead between us. There are times when I sense that it moves her, my being there. She does odd things, you know. There are times when she comes to me, there's a softness in her, but she's wary. I don't say as I can blame her, the truth being that I must always fight with myself to keep from looking for the first train west. But still I like to think there are possibilities for us."

My last conversation with Guinevere was quite vivid. "You've a sentimental idiot," I said to him.

McLeod lit a cigarette. "And you are taken in by appearances. No doubt she had a few choice words to apply to me."

"More than a few."

He rode past this with a shrug. "Lovett, you've got a deficient imagination. You can't conceive how she and I could construct something together. But that's because you think love is a spirit vapor."

"It's as good an explanation as any."

He laughed at me. "Love is simple to understand if you haven't got a mind soft and full of holes. It's a crutch, that's all, and there isn't a one of us doesn't need a crutch. You take a mixture of lust and compassion, affection and ego, you shake it well, and you pour it into the mold of your own need. And after that you got a crutch. Makes it easier to rear back and look at the cosmos."

"Still, it can't be just anybody," I protested.

"Not today, no. Existence warps too much. It sets us so we can only receive certain kinds of opposite numbers. But in the abstract, in essence, any two human beings can find warmth together. It's a primitive notion, and history won't set it free again until socialism is established. That's the human assumption of socialism, to find relationships with everybody, and none of your dope needles about marriage, family, and the spirit vapor of love and God." The expression on his mouth of a man who sips vinegar, he added, "And it's in the Soviet that you'll find this freedom."

With that, he looked at his watch and said to me, "Now, I hope you'll excuse me, but I must ask you to leave, m'dear. And if you'd take Monina down to her mother, I'd accept it all as a favor."

"I intend to stay here," I announced.

He looked at me with no humor whatsoever. "Are you serious?"

I nodded.

McLeod turned to Monina and in a quiet voice said, "Go downstairs now, baby."

She shook her head. "Monina, you go downstairs," he repeated firmly. She made no more than a gesture of rebellion, and then accepted his decision. "Daddie play with me later?" she asked.

"No bribes," he told her. "We'll play when we both feel like it next."

To my surprise, she obeyed him. He locked the door behind her, motioned me to a chair, and sat himself on the desk in such a position that his face was looking down into mine. "What makes you think you want to stay?" he demanded.

"Perhaps I'm curious."

"I never buy curiosity no matter how cheap it comes."

"There are other reasons too."

"You think you can be of assistance to me?" He laughed. "Hollingsworth wants me to continue his political education, and since our discussion on the bridge . . . well, you're not exactly sympathetic."

"I hardly know why," I said, "but I believe you misrepresented yourself that night."

He drummed his fingers on the desk, debating what I had said. "Perhaps, perhaps." In aside, he murmured, "The fact that I've been drinking is hardly promising." When he looked up, there was an odd expression on his mouth. "So you stay in spite of my political opinions?"

"I reserve decision."

His mouth twisted. "I know very little about you." Running his finger along the desk, he held it up to see how much dust he had garnered. "Lovett, I don't think you appreciate the situation."

"I've never pretended to," I told him.

"If you stay, you'll be committed to this."

"I'm aware of that."

"It may have certain consequences for you." His voice had become so soft I strained to hear him, and it was in the resolute absence of any threat that I felt the force of what he said. He had succeeded in frightening me.

"Perhaps I look for consequences," I muttered.

"You?"

"I don't know why," I told him. "Or maybe I do. But there it is. In any case what have I to lose?" I blurted out suddenly.

McLeod shrugged. "I can hardly decide what to say, and

yet . ." For himself, he murmured, "There's a limit to what a man may support."

Someone rapped gently on the door.

"Well, he's here," McLeod said. He was quite pale. "Stay then, Lovett."

Turning the key, he turned his back as well and returned to the center of the room. Hollingsworth opened the door and held it aside for Lannie who followed behind him. He was dressed nattily in a gabardine suit with a knit tie and brown-and-white sport shoes. His blond hair was plastered down with oil, and he looked as if he had just taken a shower. "My, it's a warm day," he said pleasantly. He looked about the room, took cognizance of me, and in a continuation of the same movement, perhaps to mask his surprise, took the leather brief case he had brought with him and laid it on the table. Then he took a chair from the wall, set it at one end of the desk, and motioned Lannie to it. Looking at neither McLeod nor me, she drifted into it, set her hands on the desk, and seemed to stare at them, examining indifferently the frayed cuff of her violet suit.

Then Hollingsworth sat down, opened the flap of the brief case toward him so that he might lay his hand on any of the contents and lit a cigarette. McLeod had not yet taken the remaining chair, and I stood almost behind him, near the bed, waiting diffidently for a position to be assigned.

Hollingsworth cleared his throat. "Before we begin," he said, "I think Mr. Lovett ought to leave the room."

McLeod's voice was unexpectedly husky. "He wants to stay."

"That's all very fine, but I think he'll have to go." Hollingsworth had disposed of the problem.

"I haven't made up my mind about it," McLeod drawled, "but I'm half inclined to let him remain."

"One would have to say you're not in a position to . . ."

McLeod cut him off. "I've agreed to this procedure. You're not obliged to follow it. You've got an alternative. Until you choose to use it, I'll insist on my prerogatives."

Hollingsworth jabbed out his cigarette. "This is entirely unforeseen."

McLeod studied him intensely. "There's a good deal that's unexpected," he murmured.

"I want him out," Hollingsworth said.

"Then he'll have to take your . . . colleague with him."

A breeze might have ruffled Lannie's hair. She looked up at us for a moment, before returning to her study. With a concentration of which she was probably unaware, she picked at dead skin on a fingernail.

Hollingsworth slid a sheet from the brief case. "I think a fellow ought to sit down," he said to McLeod, "and if Mr. Lovett does not mind staying on the bed, owing to the informality. . . ." He adjusted his tie. "I suppose we may as well begin."

TWENTY

O NE moment," McLeod told him. He circled past the desk to the window, and fingered the shade. Then he pulled it down and returned to his seat. With one of his long arms he reached for the lamp bulb, switched it on, and adjusted the shade so the light glared into his eyes.

Hollingsworth tapped his pencil. After due consideration he pushed his chair back and reversed what McLeod had done. He went to the window and lifted the shade, came back to the desk and turned the light out. A deprecating smile played over his mouth. "That isn't necessary yet," he said.

McLeod looked indifferent. "As I've told you, I'm willing to co-operate."

"That's fine," Hollingsworth said. "A fellow appreciates such an attitude because this kind of meeting can often get to be endless if you know what I mean."

"Where do you want to begin?"

Hollingsworth tapped the pencil again. He might have been establishing order. "I'm of the tough-skinned variety, I would say, but you know there is a source, so to speak, of embarrassment for me. That is when there are lots of mistruths. Frankness is to be appreciated." He coughed apologetically.

177

"You see we know so much about a certain party that he couldn't retain in his own interest anything that was important."

"I stand by my original statement," McLeod said.

"Yes." Hollingsworth reached into his breast pocket and withdrew a paper pad. He scribbled something on it, tore off the sheet, and passed it to McLeod. "I think it will save time if you admit you are the person whose name I have written here." He leaned forward slightly.

McLeod tore the paper into bits. He did not reply immediately, his fingers working aimlessly at a button on his shirt pocket. Finally he got it open, slipped the scraps within, and closed the flap. "All right," he said at last, "that gentleman and myself are identical."

"Jim-dandy," Hollingsworth said.

He passed across the desk a yellowed newspaper clipping on which I could glimpse a group photograph of several men. "You can see the time we saved. I'm glad you also think honesty is the best policy. Now if we can just continue like this . . ."

McLeod made no response. He leaned back in his chair, twisted around slowly to look at me. Then he winked. It seemed a painful attempt.

Hollingsworth was studying some papers he had withdrawn from the briefcase. "I wonder," he said finally, "if you would be so kind as to outline for me the biography of the gentleman mentioned."

"You have it all there," McLeod protested.

"One never knows."

Staring at the ceiling, McLeod recited as if to himself, "Born of working-class background. Age of twenty in 1921. Became interested in the revolutionary movement. Worked as machinist, studied Marxist classics at night. Joined the Party 1922." And the foundation outlined, he went on in the same dry voice he always employed in talking about himself, to list a series of positions. He was in this country and he was in the other, he fulfilled one function only to surpass it with the next, so that in a steady ascent from branch to district to national, spiced with the inevitable journeys to Mecca, he outlined a history whose items were not uncharacteristic. Here, he led a strike; there, he was the focus of agit-prop; a factional fight; a stretch in jail; member of American Central Committee; each fact a brick to be laid in position and tamped with mortar, the date following the statement with careful precision. "Returned abroad, 1932. Travelled extensively, 1932-1935. In Soviet, 1935-1936. Spain, 1936-1938." More trips following upon them, a year in Moscow, a year in America, but now he was vague and the conditions were unnamed. He floundered ever so slightly, correcting himself once about a date, and then, without transition, in the same voice with which he had related the rest, stated, "In 1941, left the Party. Subsequently worked as statistician for American government bureau 1941-1942. Under assumed name. Quit bureau in 1942. Since worked at odd jobs under name of William McLeod. That's all."

Hollingsworth had been making check marks on the typewritten pages before him. "You say you worked as a statistician for a government bureau of this country?"

McLeod grinned. "Why don't you call it a first approximation?"

"A fellow can let it pass for the moment." Hollingsworth wiped a cowlick out of his eye. "In 1935 you were in a certain Balkan country."

McLeod seemed to be trying to remember. "For a week or two."

"You speak a particular Balkan language fluently."

"With a very bad accent."

Hollingsworth shook his head. "Fluently."

Leaning forward in his chair, McLeod looked at him. "What are you getting at?"

"There's some doubt as to the country of your origin."

"I was born here. You have it listed in your papers, no doubt."

"We cannot find a record of birth."

"Your concern, I should say, not mine."

Hollingsworth sighed. "It's all very complicated." He wrote something again on the pad of paper and extended it to McLeod. "You see that Balkan name?"

McLeod nodded. "Means nothing to me."

"Oh, the fellow it seems is quite a character. Born in one of the Balkan countries by a father of that nationality and an Irish mother. You never met him in 1936?"

"Never." McLeod shook his head in emphasis.

"That was the name you used in said country."

"You're mistaken."

"I have photographs here."

"Show them to me." Both of them had begun to rise in their seat.

"For the time being I'll hold them."

"You don't have photographs," McLeod said.

Hollingsworth took out his cigarettes, lit one for himself and then offered the pack to Lannie. She had come out of her reverie and was staring at McLeod with an intensity so great that he would turn away each time their eyes met.

"Taking into account the name of the first gentleman we have agreed upon," Hollingsworth continued, "would you care to admit that he came to America at the age of seventeen from that Balkan country and returned on numerous occasions?"

McLeod seemed puzzled. He rapped a finger against his teeth as though to assess whether they were hollow. "I hardly know your purpose, Leroy. It seems an extraordinary approach to me, but in any case I will state with complete assurance that the answer is no."

Hollingsworth did not seem perturbed. Unhurriedly, he read aloud from a note he held in his hand. "Proficient in conspiratorial techniques. Leader of—I would prefer not to mention the names of these organizations before your friend. Speaks English fluently with Irish inflection."

"You know quite well," McLeod drawled, "that I speak English with a bad accent."

Hollingsworth continued to study the paper. "Notorious in his activities. Reputation as the 'hangman of the Left Opposition.'" He removed wax from his ear with a finger. "Correct a fellow if he's wrong," he went on, "but they're another one of these conspiratorial organizations, I understand. Lesser importance. Not considered worthy of top urgent attention." Hollingsworth ended his recitation. "This gentleman means nothing to you?"

"Nothing at all."

"One must always be prepared for delays I suppose." He made a passing remark. "Can we think of this fellow as your brother?" In the course of saying this, he kept looking at his cigarette upon which a half-inch of ash had accumulated, and seeing no ashtray on the desk held it over the floor. "Do you mind if I drop it here?" he asked immediately after his first question.

McLeod answered the second. "I'll get a plate for you." He rummaged through the closet and came up with a single dish which he set upon the desk. "I'd appreciate it, Miss Madison," he said quietly, "if you would use it as well. You may enjoy dirtying the floor, but you'll have to curb the pleasure."

Lannie's hand trembled, her eyes seemed enormous. She was about to speak, and then restrained herself.

Hollingsworth cleared his throat. "I must ask you again to request Mr. Lovett to leave the room."

McLeod looked at me and I shook my head. "Afraid not," McLeod said.

Holding the pencil between his finger tips as though he were demonstrating the size of a fish, Hollingsworth waved both

181

hands slowly up and down in unconscious adjuration. "It would decidedly be for the better for all concerned." His flat blue eyes stared past me lifelessly. "I shall have to make a report about this. Mr. Lovett will be in the position of a gentleman possessing State Information."

"You've always got the option," McLeod said slowly, "of taking me in and barring the cell. Why is it that you don't?"

Hollingsworth made no answer.

"It occurs to me that you're making no report about this little interview."

"The department allows a wide latitude in interrogative techniques," Hollingsworth said coldly.

"Not that wide. To skip the paper work? To have no record of what we say? Man, you've already committed the first heresy."

"Much as a fellow might appreciate the benefits of your experience, I have to ask you to allow me my own methods."

"I don't think you understand yourself what's in your head. If I were your superior, and knew you made no record, I'd set a man to watch you, and a man for him as well."

Hollingsworth's cheeks had reddened. He looked like a little boy being reprimanded. "I think the best thing is to proceed," he said quietly.

"Oh, of course. To the workbench by all means." To my surprise McLeod seemed furious. "For the record I protest this approach."

Hollingsworth blinked his eyes slowly, pleased apparently by McLeod's anger. "Would you care," he said very softly, "to relate any special occurrences which took place while you worked as a statistician in the aforesaid and unnamed bureau of the government?"

"Nothing took place."

Hollingsworth clicked his tongue. "I hate to be unpleasant, but this is an outright lie as we all know. It can only lead to a fellow making certain assumptions."

A pause. "All right, it was a lie," McLeod said. "Something did happen, but I know little about it."

"If you would tell a fellow what you do know," Hollingsworth requested courteously.

McLeod lit a cigarette and watched the flame on the match as it crept toward his fingers. When it seemed about to burn him, he blew it out and watched the smoke drift upward from the molten head, a dreamy smile upon his mouth. At last he seemed to collect himself. "I have your permission to be long-winded?" he asked Hollingsworth.

"I would like the story to be complete without being extended beyond the bounds of a fellow's patience, if you don't mind," he said.

"There's a lot for you to learn in it," McLeod observed. "If you guard a machine ye're obliged to suffer its anxiety." He drew smoke from his cigarette, and began to talk. As though compelled to organize even those materials most alien to him, he delivered a long speech or more precisely a lecture, hurrying himself just perceptibly if he thought Hollingsworth about to ask a question, dallying over details when he sensed that he had our attention. The discourse was for Hollingsworth, but it was for myself as well, and there were moments when he was talking directly to Lannie.

"You may put it," McLeod began, "that I worked in one of the endless ramifications of the embryonic State Capitalism, a big place with thousands of people and thousands of desks, and this but the local branch, mind you."

He went on to describe with relish how the various parts of the organism fitted together, the circuits of the memos in their pneumatic carriers, the hierarchy of the telephones, the schedule of the elevators, the honor-guard of the secretaries, and the stenographers arranged by hundreds on the floor, geared to the communications which moved with their own laws and their own inertia from office to office, and occasionally embarked on a journey between the outside world and the inner structure. "In all this, you might say I was only a blood cell in a minor organ."

Then, after years of regular and orderly process, something happened. "I don't know, I can't tell you what it was," McLeod said, "an object of some sort or other, not too large I imagine, but it was gone, and no one knew how."

The organism reeled from the shock and trembled to its extremities. "You cannot appreciate it unless you were there, unless you'd donated your time to the tune of a thousand days, and each morning you'd passed the guards and gone to your own proper elevator, got off at your own floor and sat before your desk which rested there waiting for you all through the night. The displacement of that little object displaced a great deal else. Cysts broke, pus spread, the blood became infected and carried the fever with it. You should have seen the giant stagger. There were guards collected at every joint and operations galore. The stripping of elevators and the examination of cables, the counting of pneumatic carriers, the tapping of the telephones, the questioning of ignorant stenographers." McLeod held out his hands to encompass the enormity of the operation. "You must understand," he said, "that this was subtle as well. It didn't happen all at once, and at no time did the works shut down. The memos still went back and forth, the desks were filled, the guards would nod at you in the morning, and the stenographers like the little geese they are would take off in a flock for the john at the stroke of ten."

He extended his fingers before him and slowly made a fist. "But don't let me deceive you. The organism was not the same." He might have been glancing at Lannie from the corner of his eye. "In the beginning the fluids pass through a madman's veins in ways indistinguishable from our own, and his body divides the food he receives into the same chemical proportions we fashion for ourselves. Only no one would mistake him for us. His mind is antithetical, and in time it exercises its influence

184

upon his body until even the organs are different, and a muscle common as the sphincter is attuned to distant stimuli so that he shits to the moaning of the wind and blows his nose into his soup."

Grimacing, he sat back and folded his arms to indicate that he was finished.

Hollingsworth looked annoyed. "Is that all?" he asked.

"Not all exactly. I can't tell you the rest. I decided my past was a poor companion, so I took off, and what's happened since is a mystery to me."

"It was at this time you married?"

"Shortly after I left the job, yes."

Hollingsworth had taken out his pipe and was in the process of dismantling it. "Now," he said casually, "when did your organization tell you to take the . ."

"The little object?"

Hollingsworth nodded.

"They did not tell me to take it because I had left them."

Hollingsworth gave vent to a prodigious yawn. When his mouth was finally closed, he picked up the pipestem and began to blow through it. He looked bored. "One doesn't just say goodbye to an organization of that variety," he suggested.

"You know perfectly well," McLeod said, "the conditions under which I left."

"Why did you take the little object?"

"I didn't take it."

"Once again. Why did you take the little object?"

"I didn't take it. I don't even know what it is. Do you?"

Hollingsworth revealed his teeth long enough to bite on the pipestem.

"Let's take a recess," he said, and leaned back in his seat.

TWENTY-ONE

WE all sat staring foolishly at one another. McLeod got out of his chair, stepped carefully over Lannie's legs, and sat down beside me on the bed. The hair at his temple was moist, and in a reaction he was incapable of controlling, his spectacles had fogged and he was obliged to remove them and wipe the lens.

Hollingsworth yawned again. "I wonder if it would be permissible to excuse myself for several minutes?" he inquired, and when there was no answer, he stood up, buttoned his jacket, nodded formally to each of us and stepped out of the room.

Lannie and McLeod were absorbed in regarding their legs. McLeod looked up. "Now that your boy friend is listening outside," he murmured, "I suppose it's time for you to begin."

Lannie trembled. With a nonchalance she bore poorly, she turned slowly to survey the cold lines of the room. And when she spoke it was with an utter disregard of sequence so that one might have thought she had not been present during the last half-hour. "Your wife told me this room was open," she said to McLeod, her eyes raising at last to gaze into his, "and that I could have it for a song, and I told her my pocketbook sings a dreary dirge."

Even this effort apparently exhausting, her voice dropped.

"You see this place is so much cheaper than my own, and if I move over, your wife promised me out of her graciousness that I would be refunded on a pro-rata basis which comes to so many dollars, and I have need of money now." Her eyes crossed his and darted away again.

"But I cannot bear this room," she said abruptly. "It is dreary, and there is the smell of dry dry rot. No one has ever lived here and no bird sings."

McLeod had been examining her with a blank stare, his mouth sucking with contempt at the imaginary lemon-drop. "No bird sings," he muttered to himself, and laughed with caustic glee. Deliberately, he lay down on the mattress, his body behind me, crooked his arms in back of his head, and lay there, inert, the articulation of his limbs a foil to anything Lannie might say.

Apparently she could not bear to remain seated a moment longer. I watched her pace the length of the room, stand facing the door for almost a minute, and then return to the window. "Oh, there was a period long enough when I wanted to meet you," she said over her shoulder so that at first I thought she was talking to me, "all the time the girl with the eyeglasses was in the corner taking notes for the green filing cabinet, and laying hands upon me were all the others in their white uniforms. They are the rulers of the earth, and I wondered at the face of their chief, but I should have known it would be like yours with the eye socket and the jaw socket sucking at the bone, for you are the undertaker of the revolution, and now it is too late, and all the slugs wallow in the bar, and men live by the clock and give a three times three hurrah as they bind the chains about them. There are only people left, people here and there."

McLeod was very pale. With an effort he sneered, "A true revolutionary."

"Yes," she breathed. "People here and there with a look in their faces, and those I would revolutionize so they can live. But there is too much grass and it's all withered and I have only a teaspoon of water." By an effort she choked off what she was saying, and returned to the cot, staring down upon McLeod. "They told me that I would find you at last, his Mr. Wilson and his Mr. Court, and they were kind and took me aside and told me all, and I begged to be the one to see your face.

"And, now seeing, I know . . . I know," she cried, "that I could sit by and watch cutthroats club you to the grave, and I would shout them on, for I know that you are wholly irredeemable. I was afraid. I thought that I might have pity, that most crippling of the sentiments, or that looking into your face, I would say, he has suffered, or—and this is what tormented me most—that in helping them, what did I help? But you have buried the revolution, and it is fitting that they who exist because of you, they who rise to eminence here because you destroyed the revolution there, should have the right to flay your bones. And I shall cheer them on."

McLeod began to titter. He held a fist to his chin and rocked back and forth through a small arc. "I saw it, I saw it," he muttered. "I saw you from the beginning, m'girl." Deep within his body, violence may have been stirring, but the summons too terrifying to measure, he merely shook his head.

"So long as he lived," she whispered, "then everything didn't belong to the man with the pipe, and Soso hated the idea of that, and he sent his messenger and I was the one who introduced them, and after that I had to give myself to the people with the white uniforms and now without me they cannot exist for if I'm not there to torture they must be at each other's throat. They're all that's left and so I must love them, for if I cannot be in love. . ." She held her finger to her mouth.

"He was the man I loved, the only man I ever truly loved with heart and not with body, the man with the beard because he was a fool—a brilliant man and I loved his beard, and there was the mountain ax in his brain, and all the blood poured out, and he could not see the Mexican sun. Your people raised the ax, and the last blood of revolutionary mankind, his poor blood, ran into the carpet." By now her face only a short distance above his, she seemed to press each word upon his supine figure, McLeod the effigy to her incantation. "Have you," she asked, "have you ever opened the door to the assassin outside?"

"Leave off!" McLeod shouted. But the effort emptied him for he lay back again, a tight smile imprinted on his face, his narrow body held with rigidity.

The door opened and Hollingsworth walked in. "The recess is over," he announced.

Lannie seemed not to have heard him. She almost fell upon McLeod. "Assassin," she whispered.

"Take her away," McLeod said.

"Assassin!"

Hollingsworth shouldered Lannie aside. "The recess is over," he repeated, and stood looking judiciously at McLeod as though to assay whether the explosion were a success and foundations had shifted.

"What do you want?" McLeod asked hoarsely of him.

"Where do you keep it?" Hollingsworth asked.

"I don't have it," McLeod said.

"Sit up!"

With what an effort Hollingsworth restrained himself from using force. Slowly McLeod drew himself up on the bed. "What do you want?" he asked again. "Take me in, and be done with it."

"Do you know where it is?"

For a moment I thought McLeod was going to nod. He rested stock-still, his head down, his eyes on the floor. "No, I don't know," he said in a low voice.

"Well, what is it? What is the little object?" Anxiety was perceptible in Hollingsworth's voice.

"I would have no idea," McLeod said painfully.

Hollingsworth stood erect, the point of his pencil jammed

into the palm of his hand. "This is intolerable," he said, half to himself. He seemed deliberating how to proceed, and ten seconds might have passed while he stood alone in the room, in contrast to Lannie who sat with her head supported by her hands, still shaking, while McLeod, making every effort to recover composure, knit a crease in his trouser, the long fingers running forward and back in restless pressure upon the cloth.

"A fellow can assure you," Hollingsworth began at last, clearing his throat, "That I'm not nearly so hard on you as some of my colleagues might be, and among the reasons"—a hint of passion might have been heard in his voice—"is that you're a man who's been quite an actor in his time, and it makes it more interesting, so to speak, in my line of work, when there's a challenge. You have the feeling I don't like you, and that's not correct. I might even have a certain . . . delicacy of feeling, more or less, about the situation in which you find yourself."

Lannie looked up, startled at first by his words, and then a crafty smile came over her face, and she shook her head in agreement.

"You think there's no hope at all for you," Hollingsworth continued, "but it's my purpose to convince you of the opposite." Saying this, he crossed around the desk, and whispered, by the length I judge, several sentences in McLeod's ear.

McLeod began to laugh. "Cooo," he said mirthlessly, and then stood up and moved away, so that Hollingsworth was left bent over, an expression of curious intensity upon his face.

"That's how it is then," McLeod said.

"As I've told you, a fellow hasn't made up his mind yet, but he can."

"I had an idea of this," McLeod said slowly.

"You're not a dull fellow," Hollingsworth answered warmly.

McLeod was twisting a piece of waste in his hands. "Perhaps we had better go on." And across the strain of his face, an irritable excitement cracked his mouth into a smile. "Something you want clarified?" he asked.

"Well. . ." Hollingsworth consulted his notes. "What would you say, critically speaking, of the story you told about how the little object was lost."

"I would say there's not a bit of truth in it."

The blond hair nodded, and into the opaque blue eyes a glint of satisfaction might have appeared. "Check," he said.

"Of course," McLeod added with a wan attempt at a grin, "sifted, analyzed and re-examined, there is still a core of metaphysical truth."

Hollingsworth allowed himself to look pained. "What is that word . . . metaphysical?"

"You needn't bother yourself. Call everything I told a lie."

"I don't pretend to have your learning," Hollingsworth said, "and one would have to think it commendable the way you employ a big word, but you see I'm a simple fellow who concerns himself with the facts, and that's not so bad in its own way, because I'm sitting where I am, and you're sitting where you are."

"I apologize," McLeod said.

"There's no use crying over spilt milk. Now, to continue, and as I have said so often, frankness is the best approach to me, what is the little object and where is it kept?"

McLeod shook his head. "You see, Leroy, there comes a time when your theoretical incapacities act as a hobble instead of a shield. Suppose I ask you: What is a tin can?"

"It's a tin can."

"It's not a tin can unless one adds to it the knowledge that it's made from stolen labor. For example, what would you say if I told you that the entire physical world at this stage of history— all the houses, all the factories, all the food—are merely a coagulation of stolen labor from the past."

"I think we're getting pretty far afield."

"Hew to the point. What if there is no point and only a context?"

"It's my job to remind you." Hollingsworth was playing with the silver-and-black cigarette lighter. "You still haven't answered the question."

"I'll answer, but I prefer to do it in my own way." He popped a cigarette into his mouth, reached across the desk for Hollingsworth's gadget, and lit it with some nonchalance. "To begin with, the little object so-called, is completely a problem in context. What is it and where was it born? Oh, I'll answer your questions, Leroy. But wait. First I want you to take into account the vast structures which created it. An end product one might say, delivered into the world trailing corruption and gore, laden with guilt, a petrifaction of all which preceded it. Do you get me?"

Hollingsworth blinked slowly. Every curve of his posture announced that he could afford to wait.

"Supposing I possessed it. Where would it be? You assume woodenly that I've got it wrapped in brown paper, and it's in one of m'pants pockets. Or perhaps it's buried in the ground. But you've got no call to assume either. I might be keeping it here"—and he pointed to his head. "Or maybe nobody knows what it is. That's possible too. You don't have to know what something is to appreciate its value. You can still trace its relation to other things."

"Would you help a fellow out with some practical examples?"

McLeod looked offended. "I've explained the possibilities. If you insist I can belabor them. But what difference does it make? The theory I lean to is that nobody knows what it is."

Hollingsworth shook his head. "Ridiculous."

"Makes perfect sense. Do *you* know what it is?" Before Hollingsworth's silence, McLeod chuckled. "No, of course you don't. You're sent out to bring back something you couldn't even recognize, and that's fitting. The processes all produce elephants, and we're only allowed to touch small pieces of the hide. You see, you're in a position where you can't be trusted, and so you get a hair from the tail. And your chief, does he know any more? Not appreciably, for he's no more to be trusted than you. Like everything else the little object creates about itself a circle of acquaintance and can be understood only collectively. For such is the nature of knowledge today."

"How do you know what it is?" Hollingsworth asked.

"I don't. You're the only one makes such claims for me."

"There's reason to believe you're not telling the truth."

"I'd have been a fool to pick that up as a playmate. What furies would pursue me for such a sacrilege." He was looking at Lannie now. "In the modern heavens what is the condition most unbearable for the Gods?" The question was answered with hardly a pause. "Why it's a little object whose whereabouts is unknown. Something unaccounted for? No God can stomach that when He is collective."

"You make it sound like a fellow would wish he were rid of it," Hollingsworth suggested.

"Yes, I imagine a man could spend his life trying to find someone to pass it on to. Yet with what difficulty. For who could fulfill the specifications?"

They sat smiling at one another.

"Of course, this is all academic," McLeod went on, "for I don't have it. In outlining the situation, I think I've made it clear that a man would be mad to accept such a responsibility. Why should I do such a thing?"

"Guilt," Lannie croaked suddenly. She had come forward in her chair and was staring at him, her wide eyes ringed by their dark circles, her hand twisting through her lank hair.

Each of the men stiffened at the interruption. By a slight inclination of his head, Hollingsworth indicated that he wished her to be silent. "Yes, yes indeedy," he mused aloud, "you've given me great food for thought, and although you're a stubborn fellow, I'd have to mark you down as generally co-operative." Once more he gathered his papers. "We'll continue this upon further notice, and in the meantime, think it over." He looked at Lannie. "Will you come with me, Miss Madison?"

Lannie stood up, but she was not to leave without incident. Hollingsworth's hand was on her shoulder, and she flung it off. Staring at me, she said in a voice thick with anger, "You're a fool, Mikey, go away." And as our eyes locked, she said with an even greater passion, "Come with us. There's no place else to be."

Hollingsworth tried to guide her from the room, but she evaded him again, and pointed her finger at McLeod. "He corrupts," she shrieked, "he corrupts everything."

"Get out of here," Hollingsworth barked. Almost forcibly he pushed her to the door, and whatever it was that had made her speak failed her, and Lannie was docile. She went into the hall without another word.

"I must beg your pardon," Hollingsworth said.

McLeod nodded.

"A fellow knows you have it," Hollingsworth smiled, "but it might be impolite to ask you once again." He ducked his head toward me and followed Lannie.

When they were gone, McLeod walked to the window and stood looking out. Several minutes passed, and I had at last decided to leave when he turned around.

"You know, Lovett, maybe you ought to follow her advice."

I shook my head.

"Don't you have any idea of what's to come?"

"But that's exactly what I must find out," I said with conviction.

"To what purpose?"

"I hardly know. When you feel something strongly. . ."

194

"You're with me, then?"

"No, I'm not certain of that. I can't be with them, but to take you on trust . . . I can't do that."

McLeod massaged his chin. "And rightly so. Look, friend, don't mistake me, I want you here very much. In a way. There may come a time when I ask you to leave the room."

"Yes?"

"You have no idea what he whispered to me, and how it's tempting," McLeod said suddenly.

"Then why do you want me to be here?" I asked.

He nodded his head to himself, and when he replied I did not understand him.

"Conscience," McLeod said.

TWENTY-TWO

THAT night the weather became unbearable, and my attic room which had suffered the sun's glare upon the roof tar was baked again by a land breeze. The pavement turned soft, the air was heavy, and waiting for rain to fall, I lay sweltering on a damp sheet. Outside the leaves stirred sluggishly. A heat lightning had come up in the west, and for a long time I watched it kindle the curling plaster of my ceiling, became absorbed at last in its alternation with a searchlight which flashed a rhythmic beam across my walls. I drowsed to the muffled sound of thunder.

And while I was asleep or perhaps even waking, almost certainly a fantasy and yet I could not disprove it existed, I saw myself in still another barracks. We were one of a hundred buildings, surrounded by wire, and the flooring had holes, the walls had cracks; we slept two hundred of us on planks spread across a trestle. Each morning, and they were winter mornings, we were wakened at five and marched a mile to a long shed where we had bread and hot water if the cooks were kind, and porridge deprived of salt. That done, we marched beyond the enclosure and saw the dawn from down a long road lined with sentries and barbed fence. It was a cruel walk and at the end was a tremendous factory, almost new, but the windows were shattered, the roof of one wing was stripped, and the machinery did not always function. There we worked, hand on a lever to punch and press, and next to us, never meeting, though in the range of our eyes, were other workers with a card, and they lived in a dormitory on the far side of the factory, and were free to walk to town once work was done. We were always promised that we would be allowed to join them if only . . . if only we would produce more than our fellows.

I had a friend. He was old and emaciated and more than bitter, a worker for sixty years as he would often say. "They made me a slavey as a boy of eight, and I earned two shillings a week, and my sister died of consumption in a dressmaker's shop, tatting lace for milady's ball. I was one of the industrial reserve army and almost permanently unemployed. Sixty years, and I am still one of the industrial reserve army and it was better then, for one didn't march to work, and at the age of twelve I tussled a girl in the shavings on the cutting-room floor."

Drugged by the morning sun, I could hardly awake. Light glared into my eyes, heat banked itself in the room, and cinder dust eddied over my face. I lay in such stupor that it must have taken me through the forenoon before I thought of quitting my bed.

A fly was circling through the hot moist air, buzzing over my chest, nipping my foot, and then off to explore the cubicle again. Somewhere the fly had lodged on a pin speck of carrion and played with the booty on the floor. I turned on my side and watched the fly even as the fly was revolving its food beneath a foreleg. Minutes elapsed this way, the insect humming against the sound of my breath, the city noise carrying into my window from far away.

I must have fallen asleep for when I opened my eyes the fly was gone and someone was in the act of slipping a piece of paper beneath my door. A corner projected over the sill, and rustled to one side and then the other. I had more than time to get out of bed and look in the hall, but the effort demanding too

much of my fuddled senses, I merely gaped at the door while
the paper nosed its way to the left and to the right, and finally
halted half into my room, half under the wood, while whoever
had so placed it could be heard softly descending the stairs.

I shook my head dully and was about to navigate my feet
to the floor and the paper to my hand when the note was agitated
once more, slipped back over the dust of the sill and was withdrawn. It was only after several seconds that this seemed at all
extraordinary, and like a bobbin jogging in the wake of events,
I had no sooner decided that the disappearance of the note was
even more to be noted than its presence, when to my complete
disaster the piece of paper wiggled under the door again, and I
could be diverted for a second time to the sound of footsteps
moving away.

For such an entrance the message was more than common-
place.

It was from Guinevere. In the neat and miniature hand-
writing which seemed so at odds with what one might antic-
ipate, she had written in pale-blue ink:

> Dear Michael,
>   Maybe you forgot but we have things
> to talk about. Come on down. I'm
> dying to see you.

And with the vulgar gentility she courted, the note was
signed, Beverly G. McLeod.

I shrugged, laid the paper on my desk, and half decided not
to see her. Still sluggish from the heat, I took a shower, dressed,
and then as I was about to go out, some impulse made me put
the note in my pocket. I had breakfast, read a paper, and came
back to the house with an idea of working. But as I climbed the
brownstone stairs, jingling the change in my pocket, I felt her
message curled into a ball, and was tickled with the uneasy memory of how the note had circulated over the doorsill.

At that instant, looking up, I saw Lannie staring at me from the second-story hall window. It was only a glimpse, and then I could have sworn she started back, unwilling to let me know that she was watching. The combination determined me. I rang Guinevere's bell.

For once I was not greeted by a miscellany of lingerie and bathrobe and zippers and flesh. She was dressed for the street and wore a flowered-print chiffon with a cartwheel hat and spiked heels for her tiny feet and a pair of elbow-length net gloves covered her forearms. "Oh, Mikey, you're sweet," she said as she let me in, the wide painted mouth curving provocatively. Perfume was strewn lavishly upon her, and she moved in a cloud of musk, the sweet odor heavy on the air. She smelled like a tropical flower with all its sensuous bouquet and its suggestion, troubling and almost fetid, of tropical earth.

"Oh, I'm all up in the air," Guinevere said.

She paused and, in the interval, folded drama about herself. "Guess where I'm going?"

I asked her.

"You remember that doctor I told you about?"

I trod warily through a junkyard of her discarded tales. "You mean the one in your novel?"

She nodded profoundly. "Yes, that's the one, although as you've probably guessed by now he's more real than fictional, and he's blown into town and I'm off to see him." She cocked her head to one side. "*Brother*, will I have a time!"

"Don't you think you've got enough to handle right here?"

"Oh you couldn't understand about this doctor. He's special." She tugged lazily at one of her gloves. "What a man. He's got everything a woman could want." And she insisted upon specifying so that I was given a small treatise on his physical attributes, his endurance, his fancy projects, his attentiveness; and all the while Guinevere was reciting, her language studded with the imagery of a pornographic ditty, greed and—was it wistfulness?—peeped out of her eyes. She might have been describing the wonders of a house in the suburbs which she had visited. "Green lawn, so green, and a picture window, and all the furniture, modern but so plush, elegant," I heard her say in my mind's ear until the doctor was blooming orchids in the rock garden.

"You know what my pet name for him is?" she finished. "Lover-boy, that's what." And she inclined her head and touched her cheek with one gloved finger, looking at me sideways from half-veiled eyes.

"What will your husband be doing while you're gone?"

"Him, he's asleep," Guinevere said. "Listen, he's knocked out. You should have seen him pace the floor last night. I asked him if he thought he was in a marathon dance or what." She sighed. "He took some sedatives, and I gave him a little extra so he'd sleep good, and now he's been sleeping for sixteen hours, curled up just like a bug."

"Why did you want to see me today?" I asked.

"Well, now, wait a minute." An amalgam of slyness and caution directed her next speech. "Maybe I'm not exactly sure. You know there's lots of things." In an offhand manner she suggested, "You didn't tell me yet what happened upstairs in the conference. I mean it could be that, for instance."

"You know I won't tell you. Why did you invite me down?"

She sat back in a chair. Her hand fanning the brim of her hat with studied unconcern, she opened her large blue eyes at me. "Oh, brother, I'm looking forward to that doctor."

A realization stirred in me, became focused almost to clarity, and then slipped away again. "I seem to be holding you up," I suggested.

She looked at her watch. "No, I'll tell you when to go."

We stared at one another in an unpleasant silence. I stood up at last and began to pace about the room.

"Why don't you sit still?" she snapped at me.

"Are you nervous?" I parried.

"Who's nervous?"

I stopped and looked at her. "The doctor just blew into town, is that it?"

She nodded warily.

"I don't believe he's real."

Guinevere shrugged. "Suit yourself."

Yet she watched my movements with great alertness, her eyes, perhaps against her will, following me as I walked back and forth, until it became at last a game children might play, and in the total of her expressions and the small agitation of her limbs, she could have been saying, "Now you're hot; and now you're cold."

I happened to glance behind the living-room door. There, tucked into the angle it made with the wall, was a suitcase resting on the floor. I picked it up, and extended it to her. "Quite heavy," I told her flatly. "You may need help." The bag had been packed only too hastily; a snip of lingerie protruded past the hinge.

As though the issue were now decided, Guinevere removed her hat. "I knew you'd do that," she murmured. "You're smart, Lovett." She said this with a certain calm, but her mouth trembled.

"Do you intend to come back?" I asked quietly.

It was just the question she had wanted. "Oh, of course. Oh, listen, I wasn't going away. I mean I'm just going to be gone for a couple of hours. The bag . . ."

"Yes, what about it?"

"Well, you see, that's sort of a . . . sort of a dress rehearsal," she finished broadly. "I mean I wanted to see what it felt like to pack."

This completed my exasperation, "You're going away with a mythical doctor and you stuff a suitcase, and you drug your husband, and then to make certain that everything is kept secret, you invite me to discover all this. What in the name of heaven do you want, Guinevere?"

Her vexation was only too patent. Tears filled her eyes. "Why don't you leave me alone, Lovett?"

"Then why don't you go? Everything is ready."

"You're ruining my life," she shrieked.

"It's because you don't really want to go."

Her hand drooped from the chair and fluttered at her side. "Why do I always have to make up my mind?" she said in a voice which was close to weeping, her face puckered like a child.

"You never make up your mind. You want everyone else to do it for you."

She looked about her helplessly. "Leave me alone, just leave me alone."

But Guinevere had her reprieve. There was a knock on the door. Now anything which had been smashed could be restored again. "Oh, my aching back," she cursed in a whisper, "that's him, that's him." She looked about wildlly, but it was counterfeit. "Oh, here, what'll I do? You've got to hide, you just got to hide."

"I won't hide," I told her, and in saying it admitted I would, for I was whispering too.

"Mikey, don't argue! Get behind the door."

Sweet farce. She left the bag in the middle of the floor, and myself where the bag had been, moving to the hall entrance in the gait of a hostess, adjusting her hair with one hand, while with the other she was free to nudge a chair and turn a lampshade to another angle. "Oh, kill me," she groaned, kicking out a wrinkle in the rug, "why do they always catch me like this?" And the knocking repeated, she shouted, "Hold your horses, I'm coming," yet pausing long enough to admonish me in yet another whisper, "You stay there now, damn you, you've got to."

202

If I did not, she was lost. She could sally forth to battle, her breasts charging like cavalry, but she would have been helpless without guerrillas in the forest. So I waited, and she threw open the door to Hollingsworth.

Guinevere would play this extravagantly. He had hardly entered before she declaimed, "Oh, lover-boy, how long you have kept me waiting."

I heard him walk to the center of the room, and I imagined him turning around slowly, staring at her.

"Do you still love me?" she asked theatrically.

I was to hear another Hollingsworth. "Yes, I love you," he said, his delivery pitched in novel tones for me. As though language were a catapult he proceeded to tell her how he loved her, his speech containing more obscenity than I had ever heard in so short a space, and in rapid succession with a gusto which could have matched Guinevere's description of the doctor, he named various parts of her body and described what he would do to them, how he would tear this and squeeze that, eat here and spit there, butcher rough and slice fine, slash, macerate, pillage, all in an unrecognizable voice which must have issued between clenched teeth, until his appetite satisfied, I could see him squatting beside the carcass, his mouth wiped carefully with the back of his hand. With that, he sighed, as much as to say, "A good piece of ass, by God."

"Oh," Guinevere responded, "Oh, brother," but her voice was reflective. Probably she played for me as well as for him. I could hear her walk a step or two toward the door as if to indicate she knew I was there. Then she turned back to Hollingsworth. "Oh, lover, I'd do anything for you," she said.

"You would?" His voice purred.

"I'd work for you, I'd slave for you," she continued to declaim, "I'd get down on my hands and knees and scrub."

"That's not necessary." In offering such submission, she had thrown a switch, and now when he spoke, I had the impression he adjusted his cuffs and wrapped formality about him once more. "Oh, that would hardly be necessary I should think."

Then he giggled. "I wonder what your husband would say if he ever heard us."

"Don't think of that character as my husband," Guinevere said.

But she would deprive Hollingsworth of something very essential. "Oh, yes, he is your husband, and there's no getting away from that I would say." He must have been holding her now. "And you know, he's an unusual fellow. I can see how a girl would get a crush on him." His voice throbbed suddenly. "He's been a big fellow in his time."

"You can go for him, huh?" Guinevere said crudely.

He disregarded this. "You know I cut a figure with the ladies, so to speak, but it's different with you." Much as though he had not told her this all before, he restated the theme in a smaller voice. "I could eat you, every last bit of you." Passion, retracking its spoor, licked at the edge of his words. What curiosity devoured him. "Why don't you tell me what it was like with him?" he said huskily.

Guinevere slipped away, out of his arms and across the room. "Ah, you're always asking that," she said.

"And you never tell me."

"Let's get off the subject," she bawled.

"You're his wife."

"Yeah."

"You're his wife," he repeated, and loaded with this, I could hear him embracing her again, his breath coming quickly.

"Whoa," Guinevere said, and now it was she who giggled. "Let's have a cigarette."

There was the sound of Hollingsworth's lighter as he clicked forth the flame to her cigarette and to his. I could picture them sitting back in their chairs, blowing smoke toward one another. And to my relief, Guinevere began a new subject.

"Do you see that? she asked coyly.

"What?"

"Why, the suitcase," she said sweetly.

"I see it," he said.

Now she began to deploy her forces. "Suppose I was to ask you to go away with me now. Would you go?"

"Go where?"

"Anywhere. To the ends of the earth. To Barbary—I like the sound of that."

"I'd take you with me," he said quietly, "yes, I would."

"Why don't we go now?" Guinevere said wistfully.

Hollingsworth cleared his throat. "You know we can't. I mean a fellow has to finish certain of his obligations."

"You won't ever take me," Guinevere proclaimed sadly. "I know you. You've filled me with a siren song."

"Oh, no, I will take you," he said with sudden force, "believe me, Jimmy girl. You see, after this, it's Europe next, and missions of grave importance."

"They'll never send you."

"Oh, they appreciate me," he said mildly. "I do good work. Only today I finished up the first report."

"But you won't send it in?" she said with false confidence.

"I don't know," he murmured in a troubled voice. "You see it's the proper thing to do. And you know what'll happen otherwise."

"Listen," she said, and it was her turn for passion, "this thing is worth a fortune. A fortune."

"But we don't know," Hollingsworth protested.

"I know, I tell you, I know, and I lived next to him all these years, and he had it all the while. It's a fortune would choke a millionaire. They'd make us royalty."

"I can't make up my mind," he told her. "I know, and you don't know, what it would be like." He said this with such conviction that I could feel the weight of her silence. Yet he added angrily, "I'd like to show them." I could hear him stand up. "It's late already, and if we are to go to that hotel for this afternoon, I think a couple of fellows like us ought to make a start."

She must have put an arm on his. "Oh, honey," she said in a weak tormented voice, "I'm so confused. Will you tell me what to do? Will you always tell me what to do?"

His voice was balm, and I could sense her drawing strength. "I will tell you what to do. Over and over I will tell you what to do."

"Kiss me once more," she said.

Once again I could be treated to their language, and out of the welter of their rapid breath and quick whispers, as the joist upon which was festooned the rest, I could hear the sequence of you're his wife and yes I'm his wife and his wife and the nourishment of such a feast furnishing its perpetual circle of absorption so that the banquet once exhausted could only furnish the next, and his wife devoured became his wife resplendent, until he sleeping, the producer of wives, might almost have been merged himself, but never quite.

"I'm *his* wife," Guinevere concluded breathlessly, and pushed him away. "Come on, let's get going. Let's *go*."

Dizzied, distraught, she must have tripped upon the bag. "No, wait. No, wait," she called out in a hoarsened voice, "one second, love, let me get rid of this, just one second, honest."

And while he waited at the door, she carried the bag to my corner and thrust it in at my feet, her eyes meeting mine for one instant in a hurly-burly of triumph and terror, as though she were an infant thrown into the air with its laughter this side of panic.

"Leroy," she called out from where she stood, "nothing will happen to him, will it?"

"Oh, nothing, nothing," Hollingsworth droned. "I know he'll co-operate."

"I thought so. He'll come to no harm," she declared, and turning her back to me, she left the house with Hollingsworth, explaining with her last question why she had wanted me there, setting out of her unalterable contradiction a course with one hand the more to tip the wheel with the other, and, rigging fouled, could be the glutton only when she was blown by guilt.

TWENTY-THREE

BEFORE I left the apartment I went into the bedroom. McLeod was sleeping, curled up like a bug as Guinevere would have it, but the description was less than adequate. He slumbered heavily, limbs jammed against his body, hands over his eyes, his knees at his chest much as though he would usurp the smallest volume possible. His breath was drawn through clenched teeth, tensing his face tight as a fist. There was something infamous in watching him helpless; I had the idea he would be furious if he knew he were observed.

Beside him, Monina slept with her head next his, her arm curled upon his shoulder in unconscious trust. She breathed quietly and prettily, a flush on her child's face, her golden hair strewn upon the pillow. They were father and daughter and shared a bed, but little more; the interval from her baby skin to the gaunt stubble of McLeod's jaw was very great. I had never seen him look so old. His beard sprouted gray, and was black in all the wrinkles about his mouth. Even as I watched, the tight lips parted and a painful grunt came from his belly. He muttered something, he was protesting, and then his arms hugged his body more tightly.

I left them like that, passed back through the living room where I had eavesdropped and quit the apartment. Lannie was waiting on the other side of the door.

How long I could not know, but with what impatience I could estimate by the way she caught my arm. Her thin fingers pinched into my bicep. "I want to talk to you," she said huskily. "Come up to my room." Charged with emotion, she shook almost visibly.

As I followed on the stairs, I could see that her violet suit was freshly pressed, and that the back of her hair had been squeezed into tight anchovy curls. "What is it about?" I asked.

"I'll tell you in a minute."

She waited until I had entered her room, then locked the door. When she turned around I was able to see her clearly. She was well-groomed this once, but like new paint upon old, there was small hope it would last. Already a few wrinkles cut across the worn shiny fabric of her suit, one of the hair curls had begun to unwind, and upon her sallow skin, white face powder applied in two quick strokes, overlapped on the point of her nose and exaggerated the deep circles about her eyes.

Reaching into the breast pocket of her jacket, she took out several bills and handed them to me. "This is what I owe you."

I covered my surprise by counting the money. It was actually several dollars less than I had given her, but I could hardly believe she remembered the amount, and probably the sum was chosen by caprice. "Where did you get this?" I asked her.

Lannie was silent for several seconds and then burst into a tirade. "When you gave the money it was charity for the crippled and the drunk." Her eyes burned. "I took it as the insult you intended, and knew I could not despise you so and not pay it back." She was shaking with anger and something more perhaps; the hand which had given me the money twitched uncontrollably until she jammed it in a pocket.

"What did you want to talk to me about?"

She moved away without replying and rummaged in her closet to come forth with a new bottle of whiskey. Her poor fingers worked all around the seal, pinching and tearing at the celluloid with blunt motions which opened nothing. "Here, let me help you," I offered quietly.

She answered by digging her teeth into the cork and pulling it free, with what damage to her mouth I hated to calculate. Then, irresolutely, staring at the neck of the bottle, she tried to put it in her mouth, and gagged in reaction.

"I'll get you a glass," I told her.

I found a few dusty tumblers on the shelf of the closet and with it her booty. A case of liquor was resting on the floor. She came up behind me in a panic at being discovered, and pulled the glass out of my hand. "Where have you gotten all this money?" I was about to ask again, but the answer was obvious. I took the bills she had given me, and put them on the table. "I don't need it after all," I said.

Lannie almost shrieked at me. "What right . . . ? What right . . . ?"

"I knew you followed after him," I said furiously, "I knew you wouldn't take a breath for fear you'd miss one of his"—so much I had left unsaid was finally to be declared—"but I didn't know he paid you. To take money . . ."

"You're an idiot," she cried, and into her throat went a half-inch of whiskey from the glass. "To take money, money which is so pure, and reflects the purity of our world. But someone must have told you of the circulation of money in all its metamorphoses like the frog, until all one can say is that money carries the average rate of blood. And what a pity the great man isn't alive today so that he might tell of the manufacture of guilt, and the falling rate of love." Odd timbers of a shipwrecked culture floated in her mind. "It's all lost in blood, and that is the law of money which is a commodity." She swallowed the rest of her drink, and said almost dreamily, "But you would take money from the other one."

"I think I would."

210

Perhaps the liquor had given her ballast. She made a concerted effort to convince me. "No one ever told you that to be sentimental is to commit a crime. Do you know what he's done?"

I shook my head.

"In the end, you think, it will all be explained away, and he never touched a fly. Well, you're wrong." Her voice was filled with hate. "He destroyed the world, do you understand? He's a murderer of the best and thus he gives an impression of being one of the best, just as my friend is a murderer of the worst, and so you do not like him. One after another, through the years, *he* picked them off, all of the best, and each night he would come home and prostrate himself before the picture of the man with the pipe, and say, 'Oh, my Lord, in my thoughts I have transgressed against Thee,' and then he would spit at the picture with all the force of his puny neck, and say, 'What crimes have I committed in Thy Name,' and spit again, spit, spit, until he could only weep, and the picture of the man with the pipe never taking his eyes off him because he is waiting and it comes. 'Forgive me, my Lord,' he cries, 'for I know not what I do.'"

I did not answer her.

"You don't believe me?" she asked.

"I don't know. I don't know what to think of him."

Even as we had been talking, her hair had come undone and the oiled waxed curls were broken by her fingers one by one. Cigarette ash was dirtying her suit again, and the first of a new series of liquor stains spread over her shirtwaist.

"I don't know why I am in this," I said to her. "It makes things worse. I want to avoid everything . . . and yet I can't. So why do you talk to me?" I begged her. "Of what do you try to convince me? . . .That he should have nobody with him. Is it so painful to you that the man has one friend?" I looked at her. "You don't want to convince me."

"I do," she said.

"You want to convince yourself."

The remark had its effect. She burst into laughter. "Convince myself? Oh, Mikey, I'm convinced. It's only you who is still the fool as I was once the fool, and you will not recognize that all these years, ever since the great man sat on his piles in the British Museum and let us think there was a world we could make, when all the time he was wrong, and we've been wrong, and there's no world to make for the world devours."

"We still don't know," I muttered.

"Don't know!" Her mouth was passionate with the idea. "Listen to me. We never understood anything. There is a world, and this is what it is like: It is a tremendous prison, and sometimes the walls are opened and sometimes they are closed, but as time goes on they have to be closed more and more. Have you forgotten? Do you remember how the poorest of the poor used to be driven to the room where they were given death by gas? How was it done, and with what nobility do we all die? Let me tell you. The guards were chosen from a list, so they would come from the kitchen or standing before the gate with their gun at present arms, and they would all assemble in a room and an officer would give them orders, and each of them would rate an extra cup, and they would drink it and go to collect the prisoners who had been selected already by other men. And the prisoners would march along, and if one of them weighed a hundred pounds, he was a giant to the rest, and they would shuffle and smile and try to catch the guard's eye. And the guards were drunk, and you would be amazed how happy a man may feel at such a moment. For the comedy is about to begin. They come to the antechamber, a room with gray walls and without windows, and it's men to the right and women to the left and strip your clothes, but only a moment. The clothes off, the guards are driving them into the other room, and smack their hands on skinny flesh and bony flesh, it's bag a tittie and snatch a twot, and they can smell them stinking all those naked people, while in the heart of their own pants it's sweet with brandy so slap an ass and laugh like mad while the naked go stumbling, screaming into the last room of them all. And there one might suppose they prepare to die. For, mark you, this has been a long road, and each step of the way they have been deceived.

"Yet my story is not done," she said, holding up a hand, her eyes clear, her speech distinct as though she were reciting before a mirror. "The guards have one more resource. As they are about to close the door to the last room, an announcement is made. The State in its infinite mercy will allow one of them to be saved, the strongest. The one who can beat the others will be given a reprieve. This declaration, although it is worthy of the State, is due actually to the genius of a single guard who has conceived it at the very moment. And so through a window the guards may watch while one naked pygmy tears the hair of another, and blood runs where one thought no blood was left, and half of them are dead and scream like pigs with the head down and waiting for the knife, and as they scratch and sob and bite each other's rind, the guards turn on the gas and roar like mad for the fools thought one would be saved and so ate each other.

"This is the world, Mikey. If there had been one who said, 'Let us die with dignity,' but they went choking into the gas with the blood of a friend in their mouth."

"It was too late then," I murmured.

"Listen, my friend," she said softly, "the grass waves, and we are lost again in childhood souvenir. It is too late now. Do you understand? There are no solutions, there are only exceptions, and therefore we are without good and without evil."

"If that were so, you would not have told me your story."

Her mouth turned bitter. "You still do not know why I told you. Oh, you have not begun to look at the world. You would call the guards evil, and so you have avoided everything. But I tell you they were humane."

"Humane?"

"They allowed the inmates to die in all the fever of small passions, and that is so much better than to die together. For dying together in such a way one may feel only the sense of failure, and that is how most of us die this year. No, Mikey, the guards committed a crime, and yet it is not what you think. There is neither guilt nor innocence, but there is vigor in what we do or the lack of it, and the guard's crime was that they needed the brandy, and so were empty creatures. They were shoe clerks before and shoe clerks today, and now they probably tell themselves that they repent. And that is the crime—to drink and repent."

"I should say it's the hope."

She was furious at how I denied her. "You wanted to know," she said with an effort to restrain herself, "why I have taken money from him."

"Yes, why him?"

"Because he is with them, and they allow you a corner for small rent charged, and there I may sing my little song. And that is what I tell myself when I am convinced I shall always be ugly."

"And who is 'them'?"

"The guards, of course." She sat rigidly in the chair, as if to hold the structure of the argument for so long were an insupportable pain. "They are the guards of the country we live in, even as your friend is a guard from the other. And sooner or later, they will all meet, and one or the other will win. Then, how they will be terrified. For, you see, they are so devoted to winning they have no equipment for victory, and I am the one who will nurse their terror. They will turn to me." At the smile which must have crossed my face, she read my thought. "Or, if not me, then another. But someone must bind their wounds, someone must tell them that they don't need brandy. I'm the only one who really wants people to keep on living, I'm the only one who understands."

I had begun to pace back and forth. "And what if I don't want to choose my prison?"

"You must, and gladly. That is the secret."

"No one will win," I told her. "They'll destroy each other. And that's what you really want to see."

Her expression had become remote. "Who knows what we do want? Perhaps all that is left is to love the fire." She lay her head back against the chair. "Come with me, Mikey," she said, and she was almost pleading, "for if there is a future, it is with him."

"Yes, and you're so miserable you must draw everyone after you."

She shrugged and made no further response.

"Tell me," I went on, "was it as part of your duties, part of earning your salary, that you have followed Guinevere and spied on me and read that note?"

Her face was expressionless. She gave no evidence of having heard me.

"Lannie, why were you listening outside the door?"

"For myself, myself alone," she muttered. The sound of her voice must have opened echoes to my question, for she picked up the empty whiskey tumbler and then dropped it nervelessly in her lap.

"They went out together, didn't they?" Lannie asked.

I nodded.

"Oh, she's a bitch, she's a bitch, she's such a bitch." And Lannie sat looking at me, her face grown pale from the war she suffered, all her feelings, all her pain, seemingly concentrated into the white splotch of powder upon her face.

"A bitch," Lannie repeated, "and that I was not prepared for."

TWENTY-FOUR

I F GREATNESS is thrust upon certain men, thought is extorted from others. How apt that I who had no past and so eschewed a future, who entered neither social nor economic relations, who was without memory and henceforth privileged not to reason, should have struggled again with ideas which were not my own, that I had learned upon a time and then ignored. The paraphernalia of study, the lessons absorbed, the definitions learned and then employed, came trooping back.

I sat down and reviewed the primer. The worker sells his labor-power, and in the time he labors he creates products whose value is greater than his wage. And on the seventh day, the laborer resting, the capitalist can compute his gain, consume a portion of the take, and search for a place to invest what remains. This was Genesis in what had been my Bible, and from there one could make a voyage of two thousand pages and what other endless books, on through the history of three hundred years, while along the horizon the factories grew, the railroads were laid, the cities expanded, even into the twilight and the falling rate of love.

I contested with equations and relations. There is the worker and the machine, and as the machine grows larger the man diminishes until one can hear from the background the funereal hymn of the falling rate with the sense it gives that what is born must die and yet grows larger before it expires. To such music the hunted had given chase while the machines which pinched their rate of gain drove them out across the world. The laborer and the machine, the wage of one to the cost of the other, the variable capital to the constant, and how the one decreased as the other swelled, how the men from whom the profit must be stolen became so small in proportion to the machines that yielded none at all. Across the world they searched, the men who owned the factories, for the tin can must absorb its cost and present its dividend, and the natives of a hundred colonies and dependencies had, ergo, to be plucked from their holes and thrust into cells.

Moneybags, the haunted, for the surplus product once stolen, must be reinvested. And if surplus value had been the source of their capacity for expansion, it became as well the root of their destruction. I sat, I thought, and what I could not remember, I was obliged to reconstruct. I pondered the intricacies I could manage, and juggled the law of value against the practice of monopoly, groped through the techniques of the trust to understand again why production was limited and prices made artificial, how the living standard of half of mankind could not rise, for if it did where would monopoly find Peter to rob and pay the Paul? I sloughed through a gold standard I had rarely grasped and slashed the knot of tariffs until, my head aching, I could seize the contradiction and understand how at the moment industrial techniques were ready to supply the world, the world market was in the process of being destroyed.

I traced how they moved, cheating and colliding through every country of the globe, while as an instrument of necessity— and they called it policy—the armies grew and the armaments were piled. I mulled the history of that first war which ended probably before I was born, and the second which had swallowed me, and the third which was preparing. The man grew smaller and the machine grew larger, the horizon was broken by new factories and new ones upon them, and all the while the creation of products that men could use became less year by year. For there was a new consumer and new commodities, and every shell could find as customer its enemy soldier. That market could never be glutted; it furnished new blood for the thickening of the old, enabled millions to be employed and other millions to be put into uniform. No longer the need would exist to search for re-investment and be haunted by surplus value. I scratched my hand and knew with sour mirth, for I owned so much, that this was the last year in my time when men, if they had the money, could buy without thought whatever they wished. In nostalgia this year would be remembered.

Moneybags, my classical moneybags, would bewail it with the rest, for he was as weak as I and knew it in his heart, knew it from the bottom of all his newspapers, knew the naught in the eyes of all his men who said yes, knew it in the power of the bureaucrats he abused. He was going out and they were coming in. With every check he received from the republic, with every carload he sent to its arsenals, he was making himself smaller and making them larger. Oh, he had life yet, life enough for a year or two of war and even longer, but the end was coming. The days approached when the worker would be paid less and obliged to work more, and to accomplish such magic only a government that spoke in the name of the worker could suffice. What for moneybags but to cry his sour resignation? Small prize for him to know that the new leaders would have their profit, that the state as capitalist would buy the labor-power of all and dispense it back again with high wages for the few and low for the many. Small glee for him to cry that the new democracy had the freedom of an army and the equality of a church. No one would be listening. For he had planted the rot and now screamed at the weeds. There was the enemy, the progressively unspeakable, unmitigable, irredeemable and damned enemy; the weeds; the mirror to the future. The monopole had been closed to the enemy, they had been necessary Peter to feed the Paul, squeezed beneath so they could never rise, but now suddenly they were gone, they were the enemy, birthed from the wars monopoly had begun and they were driven to finish. They held the mirror and prophesied the future; the winner would be distinguishable by a mote from the one who lost.

I thought of the workers who would support the bastard inheritors of what was no longer a social revolution. The standard of living would be raised the promises stated, raised to the weight of a pork chop and taken back again. Their party which came to power the workers would think, and discover that the state was not their instrument but their master. An association of free producers and free consumers they once had demanded, and now would exist in a wage-relation to the party and to the state. The international co-operation of the nations they had sung, and one-half of the world would fight the other. Socialist freedom, the greatest conception of freedom, and for substitute they would be granted the enslavement of regimented labor, the saturation of the working-class mind to propaganda until even the mating bed became a duty. There had been a heritage but it was given away, and the labor boss, the hack, and the Fabian devoured it among themselves. Moneybags would die, but not by the ax; slowly he would perish and of his own contradictions, simmering away in the wars he had cooked with their juice as sauce. That way it would come, or thus I saw it, and the armies of the swindled would bleed each other for slogans that became ever more similar.

What could follow? There the questions I answered were fewer than the questions I began, and if I had thought to reply to Lannie, I quit in fear I should listen to the echo. Thought may have been extorted from me but I ended by clutching it back, and sat as motionless with my body as I was moveless with my brain.

An hour passed and I mused, throwing pebbles into the

mind's pool until the circles spread so wide that form was lost. I must have been in stupor.

How long I might have continued, I do not know, for I was interrupted. Hollingsworth came to my door, and with a greeting that was almost friendly, told me that the conversation he conducted with McLeod was to be continued, and indeed the business if it were not improper to call it that, or so he went on, was to commence in fifteen minutes. He hoped I might find it possible to attend.

I found it more than possible. As if I had been waiting for just such an opportunity, I crossed the hall and was there the first, sat in the empty room until he and Lannie, and McLeod almost upon their steps, came to join me. We resumed our previous positions, we looked at one another, McLeod facing him across the table, Lannie between them, while I perched on the bed.

"I wonder," Hollingsworth began, "if you have come to a favorable decision on my offer?" and expectorated neatly into his handkerchief.

McLeod shrugged, while in the interval, Hollingsworth arranged papers on the desk. "It's an unreal offer. You furnish no explanations how I would be protected." Time passed slowly, and with a start I forced myself to concentrate. "In any event," McLeod went on, "I have made up my mind. I do not accept your bargain."

The pencil was tapping. "Fine." Hollingsworth made a mark on a piece of paper. "In that case, I think it is time to go into details." He looked at Lannie who was slumped into her chair and seemed half asleep. "Is there anything I can provide for you, Miss Madison? Cigarettes?" the irony in his voice betraying anger.

Lannie started at the interruption and raised her eyes. She was haggard, more haggard even than I had left her. When she spoke her voice was husky, nerves wrangled by this interruption.

"No, no thank you, nothing," she said, looking about her guiltily, and by an effort she settled back into the chair, but she was hardly at ease. To each abrupt gesture one of them might make, she responded with the quiver of a finger, or the blinking of her eye.

Hollingsworth picked up a typewritten sheet. "Details, then," he sighed. "Would you mind telling me how you came to join the organization I work for?"

This question which could not have startled me more, was expected apparently by McLeod. Yet his hand, involuntarily I may suppose, had come up to the breast pocket of his shirt, and he was playing with the flap as though once again Hollingsworth had handed him a paper he wished to conceal. "There's no point in going into it," he said at last. "You know everything about that subject."

"Permit me my methods," Hollingsworth almost whispered.

McLeod could only shrug again. "The story is simple enough," he said briskly. "I knew that if I remained in my old position any longer, I would be brought to trial, and it would be m'neck. There was a certain military pact completed at the time, which I found impossible to support. I had said not a word to anyone, but there are ways of knowing when one is in disfavor, and I had knowledge that I was to be publicly attacked by a high official. Therefore, having a moderate desire to live, or so I told myself, I made inquiries, and was told I could recover my passport to this country, if . . ." Here, he paused. "If I would go to work for your organization. The price for my papers was a detailed list of information about specific events and personalities in the land across the sea. Upon due consideration I decided to furnish it."

A sneer had come on Lannie's mouth. She laughed hysterically.

"So I worked," McLeod went on stiffly. "After a time they even gave me a desk and a secretary."

Hollingsworth permitted himself a joke. "A fellow has to admit you were a kind of statistician."

"Is it necessary to discuss this any further?" McLeod asked.

Hollingsworth clicked his tongue. "Not if we can come to some agreement about the . . . little object."

"I don't have it," McLeod muttered.

"Well, we'll see about that." Hollingsworth sighed and looked at the ceiling. "How to continue?" He pulled a piece of paper toward himself as though he were selecting a card from a deck, and giving a show of reading it, he nodded his head and made small affirmative sounds. "Yes. Yes. This will do." He adjusted his tie.

"Would you care," he asked formally, "to explain why you left us? You will remember that you disappeared without a trace."

McLeod examined his knuckle. "I had come to the conclusion that I was destroyed as a person." By the slightest inclination in my direction I sensed that he was talking at least as much for me as for Hollingsworth. "I was obliged to take up a wholly new existence. You see after a decade of acts which have undermined one's revolutionary fiber, there is only one act which still possesses meaning—to save one's life. But to save it in the name of what? I had never until then considered my life important in itself. And this tormented me when I joined your friends." McLeod carefully traced his tongue over the outline of his lips as though to assure himself they were still there. "No need to specify the various crises, mental, moral, and even physical, which I experienced. I need only state that having once understood my situation, I determined to make a clean break."

"And you disappeared?"

"Precisely."

"You didn't take the little object at the time of your departure?"

222

"No."

"It was discovered missing," Hollingsworth reminded him.

"Coincidences may often plague one."

Hollingsworth nodded politely. "In other words, you just devoted yourself to doing new radical and revolutionary work, but on a small scale."

McLeod shook his head. "I devoted myself to nothing. I have merely floundered since then, and have indulged in no political activity whatsoever."

"Oh, you must think I'm completely stupid," Hollingsworth exclaimed. He drew a clipping toward him:

> With the integration of the worker into the state economy of the two opposed Colossi, the perspective of Barbarism draws ever closer.

Hollingsworth read with difficulty, moving his mouth in preparation for each long word like a schoolboy thrust into a text beyond his means:

> And to the Socialist historian of the future the tragedy of the twentieth century will become fixed on the few years following the First World War when the revolution failed to spread to Western Europe, and the young giant of the worker's movement, mortally wounded, could only degenerate into the death agony of corruption, betrayal, and defeat.

Hollingsworth looked up. "Shall I go on?"

"If it serves your purpose."

> By now, with the approach of the Third World War, the techniques of Barbarism are well established, and the vista of the concentration camp, the swallowing of all opposition by the secret police, and the war to be waged in the name of peace, comes ever into sharper focus. And inversely, the perspective for revolutionary

socialism diminishes to its limit—a point in the political horizon. It is this point which must be kept alive in the event that, after the war, the Colossi smashed upon each other, objective conditions may again exist for the successful world revolution of the proletariat. As responsible socialists, however, we must be the first to admit that this is no more than a possibility.

Hollingsworth ceased to read and looked at McLeod with a small air of triumph. "Do you admit the authorship of this?"

"No."

He coughed into his folded handkerchief. "It may interest you to know that we uncovered your whereabouts exactly because of this article. Took us months. But the mimeograph machine, the paper, the tie-up with other articles written by the same man, his knowledge of the operation of our organization and the one across the sea, it all fitted together." He took a folder from his brief case and extended it to McLeod. "Look through this. All the proof is present." And while McLeod subjected it to his scrutiny, Hollingsworth sat back and in unconscious satisfaction patted the clasp of the brief case as though it were Pandora's box and all of his needs could be furnished there.

"All right," McLeod said, "I wrote that article."

"And the others?"

I leaned forward to hear his answer, my heart beating with surprising rapidity. "Wrote all of them," McLeod said, and elation I could hardly repress leaped up in me. Forgetting myself I turned to Lannie. "You see?" I said aloud.

But she was on her feet with quite another reaction. "He never wrote that. He lies."

"Sit down," Hollingsworth said quietly.

"No, he can't have written that. He tricks you all." She froze into silence, eyes transfixed before her, muscles tensed.

Hollingsworth got up, offered her a cigarette, and lit it very carefully. "I told you there would be twists and turns," he said evenly.

"I know, I know," she murmured.

Hollingsworth took up his position behind the desk. "These interruptions must cease," he said severely. "I will continue only if Mr. Lovett remains silent." When I made no response, he smiled politely as though to blunt the adjuration, and went on in a matter-of-fact voice. "You claim then that the last few years have been spent in writing such articles?"

"In writing and in study."

"Nothing else?"

"Nothing."

"In anticipation of just such an argument a fellow like you might give, I have had a report compiled of historical figures. There is not a single case of that expression I've heard you use, a bureaucrat, ever turning to writing and study about Bolshevist theory. . ."

"Marxist theory."

". . .after many years spent in that country," Hollingsworth was almost apologetic. "Therefore one gets to thinking that maybe what you're doing now is camouflage, if you know what I mean."

"I don't follow."

"That you are conducting revolutionary theory only to mask the fact that you still belong to the organization you pretended to leave when you came to us. Because, a fellow asks himself, why didn't they dispose of you?"

"They never found me."

Hollingsworth sniffed his fingers. "Unlikely."

"Leroy, you claim I have the little object. If I have it, how could I still belong to the. . .

"Bolshevists," Hollingsworth finished.

"If I belonged, I would have given it to them long ago."
Hollingsworth closed the trap. "But you claim you don't have the little object."

McLeod burst into laughter. "That was well-managed, friend," he said.

"I do think we have made some progress," Hollingsworth sighed. "Let me sum it up. Either you have what we are looking for and belong to no organization, or you do not have it and you have never left off allegiance to the enemy flag. You are just making believe you are a fine fellow and sorry for your past. These are the only two possibilities a fellow can accept. Can we work on this understanding?"

"It's a waste of time."

Hollingsworth took a penknife from his pocket and began to sharpen a pencil. He did this slowly and thoroughly, McLeod's eye upon him, and when he was finished he gathered the shavings in the palm of his hand and dumped them on the floor. "Oh, I beg your pardon," Hollingsworth finished, and scattered the waste with his foot. McLeod nodded, his mouth drawn.

"If a fellow had decided to leave us and go in for theory," Hollingsworth speculated, "why should he want to take the little object?"

"You want a hypothetical answer?"

"Oh, yes, present company excepted."

"Again, it's a problem in context, Leroy. On the surface, it's a foolish gesture, and will merely add to the urgency with which our imaginary friend will be hunted. But what is his situation? He is going to reform himself, he must overturn the habits of the last ten years, and he cannot retreat. Moreover, he is barred from joining any group with whose program he might be sympathetic. Therefore he will be all alone, and the theft will stiffen him. Action always gives ballast to theory. But there is another consideration even more important. If possession of

226

the little object by neither power is a disadvantage to both, to deprive them is a moral act."

"This all sounds farfetched to me," Hollingsworth said.

"Believe what you wish."

"Do you have the little object?"

"No."

"Then I can't believe you." Hollingsworth extracted a file from the brief case. "Let's see if you're the kind of fellow who's capable of being unselfish. I want to return to our Balkan friend whom I introduced in the last session. Do you still deny all knowledge of him?"

McLeod took his time to answer. "I've been thinking it over, and I believe that I met him once or twice."

"That's all?"

"All I remember in any case."

"Let's take a look at the facts," Hollingsworth said with an obvious love for the sentence. "This Balkan gentleman appears in a Mediterranean country in, shall we say, 1936? Said country is in the middle of a civil conflict, and the power he represents is giving aid to one of the two factions, the faction of the legally constituted government. Our friend takes over a high function which is related to a particular brigade of soldiers who are international in character, and he is in charge of the counterespionage. In going through our papers on him, we find that he has previously made speeches which may account for his position. If you wait, I will read you an excerpt."

Hollingsworth plucked still another paper neatly from the file, and spread it before him on the desk. "Here is what he says:

> It is not enough to work for the revolution. One must put oneself into the very heart of the fight, one must accept those tasks which, quite to the contrary of those missions most gratifying to our socialist heart, the building of collectives, the industrialization of the

wilderness, and other of our remarkable achievements, is in contradistinction to these, tasks of a less pleasant character. One tests one's revolutionary fiber by accepting with joy the most difficult, the most unrewarding, indeed even the most painful of assignments. It is in no way to be construed that I offer other than the highest praise to our national security organization, the watch-dog of the revolution, when I say it is with great joy I accept my new high position in the heart of the fight where one is tested a thousand-fold."

Hollingsworth nodded. "The potentate of that very country spoke with praise of the author."

"He would not today," McLeod said.

"One never knows." Hollingsworth coughed. "This is a fellow who says he wants to test himself, and conditions being what they are in said civil conflict, he has plenty of opportunity. The first case which comes to my attention is a minor one. Elements in this brigade are ranged on the battle front next to other political elements with which they are not sympathetic. I have to admit I never get it clear in my head because all the parties and groups are so complicated, but the said other elements are made up of workers who claim to be revolutionary—if I remember they are called something like the Pow-wow—and they don't get along politically with the brigade. One time ammunition comes through under the aegis of the great power which supports the brigade, and the arms are so distributed that the elements of the Pow-wow receive nothing. When the enemy attacks, the Pow-wow is routed, and the result is disaster for the flank is turned and much ground is lost. Afterward there is dissension in the brigade. Why, they ask, was our flank given no arms, and this dissension reaches the point where a delegation goes in protest to our Balkan friend. He argues with them, he attempts to dissuade them, but his efforts unavailing; he is obliged to order imprisonment, and word is sent back that they have been discovered to be enemy agents. Moreover, the rumors that the Pow-wow was not provided with arms proved to be false, our friend announced. They were provided with arms but sold them to the enemy, and retreated from cowardice and not from lack of munitions. This story is distributed by all the best propaganda agents. The Balkan gent in question confided to one of his subordinates that a terrible blunder had actually been made in not supplying arms to the Pow-wow, even though they were some kind of anarchists. But, and I quote directly, 'It is better to carry through a blunder with all one's energy, than attempt to halt midway and retrace one's steps.' Now, what do you think of this fellow?"

"He was the product of a system," McLeod muttered. Perspiration had begun to form on his forehead.

Hollingsworth offered a cigarette and was refused. "Our information is extremely detailed on these points, for several subordinates sent continual reports on the fellow to the mother country, and through certain special contacts we were able to obtain copies. So another case comes to mind. Of a prominent Pow-wow leader, or maybe he's an anarchist or whatever, who refuses to collaborate and is attempting to incite the workers to a revolution before the war is ended. This is against the policy of the great power who supplies arms. One fiery evening the leader makes a speech to some kind of Pow-wow council." Hollingsworth sighed. "The speech is to the effect that they will lose the war unless the workers know that they are fighting for their own revolution and not for the promise of one. There is activity in the air, and who knows what is possible? The Balkan fellow apprised of the situation moves fast on orders from above. A couple of paid killers murder the particular leader and several of his companions two nights later, and forged documents are distributed showing that he too was an enemy agent."

"Workers bled," Lannie said suddenly. Her voice was hollow and resounded in the room. McLeod supported his elbow upon his hand and lit a cigarette.

"I've made a study," Hollingsworth went on, "of this Balkan gentleman, and one has to admire his efficiency. Let me cite another case. . ."

But another was hardly to exhaust it. While my mind whirled and my reason grew leaden, incident tumbled upon incident, and forgery upon weapon, until arrests and murders, betrayals and slander, jumbled into an olio of secret inks, Magyar knives, and the swollen spider mesh of the Balkan gent. Hollingsworth ticked it off in a mild flat voice, a clerk reciting from his ledger, fingers extended one by one as Case Three, Item Four, and Subject Five were elaborated and folded back into the brief case again, until the first hand enumerated, he must employ the second, and Project Seven, Case Eight continued the list. With the expansion of the dossier, McLeod fought a rear-guard action, listening in silence to story after story while the perspiration gathered on his forehead and wet the front of his shirt, listening with such apparent patience that I was on the point of protesting myself, only to attack with all his resource on a detail I might have considered trivial. Lannie listened, her lips parted, her eyes bright, shaking her head and clucking her tongue, an audience animated beyond the expectation of any actor, attention given wholly to whoever was speaking.

"I come now," Hollingsworth said, "to a special incident which attracted my attention when going through these files. It's a minor problem I should say, but I found it of unusual interest. There is a young fellow who works in the field organization of the gentleman we have been talking about, a nice young fellow from all reports, but a little impractical. And after a year or so in which he's up at the front and back again all the time, he begins to act in a manner which is very unusual. Our reports say that he goes around to everyone telling them things like this, 'We are losing the war and it is all our fault. We are murdering innocent men. The anarchists and the Pow-wow are genuine revolutionaries, but are we? That is what I ask.' And it is amazing how little discretion the fellow has. Reports bombard his Balkan boss about what he is saying, and indeed he even says it to that very fellow himself." Hollingsworth looked at each of us in turn, his pause manufacturing drama. "Orders come through. The young man is counterrevolutionary and must be eliminated. A simple enough case up to this point." Gently Hollingsworth was rubbing the end of his nose with the eraser tip of the pencil. "What does the boss do? Something one might say is unforeseen, judging him on his past actions. He doesn't kill the young man. He hides him away in a secret place, and sends in a false report. A very unusual action. So unusual that he almost gets away with it. But somehow he's found out, and then he's told in no mistakable terms that if the young man isn't disposed of, he himself will be."

"Ohhh," Lannie breathed.

"Yes. He then does what one would expect him to. The young man is eliminated. Only, for reasons which I suppose are psychological, he does something very exceptional. He kills the young man himself."

"What's exceptional?" McLeod asked flatly.

"Well, you see the boss has never done any of this in the past. There are lots of employees for that. But in this case he goes to see the young man who trusts him implicitly, surprising as that may seem, and after hours of talk, he carries out the orders. And when he goes home he sits down and writes out the whole thing for himself alone, never knowing that eventually it will turn up in our files. What would you say to all this?"

"That's so cruel!" Lannie exclaimed with a smile.

Hollingsworth shook his head. "He was commended for it, and they were right. That gentleman might have been ready to . . . deviate, is that the word? But when he alone killed the young fellow, I guess they figured that would straighten him out. Maybe he did it to straighten himself out. Cause you know he committed another murder after this. All by himself again."

"What was the condition of this second murder?" Mc-Leod asked hoarsely.

"Oh, a more routine affair." And Hollingsworth went on at even greater length. There was a friend, a great friend, of the Balkan boss, and they had known each other for years, and had worked together more than once. He was sent on a mission to the very capital of the very Mediterranean country where our protagonist disported, a mission from the mother country as Hollingsworth described it, an important mission, and yet before he had been in the city two weeks, it was obvious that his behavior was odd. He drank, a man who had seldom touched liquor; his hands shook, a man with nerves of steel, veteran of an earlier civil war; and although he had been a big man, none of his clothing would fit. He completed his work, and went to his hotel room, and there he stayed for three days, seeing no one, and only drinking. A passport arrived for his return to the east, and he mailed the passport back to his Balkan friend in the very same city. So the Balkan went to see him, and as Hollingsworth told us with relish, they once again talked for hours, and they had a discussion. "We have sabotaged the revolution," the old friend said, "and we have eaten ourselves. The trials. Do you know the lie of the trials.? Do you know that equality is a bourgeois principle, and we have cheered for piecework, and our wives wear fur coats. We have put dung in the milk and poison in the honey, and we have retarded socialism a hundred years. For socialist morality is dead, and I have come to the conclusion it is the head of a pin, and unlike angels not a single lie may dance upon it." And so they argued, or rather the old friend declaimed, and finally the man swore that he would not return unless it were by force, and he dared his old comrade to employ the force.

"At the end of it," Hollingsworth said, "this idealist fellow

232

was dead. An extraordinary case. You see the boss overstepped his authority. All he was supposed to do was give him the passport. He should have left the rest to somebody else."

"I say," McLeod muttered thickly, the skin of his face drawn back against the bone, "that a man who would perform such acts had become untrustworthy, and divided painfully by his own doubt, could only resolve it by driving himself further, by forcing himself into the position he now dreaded to place his subordinates."

"I'm sorry to disagree," Hollingsworth murmured quietly, "but this goes against all the facts. Even by his own admission the fellow remained with the organization through to the end of that Mediterranean ruckus, and then quite a while after that. There is reason to believe he is still with them."

"I am not that man," McLeod said desperately.

"One never knows exactly. You defend him."

"I explain him." McLeod wiped moisture from his upper lip with a quick motion of his tongue.

"That is possible," Hollingsworth nodded, "but still it's interesting. In each case they talked for hours. A lot must have been said in that time."

High on McLeod's temple a pulse was throbbing, the vein standing out against the skin. "You assume these acts were done coldly."

Hollingsworth seemed indifferent. "I've discovered in my line of work that it's actions which count. A fellow, after all, can get to feel one way and then he can feel the other way, but in the long run it's what he does that keeps me busy. Now, in this particular circumstance, the man we're discussing goes in with a weapon, he feels it against him, so to speak, all the time he's talking. Suppose once or twice during all those hours, he even decides he won't use it after all, he likes the other fellow too much. Still, no matter what he thinks, he ends up by pulling the trigger. He comes with the lethal instrument"—Hollings-

233

worth was outlining the brief on his fingers— "and he goes away with same said lethal instrument . . . fired. A lawyer fellow can argue about cold blood or not cold blood, but it seems to me if his mind isn't made up at bottom, then he doesn't bring the murderous weapon in the first place. You know, I ask myself a question."

"What?" McLeod croaked.

"Isn't that fellow still doing the same work right up to this day? That is, unless he can show proof to the contrary. According to my modest opinion, he must be, because nobody could admit they had been that wrong. That's proved by statistics. None of the bureaucrats, as I have said, turn back to theory. For a fellow to admit all those things and then say he was wrong, why he couldn't set himself up over anybody. He couldn't set himself up over me, for example."

"It is only by admitting your guilt that you can ever judge," McLeod said slowly.

"Fiddlesticks. You're a fellow likes to turn everything into a discussion. But it's facts and not words a fellow like me must accept."

McLeod's eyes, burning out of his gaunt face, looked across the desk at Hollingsworth. "I am not a servant of any power."

"Then you have what we are looking for."

"I do not."

"Are you the Balkan gentleman I was referring to?"

"No."

"What would you say if you were?"

"That one of the two propositions you have outlined would have to be correct."

"Finally." Hollingsworth sat back and lit a cigarette. But though his arms were folded neatly in his lap and his shoulders touched the wood of the chair, he was hardly relaxed, and the

234

sense of continuity he had pursued was so painfully close that he could not contain it.

"Miss Madison," he said, "will you please leave the room for a moment?"

She stood up without a word and obeyed him, closing the door behind her. Hollingsworth leaned forward and switched on the lamp so it shone directly into McLeod's face.

"You see," he murmured, "I have the utmost admiration for you, and it makes a fellow feel bad to have to tell you all these things. There's no need for you to have to go through all this. Everything would be so simple if only you would accept my offer, and you could go away."

"The offer has never been definite," McLeod managed to articulate.

"It is now. I can't tell you the respect I feel for a gentleman like yourself who commanded so many men, and if he so desired could have supped in the lap of luxury." Lust marched in Hollingsworth's speech. "A fellow could buy an army." And his voice dropping until all feeling was suppressed, he added, "It's only hard times has come upon you, and one should never aggravate himself for nothing."

He paused, and in the pause he struck his little lightning. A hand scratched on the door outside as it scratched once weeks before, and continued with mounting hysteria until a finger was crying at the wood and nibbling at our ear. The lamp bulb glared into McLeod's eyes, the finger scratched and importuned until it might have been beneath our flesh, and all the while Hollingsworth was watching him.

"Stop that sound," McLeod said.

"It disturbs you?"

"Let it continue."

But he was gripping the edge of the desk, and across the rigid muscle armor of his mouth, a tremor rippled as though

235

another mouth long concealed would present its frail credential.

"This was the sound," Hollingsworth stated, "which the Balkan gentleman employed on certain secret work. It is a password one might say, and he used it the night he visited his old friend. It is obvious from your reaction that this same sound is not unfamiliar to you."

McLeod made no answer.

"Are you the so-called Balkan gentleman?"

Half a minute might have elapsed, the scratching continued, the lamp burning.

"Yes," McLeod said.

"Did you really leave that organization?"

McLeod nodded.

"Then you still have the little object?"

"Yes," McLeod said.

"Where is it?"

"No, that's enough, that's enough," McLeod shouted. "Not today. Give me time." In his agitation he had come to his feet and was leaning over the desk. I thought he was about to weep.

"All right, that is enough," Hollingsworth said. "Easy does it, easy does it." And to my bewilderment he crossed the desk to McLeod's side and stood patting him on the shoulder with the gentle sympathetic attention of a man who has told another some tragic news. "Yes, easy does it, and pull yourself together," he murmured in a demulcent voice.

"Go away," McLeod said thickly.

"We'll adjourn and continue this upon further notice," Hollingsworth said quietly, "and may I thank you, sir, for your co-operation."

With a last soothing touch of his hand on McLeod's neck, he gathered his papers and quit the room.

TWENTY-FIVE

Now, in the short time that remained, in the evening after their audience and the next evening, McLeod came to my room and talked for hours. And like a man who carries his mortal illness within him, and obsessed with the death he contains, must constantly exhume it, he would pace my floor through the middle of the night and relate from his incalculable necessity a list of the crimes he had performed. Fluvial, torrential, he could have dammed it no more than I could have stopped my ears, and while the night air stagnated in the attic room and insects battered themselves in frenzy against the wall looking for the window from which they had entered, it poured forth over my head in a storm of recrimination and justification, of places I had never known and names I could hardly untangle. He would lacerate himself, searching deeper and deeper into the mesh of motive until each successive reason for what he had done became more frightful than the one which had preceded it, and when he had finally, to his satisfaction if not to mine, exposed the last festering cocci of the sore, he would close the incision only to open another. And if, at last, I could begin to shift from the mystification of such an ordeal to the first perception of its extent, he would halt me, before I had even succeeded, to demonstrate with what desire he could hardly support that in such an instance, all perfidy granted, he had nonetheless . . . he had made efforts, he had tried . . . he had even . . . So through one night and most of another I listened to him, not knowing what to say, while he continued, half for himself and half for me, defense combined with prosecution, the moralist and the criminal brought to dock and each arguing at odds, for even as I, the judge, would pardon the accused he was delivering himself to execution.

"You, of course, would have been unaware of this," he was going on, "but I watched you during the entire time, and there was one expression on your face. It was disbelief. You couldn't accept the fact that the corporeal face and body of McLeod could ever have performed such capers. All the while you were waiting for me to deny it, I could sense that. You still don't accept it completely. For you, there's a magic word, and I've only to utter it and the explanations fall into line. And I could tell it to you, I could show you with dates and facts that I am not the Balkan gentleman as Leroy puts it in all his humor, but what would that avail? Because you see the truth is that there are deep compacts between Leroy and myself, you might almost say we are sympathetic to each other, and there was your presence and the girl's, and who knows what she'll babble, and then there are his artistic qualifications for the job which must not be discounted—whether it's organizational insight or more probably an accident, I must say that from their point of view they couldn't have chosen a better man because I can assure you that all through it, all through the fiction and fancy of all the things I was alleged to have done in Mediterranean waters, there was not a word of legal truth and all the parallel truth in the world because if it were not one act I committed it was another, and you must notice his devilish cleverness, unconscious I'm certain, for his instincts are perfect. He knew how I would react if the specifics were given. I've covered that over for myself these many years, oh, aware what I did, but none the less there's a certain crutch to the name of a thing, it all seems more reasonable and possible until you put it figuratively, until the metaphorical end, which is always the muzzle if you come down to it, blasts you in the face. And all the while, the detached portion of my brain which feeds on ice water, and that's true, was admiring him for an aesthetic performance, so that you see no matter how I suffer there's a counterfeit touch, and even at this moment I find a basic amusement because I'm not suffering at all, I'm merely trying to suffer and with such exertion that I suffer from the effort, and that's how cold my tit has proven."

He ceased talking, but the transition was only external, for he continued to pace back and forth, the latest of the continual cigarettes he smoked drooping from his mouth and laying its trail of ash beside him. In his head the words undoubtedly continued, jostling, burbling, stewing until the pot must have rattled, and from the force of the soliloquy his lips formed a soundless equivalent of what he might have said.

With no more reason he was speaking aloud again. "Yet I ask myself if it is entirely a swindle that you should have had such confidence in me, or whether it is an indication that I have altered in these past years and could have given an impression of personal integrity and the capacity for theoretical speculation, for you've involved yourself on my account. May it be that the potentiality I possessed once as a revolutionary has not been completely dissipated, and there is still hope for me if only I can slough the hundred crimes upon my head, shake free once and for all, and strike out again with vigor instead of by the half-crippled steps I have employed? But, no!"—and here he struck one hand against the palm of the other—"this is rationalization, and I can be trusted to scrape the meat off the last rotten bone, looking for anything to find my out, and even enlisting you with all your poor sad dependencies to make my brief."

So he continued on and on, expressing at last outwardly the

239

total of all the nights he must have lain in his bed, all nerves alive, limbs aching, while in relentless turmoil each thought birthed its opposite, each object in the darkness swelled with connotation until a chair could contain his childhood, and the warm flaccid body of Guinevere slumbering beside him expanded its bulk to become all the women he had ever known, but in their negative aspect, so that whatever pleasure he might have felt was not felt now, and he rooted in all the sweating and lurching of unfulfillment until the flesh of his wife had become just that, and as flesh was the denominator of meat and all the corpses he had ever seen and some created.

"I'm the only one he says who ever turned back to theory, and this he delivers with a smack of the lip for he's seen the statistics and that's enough for him. It's all the key he needs. But do you know what it means to turn back? It's the one achievement of my life, yes," he said. "Think of it, you've got to make the imaginative reconstruction, don't forget you're dedicated to the land across the sea, you've come to understand finally the gory unremitting task of history and the imperfect men with whom you change it, and it's a whole choice, you tell yourself, with all the good and bad of one against all the bad and good of the other, until I can tell you it's with a gloomy but nonetheless delicious satisfaction that you hear about some particularly unpleasant piece of work by the side you're on because it's a test of yourself, and you don't shrink back. It's hard is it, well then make it harder, burn out the pap and the syrup and make yourself harder because it takes that; it takes all of that." He halted in the middle of the floor, looking at me expectantly with a puckering of his mouth. If there had been a glass of water in his hand, he would have swallowed it at a gulp. "And that's only the preliminary, because soon you know that it's all renounced for yourself, all the pleasures of the plump belly, and you're burned out, burned out for the generations to come, and so you can only drive yourself. Cannot you understand, you crippled prig," he shouted at my impassive face, "why we remained so long in a situation now reactionary and stoked fuel to the counter-revolution? You have no life, and so you do not know what it means to deny what has been the meaning of your life, for if you've been wrong, mark you now, if you've been wrong, then what of the decamillion of graves, and so you're committed, you're committed wholly, do you understand? and each action you perform can only confirm you further in your political position or what I would now call the lack of one, and there's only the nightmare of yourself if you're wrong, for you see it gets turned inside out and after a while the only path to absolution is to do more of the same so that you end up religious and climb to salvation on the steps of your crimes. And in all this, in all the activity and activity, do you dare lie awake and resurrect all the old tools of surplus value and accumulation and the exploitation of one class by another, or do you sink your teeth into the meat you're permitted, no private ownership and therefore . . . therefore therefore . . . I exist, therefore I am, and so there must be socialism, except that the weirdest statements go through your head, and once I jotted it down on a piece of paper, a perfectly ridiculous remark, 'The historical function of La Sovietica is to destroy the intellectual content of Marxism,' except the underworld was beginning to win out in me, and how I turned on the others who deserted, and deserting were not dead for there was another exploitation they could join. Oh, none of those went back to theory as Leroy can point out with all his little numbers on the paper, and small wonder with their heads stuffed with all the fetid paraphernalia of factology and commission and how many divisions have you? The whole choice they've made on one rotten boat, and what can they do? they're sailors they say, and so it's the other stinking bark for them, and the old exploitation for the new, and in the swap Leroy comes in, and the rich old exploitation lulls them with its living standard and how they've forgotten that it exists at the cost of the misery of the rest of the world and a million ton of cannon."

But his invective could flay outward only so long before he must reverse it upon himself. "And yet. . yet what did I do myself? Did I drop out of sight with one clean break, or did I have to play out the comedy to its last unpleasant detail? Oh, I was forced to work for the others, they admitted me here in return for services rendered, but that's small excuse, and there were times in the early months when you might say I was almost eager, for I was attempting to reverse what I had once done, and merely succeeding in doubling it, but I was charged with hate at that time, hate for the party and for the past as protection against the hate of m'self and all those wasted years. And in such a state you can imagine the labor it takes to see yourself for the second time clearly, and prepare your theoretical retreat, but how, with what distrust, by making it almost impossible for oneself to continue to live, by grafting the little object into my flesh, so that now I could be hunted not by one but by two, as if I had to make certain that any return was absolutely impossible. And marrying on top of that when what I wanted was isolation, and petrified in my bones that I was already dead so I must call on her to thaw me out, and I've never given her the time of day. Thus, notice the admirable path I have taken from the bureaucrat to the theoretician. Still such is the arrogance of my species that I resent Leroy for my judge and the fact that he makes me a smudge on the paper and is indifferent to what I have endured I find intolerable. I tell myself he's got a policeman's brain, and it's only the murders he can understand, but what of the capitulations which he would undoubtedly approve? those are what torment me now if I think on the past, every time I opened my mouth and sullenly, hysterically, or even happily, depending on circumstance, I would renounce all my despicable, counter-revolutionary, depraved, degenerate, wrecking and inconsequential objections to no matter what, and so forth and so forth, there was the commitment step by step, there was the betrayal of myself as a revolutionary, and the rest, the legal crimes, merely the confirmation. It is only possible to come at last to the conclusion that Leroy is right and I should be just a cipher on the paper, and justice is justice, and it's only the fool expects a mother's milk.

"For I tell you"—and now his engine running without governor, he must grasp me by the shoulder, squeezing it with a desperation to match his eyes—"that I haven't begun to plumb the rottenness of it, and it's when I think of the other one with the ax in his gray hair, and your friend Miss Madison who'll never be able to live past that moment, and it wasn't the direct participation of myself in it, oh, I have no concrete blood on my hands, I was just a cog in that one and arranged a passport, and smelled a little of what was to come, but you see I did nothing and all the while I was managing my infinitesimal part of the operation, working on it while I was at the height of a crisis for it was the time of the pact, and I no longer believed a minute in what had been the external and objective reality of my life." He had begun to mutter. "This detail taken care of and that. I could not have known who it was for, and yet I knew it was him out in Mexico, and on the dark sly I was reading his works behind my barricaded door.

"I knew," he shouted suddenly, "I knew. There's the crime. No longer believing and I went ahead, I let him be murdered you see. Why did I do this? Was it out of fear, can I extract that last extenuating circumstance? Can I plead that out of mortal fear which may assail any human I was a craven, and harsh as the word may be, a drop of pity may be dispensed. No, that's not it at all. Because I wasn't afraid at the time. I'd nibbled at death like salt, and for years. My system was full of it. I expected it myself. No, I let him be killed because I hated him, because the thought that all through the years with all his theoretical bilge about a degenerated worker's state, he was still

243

nearer the truth than I had been, and my life was the lie, and the thought of him was unbearable for he had a knack to activate the tumor in all of us until it gave no rest, and I was making herculean efforts to regain conviction, and as long as he remained, he was there, you understand? I hated him, I wanted him dead as if that would prove he were wrong, and with all this stuffed as I was with the desire to quit, ready to burst."

But there were circles upon circles yet to be traced, and if he attacked himself, my turn was to be next. "It's when I go through all of this and face the actions I've taken, and the years I've spent in the room right across there when you know what was tormenting me? That I was out of things. The biggest of all the obstacles I set against myself in doing my little theoretical work, the biggest of them all was that I was alone, and time was passing, and how many divisions had I? Because that's the other part of the swindle, and if you start with a whole choice, you end with a whole office to run, and it's not easy to give it up. You want to be treated with the bourgeois dignity befitting your position, and I can tell you it goes deep enough so that one of the things which excruciates me now is that brought to book with my hands and legs all properly tied, who do I face as prosecutor but a child, one of their youngest men, promising perhaps but you'd think they need more than that for me, you see the petty things mixed in all this, you see how I complain, and if I'm to be honest there's a word or two to be said about yourself. What is your function in all this, and you have hardly the least idea, but I treat you as a confessor monk with the part of myself that never sloughs the Catholic, burn their black robes at their own stake, and that galls in me as well, for if I'm to have the prelate, you might suppose a cardinal would be on demand with all their techniques for such a thing, or even a pope in white and gold, but what do I get instead, a poor little friar like yourself with all your blunted flattened spirit, your lack of understanding, a castrate in short. Poor little monk from a third-rate monastery with the patches showing in your frock, and nothing left to yourself so that you can only sup for emotional wares at someone else's table."

He must be all things now, sword-bearer, warrior, and doctor; no sooner did he open a wound in me then he must salve it. "The mark of my irredeemable corruption," he cried out, "is that I turn against you when you're the first human being who has offered me friendship in so many years that I've lost all aptitude for it. And it is impossible for you to know the excitement I felt that night on the bridge when I heard you talk with precision enough for me to realize that here was one of the young generation with a socialist culture, and that if my time was passing on another was coming, a new generation with new strength, and the pain it cost me to masquerade as something else, but I couldn't reveal it to you that night, not when I didn't know how much Leroy had found out, and that by the side, for if I speak bitterly to you, it is because you raised an expectation, and I realize now that your equipment counts for nothing, and like the others you will await the flood with despair. And if I find that intolerable, it's due to my own itch. What after all is at the bottom, what has sent me helter-skelter across the hall to entertain you all this time with the sound of my voice, and the answer is simple enough now that I come to it. I ask," and here he paused, stood looking at me with eyes which had become expressionless.

"Lovett," he said, "why shouldn't I save myself?"

And with an eagerness which would suffer no answer to his question, he went on before I could reply. "The more I consider, the more I'm filled with a technical admiration for Leroy, and I've come to decide he's the perfection of the policeman for it's never enough to bring the man in, you've got to swallow him first, and with the natural anxiety of the average human I resist his intent, but there's no getting around it, I'm tormented by the thought, and it's a simple one. For what? For

245

what do I resist, and to what purpose, because you notice I'm caught in all the unspeakable discomfort of a grave contradiction. If it is possible, all past considered, to function as a man and to create work which satisfies my moral appetite, to wit contribute to the body of revolutionary theory for the future, and so resist him, then I have no choice at all. I'm a dead man. Whereas, if I capitulate again, and after all says the worm, what is one capitulation when I have contributed to a hundred? then, oh then, worked with all my skill and playing upon his cupidity, there's a tiny passage into the clear, and what do I have for my pains, I go out alive and better off dead. So, you see, alive it's dead, and dead I'm alive, and yet I prefer the second and a corner still kept for myself, and all the while he put me through his paces, I bled to confess, I wanted to tell him, it was with a relief you cannot know I told him I had the little O for that brought me a step further to the ultimate of conceding it privately to him, and I must tell you that I know against the voracious appetite of Mr. Hollingsworth there is only the fatigue in my own bones, and the heartlessness of no political future for any of us, and then I wonder if I have actually, if I care actually to resist him to the end. For what?"

He paused for breath and was off again. "You see, there is something actually. What I come up with in this the irony of ironies is that I who married for many reasons and few of them good, now find that I could feel the most intense love for my wife, and would be willing to accept a nook for the few years left, indeed hunger for it with a passion that surprises me now, so like the love-torn youth I build a mountain of innuendo on which to feed if there is an exchange between us of even two pleasant words. And it's her who has to love me, for if she does, he can have the thing he wants, and she and I'll disappear again, and what's one more defeat when we have lost every battle but the first? You see, Lovett, the problem"—he grasped both my wrists with his hands—"is that I can no longer approach the idea of Guinevere and myself with anything like detachment, and I'm completely adrift and cannot discern up from down nor left from right, and yet at the same time my hunger to know the truth of this situation, which is at least the shred of integrity I possess, has become immense, and I want you to come down with me, tomorrow or the day after so long as it's soon, and listen to her and me talking, and form your conclusions from that to see if there is any promise whatsoever, or whether out of her own mixed beginnings and the race I've run her, there is nothing but her own limited capacity for hatred, and I am literally at zero."

"How can I ever judge..." I began to protest.

"How, indeed?" And he threw up his hands in the air, and declared, "But I can't give it up. You see I can't capitulate still another time. No, no argument," he mumbled, "you've got to come down for you're the best observer possible, and that's an end for now. What will I do?"

For the first time in over an hour, he ceased pacing back and forth long enough to drop into a chair, and there he stared at me as though to assess for still another time whether I could help him, or if this, without the trace of a hope for alleviation, were indeed desperation alley.

TWENTY-SIX

So I went down the next afternoon and suffered an eventless hour of what Engels once called "that state of leaden boredom known as domestic bliss." Guinevere sat in an armchair, a miscellany of sewing occupying her hands, while a comfortable distance away McLeod was installed in another seat with Monina upon his lap. One of them would say a word, the answer would come, and conversation would die. I, who might have been the casual Sunday visitor, perched on the sofa and looked first at one and then the other.

"It's a long time," Guinevere murmured at the end of a ten-minute silence, and with more than a glance in my direction, "since we been here like this."

McLeod nodded. Monina was in the process of climbing over him, and both hands enmeshed in his black hair, scrambled her feet over his stomach. "Yes," he said finally, "it has been a long time." In what must have been a reaction from the night before, he sat lifelessly in his chair, depression heavy upon him. Yet, apparently, he had decided to begin. "I wonder," he added casually, "if you find this pleasant?"

"It's all right," she said flatly.

Perhaps it was my presence, perhaps even the sunlight which entered through the basement window and set its rectangle upon the carpet, but in any case, no doubt despite him-self, he must treat her as a stranger, and all the boredom, all the restive desire each must have possessed to be somewhere else, could hardly be contained. The result, irritating to her and pointless for himself, was a long discursion.

"I've spent the better part of my life avoiding just such moments as these," he said formally, "and I must admit that in the past the sight of a house in the suburb of some city or other was enough to depress me with that damn afternoon sunlight and the shingles in *kitsch* and all the bloody papamamas with their brat in the baby carriage. To anyone who attempts to change the world, that's the specter. Subjectively, there's al-ways the fear: that's where I end up. And objectively it's even worse, for you know that the end product of your labors, if you are successful, is that the multi-millions in misery will graduate only to that, and the brotherhood of man is a world of stinking baby carriages. It's the paradox of the revolutionary who seeks to create a world in which he would find it intolerable to live."

Guinevere yawned.

One of Monina's feet was prodding his ribs, and he caught it with his hand and boosted her upon his shoulder. "You might say the human function of socialism" —he was now talking to me— "is to raise mankind to a higher level of suffer-ing, for given the hypothesis that man has certain tragic contra-dictions, the alternative is between a hungry belly and a hungry mind, but fulfillment there is never."

"You're off again, huh?" Guinevere commented.

"No." He brought himself up short. "I was disgressing, that's true. All I wanted to say is that I'm turning mellow, for with all the shortcomings I've enumerated, this kind of afternoon, given my objections, no longer stirs me into anger. I might say that I can even enjoy it for a short period." His face, however, would hardly agree. His long features had grown longer still, and his mouth puckered about a quinine tongue.

Her needle whipped through the cloth, into the fabric and with a quick pull out again. She might have been drawing a noose. "I never can understand a word of his," she muttered.

"Well, maybe you can understand if I say that it's been my fault and not yours."

Nothing could have awakened her more. "Why do you say that?" Her eyes came to meet mine. A quick look, very much ill at ease, and then she was at her sewing again.

"I'm willing to state, Beverly, that I have given you neither the attention, the interest, nor the affection your nature demands, but I intend to make all attempts to alter my conduct."

She stared at him, then at me, then at him again. And when she spoke she was angry. "I swear you can work out anything as if it's a cross-word puzzle. But just tell me this. Why did you pick a time for your New Year's resolutions when Lovett is around?"

Monina had clambered down to the floor and was playing a game with McLeod's shoe. "Pooey, pooey, pooey," she said aloud and giggled.

"Why do I talk with Lovett here? Yes, that's a question, isn't it? And there's probably more answer than one." In the stiffness and constraint of his speech—excessive even for Mc-Leod—was the hint of much else. He conducted himself more like the high priest than the rejuvenated lover, and, the world lost, could only perform the ritual. "I wonder, Beverly, if you can remember when we first married, if you can recall any of the emotions you felt at the time?"

She sat with her needle poised in the air, nose pointed before her with the attention of an animal who has caught the scent of something wholly unexpected, and in the separation, be it only seconds of this first apperception and the subsequent discovery for good or for ill, has wholly and resolutely set herself upon guard. Her arms held out, her back no longer touching the chair, she stared at him. And her little mouth, revealed by its lack of lipstick, parted unhappily. "Maybe I remember," she said.

"You do, probably, or could if you made the effort, but I've discouraged such things. So perhaps it's best for me to tell you. Because, you see, when we married you were ready to share yourself with somebody. It was a short period, but the only period in your life, I think, when you could have been in love. And I betrayed that potentiality. You needed a man who would give you a great deal, and I gave you very little."

"Yes," she said. The confession from him evoking only bitterness in her, she returned sullenly, "You had your chance."

"I know, but I want another."

"Another?" She snorted. "Boy, you're a character."

"You've got cause to be resentful," he said, "but the point is you still need all the emotional contact I failed to provide. There were moments, if you look back, Beverly, when you were not unhappy with me. For instance, I might mention the trip we took in the old car I bought in the first year of our marriage. Do you remember that?"

He had touched some depth in her. By the slight shifting of her seat, in the attitude of self-protection with which she hugged her arms to her bosom, I could sense the center of discord in herself. "Lots of men gave me just as much," she declared. "It's the woman makes the man anyway."

As though he sensed by her opposition that she was hungry for his plea, he worried the exposition even further. "I understand you, Beverly, and you know that's worth something"—echoes of the conversation I had had with him once about Mr. Guinevere. "If you're willing to make the attempt, we can try all over again."

He wiped his glasses with a handkerchief and set them up on the thin bony ridge of his nose, but in the interval they had been removed the dark shrunken sockets of his eyes blinked painfully. They were both silent, both considering what trying-all-over-again would mean, and the thought two-faceted for each of them balanced precariously between the antipathetic past and the moot future.

"And what'll we do?" she asked at last.

"We'll have to go away. That's the first thing."

"How'll we live?"

"Modestly. Modestly. We'll be more or less in hiding, you understand. It'll hardly be pleasant." He would reveal it all. "I've considered going away myself, but to be underground . . .I'm more than weary, you know," he said softly. "And then perhaps we can't get away. Surveillance is hard to determine." In the act of arguing the proposition he twisted upon himself and found it intolerable.

"You mean going on like it is now?"

He nodded. "Yes. Except, you see, I would be a different husband to you."

"We'll live in a place like this?"

"Maybe less."

On into the years ahead, the two of them sitting in just such a room, afternoon sunlight on the floor, the child playing between them and the minutes ticking past.

"I love you, Beverly," he declared.

"There's a way," she said quietly.

"Yes?"

"The thingamajig. I was wondering if it was what they call convertible into cash." She insinuated this delicately, her fingers not missing a pass of the needle.

If this had been what he was ready to broach, the sound of it coming from her made the prospect intolerable. "Sell it?" he said slowly.

She nodded. "I'm only asking." Her tone was almost gentle. "You hinted that you might."

"Why don't we try to get away?" he said abruptly. "On the

sly. We can manage it, and not give it up at all. You see . ." His face was rigid. "I've tried to give it up. I don't think I can. Wouldn't you go away with me if I still kept it?" Enthusiasm was betrayed for just an instant. "I've realized something. You loved me when we married, and I could love you now. I would devote the energy I possess, for you and for the child. Do you understand? You could blossom in the admiration I would furnish, and there's a part of you never given up the idea." So he would woo her.

Only after the gate was closed. "You got a crust," she shrieked suddenly. "Anybody else offers me . . . offers me lots of things," she finished lamely, "and you won't give me anything, not even when you can."

He shook his head. "Listen, Beverly, I know you well enough to say you're miserable and tormented with your two companions. Each of them represents an existence filled with uncertainty and with terror. Neither will provide anything for you."

"Oh, shut up," she cried.

They were silent, the charge gathering between them so dark and ugly that Monina looked up from where she played and whimpered almost without sound.

"Listen," Guinevere said, "listen, you!"

"No, you listen to me."

"I wish you were dead!" Guinevere shouted suddenly.

A pause. Guinevere gathered the sewing in her hand, wadding it between her fingers. I would not have been surprised if she had thrown it at him and the basket to follow.

"Tell me," she asked sweetly.

"Yes?"

"Do you love me?"

He nodded. "Yes, I do, Beverly."

Her mouth twisted. "I'm your bloody salvation, that's all."

McLeod's face became pale. "Not true," he murmured.

"I'm your bloody salvation," she repeated, "and you don't even want that. You want the ship to go down."

"Do I?" he asked aloud, and half rose in his seat. "I don't know. It's possible. Maybe I do," he muttered.

Nothing could please her now, no admission, no concession. She must drive him out of the room and out of her sight. "It's just like you to come smelling around after everything's been decided. Why don't you find out what's going on?" Her face swelled from rage. "Ask your friend here the sights he's seen. He could tell you a thing or two."

"I don't want to hear about your dances. How I know they're ridiculous."

". . .about Leroy and me, but he won't tell you, no, sir, because he'd like to get his finger in the jam too. All of you would. All you men. You'd just like to grab in me and grab in me." She was almost weeping. "Why don't you get out of here?"

McLeod was on his feet now. "What is she talking about?" he asked me.

"I think it's best not to go into it," I murmured.

"Get out of here," Guinevere screamed at him.

He lit a cigarette and sighed once remotely. I could almost have sworn he looked relieved. "Perhaps it's best I take a walk."

"Oh, get the hell out."

When the door closed behind him, Guinevere sat back in her chair, but her body was tense. "And you can get out too," she said to me.

"All right."

"You just want to torment me, and make me feel like. ." Imagery failed her. "Like two cents."

"Do you care what happens to him?" I asked.

It was an unpleasant question. Why must something happen? she might have screamed. "He doesn't care about me," she said in an excited voice. "He says he loves me. Did he act like a man in love? Did he say he liked me? You were here. Did he give me a single compliment?" She was close to weeping. "That's the way he's always loved me. He loves me by telling me what my faults are, and I used to think he was a fine guy once." She held her hands to her head. "What am I in, anyway? What's going to become of us all? Oh, I'm so tired I could bust."

Monina was pounding the floor with her fists. In a grief almost incommunicable she began to wail.

"Keep quiet," Guinevere cried at her.

Monina hate you, hate you, hate you," the child sobbed.

Although she shouted, Guinevere's voice was not without its plea. "He's okay, though, he's okay, isn't he?" and the sarcasm failed.

"Monina hate him too." The child wept only more.

"Oh, shut up," Guinevere shouted, "or I'll get the strap." She seemed about ready to join the child on the floor. "Oh, murder mia, shut up, will you, Monina?"

In answer, Monina continued to pound her fists.

TWENTY-SEVEN

THIS was the tableau which greeted Lannie. I stood in the corner virtually concealed by the heavy shadow of the stuffed armchair, while in the center of the carpet, her head illumined by the indifferent light which sifted tnrough the basement windows, Monina sat weeping, her agitation translated by now into a thoroughgoing tantrum. And Guinevere towered above her, helpless as the child sobbed.

Small wonder Lannie did not see me. She must have noticed Monina, but without pause she crossed the room, threw her arms about Guinevere, and kissed her upon the mouth. For one instant Guinevere shuddered in the shock of awakening from a nightmare to see a stranger by the bed. But in the next moment all had been restored again, the body was familiar, and Guinevere returned the embrace. They met like lovers who tryst in the dark, consumed with impatience, their hearts beating, all fear of discovery melting at the touch.

"I thought he'd never leave," Lannie whispered. "It was terrible. He passed me on the street and he smiled. He knows!"

To draw attention to myself, I tried to clear my throat. But as if this were wholly inadequate, I gave vent instead to a furious spasm of coughing. Each of them started from the embrace. Lannie stood rigidly, her eyes fastened upon me. "Ohh," she breathed. "Ohhh, why did you have to be here?"

Guinevere pulled her dressing gown over her halter, and the motion completed, looked at me with a silly expression on her face. She began to snicker. "I forgot you were coming," she blurted to Lannie, bewildered, I am certain, that she had been rendered so unaware. "Oh, brother," she offered in diminutive. Yet she could hardly conceal her delight. If the first diversion could not have come at a better moment, the second relieved her entirely. "Brother," she repeated, and not without gusto.

Hands against her forehead, Lannie dropped into a chair. "I'm sorry," I said.

Despite myself, I began to laugh, and if the coughing had not exhausted me, the laughter would finish me indeed. I roared at Lannie as the duplicate of myself, and at Guinevere who must run all her trains on the same track and cannot remember if the freight has passed and the express is coming. I roared at McLeod who dropped all his bets on a crooked wheel. I roared at ingenuity which filled the same hole necessity has dug, and thought of Lannie who waited outside for hours. And in seeing the two women together I saw myself alone with each of them, and laughed even more.

Lannie was grasping the arms of her chair. "Don't look like that," she snapped at Guinevere, whose mouth was open at my reaction. The rebuke effective, Lannie added furiously, "Pay no attention to him. He's a fool."

Guinevere's eyes came up to mine, flinched, and moved away. "Oh, you characters will drive me nuts," she shouted.

Lannie lit a cigarette, her quivering fingers negotiating the contact between the match and the tip with obvious difficulty. "You must never say that," she told Guinevere; "you must never try to catch the favor of anyone who is not your equal, for there is no shame equal to that."

257

"I don't know. I'm no different from anybody else," Guinevere proclaimed. But the smugness with which normally she would have mastered the statement was not quite successful. If she had used this a score of times with that part of her equipment which acted the housewife and had noted it to be a convenient rest in any conversation—yes, we are all alike, we are not fools nor radicals nor thieves nor clowns—where one could nod his head and mutual self-esteem could lap about this bond, she could employ it no longer with complete satisfaction. For the speech Lannie must have made many times had caught her at last in its attractions. She would be a thief or a clown or a radical or a fool and flourish in the novelty. "I'm no different from anybody else," she said, but offered it as an obvious gambit, panting to be contradicted.

And Lannie satisfied her. "Why must you be so silly? You are different. There is no one else like you, and you are beautiful." I might not have been there for all the attention paid me. "To think of you years ago," she said in her husky voice, "and how everyone passed through you and over you, and if you became drunk enough you could think you loved them, but it was never true. You were too beautiful, and what did they know of you, what does a boot know of the ground it soils? You gave yourself to them, and yet you were always free, for you wanted more than they did, you agreed to them and followed their ways, but you were miserable because that could never be for you. How could you love them when it was only yourself that you loved, and you were so right in that because we are born to love ourselves and that is the secret of everything. All your life you searched for a mirror to find your beauty, to see how your skin glows and your body swells in rapture and the hymn that is in you may be sung to yourself." Caressing, delicate, her voice must seek to create a spell. "But no one could give you even a tarnished dirty picture of yourself, for how may a boot

258

reflect beauty? And how could they see that you were alive and that your face could shine and there was color in you and such a sweet song, when they didn't want that, they wanted to swill and grind you into the dirt and tromple tromple. What an island you must have lived in, what a cry there is in you for deliverance. And that is why you love me, for I would be a mirror to you, and we escape only when we follow our mirror and let it lead us out of the forest. I can let you see your beauty, and so you will love me for I adore you and unlike the others want nothing but to lie in your arms, the mirror."

Guinevere heard this with her lips parted, her eyes far away. Bliss animated every curve in her face. "Yes," she murmured, "yes," dropping her voice into a gentle reflective sigh. The nectar she tasted rolled in her mouth until she could have absorbed her tongue in the sentience of the moment. Unconsciously, she clasped her breast. If it had been possible she would have kissed herself upon the throat.

"There is no one," Lannie went on, "who loves you as I and is devoted to your beauty."

"No one." Response to the invocation, Guinevere chanted the words.

"Then why oh why," burst out Lannie with sudden anguish, "do you cheat upon me in a corner until only the worst in Blondie can meet the depraved in you, and both must wallow in stinkheat?"

Marvel of anger, Guinevere's nose turned red. "Leave me alone," she said raucously, "I got to think of the future."

"There is no future," Lannie told her. She caught Guinevere by the arms. "It is shameful to entice him and worse that he forgets himself."

"Leave me alone."

"It can't be true that you and he really plan . . . ? Oh, but that is impossible!" she cried aloud, hands at her temple. "No,

259

listen"—and now her hands fluttered to Guinevere's cheek— "there must be honor in punishing the other. Justice must be done I tell you, and not profit."

"We've got our plans to worry about," Guinevere muttered.

"Oh, no, the evil state," Lannie rambled, "has beauty because it is so strong. But my friend must not leave them or it means that he is . . frightened of what is to come, and I was so certain that they were so strong." She collected herself. "Oh, he will take you away from me, and you don't care. Not even you will they allow me."

What Guinevere would do I could hardly imagine. Anger swelled in her face until it bulged her eyes, and yet she might as easily have given herself to Lannie's arms. "Why don't any of you ever leave me alone?" she blurted out for still another time.

Monina made the decision. Motionless on the floor since Lannie had entered, her tiny fists frozen at her side, head cocked rigidly in the straining attitude of a foreigner who would overhear a conversation and is baffled by his equipment, she was nonetheless an audience for all that passed. Words may go by and the sense be retained. Though the child remained seated, she was no longer silent.

"Mommie hate you," she whispered, "Mommie hate you." And hardly moving, her back curled, her eyes distended, she spat at Lannie with the intense venom of a cat.

"Monina!" Guinevere shrieked.

"You kissed her. You kissed her." Monina began to cry. And turning on her mother, she struck a blow. "Mommie will die."

Guinevere blanched at the child's words. "You keep quiet," she bawled. But when Lannie attempted to touch her cheek again, Guinevere threw her off with a shudder of revulsion. It must have burned Lannie's fingers.

"Oh," Guinevere moaned in her fishwife voice. "Oh, I'll go nuts."

"Stop that," Lannie snapped. We had completed the circle.

If Guinevere muttered, "Oh, I don't know, I don't know," it was only to furnish momentum. A second later she turned to Lannie and said, "Look, girlie, you better leave."

"Leave?" Lannie repeated.

"I don't know what to do," Guinevere protested, "I don't know what to think, maybe it was wrong to do what we did, oh brother, I don't know if I can get it out of my head. Just go, fellow," she begged at Lannie. "If we had a good time once, well I can always say I tried everything. . . ." And the last sentence rolled out with a swagger.

Did Lannie bear defeat well, or did she sup on it with nearly all her heart? "All right, I'll leave," she said, a faint smile upon her face. She moved toward the door, Monina watching her with intense suspicion. Lannie halted, fumbled through her purse in characteristic distress, and came up at last with her hand crushing a few dollar bills. "Do you know what I shall do with this?" she asked of me.

I made a meaningless motion in answer.

"I'm going out to buy a can of dark dark paint, for there is something I must cover. The little mouse who came to me and said he was Jesus will leave me alone no longer. This morning I found his hole, and once I have the paint I'll cover it, and he will die." She said this with resignation. "I had hopes for him, but this"— she waved her hand benignly about the room— "has made me realize that there is small future for such a mouse." She closed the door carefully behind her.

"Oh, Jesus," Guinevere declared. But moving about the room to empty an ashtray into a basket, straightening the corner of the rug, she was also settling herself.

"It's my fault," she announced with her back to me, and then immediately burst into laughter. "How I can send them away." The laughter exhausted, she was yanking at her hair again in distress. "Christmas, you tell me, why did I tell her to go?"

"She frightened you," I suggested.

I aimed too hard and stabbed the air. Guinevere shrugged and pointed to Monina. "It's your fault, that's what it is. Why can't you give me a moment's peace?" Monina took it like a puppy, smiling from ear to ear, her eyes shining.

"You know, all kidding aside," Guinevere told me, and she would brush it thus away, "that Lannie is quite a character. She's a very wonderful and strange girl." Guinevere delivered her last remark as though it were a manufactured article she sold across a counter. "Wonderful and strange," she repeated.

"Exactly," I said.

"No, there's something about her. I'll tell you the truth, Lovett, she does me good. I don't know, maybe I am that way . . . she makes me feel like I haven't felt in years." Secure now, Guinevere could become the captive of what she said. "You know, I believe in happy endings. I love her, I guess." And for the moment she was in love.

"Fine."

Only for a moment, however. She chuckled. "Boy, I got to admit it, that dame does have a line on her. I used to think I could hold up my end in a conversation, but your friend Miss Madison makes me look tongue-tied." She tossed this off so casually that I might have wondered if I had ever seen them together.

"My friend?"

"Yeah." Once again I could be charmed by Guinevere's powers of recuperation. "Don't think I don't know what's gone on between you and her. From what I heard your ears ought to burn." She shook her head. "I used to think it was a compliment you went for me, but I should have known. You'd chase anything." And in a crude burlesque of Lannie, she crooned,

262

"Oh, I don't know what I'll do, I'm sooo wild about you." In chorus, Monina laughed with her.

"Ah-huh," Guinevere said, "you like that, don't you?"

Monina nodded, roaring indecently, her baby cheeks quivering with mirth adequate for a middle-aged woman. "You're a devil," Guinevere said to her.

That way I left them.

TWENTY-EIGHT

"**A** FELLOW has to ask it of himself because there are so many problems," Hollingsworth was saying. "You know, we have courses now, and some of them in very abstruse subjects I can tell you. To be a good man in the organization a knowledge of the psychological is essential." With that he had finished cutting his nails, the product deposited neatly on the flap of an envelope which he kept to the left of him on the desk as though in opposition to the other envelope to his right, also open, which contained the shavings of three pencils he had carefully sharpened at the beginning of the interview. So he sat, the lamp behind him shining over his head into the eyes of McLeod, the envelopes serving as balance pans for the justice he would dispense.

"I've considered your allegations very carefully," Hollingsworth was continuing, "but one gets to wondering what the psychological part of it is." In reproduction of a gesture which had once belonged to McLeod, Hollingsworth touched his finger tips together lightly, judiciously. "It's part of a case I would say," he offered mildly, and hawked his throat. "I wonder if you would object to my just thinking aloud for a little while?"

Before there could be an answer, Lannie had interrupted. "I have a question," she said in a low voice.

"Not now," Hollingsworth snapped.

"No, but I. . ." she began.

"I said, 'Not now.'" Reaching across the desk he lit a cigarette for McLeod. "Here is the way I put it to myself," he said thoughtfully. "We have a fellow who one could call intelligent like yourself, and yet I must say it, one can't help being struck by the idea that he acts like a fool. Now, the last thing I want to do is to be offensive"—Hollingsworth radiated geniality—"but still there's not an awful lot he does which makes sense."

"Would you care to specify?" McLeod slumped in his chair, the top of his head barely visible, his long legs propped for support against the table. Arms hanging at his side, his finger tips must have trailed the floor. He might have appeared wholly patient, wholly passive, if it were not so evident that the glare of the lamp had begun to affect him.

"Let's look at it. It seems to me that for something to make sense, there's got to be a balance; you know one side has to weigh as much as the other."

"No balance here?"

Again the finger tips touched. "Not much, a fellow would have to say." Hollingsworth separated his hands, then pressed them lightly against the table. "In one of the courses we were instructed in, there was a great deal about what we called the psychology of the Bolshevists, and in it we were taught that these fellows thought they could change the history of the world, and naturally like everybody else they thought they were doing it for world betterment. Now, to take the fellow we been talking about all this time, he undoubtedly reasoned that way, and so everything he did there was a purpose to it. And no matter how terrible we might think those things would be, world betterment was the idea. So he could go ahead and do all that." Abruptly, Hollingsworth chuckled. "Only the poor fellow decided he was wrong, and so he quit them. What is his psychology now?"

"You want me to answer?"

"I'll go on, thank you. He feels very bad we can suppose. Here are all those terrible things he's done, and how can he change all that? Well, first of all he goes to work for the people I represent, and that doesn't pan out so well, now does it? He feels even worse, and so he has to take something to make up for it, and that he does, and then here he is now."

"Except for his theoretical work."

"Yes, I'm so glad you mentioned that. Except for his theoretical work." Hollingsworth reached deftly into his brief case, and deposited a pile of mimeographed pamphlets on the table. "We have here the sum total of the said fellow's work. I can enumerate all the categories of subjects treated, but why bore you with something you know already? The thing that's more interesting is that out of all these articles and pamphlets we've made a list of the circulation, and the one that was read by the most people numbers five hundred readers." He fanned them out upon the desk, and touched his finger to one and then another as though he were examining samples. "This one had a hundred and fifty readers; this one, two hundred twenty-five; this one, seventy-five; this one, fifty." Hollingsworth yawned. "These figures are all in round numbers, of course."

"What point do you make?" McLeod asked.

"Well, it's very difficult for me to understand," Hollingsworth began. Before he could continue, however, Lannie had clutched a page from one of the papers, and read the title. She put it down. "You didn't write this," she said to McLeod in a strangled voice.

He nodded.

"No, he didn't write it," Lannie was on her feet now. "It's you he's swindling, you!" she screeched at Hollingsworth.

"He wrote it," Hollingsworth said quietly, studying her outburst.

266

"It's impossible," she cried, and now she was pleading for herself. "Contradictions and class relations in the land across the sea, as he puts it. Yes, he may have written it, his hand, his ink, and so you're convinced, but all the while he was writing he laughed because he never believed a word of it."

Hollingsworth merely stared at her, his silence weighing upon her speech until the effect cumulative, she was quiet at last. "I told you," he said, clearing his throat, "that there would be twists and turns."

"You're wrong," she managed to blurt out.

"Very well, then, I'm wrong," he said, and unable to restrain himself, began to laugh at her. "Yes, I'm sure wrong."

She was back in her seat, but the chair gave small comfort. Her body pressed against the wood, her stained fingers plucked cuticle from her ragged nails, and her poor soft lips fluttered one against the other. "I . . ." she started to say.

"Be quiet now," Hollingsworth said. With evident distaste he rearranged the papers she had strewn and consulted his notes.

"Applying statistical methods," he informed McLeod, "a fellow can see that the average circulation of these pamphlets is one hundred and ninety-eight point three people per unit of political propaganda."

McLeod said wryly, "I'd often wondered what it was."

"This is the point I've been trying to make," Hollingsworth went on. "A fellow who has as many things to keep him up at night as the gentleman we've been discussing, seems to think that to balance it out, all he has to do is to write these articles. I suppose he's trying to make the plus equal the minus. But one is forced to think this fellow in question has a very interesting arithmetic. Because the way I figure it is that he's down about a million, and every one of these things is worth maybe ten off the score."

"The difference between you and me," McLeod said, "is

that I depend upon potentiality. Who are you to state that in a decade there will be no possibility for new revolutionary ferments?"

"Assess the plus and minus," Hollingsworth intoned.

"There is still the future. And if there will be a revolutionary situation and revolutionaries of stature, then it is of the utmost importance the lessons of the last revolution be learned." He sat there blinking his eyes slowly into the glare of the light bulb, while across the tight skin of his face, steadily, involuntarily, a tremor rippled through the flat muscle of his cheek. "Why do you insist?" he asked finally, querulously.

"Because you want to influence people," Hollingsworth said shortly. "And when people want to influence people, then that falls into the area of my occupation." He sighed heavily. "And I am obliged to question your qualifications. For example would you say that the gentleman mentioned was in complete possession of all faculties at the time he was so active in said and aforementioned Mediterranean country?"

"What do you mean by faculties?"

"There's a better answer than that," Hollingsworth suggested. "Take the time he goes with the revolver in his pocket to see his old political friend. Can you say he found no enjoyment at all in the events of the evening?"

"None."

Hollingsworth made a deprecatory sound with his tongue. "You're an intelligent fellow. Would anybody feel bad for all of four or five hours, talking to somebody, knowing he's going to kill him?

"I don't know any more."

"No pleasure at all?"

McLeod raised a hand to his temple. "How can I remember?"

"In other words, some pleasure. That's looked down upon,

268

isn't it?" Hollingsworth nodded to answer his own question. "The fellow we're considering has an unhealthy psychological part to him one is forced to conclude."

"All right."

"This unhealthy part affects all his actions. An eminent specialist in these matters told me so. We think we have an idea just cause it's an idea, but the truth is we have such and such an idea because we want it so."

"All right," McLeod said tonelessly.

"One is forced to conclude politics is the bunk and so are opinions."

"All right."

"Then," Hollingsworth continued rigorously, "how can a fellow pretend to act for the future?"

"All right, all right. All right," McLeod said.

Hollingsworth adjusted the lamp so it shone equitably between them. In a gentle voice, he continued. "Now, unlike most people, I don't look down on such a fellow. We all have our different characters, and that's true. It's just that we mustn't be stubborn. You've been an unhappy man all your life, and you didn't want to admit it was your own fault. So you blame it on society, as you call it. That isn't necessary. You could have had a good time, you could still have a good time if you'd realize that everybody is like you, and so it's pointless to work for the future." His hand strayed over the desk. He might have been caressing the wood. "More modesty. We ain't equipped to deal with big things. If this fellow came to me and asked my advice, I would take him aside and let him know that if he gives up the pursuits of vanity, and acts like everybody else, he'd get along better. Cause we never know what's deep down inside us"—Hollingsworth tapped his chest—"and it plays tricks. I don't give two cents for all your papers. A good-time Charley, that's myself, and that's why I'm smarter than the lot of you." His pale face had become flushed. "You can shove theory," he said suddenly. "Respect your father and mother."

"He's absolutely right," Lannie exclaimed. "But then he isn't. I mean. . ." she finished lamely, jerkily, the outburst of her private thought amputated as she heard her voice. And flushing at her inability to express what she would say, she continued to stare at her hands, and in a morose energy pulled cuticle from her nail.

McLeod smiled wanly.

"Have you got a cigarette?" he asked. "It seems I'm out of them."

"I'd be delighted," Hollingsworth said, furnishing tobacco and flame in what was almost a single gesture.

"Would you call yourself a realist?" McLeod asked almost dreamily.

"That's the word a fellow would employ for me."

"Then, philosophically speaking, you believe in a real world."

"More words," Hollingsworth sighed. "I'll say yes."

"A world which exists separately from ourselves."

"Oh, yes, that was what I wanted to say."

"You didn't," McLeod told him. "I want to point out to you that no one may be disqualified from coming close to a knowledge of the relations of such a world. One's psychological warp, upon which you harp so greedily, may be precisely the peculiar lens necessary to see those relations most clearly."

"You're trying to confuse me," Hollingsworth said.

McLeod was silent for almost a minute, and as if the brief foray had encouraged him by its success, he looked up at last with a grin. "I would like to make a speech in my defense."

"No." Hollingsworth almost stood up. "We've gotten nowhere today, and none of the practical issues have been decided. You don't need a speech."

270

"I insist upon my right."

"First you must fulfill conditions."

The muscle quivering, the eye blinking, McLeod held up his hand and watched it tremble independently of himself. "I am prepared to," he said. "But I want to know whether it goes to you directly or to your organization?"

"I haven't made up my mind," Hollingsworth said, "but that shouldn't affect you. You have to be willing to concede either way, or no speech."

"Either way," McLeod said with a shrug. "May I proceed?"

Hollingsworth nodded.

"You know," McLeod said, "there was a time when I thought the last speech I might make would begin in quite another way. Once, I even composed it. 'Citizen comrades,' I began, 'there seems small justification possible that a renegade like myself, a wrecking dog of the lowest litter should even open his mouth.'" McLeod's mouth opened in a soundless laugh.

"One of the small benefits I can permit myself is to spend no time apologizing for my past. It is what it is, and in the time permitted me here, I should prefer to indulge in the only meaningful defense, to transmit the intellectual conclusions of my life, and thus give dignity to my experience. I shall not treat the past as personal history, and I will attempt to delineate what I believe to be the future, for it is only as ideas are transmitted to someone else that they attain existence."

Hollingsworth interrupted him. "You talk like a fellow who doesn't think he's going to live long."

"You misunderstand. I speak metaphorically."

"All I care about is that you concede," Hollingsworth said sullenly.

"I told you I would. Now, may I go ahead?"

"Who are you making this speech for?" Hollingsworth asked peevishly. "Me? Miss Madison?" His eyes met mine, and he shrugged. "Well, if you think it's worth your waste of time, go right ahead, but I don't hold the high opinion of your friend that you seem to." He looked away and tapped his fingers. "Go ahead, make your speech," he said in what was almost a woman-ish voice.

TWENTY-NINE

" MAY I begin," McLeod asked rhetorically, "by discussing the argument of the sophisticated apologist? When I discover myself in a mood of assessment, I'm often struck by the number of brothers I once had, and how different are the roads we've taken. Yet of them all, the apologist is the only one who flourishes today. You might even say he has a vogue.

"This gentleman admits everything. He will agree that state capitalism is not to be confused with socialism; he will even grant, although his language will differ, that the new society is not without privilege. But, look, McLeod, he is always in a rush to tell me, it is time to take an accounting. And he will shake his head wisely. The revolution has failed to come. The proletariat has never gained political consciousness in sufficient degree. It is very doubtful they ever will. What is important, says the apologist, is that civilization be saved and human life not cease. The problem of our generation is not to make a revolution, nor is it to bewail standardization, militarization, and all the trends which you and I have found distasteful. We must agree, if we are historians, that equality has not existed since primitive man, and freedom has occurred only in the context of wealth and leisure. Probably that is the only way it may ever appear. It is a luxury, and equality is a dream. What we must accept today is, precisely, standardization, even the temporary abdication of the best in human potentiality. Periods like ours will pass. The problem for today is to end the crippling conflicts of the economic system. You see, McLeod, my mythical brother is always declaiming, you have never understood anything at all. Your problems are not the problems of the world. Bellies must be fed in Africa and for that production must follow a world plan. We have overestimated human nature. It is impossible for such a plan to provide the equality of socialism, but what matter? It's the mass who must be fed and in an orderly fashion or the world is destroyed. Our problem is not to end exploitation but to resolve contradictions in the economic structure. Indeed, we may have been wrong all the time, and the bourgeoisie have been right. Man is only capable of founding societies based on privilege and inequality.

"As I have said," McLeod went on, "the apologist admits everything. It is true, he tells me, there may be a war, but it is also true it may be avoided. You cannot know, McLeod. History is unpredictable. How can you say that war must come definitely? But even if it should come, there is no reason to suppose that everything is lost. We find moderation in everything, even in war, and after all, no matter what the cost, no matter how severe, one side finally will win and will control the world. Permanent peace will then be possible. The winners will administer the spoils of exploitation in a rational manner. Why shouldn't they? All the contradictions will have been resolved."

Hollingsworth seemed interested. "You know, if you don't mind my saying so," he interrupted, "I think that's been very well put. I'm not a political fellow, although I've always considered myself sort of liberal, but it's often occurred to me, if I think on those lines, that it's real democracy if you can make the stupid people happy, cause if you're not stupid you're never happy anyway. Now, I know you'd say," he murmured as

274

McLeod began to frown, "that the stupid can't be happy because they're, if I may use your word, swindled, but it seems to me that people don't mind being swindled if only they're told the opposite. It's when you tell them they're being swindled that they can't stand it." Hollingsworth giggled. "You know, I've been talking too much." A quick look at his watch. "I wonder if your remarks could be more brief?"

McLeod looked at Hollingsworth almost without recognition. His eyes knitted together to form a vertical line between, and with a sigh, as though to hew to the line of the argument were even more demanding upon himself than upon us, he reached into his pocket and withdrew a pack of small papers upon which he had scribbled some notes.

"The plausibility of the apologist's argument depends upon a logic which is as attractive as it is superficial. Everything he said was complete nonsense." This was worth a pause. "It may be noted that the apologist was an abstract conception. In life, since he claims to be a realist, he finds himself inevitably espousing the cause of one side or the other. He can hardly argue for both. Need I add that he hopes the bloc for which he pleads will win in the war which is to come. And if one asks him what will happen if the other side wins, he will answer: disaster, complete disaster. So, by adding two separate halves of the truth, one arrives at the conclusion."

For the first time McLeod's voice showed some animation. He remained still seated formally in his chair, hands before him on the table to examine the notes, his spectacles set resolutely upon his nose, but in completing the introduction he seemed to have purged his fatigue. "I need hardly depend, however, upon such legerdemain. I prefer to answer more fully. My political formulations are based on the thesis that war is inevitable, and I think it is reasonable to assert that if either of the two powers is unable to solve its economic problems without going to war, it

275

must follow that war will come. But what if both of the Colossi suffer such contradictions? *A fortiori,* the inevitability of war receives its double guarantee.

"Proper analysis must be virtually exhaustive. I have been reminded that my time is not without limit and so I will confine my remarks to assertions. The situation of the bloc which may be called 'monopoly capitalism' is critical." McLeod went on to repeat what I had already analyzed for myself. The productive capacity of monopoly had become so tremendous, its investment in machinery so great in comparison to the labor force it could exploit, that only the opening of the entire world market could solve its search for investment and profit even temporarily. "Those backward areas of the globe so necessary to monopoly cannot be lost," McLeod droned. "Without them, monopoly cannot continue its operations on an adequate scale, without them there is no choice but to engage in the production of armaments or to suffer economic collapse. Yet those same backward regions, finding their own development to capitalism blocked by monopoly, whose interest it is to keep them retarded, are obliged to move at one historic bound from feudalism to state capitalism. Thus, half the world is now closed to monopoly, and the other half, still nominally in its possession, has moved a long way on the road to nationalization.

"The crisis of the major state capitalist power is even graver. Upon the mountains of rhetoric which have been deposited, it is not my intention to add more than a stone. I wish merely to underline the notion that socialism does not come about by an act of will. It should be axiomatic that, where conditions do not exist which make it possible to raise the standard of living, a socialist revolution can only degenerate into its opposite, and when the events of 1917 failed to induce similar proletarian uprisings in the countries of the West, the revolution was doomed. Surrounded by enemies, forced into the herculean labor of raising production by the bootstrap, all possibility for so-

276

cialism was lost in the necessity for survival. The portion of the economy devoted to goods and services for the mass of people had to be limited. The more production which went into the creation of the tools, elements, and articles making possible further production, the less could be provided for human consumption. Such a project of expanding one's industrial capacity has potential enrichment only if it is not necessary to continue it too long. For, mark you, the results. If benefits do not follow deprivation, the proletariat diminishes its rate of productivity. A man is capable of participating efficiently in the modern industrial process, with all its demands for skill, intelligence, and intense labor, only if there is a reward possible, to wit an adequate scale of living and the promise of an improved future. Deprived of the minimum of comfort and hope, workmanship must degenerate. Little balm for the laborer if factories swallow the earth, when they fail to provide him with creature comfort, and less balm for the bureaucrat when the failure to produce what is socially possible becomes increasingly more serious.

"Do you find this hard to follow, Leroy?" McLeod interjected suddenly. Hollingsworth answered by yawning in his face.

"Witness the problem the bureaucrats of state capitalism must face. If they are to retain their power and privilege, there is a limit beyond which they cannot depress the standard of living or they are left only with slave labor and the complete deterioration of their economy. Yet the working class can be neither coerced nor driven to begin to match the productivity of monopoly. Their morale is too low. Only the adrenalin of the last war with the incentive to fight against a foreign invader could solve that problem temporarily. Therefore, no matter how they suffered in that war, no matter how the mass may want peace, peace is impossible.

"The inescapable corollary is that state capitalism as a social organism has lost hope in its own ability to improve productivity. It must now depend upon seizing new countries, stripping them of their wealth, and converting their economy to war. In short, plunder. Alas for the project, this plunder is a flask which contains no bottom. The wealth newly acquired must be immediately converted into armament, the living standard fails to rise, and the process must be repeated. Thus, each bloc from its own necessity to survive prepares for war. The process is irreversible.

"It is a war fought by two different exploitative systems, a system vigorous in the fever of death, and another monstrous in the swelling of anemia. One doesn't predict the time precisely, but regardless of the temporary flux of military situation, it is a war which ends as a conflict between two virtually identical forms of exploitation. State capitalism occupies the historical seat. The state, the sole exploiter capable of supporting the ultra war economy and the regimentation of the proletariat, absorbs monopoly either peaceably or by a short internal conflict. There is no alternative. The historical imperative is to reduce to the minimum the production of consumer goods in order to expand the critical needs for armament. Such a change occurs against the background of military losses and military destruction. To a people who depended upon commodities as the opium which gave meaning to their lives, the last of the luxuries is inexorably wiped from the board. Problems permitting of only a single solution follow upon this in quick order. More money than goods to buy, an inflation of vast proportions can be prevented only if wages are reduced and exploitation increased. The result is a diminishment of the will to work and a drop in the velocity of industrial performance. Discontent is everywhere. The first examples of random sabotage, motivated by no more than brute exasperation, begin to multiply. The police system which had been already expanded at the moment of entering the war, when hundreds of thousands of people politically suspect had to be found and imprisoned, now receives a new levy. The police are everywhere, within the unions, in the military, at the seats of government power; they have almost reached the point where they co-exist with all of society. State profit and state surveillance, state-enforced poverty and state-endowed wealth. The bureaucrat drives his limousine and he is the only one. Poor proletariat. Cheated still another time. They are fed the turnips their masters would have them become."

McLeod was speaking in a mournful cadence, so slow, so spaced, so sad that emotion was betrayed by irony and he was almost mocking himself. Across the desk Hollingsworth sat in the perfect pose of boredom, one arm supporting the elbow of the other while with his free hand he picked languidly at his nose, much as if he lay upon a couch and plucked grapes from a bowl. Lannie seemed to have fallen asleep, or was she in coma? Her legs stretched out before her, breath rattled from her throat, and her eyes, pressed tightly closed, twitched with the anxiety of the hand that holds a lizard.

"Very well," McLeod sighed. "The process takes surprisingly little time. Nations which come late to a new organization of society seldom take as long to trace the history of their predecessors. Moreover, the character of economic production must undergo so profound a change that little will remain of the bastard civilization we now possess. Consider it carefully. For the first time in history, the intent of society will be to produce wholly for death, and men will be kept alive merely to further that aim. Through the worst excesses and inequities of every culture which has preceded us, the natural function of economy was to produce for life. Even capitalism in its search for profit assumed automatically that life and profit were compatible. Perhaps a little less life and a little more profit, but nonetheless the body of man's production served to keep him alive. In the advanced stages of state capitalism this natural function must be discarded. Hereafter the aim of society is no longer to keep its members alive, but quite the contrary, the question is how to dispose of them. With your permission"—a nod at Hollingsworth—"I should like to illustrate my remarks."

"Do as you wish," Hollingsworth said sullenly.

"The factor never to be forgotten is that the economic crisis is now permanent. If the parasitical layers of capitalism have been destroyed, they are replaced by the elephantiasis of the bureaucracy. From that moment the rate of production is never again capable of steady increase. The search begins for methods to stimulate it. State competition becomes substituted, and artificial campaigns between state corporations, accompanied by all the machinery of propaganda, make exhaustive efforts to match the requirements of armament. Piecework reappears. Such a process is narcotic. The injection must become progressively more intense, until the price for losing a competition becomes the neck of a bureaucrat. The first stage of cannibalism has been reached, and the bureaucracy finds itself obliged to dispose of the same personnel it needs so desperately. They are a class which comes to power at the very moment they are in the act of destroying themselves."

Hollingsworth was giving his attention once more. There was a little sore at the corner of his mouth and his tongue came out to explore it, moistened the lesion and then wet his lips.

"You must realize," McLeod said to him, "that these gentlemen are subject to the most extraordinary pressures. They dare not commit an action which is against the interests of the state, yet the interests of that body change constantly; they are terrified of the price for error and would content themselves with the minimum of initiative, yet extraordinary efforts are constantly demanded of them. They are not able to consider their own needs before their duty. There is a conflict between their desire for a private life and their public and party obligation. They function for the collectivity and the most terrible greeds for personal enrichment begin to torment them. Psychologically, the check must at last be paid. The bureaucrat becomes driven to express his personality through anti-social action." Here, Mc-

280

Leod stopped, and he and Hollingsworth stared at one another, as if the one had said too much and the other had listened too long.

"I follow you, yes I do," Hollingsworth whispered, his tongue worrying the lesion.

"They become obliged," McLeod said hoarsely, resolved I thought to mutilate every retreat, "obliged to commit some act against the state. Its content matters not. It suffices only if it is illogical, unfounded, and disastrous for them. You see they have lost the sense of their own identity, and if it has been the state which began to devour them, they end by collaborating with the process.

"But let me waste no grief for those gentlemen. They are merely a parallel to the destruction between armies and within economies. War has become the only method of accumulation, and by the orchestration of patriotism's mad opera that pace of manufacture which insists upon diminishing may be resuscitated for its brief time. Yet what is one to do? As the strength of the working class is progressively exhausted, the quality and the rate of work continue to diminish. No longer will any measures but the most drastic be effective. The armory of compulsion must be employed. Forced labor appears, and since even hell must have its stages, at the end of forced labor is the concentration camp."

"The gas chamber," Lannie said loudly. She might have been awakening from a dream.

"The concentration camp," McLeod repeated. "And its mate, the secret city, where new weapons of more extraordinary capacity for destruction are developed. These phenomena accompany the most significant phenomenon of all—the degeneration of knowledge. In the past our collective understanding was limited only by the capacities of the human mind; now it is to be restricted by the social organism whose necessity is to maintain ignorance of the whole. Thus, millions will be destroyed in the concentration camps while a few miles away people will conduct the routine of their lives and know nothing but the suspicion of rumor.

"The techniques of the last war provide only a hint of what is to come. On a quasi-systematic basis an attempt was made to eliminate that portion of the population which was incapable of producing for the economy. But the lines were blurred by religious and political categories. As the next war progresses it will become even more impossible to maintain the luxury of nonproducers. They will have become intolerable for society. The aged and the children will be killed, but such selection will serve as a beginning rather than an end. For the organ has been created, it is a part of the social structure, and may be dismantled no more than the state. If Moloch is not fed, the last stage of hell will vanish, and with it, the apparatus of hell. So, year by year, the useless millions are to be eliminated, until in the final crowning of contradiction, even the producers will go into the machine. Stability depends upon it."

McLeod drew his breath. "War is permanent and the last argument of the apologist is no better than the first. If one bloc should vanquish the other, it will find itself almost totally impoverished. It will repeat at even a lower level the necessity to wage war which now besets the sole representative in the world today of state capitalism. Its impoverishment enormous, the winner will find it impossible to set up the rational exploitation which could solve his problems. Instead, he must exploit as extravagantly as he dares not only the vanquished but his former allies as well. His demands must be so great in relation to what is left that a new military situation develops before the last has ceased. The war begins again with a new alignment of forces, and to the accompaniment of famine and civil war, the deterioration continues until we are faced with mankind in barbary."

"Is the speech over?" Hollingsworth cried.

"So you come soon to power," McLeod said quietly, "but you have merely inherited the crisis, and yours is the profit of cancer."

"Finish!" Hollingsworth commanded.

Like caps attached to the same cord, each detonation induced the next, until abruptly the air was clear. "I am obliged to discuss the perspective for socialism," McLeod said in a slow voice. "It will take still a few more minutes and then I will be done."

Hollingsworth hitched himself back in his seat. "I am not here to be insulted. Your remarks must be indirect."

"There is a choice to reverse the process I have outlined. It occupies no prominence at present, and yet it is all we have. I speak of that body of ideas and that program which may loosely be called revolutionary socialism. It conceives of a society where the multitude own and control the means of production in opposition to what exists everywhere today. It holds the true conception of equality where each works according to his ability and each is supplied according to his needs. It views the end of exploitation and the beginning of justice. It is the antithesis of all I have predicted.

"But how may it come about? Here we arrive at what is the knot of history. We assumed for far too long that socialism was inevitable and the error has reduced us to impotence. Socialism is inevitable only if there will be a civilization. What we have never considered is the condition that there would not be. For socialism as I have remarked is not a passive rag to be cut to shape by the politician's scissor. It depends upon the potentiality of the human, and that is an open question, impossible to determine philosophically. Well may it be that men in sufficient numbers and with sufficient passion and consciousness to create such a world will never exist. If they do not, however, then the human condition is incapable of alleviation, and we can only witness for a century at least and perhaps forever the disappearance of all we have created.

"I speak in the most abstract and general terms and that explains little. We face today a situation which is almost hopeless. The splinters and fragments of revolutionary socialism are scattered, shards of a black time, and the world proletariat, inert and in historic stupor, belongs almost completely to one bloc or the other. Beyond the horizon, in the most backward continent on earth, revolutionary ferments are breeding, and the pity is that they are already dominated by the representatives of state capitalism. With the war little is calculated to improve. It is likely that the degeneration of humanity will occur even more rapidly than the deterioration of the state, and by the time the Colossi will have butchered each other to the size of a hundred Lilliputs, it may not be considered probable that revolutionary socialism will play a prominent part in the civil wars to follow. Certainly the destruction of the greater portion of the productive capacity of the world will be an almost insurmountable problem. The hope is that the state deteriorates more rapidly than the people, and in counter to the fantastic atrocities and inequalities of state capitalism, there will remain in the masses strength and conviction to deal with it. Such a condition will produce, I believe, its revolutionary consciousness. If once within our time the locomotives of history were running, and in contrast to the ten years which passed like a day, there was the day which was the equivalent of ten years, then the Lenin of tomorrow may be presented with a century in an hour. It is my hope that a revolutionary determination, the like of which has never been seen before will sweep the earth, and these theses, difficult, recondite, and often incomprehensible, will match the experience of even the most inarticulate peasant, so that the socialist theorist will once again find language to reach the many.

"That there be theorists at such a time is of incalculable importance. The culture of a revolutionary socialist is not created in a day, and not too many of us will be alive. Yet there must be some to participate, for revolutions are the periods of history when individuals count most. It is not a question of a party now, nor recruiting drives, nor attempts to match the propaganda of the blast furnace with the light of our candle. It is the need to study, it is the obligation to influence those few we may, and if some nucleus of us rides out of the storm, we shall advance to the front of any revolutionary wave, for we alone shall have the experience and the insight so vital for the period. Then we shall be the only ones capable of occupying the historical stage.

"The problems we shall face. A specter will haunt us and fittingly so. The ghost of that other revolution will be always with us. For if we forget, if we ever suppose that the party or parties which form can answer everything, then our action and our suffering as well as the sacrifice and determination of millions of men and women may again be lost. There is no dogma we can carry with us, no legal machinery we can invoke. There are only two principles, freedom and equality, and without them we are nothing. The absence of the one involves obligatorily the corruption of the other, and this is the lesson which must be learned. There will be crises if we are resolute; there will be voices who speak who would be better silent, there will be idle machines and men who refuse to work, there will be disruption and inefficiency, but if the mass and we cannot surmount that, if we cannot find the means to guarantee the freedom of all and their equality, then the revolution shall be lost again, and the potentiality of man will not have proven equal to the challenge.

"But, if we succeed, what a period will follow! I am not a prophet dreaming of heaven, I do not assume that we leap at a bound from hell to Arcady. At last there will be, however, a soil in which man may play out his drama. It will be a time of the most extraordinary contrasts, a time of despair as well as of hope, a moment when each injustice which is ended may birth another, one we cannot conceive as yet. There is so little we know about ourselves, our historical life has been spent in battling nature and each other. This will be the opportunity to discover of what we are capable and what we shall never achieve. We may even learn if we can attain a rational life or if we are condemned to remain forever the most tragic of the animals. It will be the first time in history that man freed of hostile environment shall be able to discover his real dilemmas and real fulfillment if there is any. How I wish I could see the day. It would be so much more interesting than our own."

He had come forward in his chair, his face animated. He had forgotten himself and where he was, and for an instant the future might have opened before him with its promise to a youth of spring, adventure, and reward. He blinked his eyes slowly, as if this image were the most difficult to capture and the most quickly lost.

Hollingsworth spoke with ferocity. "You indulge yourself. Hear, hear!" and he clapped his hands. "You're an old man and you indulge yourself."

McLeod's speech ended. The lines came back to his face, the twitch regained its rhythm, and his voice grew dull. "I have been talking a long time," he said in answer.

"A long time?" Hollingsworth was shrill. "You wasted a fellow's patience. And for what? All that abuse. You talk about this high-and-mighty project, and then you talk about the next one. If I didn't understand the value of politeness . . ." He cut himself short. "Would you say," he asked in a penetrating voice, "that a fellow like yourself with all the things you've done, would you say that such a fellow isn't a little tired?"

Apparently McLeod did not trust himself to speak. Slowly his head nodded forward and back.

"You think such a fellow is energetic enough to live through all he says is going to happen? And then at the end of it he's

286

going to make a big revolutionary spiel? You're just like an old thing," Hollingsworth said furiously. "Babble, babble, babble about how sweet it used to be. Only you make it the future."

Stony fruit to stony palate, McLeod sucked upon his knuckle, resting motionless but for the action of his lips, so that he might have been a statue, the marble curved upon itself. Deprived of nourishment through the years it was only now his mouth could water.

"And if you ever did live to such a time," Hollingsworth continued, "and the revolutionaries could get together, what would you do there? We checked up on you pretty thoroughly. You don't have any contact with anybody now, and for good reason. Even those pieces of paper you write. You mail them anonymously to people you think might be interested. You're ashamed of yourself," Hollingsworth shouted. "You think you're so superior, you still look down on me. But I at least talk to you. Those wonderful revolutionaries of yours—why if what you say comes to pass, they won't have anything to do with you. You're beyond the pale. Don't forget your record. Don't ever forget that."

"Nor will you let me," McLeod said in a small voice. He removed his finger from his mouth and watched the light shining on the moistened skin. "It's true," he whispered. "What more do you want?"

"I want you to concede," Hollingsworth said.

"But I told you I would."

"Yes, and I know you. While you were talking you had the idea that maybe you wouldn't. And with me a bargain is a bargain. I hold you to it."

McLeod looked at his knuckle. "Is it to you, or to your department?"

"Oh, I'm ahead of you, don't worry about that," Hollingsworth said in the same furious tone. "Trying to frighten a fellow. You have the idea you can make a better deal at my office.

Well, you can't. I'm your best deal and . . you're to give it to me."

"I concede," McLeod sighed.

Lannie had begun to weep. "What are you doing?" she cried aloud, but I could not tell to whom she spoke.

"I suppose we must have a private conversation," Hollingsworth said. "It'll take time, won't it?" McLeod nodded. "Well, I don't mind so long as the bargain is kept."

Much as if he were revolted to look at Lannie or at me, McLeod said quietly, "Lovett, I'll have to ask you to leave the room."

"I don't want to leave," I said. "You can't give it to him."

Now, he did look at me, and his eyes were blank. "Ah, but there's not an alternative. You might as well go, Lovett."

Lannie had finished weeping. Her eyes dry, her face stiff, she stood up slowly and drifted toward the door.

"Oh, go now, go, will you!" Hollingsworth exclaimed with irritation.

So we went, Lannie and I, stood looking at each other in the gloomy silence of the attic hall, and then separated, she to her room, and I to mine. Behind us in the room, the battle over, the casualties counted, terms were being drawn.

And it was I who felt the shame.

THIRTY

I MUST have lain awake all that night, sometimes in darkness, sometimes—fear swelling each sound—with the lamp burning by my bed. And through the night the casual noise of the house and the city outside was repeated for was this the hundredth time? and yet, repetition or no, I shuddered with terror and undefined sorrow, as unashamedly miserable as a child in the immensity of an empty house.

Sometime during the night I heard them leave the room across the hall and walk silently down the stairs. Later, my flesh roused like water over which blows the wind, I thought I listened to someone sobbing, and from my solitude I was marooned in equal grief. Somewhere—was it in the distance or from one of the rooms in the house?—I could hear a baby crying against the wash of a drunken quarrel.

Each of them passed before me, magnified, exaggerated, conducting a monologue to which I was audience, justifying, condemning, pleading, merciless, until vertigo-spun, the night might have carried me in all its heat to a ship at equator. Lannie sang her songs, Hollingsworth giggled, and McLeod sucking at the mordant candy-drop he must always pouch in his cheek, said from his great distance, "Grieve not, m'bucko, for it's kismet, and that's the secret of it all."

And Guinevere holding Monina at arm's distance while the child pummeled the air and screamed in frustration that she could not wound her mother's flesh, delivered herself of a protest. "I'm a young woman, Lovett," and a young woman, Lovett, "I'd a gone off and eaten the hey nonny nonny. But there's the child you see, and I'd mug her to death, but she won't leave me."

So they danced, and the night opened its furnace, and my head burned.

I greeted the light of morning with all the sick, sore, and nausea-ridden appurtenances of a thundering drunk. The heat straddled my limbs and I wrestled my bedding; if the night were bad, the day promised little improvement. Had I conducted dialogues with them through the night, and had they sat up my bed? At least one I had to see, Lannie at least, and suffered the panic that a train had left and I had missed it by a minute. Yet after I dressed and descended the stairs, I found myself going back to the room again. There was my typewriter, and somehow I did not want to leave it there. Why I took it with me I hardly knew, but within the hour I had dropped it in a pawnshop and following my impulse to the end, the name I gave was not my own and the address I wrote was a street which did not exist. There was still the novel and that I put in an envelope and mailed it to my new name at the central post office. In a day or two, or perhaps a week, I would pick it up. These errands done, I felt it was possible to return to the house and visit Lannie.

Her door was unlatched and yielded before my knock to swing slowly open. I entered, and in crossing the threshold a curtain might have dropped, for I was returned to the night I had quit with such pain, and all of it was back upon me. Giggling from what I saw, shock tickled the sound from my throat. I was frozen where I stood. Someone had run amok.

For the room was dark. No sunlight entered, and the feeble

electric bulb one may foresee at perpetual night shone like a wan moon in the silence. The air was foul. Turpentine and pigment crossed odors with the stench of spilled liquor. Black paint was spattered everywhere, upon the carpet, the walls, even a puddle upon the floor.

Lannie had killed her mouse.

The windows were painted black. Up and down, cross and back, the brush strokes furious, effort discharged in spasm and her breath sobbing, she must have thrown it on like blood, relishing the drip and gore, grinding the handle upon the glass. In blots and swashes, thick wet coat upon thick wet coat, the windows reared their socketless eyes back to mine, and stood still wet, still wounded, their paint dripping the woodwork.

I saw Lannie then, sprawled morosely on the sofa, her face to the wall. She sat unmoving, not aware of myself nor of the door which had resounded to such knocking. I slammed it shut behind me with enough of a clatter to have started her from an opium sleep, but her senses were numbed; she turned to me with mild surprise as though I had muttered a soft word.

"Oh, hello, Mikey," she said, lethargy weighting her words. She elevated her chin languidly, exposing her head to the electric bulb.

She was hardly an attractive sight. "What happened to you?" I exclaimed.

"Did something happen?" she asked vaguely.

Her features were puffed and an ugly bruise purpled her cheek. She exhibited a lopsided smile, mouth swollen at the corner. "What happened?" I asked again.

Lannie stared past me vacantly, and I realized that she was fuddled. An empty bottle lay at her feet. With her toe she nudged it gently from side to side. "Is it morning yet?" she asked.

Drunk, she gave this once the impression of being sober. Exhaustion hung upon her and slowed her speech, made visible the slow rise and ebb of her breath. With what fury she had worked. Paint spattered her face and hair, and upon her chin was wiped a black smudge. "You know I feel as if in an hour or so I'll be able to sleep," she murmured.

"How did you get hurt?" I insisted.

She shrugged. "Hours ago, was it early this morning? I remember when he left I could not bear the sunlight coming. Before that it must be, he came down and brought this bottle. It was so kind of him, for he had taken the case he gave me once, and then up in his room, oh, he could not bear to be alone last night, so frightened in triumph and *vive* the worm, and he had to talk until every last suspicion I had ever known was more than true. He's so unworthy, and it's only a big man should commit a crime. So we drank and we talked and I told him all this and why he loves her, moxie I said to take your Jimmygirl for proxy, and he raised his hand and he did this to me. I suppose he felt that I would like it. And when he left I remembered the paint I had bought, I was crying in the store and the man said flat black miss? Then I went to work. The windows hated me." She stared up at the black glass. "It's still there, isn't it, oh that's silly, of course it's there, but somehow I had expected —her eyes faced mine—"that it would go like everything else. Oh, I shouldn't have painted it."

"He did it then."

"What difference does it make? Don't stand there so stupidly. Sit down. I'm tired. I don't want to look at you standing."

"He ought to pay for this," I said angrily.

She shook her head slowly. "You're very silly, Mikey. I don't mind that he struck me, for I owed him a debt. It was not you who came with the bottle, and I was so alone here." She watched the wall before her. I said nothing, and in a moment or two she continued, perhaps not knowing she had even paused. "How I adored her"—fingers caressing the bruise upon her cheek. "When I would see her coloring, the red hair and her pink flesh, baby bubbles in the fat, and for the first time in how long since the sugar itch was dead it was dead no more and it was myself a round honey in the heat, myself you hear, so that it became bubbles, baby, bubble that fat." Her mouth twisted. "But he wouldn't leave me her, oh no, he must betray me. It isn't that I was not ready, he could betray his mother and I would cheer him on, but he has betrayed himself." She nodded wearily. "I knew that there were others behind him and above him, but I thought that really he was free and had the same contempt any honorable man would hold for his superior. When he beat me this time . . . oh, I could have borne it, and with pleasure if he had struck me out of contempt or because the whim had seized him, but he revealed his face and that was disgusting. To defeat me and he so afraid. I will not suffer blows which are given me out of fear, and yet he was stronger than I and very unpleasant." Breath charged with resentment was expelled from her lips. "Afterward he was greasy and paid me compliments and tried to make me think that all of it, the liquor and the smack-smack had been a present, and he had taken the time to please my taste."

McLeod was at the doorway. His thin mouth bearing a grimace, he examined her room, stared at the paint on the windows.

Lannie bolted upright. "What do you want? Why are you here?"

"I wanted to talk to you," he said in a gentle voice. The long thin nose sniffed delicately at the air. He gave no more than a covert glance at Lannie, afraid perhaps of arousing an outburst. "You've not been feeling too well, have you?" he suggested quietly.

Her head stiffened. She was prepared to accept this as a taunt, but his voice had been too soft. Warily, she told him, "I'm fine, thank you." As though he were a threat to her so long as he believed her ill, she moved away from the sofa and stood erect with a smile upon her pale lips. "I'm fine," she repeated, "I've had an enormous meal, and my pockets are bulging with money. A man passed and clapped a fifty-dollar bill into my palm, like that! and fled down the street." Obliged to prove what she had claimed so many times, the stained fingers fumbled at her breast pocket and came forth with a crumpled banknote.

"He beat you and you took his money," I exclaimed.

"A stranger," she said.

"Leave off," McLeod muttered suddenly.

"I. . ."

"Leave off," McLeod repeated, one of his bony hands at my shirt, his face, twisted into a startling rage. "Leave off, and a little mercy, insufferable, unfeeling, and ignorant. . ." He could not find the word to cap it. "By what right do you claim authority?" He was trembling, and as abruptly as he had grabbed me, his fingers flew loose. He stood with his back to me, thin shoulders pressed upon one another. A minute passed, and when he turned around his face was composed in its harsh lines.

"I took it," Lannie said, half to herself, "because money is nothing, and it gave him pleasure to befriend me. And then he ran down the street so ashamed of his kindness."

McLeod nodded. "Go to sleep," he said almost tenderly, "and when you wake everything will be better."

A mist from childhood came near to whisking her away. An echo lingered from the past. Lightly she touched the bruise upon her face. But the finger of pain which met her own poked it all away, and cobweb silver came down to dust. With a little sob she pressed upon the heart of the swelling as though she would search out the flesh beneath the ache and vanquish the wound. She pressed and it was too tender. Her hand quivered back to her side.

If this were a token, the symbol had cheated her. "Don't be kind to me," she shrieked at McLeod. "I can't bear kindness now."

"You need it," he muttered back.

"It is I who must give it to others," she cried. Weakly she tottered on her feet. At that instant she could have fumbled toward McLeod and accepted the support of his arms. As easily she could have attacked him. Instead, swaying miserably, hand at her forehead, she whispered, "Why did you come here?"

McLeod studied the ash on his cigarette. He was about to say something, but he changed his mind. Lips clamped together tightly, compressed until they were white, he shook his head. "I don't know."

"Why me?"

"Because," he said slowly, and he was trying to phrase it for himself, "it was you and not him who wore me down."

To my surprise she nodded her head at his words, and in a reply which was more direct than I could ever have anticipated, she said, "It's true, isn't it? You haven't been with *them* for a long time." Waiting for the answer, she stared at the floor.

"It's true," McLeod said.

"Oh, I knew, I knew," Lannie cried out. "I knew and yet. . ." She trailed off. "What have I done?" she asked. But too much crowded upon her too rapidly. "You gave it to him, though," she stated, "you gave it up to him. Why come to me now?"

"I haven't given it yet," McLeod answered, his speech so soft that we were bound together. "It takes time I told him, and so I have until tonight or maybe the morning."

"And you don't know what to do?" she asked.

"I can't let him have it," McLeod said hoarsely, "and yet I suppose I will."

"No, you mustn't," she declared, "you mustn't at all."

He was on her, his hands clenching her hands. "But why resist? For what?" He released her arm, refusing resolutely to look at me. "Still, I come to you," he told Lannie, "I look for some way. What do I want you to do? Encourage me? I tell you

I don't know myself why I'm here." And rubbing his neck against a circulation which persisted in leaving him cold, he muttered, "If only I could have made you understand earlier. I swear that. . ."

"Don't swear for me," she said in a muffled voice. "I don't know. I don't know." Lannie began to weep. She cried with the dignity of a child, her back straight, her head high, arms at her side. There could be no attempt at concealment, for that was the disgrace. She talked rapidly, her poor bruised face wrenched with anguish. "Oh, so many years gone by, and they labored over me, all the people in white, and if you're to be destroyed you must love your destroyer, for who else is there to love when that's the world and all space filled? You were prepared for me, they allowed me you to hate and that's so necessary, and yet even the first time I saw you, now I know I knew then that you were not the man they represented as you and if guilty before innocent now, but how can I admit that, when you see they gave the other to me with his blond hair, and he was to carry me away and save me for even the cruellest father puts you in his house. And so you must forgive me." Weeping, she dropped to her knees, and in a fit of torment fell forward without protecting herself. In dead weight her head struck the floor.

We brought Lannie to her feet and led her to the bed, but as we lay her down she flung us away, and sat up rigidly. "You ask me what to do? Don't give it to him." But her face twisted. "I tell you that, and yet, let someone help me for I cannot, I must tell you that even now all confession made, I cannot . . . I cannot find it in myself to do otherwise than hate you." The effort exhausting her, she lay back upon the bed. "Go away," she cried at McLeod, "go away."

He started to obey her. "Tell me," she called out in a strangled voice, "do you think that I, too, am beyond the pale?" A touch of conviction appeared in her eyes. "You see, once, I was so respected in the movement, culture they said and the heart of a fighter. I can regain it all. I need only rest and . . . gather myself. For if it is really coming, if everything is not dead, and you seemed so certain yesterday that it was not, then they will need me, will they not? Or will they say, they are so cruel, you cannot be with us?" As though she had heard the sound of her voice, and was now reduced to the whisper it had been, she shivered. "Get out of here, oh get out, get out," she pleaded.

And with a wise sad smile upon his face, he kissed her hand. "I'll see you later, Lovett," he said, "later, I hope," and I could hear him close the door.

Lannie rose from the bed and traced a few steps. "Is he gone?" she asked, fingers trembling at her chin. "You must leave me, too," she said. "Everybody." She lurched about, and in the sudden motion her body blundered against the floor lamp and set it swaying. Her arm shot out, perhaps to catch it, but she succeeded only in knocking it over. "Oh," she said out of some remote frustration, and in reaching to pick it up, fell herself and struck her forehead one more blow against the floor. As she struggled to rise, I extended my arms to assist her, and she raked her nails across my hand. "Leave me alone."

So, arms folded, I watched her move, body all at odds and co-ordination a paper she chased in the wind. Effort sweating her forehead, she crossed the room to the bed and without a word lay down upon it, staring at the ceiling while I, following helplessly after, could only perch at her feet.

Hours passed like this, Lannie on the bed and I watching, my body receiving her distress. If her forehead burned, mine ached; if her limbs quivered, mine itched; and when from the sleep in which she tossed a cry was uttered half from the dream and half from pain, her dread was communicated to me and I sat beside her with a leaden throat. Outside, the afternoon passed, the sun beating against a blind window until the air in our dim room became unendurable. Once, with great difficulty,

I succeeded in raising the sash from its binding of paint, but the sudden shaft of light clapped Lannie upright in bed with a dazzled cry, and I could only shut it again. Thus the sun went down, and the gamut spread in the sky from illumination to darkness could induce only its most subtle reflection behind the raven pocket of the glass. Obscurity banked upon itself and the walls turned darker and darker, until with what sense I hardly knew, I was certain night had come.

Lannie's eyes were open again. Head turned to the side, she looked into the feeble globe of the electric light.

"Oh, I'm tired, tired, tired," she breathed.

"Rest more," I told her, even as she was struggling to a sitting position.

"No, there's no rest, not anywhere." Her hand journeyed over her face. "There's too sad a story to tell of the princess who searched out evil for only that was left." Her eyes stared out at me, luminous and swollen in the bruised curve of her face. Even as I was certain she did not know I was before her, she would address a remark to me, and then before I could answer, her eyes were staring at the shadowed walls with all the certainty of one who sees before him a continent or a heaven.

"Oh, there are theories today," Lannie said in singsong. "There are so many ways to make an apostle and no way to keep one until the princess could weep." She fumbled through the pocket of her pajamas, and delivered a wrinkled cigarette, half voided of tobacco. I started to light it, and she pulled away her head. "No," she said, "it's all I have left." Between her fingers she kneaded still more tobacco from the paper. "She would have remade the world, giving each to each what was their due, so they should be proud in their vice and know that it is beauty which blossoms on guilt." Her voice droned on. "But she planted them with roots in the air and buds so deep in the muck. They dripped upon her until she was only their instrument, no more, nothing but their servant, and that she could have borne if they

298

had been of stature, but they deserted her only too cruelly and tore the bandage from her eyes, and said look upon us for we are mud, and you have altered nothing, and you who are beneath are also mud and not a princess. And thunder came, the sky darkened, and the princess saw herself and screamed, for indeed she was not the princess at all, she was nothing, she was this cigarette with the tobacco falling and afraid of the fire. . ."

THIRTY-ONE

IN the middle of the night I had a dream, or did I imagine it while I was awake? I stood with a crowd of men in a
tremendous hall, and we rested on one foot and then the other.
The speaker had been talking for an hour, and we listened with
our eyes down, looking at cigarette butts wrapped in newspaper
and the sullen spittle of a dirty floor. Whenever the speaker
would pause, a signal must have been given for we would open
our mouths and cheer at command. After a while I was able
to hear what the speaker said:

"I been called a hack by those who got their reasons, sabo-
teurs and agents of the stinking enemy country. Listen, you
men, I spit on sonsofbitching hacks who love another country
than our own. If you find one, even one, in this here union,
string him up, I say, string him up. I been called a hack, they
say I used to be one, but it's a lie, and I swear it on the sweet
dead flesh of my mother, may God keep her."

So we cheered, for God had been mentioned.

"I work to give you men more money, that's the Lord
loving truth. But there's a war on, men. Reds and gooks and
giminy ginks, we've got 'em all to fight. I work to give you men
more money, it's just an accident, so help my heart, that right

now you got to take less. I been hearing that some of you talk revolution. Men, skip that stuff. Labor is respectable now. We don't need revolution. There's production for war instead. We submit to the speed-up, but willingly, willingly, that's the word. And we don't criticize because the speed-up means more production. And that means we're making more wealth. Agitators among you are claiming that armaments are not wealth, but I tell you armaments are wealth cause they belong to all of us. So these agitators got to shut their hole."

Suddenly, he was pointing at me. "You, Lovett, you I mean!" And in desperation I shouted back, "You're swindling the workers, you're swindling the workers, you're swindling..." and I was still crying that as my arms were pinioned behind me and I was hustled from the hall to the street outside where men in uniform were waiting.

Then a wall might have crashed for I was fully awake and fully dressed, my head stuffed into the pillow, my hands gripping the iron posts of the cot.

What time was it? My anxiety, balked in its course, must drive me out of bed for a drunken search to find the alarm clock. There, standing on the floor, with my feet shuddering in my cold shoes, I heard a soft familiar voice.

"McLeod. I say, old man, McLeod."

It was Hollingsworth. I opened my door a crack and peered out into the hall. McLeod had closed the door to his room behind him, and stood before it, his tall pinched body drooping forward. Although they did not touch, Leroy might have been supporting him.

"Took you a long time to answer," Hollingsworth complained.

"I've been thinking."

Hollingsworth looked at his wrist watch. "I'm come up here to inform you," he said apologetically, "that in fifteen minutes you must come down and the transfer must take place."

301

McLeod wiped one hand against the other. "You gave me until tomorrow morning."

"Sorry."

"I suppose you have your troubles," McLeod said.

His foot ticking the floor, Hollingsworth shook his head. "A fellow can change his mind, that's all."

McLeod grinned. "They want you at their office right away. That's it, isn't it?"

"They're fantastic, they have no right. . ." Hollingsworth said in a choked voice.

"To suspect you?" He chortled. "They've been slow."

Hollingsworth looked at him, his thin lips moist, his forearm extended in the futile gesture of a man who has something difficult to say, and frustrated, may only pinch his finger against his thumb. "No, you must listen to me," he piped suddenly, his dull eyes expressive at last in the tears which clouded their surface. A whimper, small and involuntary, came from some depth within. "Everybody wants to hurt me," he said like a boy of twelve.

"You're tired, too," McLeod said quietly.

"I can't go back to working for them," he burst out suddenly. "They go at a fellow so. You ask yourself, 'Who am I anyway?' Do you understand? But of course you do. You are so understanding," he said tenderly. "Why the dear experiences I've had with some of my colleagues, and now they're persecuting my friends and myself. And they're just like us although they don't realize it." His outpour halted momentarily, and he took off his straw boater, and reached down to massage the toe of his pointed orange moccasins. "I must apologize for hurting you the other day, but you see I knew you gave your talk for Mr. Lovett, and my feelings were terribly hurt. I can't express the admiration I feel for a gentleman like yourself. I think if conditions had been more, so to speak, propitious, we could have been dear friends." He put his hand on McLeod's arm.

302

Subtly, McLeod disengaged it. "I'm sorry," he said stiffly, "but I'm afraid I have strong prejudices."

Hollingsworth would not make it a rebuff. "Oh, it doesn't matter. We'll see each other I hope when all this is quiet. And I'll take good care of your wife. Opposites attract, as she says, but then at bottom they're so much the same." He hesitated, but this was the last opportunity, and it must be said. "I can't tell you how glad I am that you decided to give it to me. Because otherwise I would have had to bring you in, and that would have made me feel very bad. You know, I think I first had the idea for my offer when it occurred to me that I could also save you." And he said this with passion so suppressed that the effort made him lean almost against the body of McLeod. "You're such a stern sort of fellow," he murmured. "I've always liked your type. And deep down, now don't answer cause I know better than you, I feel that you could get to like me." He caught himself short.

"All this is by the bye. Will you be down in fifteen minutes?"

"You've told me once."

"And you take care of yourself. Make plans to leave at the same time I do. It's not advisable to wait." He seemed about to shake hands, and then turned around, walked quickly down the stairs.

McLeod went back into his room. I waited to cross the hall until the sound of footsteps had completely disappeared. Pushing forward the door which was open, I found McLeod sitting in a chair. Across from him was the desk and the empty seat which had belonged to Hollingsworth.

McLeod looked up at me. "You heard it all?" he asked.

I nodded, and he plucked some lint from his trouser leg. "I've finally made a decision," he stated.

"Yes."

"I'm not giving it to him."

303

We were both silent after this. "Well, what are you going to do?" I asked.

"In a few minutes I'll go down to see him."

"Why don't you. . ." I began.

"Disappear?" He laughed softly to himself. "Well, for that I'm afraid I don't have the strength. You see he's waiting down there, and his ears are not inconsiderable. No, he waits with the woman who was m'wife and the child, even the clothing's been packed, and there's only the last detail to be finished."

"What about Guinevere?"

He shrugged sadly. "All my life I've loved ideas. So I loved the idea of loving my wife. And perhaps the child as well. I may face it now. No, Lovett, I've killed the alternatives. It seems to me I wanted to fail in every case, for it's the alternatives cut your will to make the decision I have come to." He shivered suddenly. "Except for one."

"What will happen in the next few minutes?" I asked.

He jeered at me. "Oh, you assume too much. There'll be a scene and threats, and then I'll be on my way."

The way he said this gathered my flesh. "And you leave nothing?"

"Nothing."

"Then why don't you give it to me?" I said carefully.

He was out of his chair and squeezing my arm. "Are you sure?" he asked in a tense voice.

My heart was beating so powerfully, I did not know if I could speak. "I've thought about it," I managed to say. "I'm not a brave man, I know that. . ." It was expressed at last. "I have no future anyway. At least I can elect to have a future. If it's short, small matter."

He punched me lightly on the chest. "Old sonofabitch Lovett." A smile illumined his face. "Ah, there's so little time and so much to tell you. You're romantic, boy, and you must guard against it. And you're innocent, and you have much to learn."

304

He walked around nervously in a circle. "It's impossible to give all advice in a minute, and even then you must learn yourself." Able to contain himself no longer, he caught me in a bear hug and wrestled me about the room. "I'm proud of you," he said loudly almost before he had thought the words, and laughed in pleasure. "Here." He sat me down at the desk. "We've only a minute or two, and I must explain it to you. The details, the conditions, and the characteristics you can work out at leisure if you have any."

When he was done he looked sternly across the table and said, the pedagogue again, "As Lenin said to the priest Gapon, 'Study, little father, or you will lose your head.' You hear, Lovett?"

I nodded.

"All right. Then I'll be going down."

"I'll go with you," I said.

McLeod was on his feet. "Oh, no. No, no. You don't ruin it now." He was suddenly furious. "You come down and that's the finish of both of us. No, look, m'bucko"—and he had me by the shirt, his pale eyes glaring—"I'm an old hand, you know, and you don't think I've spent the last few days without working over certain tactical questions for myself"—his breath coming hot against my face—"I mean, you don't think I'd walk down there with no more than m'legs and not an idea in my head. No, I have a procedure, you see I discovered it today, and I can tell you that your presence, oh, I assure you, it would be the worst thing possible." Releasing me, he muttered, "No, you stay here, and if something goes wrong, there is the chance, clear out and I'll meet you in the alley at the end of the street."

"If you . . . If you're sure?"

As though he were drunk he bent forward with a half-comic, half-conspiratorial gesture, and said, "Mind you now, boy, don't come down, or ruin it you will. When I get back, I'll enumerate how the old fox McLeod has stolen the grapes again."

305

With that he pressed an envelope in my hand. "Just a few words. I was going to slip them under your door. Don't read it now." Lighting a cigarette, he passed into the hall, patted the banister rail, and moved out of sight.

For many minutes I obeyed his injunction, sitting in the darkness of the room, while slowly, my body motionless, heat drained from my limbs, the walls grew cold, and the stagnant attic air which had oppressed me for so many weeks, lost its warmth. My nose leaked, my hands were ice, and the silence of the house worked relentlessly at my nerve. I waited, until my ears selecting at last the momentous rhythm of water dripping from a pipe, I must attempt to determine from where it came— was it only across the hall, or could I hear it even from the cellar of another house?—and received each drop as though I were bound and the water tapped upon my skull. So, in the cave I waited, while stalactites offered their deposit to the floor.

The silence no longer endurable, I left his room for my own, and in the hall, my ear at the stair well, thought I heard the cadence of Hollingsworth's voice. I descended a half-flight, and a footstep might have been heard. Or in its weariness did a timber creak? Thus, deploying at the end of a rope for certainly I would return, I passed the third-floor landing and then the second, pausing beside Lannie's door. On the other side, in her room, the light would be on, the bulb burning into the darkness, while her windows still damp with their wound would stare at her face as she lay on the bed, and the paint not yet cold would voyage downward in its thick slow passage upon the glass. There I waited for another minute, tarrying at the last familiar outpost.

In the downstairs hallway a dusty lamp sat on a battered table, and encouraged an insect which circled above mis-addressed bills and dead letters bearing the name of people who could no longer be found. Weight on my toes, body clenched, I paused there too, my fingers shuffling the envelopes, my eyes reading nothing.

They were talking. Now, on the stairs which led to the door of Guinevere's suite, I could detect their voices, each whispering, and yet the rapidity with which they spoke and the lash of one whispered voice upon another betrayed their haste. Whisper to whisper and a low cry from Guinevere, Monina's voice breaking out once in a whimper and silenced immediately. My head was at the keyhole, and they muttered back and forth, each voice becoming more resolved until the threat at last specific, the defiance was even clearer, and Hollingsworth's voice was shrill for a single instant, crying out with the pain of a boy.

"You gypped me. You gypped me," I heard him say.

"Crybaby, cry," Monina sang.

What they were doing I hardly knew, but silence descended again, so filled, so complete, that I might have been upstairs in the other room frozen by the sequence of water falling, drop upon drop.

"You've hurt a fellow's feelings," Hollingsworth said in the mildest voice I had ever heard him use, "and that is why I am forced to punish you."

Perhaps it was the way he said this, perhaps the hush which followed. But now the silence was impossible to bear. I heard the smallest creak of a step, and I could almost see the weapon uncovered and the slow rapt movement of each man about the other. There was some sound of attack, a thick cry which followed, and at that moment I flew against the door and came careening into the room to see McLeod collapsing before me. That in the fraction of a glance, and an instant later I must have been struck from behind, for something seemed to burst in my head, and I saw the floor rushing to my face, fell headlong with force enough to shatter consciousness.

So, helplessly, my arms groped before me while the floor yawed to my half-shut eyes like a raft floating on the swell. And with the shrieking and caterwauling of animals washed over the dam, I heard voices screeching: Guinevere, from a long way off,

"I'm doomed, I'm doomed," and Hollingsworth cursing and weeping, running first to one corner of the room, and then pacing to the other. "The car is ready," I heard him cry, "and now we must go," and an attack of sobbing which followed it. "Leave me here," a woman's voice was begging, Guinevere's I knew at last, "just leave me here and let me lay," whimpering in a panic, until he must have seized her with his arms and borne her to the door. "It's off we go," he said hoarsely, "and no time to lose, and now nobody will ever have it," blubbering this, "nobody will ever have it, and what have I done?" until he screamed, "Come here, get the child, get her, I tell you." Over my paralyzed head tumbled the chase, Monina yipping in fright, and the breath of the others sobbing at her neck. With a thump she was caught and with another hauled into somebody's arms, and then I heard them stumbling out the door, and Guinevere crying, "It can't have happened, it never does," and a moment later or so I thought, the floor revolving with me, I heard the motor of some machine, an automobile I knew, and they were driving away, and into my head with a clarity which makes me certain it was said, Monina's voice gave one last bleat.

"I want my daddie," she wailed.

And the car disappeared, and the floor came up like a grappler, threw me off my knees and gasping on my back.

THIRTY-TWO

Finally, I managed to stand, and if I extended my arms far enough, the room would balance. I navigated the floor, and kneeled beside his body. The long thin arms covering his face, I did not try to see with what heart and what loss he had received his death. I touched the flaccid fingers and then I reeled away and stood leaning against the wall, remembering once to touch the envelope he had given me.

Lannie came through the door. Dressed in the sodden black rags of what had been once her pajamas, she wandered aimlessly back and forth, hair fallen over her eyes, and mouth crooning a tuneless song. She saw McLeod before she saw me, and stood singing tonelessly, her frail body lost in its wrapper. Then she drifted forward and looked into my face.

"Oh, you are my brother," she said softly, "for there is blood on your cheek, and so we are wed." And she gave me her hand.

We stood together against the wall, while outside the sound of automobiles descended upon us. One motor came racing down the street, braked to a halt, and its light which had traced a swath across the room, blinked out, and was replaced by the glare of a second car, which birthed from its twin, must come racing, braking, and blinking into position behind the other. When a third car turned the corner and roared to follow the others, I slipped away from the wall and drew Lannie after me into the bedroom.

After thirty seconds in which car doors slammed and men's feet drummed upon the pavement, and my head absorbed them both, the iron gate to Guinevere's apartment clanged open, and agents of the country we live in ran through the door. Three men with athletic bodies and business suits and gray felt hats came into the foyer. I sought Lannie's mouth too late. She had begun to croon again, and even as they were looking dumbly at one another, she moved out of the darkness toward them. "You've come, I see," she said in a loud clear voice as though they were deaf. "And I have decided to meet you." As she raised her wrist the stigmata of cigarette burn was revealed upon it.

One of the men looked at her carefully.

"Book her," he said.

When the others came forward, she smiled. "I love you even if you torment me, for you suffer," she said. But as she passed with them through the door, light and shadow rippled across her face and terror with it. "Oh," she said in a piteous little voice. And for a moment she must twist her body free.

"Oh," she whispered, "I run through a field of tall grass and I fall. Does it choke me or do I sleep here?"

They led her onto the street and other men took their place. But I could hardly attend them. For as they entered the front door I was stealing through the back window, and when hubbub broke at the sight of the dead man on the floor I must have been halfway down the alley.

THIRTY-THREE

THE envelope contained McLeod's will:

> To Michael Lovett to whom, at the end
> of my life and for the first time within
> it, I find myself capable of the rudiments
> of selfless friendship, I bequeath in heri-
> tage the remnants of my socialist culture.

Almost as an afterthought he had scrawled:

> And may he be alive to see the rising
> of the Phoenix.

So the heritage passed on to me, poor hope, and the little object as well, and I went out into the world. If I fled down the alley which led from that rooming house, it was only to enter another, and then another. I am obliged to live waiting for the signs which tell me I must move on again.

Thus, time passes, and I work and I study, and I keep my eye on the door.

Meanwhile, vast armies mount themselves, the world revolves, the traveller clutches his breast. From out the unyielding contradictions of labor stolen from men, the march to the endless war forces its pace. Perhaps, as the millions will be lost, others will be created, and I shall discover brothers where I thought none existed.

But for the present the storm approaches its thunderhead, and it is apparent that the boat drifts ever closer to shore. So the blind will lead the blind, and the deaf shout warnings to one another until their voices are lost.